In The
Moonlight

In The Moonlight

Sarah Helton

authorHOUSE®

AuthorHouse™
1663 Liberty Drive
Bloomington, IN 47403
www.authorhouse.com
Phone: 1-800-839-8640

First published by AuthorHouse 4/12/2011

ISBN: 978-1-4567-6656-6 (sc)
ISBN: 978-1-4567-6655-9 (dj)
ISBN: 978-1-4567-6654-2 (ebk)

Library of Congress Control Number: 2011906506

Printed in the United States of America

My Thanks

I would like to thank my loving husband for all the support he has given to me while I worked long hours on this book, I love you. To my beautiful boys that has given me the time to get this done. I thank and love you both. To my mom and sisters who always knew how to get me out of sticky places by making me laugh at myself when I messed up. Thanks guys I love you. To my sweet friends Becky and Chris who pushed me to get this finished just so they could read it, I love you guys.

A Special Thanks Goes To…

Seether for being my best friend while I worked. I don't think I could have got this done without you on blast in my head while I wrote. Thank you for being there for me every night.

Love,
Sarah

All cover illustrations were done by Timmy Adkins, I love you. Thank you for all the hard work you have done for me and thanks for not smacking me when I changed it up on you.

Chapter 1

It has been three months since that cold January night. As I sat there and looked around the room filled with boxes, I felt like my life was over. On that January night when my husband Brandon and I moved to this little town of Hinton, West Virginia. We were moving in and unpacking when we planned on dinner. We decided to walk to the little restaurant together and finish tomorrow. We ate and talked just enjoying our time together. As the evening pressed on we needed to get back to finish unpacking our belongings. We walked hand in hand in the crisp air when out of no where a car came speeding down the road and slid on ice. It happened so quick, Brandon screamed my name "Piper!" as he pushed me out of the way. The car hit him and then the tree, I rushed to Brandon's side to help him. I sat there in the moonlight as I held Brandon while he said his last few words to me, "Piper I love you always have. I will watch over you always." he said as his life left him. Brandon and the driver died that night, now here I am trying to put my life back together. I worked at the hospital every day so that I didn't have to be home but today was my day off. I started to unpack the boxes and put things away finally. I worked until I couldn't stand to see anything else of Brandon's, the heartbreak was to hard for me. I woke to the sun coming into my bedroom not that I slept very well with the dreams of the accident coming to me every night and Brandon's last words running through my head. I hurried to get out in the fresh air so I could walk to work like most days the crisp air help me clear my head.

As I got to work it was busy like I liked it most of the time busy meant no time to think. My best friend and head nurse, Michelle who

1

had taken me under her wing happily pointed out the new doctor who was working with us. "Piper he hasn't taken his eyes off of you all day, or for weeks for that matter well ever since he was put on this rotation." Michelle said. I just looked at her and shook my head glancing his way. As the day slowed Michelle and I walked to the drink machine for a soda. She began to fill me in on the new doctor who she said was watching me. "I barely noticed him Michelle, I'm not ready for that stuff ya know? Its been three months since well you know." I told her. "Oh I know but come on Piper he seems very interested in you." she said with a giggle. "Ok Michelle what is his name again?" I asked not wanting to hurt her feelings. "Xavier Matthews." she replied happily. As she got ready to say more about him the intercom screeched out "Doctor Danvers to the ER STAT!" Michelle and I ran to see what the emergency was only to find that it was a car accident. I choked back the tears and the visions so that I could work on this poor soul that was laying on front of me. Still I was haunted by the memories of Brandon and that night so long ago. I washed up getting ready to go to the place I dreaded to be now that my shift was over. "Hey nice work, I'm Xavier Matthews nice to finally meet you." he said offering his hand. "Piper Danvers nice to meet you too. Umm see you tomorrow?" I said as I gathered my stuff and headed for the door. I could hardly wait to get out in the crisp air to clear the day out of my head. At first all I could think about was Xavier's voice and his touch, "Ok Piper get your head together." I thought to myself. I stepped outside to find it pouring the rain and me not prepared for the weather still getting used to this town. I sighed heavily, tightened my jacket around me and started for the walk home. I was hurrying along with my head down while the cold rain beat down on me never noticing a car approaching until I heard my name, "Piper, hey Piper can I give you a ride home?" he asked. I bent down and looked in the window, "Oh no thanks Dr. Matthews I'm fine." I said. "Come on its a cold rain and I really don't mind." he insisted. "Thanks." I said as I got in. "Your very welcome and it Xavier." he said with a smile and his voice like magic to me.

I watched him take a deep breath as I began to speak, "Wow nice Charger." I said not knowing what to say. He turned to me with a shocked look on his handsome face, "Yea I cant believe you knew that." he said with a smile. "I like older cars I have a 69 Camaro." I told him. As we talked back and forth I noticed the car slowing to a stop, "Where are we?" I asked. He put a sly grin on his handsome face, "We are going to have dinner here, you like steak right?" he asked. "Oh Xavier you don't have to do that I'll be just fine, I really should go home." I said not knowing if this was a good idea or not. "I just thought since I was alone and you were alone we could have dinner, its been a long day and you should eat." he said smiling. I just looked at him not knowing what to say to that, "Come on no need to eat alone more fun if you have someone to hang out with." he insisted. "Ok." I said slowly. He got out and walked over to my side opening the door and offering me his hand with a smile. We went into Applebee's and with me being wet and cold it was warm inside, although he didn't seem as cold as I was. The waitress showed us a table and took our drink and food orders, "Dr. Pepper and ribs please." I said with him ordering the same drink and a rare steak. "Tell me about yourself Xavier." I said when she left the table. "Well lets see I moved here with my brothers and sisters about two years ago. My parents adopted them and they are good kids still in school ages 16 and 17. Now with my parents gone it is up to me to care for them but they keep up with your grades and chores while I work all the time. What about you Piper you have any siblings? How did you end up here?" he asked. "No I sure don't I'm an only child even though I wish I had a bigger family. My husband and I moved here about three months ago his job brought us here. I like it and I love my job but my parents live in Virginia." I said not really looking at him as we ate. "Your husband?? I didn't know I should have asked." he said quickly. I smiled lightly at him, "No that's ok I'm a widow, car accident." I said with a bit of sadness and a deep breath. "I'm so sorry I . . . ." he began before I interrupted. "Wow its getting late maybe we should go." I said as I looked at my watch. He got up quietly and offered his hand to me as I got out of the chair.

On the way to my house nothing was said just the sound of the rain hitting the window. "Will you be walking in the rain in the morning?" he asked finally. I just looked at him and his sweet smile, "No I'll drive tomorrow." I said with a smile of my own. "Awe I was hoping you would need a ride I'd love to come and get you." he offered. "That's sweet of you Xavier but I'll be fine thanks again for the ride and dinner. See you tomorrow alright." I said. "Anytime, hey Piper how about tomorrow?" he asked smiling that sexy sly smile. "What's tomorrow?" I asked. "There is no need to eat alone." he said. "I don't know let me think about it okay thanks again Xavier." I said as I waved bye to him and ran inside. I could hear the Hemi engine as he pulled off while I took off my jacket. I grabbed my mail and the phone to call Michelle. It rang about two times and she answered, "Piper tell me everything!" she said excitedly. "Ok ok hello to you too. Nothing really he just gave me a ride and took me to dinner, we talked some and he asked me out again." I told her. "Are you going to go? I mean there is no need for you to be alone Piper and he's very good looking plus he seems very interested in you. He has been here for about two years and I have never seen him ask anyone out." she said. I laughed, "Its just dinner not having his children, look I might go but only if he asks again. I've gotta take a shower see you in the morning?" I asked. "Sure I have a date anyways see ya." she said as we hung up.

I showered and got into my jammies, tossed in a load of laundry, loaded the dish washer. Grabbed my mail and tossed in a movie that I halfway watched, paid some bills and checked my email. Before I knew it I was asleep with more sad dreams of Brandon, I never slept well with the dreams coming to me. The dreams were a little different each time, this time I felt like my face was being stroked, I knew that I was alone or I thought I was. I dreamt of the night Brandon died but this time he had a smile on his face, and his lips saying be happy. This time I felt my hair being moved from my face, I jumped awake to find me alone and still on the couch. I gathered my thoughts took a drink of my Dr. Pepper and took myself to bed. Morning came without much sleep to me so I got up and took a hot shower. Grabbed my keys and hospital id and went out the door to find him leaning against his front fender and smiling that sexy smile. "Xavier what are you doing here?" I asked. "Good morning Piper looking lovely today. I'm here to drive you to work so we can have dinner tonight." he said. I just smiled at him, "And what makes you think I'm having dinner with you tonight?" I asked. "Well I can be very convincing when I want something." he said as he opened the car door for me. I waited a few seconds, "I just thought you would like to meet my brothers and sisters. We could have dinner at my place if you wish, anything you want." he offered. "Alright I guess but I can drive myself." I said. "Awe come on Piper I'd love to drive you to work and after dinner I'll take you home anytime you wish." he said. "Ok nothing fancy for dinner then." I told him as I got in. "Salads from Wendy's it is." he said with a chuckle. We talked back and forth while he drove us to work.

It was slow and I liked slow sometimes that way I could take more time with my patients. Time seemed to tick by and I was a little nervous about dinner. Michelle told me about her date with some guy named Jerry, "He's nice and all but I don't think I'm going out with him again." she said as we sat at the desk. "Why not?" I asked half way listening. "Sloppy kisses. Hey what's up you look distracted? YOUR GOING OUT WITH HIM AGAIN ARENT YOU?" she accused. "Well yea he showed up at the house this morning and offered me a ride. He wants me to meet his brothers and sisters tonight. Michelle do you think I should go I mean I'm not rushing am I?" I asked her. "Piper you need this there is more to life than work and DVDs." she said. "Your right, all I do is work and watch movies. I don't even know why I pay for cable. I'm going and I'm gonna have fun." I told her. "Good girl." she said with a smile. Before I knew it he was up behind me with his hand around me, "Are you ready Piper?" he asked with velvet words. "Sure I guess lets go." I said with a smile feeling nervous. The sun was bright and warm on the drive to his house. He pulls up and hurries around to help me out of the car. He pulled me to my feet to meet my face with his. His eyes were the most beautiful blue I have ever seen, and his hair was black with blonde slits running through it. "What, something wrong?" he asked. "Oh no, you have the most beautiful eyes I have ever seen, absolutely breath taking." I said a bit embarrassed. "Thank you Piper. Piper are you?" was all I heard him say before everything went black.

I opened my eyes and at first everything was blurry, then things started to clear up. There he was bent over me, "Piper can you hear me?" he asked with worry in his voice. I shook my head, "What happened?" I whispered as I tried to sit up. "You told me that my eyes were breath taking, I didn't think you meant it literally." he said with a laugh. "I'm so sorry if you take me home I'll make dinner up to you I promise." I said. "No way I'm taking you home you need to have something to eat and then I'll take you." he said. "Thank you Xavier sorry again for messing up dinner." I told him feeling bad. "Regina will you bring Piper something to eat and drink please?" he called to her. "Sure thing Brother." she said and quickly exited the room. Within a flash she was back with a salad and a Dr. Pepper for me, "Here ya go Piper my brother cant cook unless its on a grill so he set us out for you." she said with a smile. He narrowed his blue eyes at her and she giggled, "I'll leave you two alone but the others want to meet her." she said. "They can meet her some other time." he told her. "That's ok Xavier Id like to meet them." I told him. "As you wish." he said handing me my drink. They all came into the room looking as beautiful as Xavier, "Hi I'm Jonathan nice to meet you Piper." he said. He had sandy blonde hair and very blue eyes standing tall and slim. "This is my older brother Michael, my two sisters Cyndi and Regina." he added. Michael had red hair, Cyndi had long blonde hair past her waist, Regina had satin black hair. All of them were tall and beautiful with blue eyes. "Very nice to meet you all. Sorry about dinner guys I haven't eaten all day I guess I need to stop that." I said. "That's ok Piper maybe next time I have homework so if you will excuse me." Michael said.

I started to eat my salad as they left us, "Would you like to watch a movie or something?" Xavier asked. "What you got?" I asked. "I've got all kinds." he said showing me his collection. "Just pick out anything I don't mind." I said with a smile. "Vampires it is." he said with a sly smile. "Ooooh I love vampire movies, I have a bunch of them." I told him with a laugh. "You like the scary, bloody, gutsy stuff?" he asked. "The more the blood and guts the better the movie." I told him. He just smiled at me while we watched Underworld although he watched me more than the movie. "Can I get you anything else?" he asked. "No thanks by the way why were you watching me instead of the movie?" I asked. "I've seen this movie a dozen times besides I'd rather watch you. You move your lips with the words, how many times have you seen this one?" he asked. "I don't know twenty times I think. I love vampires, zombies, witches all kinds of movies." I told him. He just smiled at me when I looked at him, "You are very beautiful, your eyes are the most green I have ever seen and your burgundy hair is so soft around your shoulders." he said softly. I felt my cheeks blush, "Thank you, no one has ever said anything like that to me except my husband and well he never put it like that." I said a little bit embarrassed. "I'm sorry if I have embarrassed you but you are quit stunning." he said. "I think maybe I'm ready to go home, would you mind?" I asked. "Sure thing let me grab our coats." he said as he got up. I threw my trash away, folded my blanket and put on my shoes. I sat there trying to figure out why I was more comfortable with him than with anyone else in my whole life. "I didn't mean to make you uncomfortable you don't have to leave." he said as he came back in. "Oh I don't feel like that I just gotta go, maybe you can come over and we can raid my fridge one night. I've gotta go to the store to get some Dr. Pepper so let me know what you like and I will pick it up." I told him. "Ok then the next day we are off I'll come over Friday right?' he asked. "Yes Friday is good for me." I said getting on my jacket. "I'll wear my shades so you wont pass out again." he said with the most convincing smile I had ever seen. "Very funny." I said as he led the way to the car.

He dropped me off at home and I went to the store to get the few things I needed. I got home and got the day over so I could start a new one. The next morning I went out to go to work and there was Xavier waiting on me. Everyday after that he came to pick me up and take me home after dinner and a movie. We dated like that for weeks, him picking me up and taking me home. Many nights I had to pull a double and he would work out the schedule so that he worked with me. The end of the long two weeks and I was excited about friday. We planned to spend the whole day together. He waited on me at the car after work, "You want to grab dinner or something?" he asked as he helped me in. "No thanks I have to go to the store I'm bout out of Dr. Pepper and I'm freaking out about it. You can drop me off and I'll see you tomorrow right?" I asked. "I can take you if you wish." he offered. "No I have taken you from your brothers and sisters for weeks now so I can just go but thanks your so sweet." I said. "Come on Piper let me take you." he offered. I felt unbelievably comfortable with him I couldn't believe it like I couldn't stay away from him or wanted him far from me. I agreed to let him take me to the store, "You coming in or waiting on me?" I asked. "Oh I'm coming in with you I want everyone to know you belong to me." he said. I blinked my eyes at him for a second, "I mean that we are dating." he quickly corrected and smiled. The way he smiled at me with that sly sexy smile made me forget what he said, made me feel comfortable. We shopped around getting the things I needed to make it through the week and our day together. "Wow I hadn't noticed how much stuff I got!" I said with surprise. "You just kept throwing things in so I added a few of my faves." he said as he pushed the buggy. "Maybe we should get something new because I know all the words to my movies." I suggested. We walked by the entertainment department and found a new scary movie and grabbed it. I checked out all my junk that I had and he drove me home, "I'll help you unpack." he said as I started for the front door. I started to say thanks but I stopped short, "What's up Piper?" he asked walking up to me. "My front door, its been kicked open. Damn I bet they got everything!" I said. He led the way into the house, "Call the police Piper, I'll look around and see if they are still here." he told me. I took out my cell and dialed 911. About five minutes the chief of police showed up, "I'm Chief Tim Adkins what happened here?" he asked as he took notes. "I went to work and then my boyfriends house and I went to the store when we got home it was like this." I told him. "Is anything missing?" the chief asked. "I don't know we just got here let me look and I'll let you know." I told him as I went inside. I soon came back out to them, "Well all that is missing is the clothes I took off last night which is weird but nothing else." I told him. "This could have been kids looking for cash or drugs let me know if you find anything else missing." Chief Adkins said.

I told the cop good bye and went in to be with Xavier who was on the phone, "Thanks Bro." he said and hung up. "My brothers are on their way to get you new locks and they will put them on for you." he told me. "They don't have to do that Xavier I'll be fine." I told him. "You look a bit shaken so I'll be here until you kick me out." he said with that irresistible smile. "Fine." I said as I started on the kitchen. There was a knock at the door and I jumped out of my shoes, "It ok Piper just my brothers." he said as he answered the door. They quickly put on the new locks, "She is coming to the Great House tonight right X?" Jon asked. "Come on guys I've got new locks I'll be fine." I said. "I'll take care of it guys thanks again." he told them. "See you later Piper." Mike and Jon said together. I told them bye as Xavier came into the kitchen, "I'll hang around for awhile if you don't mind." he said putting his hands on me. "Well if you want we can watch the new movie." I said forgetting all about the events that just took place. "Love to." he said smiling. "Do they call you X a lot and the Great House?" I asked. "Yea my parents called me X a lot and we have always called home the Great House. Don't you like it?" he asked. "I like it I was just wondering that's all." I told him as he took my hand and led me to the living room. "You can call me X if you wish." he told me. We ate chips and watched the movie although he watched me more than the movie. Afterwards I turned to him, "I want to thank you for all you have done today." I told him. "Your very welcome Piper, I was thinking that I would stay the night, I could sleep on the couch." he offered. "That's very sweet of you but I would never get to sleep knowing that you were on this uncomfy couch." I told him. "How bout this we can talk or I can watch you mouth the words to one of your favorite movies." he said smiling that smile at me. "A movie or two how's that?" I asked. "Cool." he said shaking his head.

Before I knew it I was waking up in his arms still on the couch. He was stretched out with me leaning on his hard chest, his muscular arms around me and him sound asleep. I just stayed there and went back to sleep until the sun came up the next day. He made me so comfortable that for the first time in many nights I didn't dream any about Brandon all I could ever see when I shut my eyes was Xavier. When the light came up well enough for me to see I got up and went upstairs to get a quick shower. I came back down to find him in the kitchen fixing bacon, "Would you like eggs this morning?' he asked. "Na just the bacon. Hey wait a minute Regina said you cant cook so don't burn down my kitchen." I said with a laugh. "Were you comfortable last night?" he asked. "Sure haven't been that comfortable in a long time how about you?" I asked. "The best night sleep I have had in a very long time. Never met anyone like you before Piper ya know someone I'm comfortable with." he said. "Me to but that's good right?" I asked. "Yep, bacon up." he said as a knock came to the door. I let Michelle in as she asked about the cops over here yesterday and stopping short when she saw Xavier in my kitchen cooking. "Oh hi Dr. Matthews." she said smiling. "Xavier please, would you like some bacon?" he asked. "Maybe a slice or two." she said setting down. "Hey Piper I'm going to go and check on my brothers and sisters I'll be back in about an hour, then we can have our day." he said. "Sure thing tell them hi for me, see you soon." I told him. He bent down and looked me in the eyes, and kissed me on the cheek for the very first time and left. I gave Michelle the inside scoop on everything before she left and cleaned up the kitchen waiting for him to return.

Chapter 2

When I heard his Charger pull up my heart skipped a few beats just knowing that he was coming. I peeked out the window as Xavier got out if his car. He was wearing dirty looking jeans with holes cut in them, a blue shirt with the sleeves rolled up showing a small Egyptian ankh tattoo on his forearm, and timberland boots. "Good Lord that shirt lights his eyes up." I thought to myself. He walked up on the porch carrying a single red rose and knocked. I waited a few seconds and then answered, there he stood looking totally breath taking with that sexy smile as he handed me the rose. "Come in Xavier thanks for the rose its beautiful. What's the plans for today?" I asked. "I was thinking we could get some lunch and then head to the Bash." he said. "The Bash what's that?" I asked as I put the rose in some water. "Its a club ya know dancing, food and drinks, you dance don't you?" he asked. "A little bit hey will your sisters be there?" I asked. "Yes they are coming." he said. "Cool I have never had sisters before it should be fun." I said. "Yea the sisters, they better be right." he said lowly and looking like his mind was somewhere else. "Xavier what's up?" I asked. "Piper do you remember when I said that I have never met anyone like you before?" he asked. I shook my head and took a seat. "You are nothing like I have ever met before someone I can share my secrets with, someone who I have to tell everything to no matter how hard I try to keep shut." he began. "Yes I like to think that you can trust me with anything you have to tell me." I said trying to get a grip on him. "I was thinking about what you said to the chief yesterday about me being your boyfriend." he said and stopped. "Yeaa should I have said something else?" I asked softly. "Did you mean it, because I have been looking for you my entire life?" he asked. "Yes I meant it every word I feel like I have known you forever. I mean if you could be with a crazy person who loves scary movies and drinks excessive amounts of Dr. Pepper. X where is this going?" I asked not wanting my heart broken. "Yes, but I have secrets that you may have a hard time dealing with." he said taking my hand. "Maybe you should start from the beginning." I said. "I don't want you to be afraid of me I would rather die than hurt you ever. I am over three hundred years old, but I will look thirty for the rest of my days." he said and stopped. I laughed lightly, "Are you crazy or something?' I asked getting up. "Wait its true I am a vampire a Day Walker. Piper I didn't want us to start a relationship of any kind without you knowing and I don't know how long I could have kept it from you. You hold me so tight that I cant keep anything from you. I wanted to tell you the first day I met you before I even knew your name. If you never want to see me again I will never darken your doorstep and I will understand." he said. I just set there not believing any of this, "Piper please say something." he pleaded. "Xavier this cant be vampires don't exist!" I said quickly. "Where do you think these movies come from." he asked as I walked off.

He stayed away from me for a few minutes, "Would you like me to leave, to give you some time to think?" he asked. "Are you for real this isn't some stupid prank or something?" I asked. "I'm afraid not we all are my brothers and sisters. I just hope that you can except me for me not what I am. Ummm I could show you if you wish." he said softly. "Show me how?" I asked. "I have super human strength and I can move at the speed of light, hear the lowest of whispers and I can feel only a small amount of your feelings." he said staying away from me. "What about fangs and what do you do for blood, do you feed on humans?" I asked. "We never feed on humans just blood banks and wildlife, we can eat and live off of human food like steaks. My family isn't allowed to feed on humans ever and we hunt for fun mostly, and for the fangs just really sharp teeth. We are different than what you see in the movies the whole day walker thing lets us blend in with humans and we can stand daylight. Something about our human genes and vampire venom that makes us somewhat normal." he said. "I think I'm crazy but I'm ok with this I have always wondered about this stuff. So when you said that you wanted others to know that I was yours at Wal Mart?" I asked. "Yes word gets around in the vampire communities and they will stay away from you knowing that you are mine. I'm very addicted to you its something about the way your blood smells to me very sweet. If another vampire looks your way I would kill him before he had a second look. It is like that in all vampire communities the other night you fell asleep on the couch and I watched as you dreamt. You became very sad inside and I could feel your sadness, I tried to comfort you before you woke up. Another vampire had looked at you so I made my presents known and he has never shown again. Are you sure you are ok with this?" he asked. "Yes I'm sure but I'm going to have questions and I want to know everything with no lies." I told him. "As you wish. You will be in everything I do I knew from the very first moment I met you that I love you." he said from his knees. He looked into my eyes with his glistening blue, "Would I be out of line if I kissed you?" he asked. "I would like that." I said softly. He started at my neck and kissed all the way up to my lips, then he kissed me with so much passion and carefulness that my heart melted.

He pulled away and I gathered my thoughts, "Maybe we should walk for a few minutes." I suggested so I could think and put it all in the right folders. "As you wish." he said getting up and offering a hand to me. On our walk we held hands, "I don't think there should be any fighting, I mean you can trust me." I told him. "It isn't you that I worry about its others, when you have waited on your soul mate for as long as I have you would fight to. I have waited hundreds of years for you Piper. The very minute I saw you I knew you were the one for me. So no unnecessary fights I promise. If I don't let it be known that you belong to me another vampire could bite you and I would lose you forever, and you would belong to whoever bit you." he explained. "Ok that's interesting to know. So the Bash is it a vampire club or something?" I asked. "There will be other vampires there so I need you to stay close to me but there will be humans there as well." he said. "Lets get something to eat." I suggested. We walked on to the nearest restaurant and grabbed a seat. He kept watching me while we ate although he didn't eat very much. "Are you sure that you are ok with all this, we could go to the Bash another night if you wish." he suggested. "No I'm fine this is my chance to find out some cool stuff, I just have to put things in the right folders." I told him. "Come on lets start back to the car." he said getting my hand.

The walk back did me some good I had time to get things in order for me to have fun tonight, "Hey can we take my car it really needs to be started?" I asked smiling at him. "You know my sisters were thrilled when I told them about you." he said. "Are you sure cause Regina didn't seem to happy to have me there?" I asked with a shrug. "Sure she is its just that she is very protective that's all. Cyndi on the other hand is ecstatic to have you in my life. Now X can get a life and stay out of mine, she tells me." he said with a laugh. "And your brothers what do they think?" I asked. "They cant wait to have you in the family." he said as we pulled up. He came over and took my hand, "Remember stay close." he reminded me. Cyndi grabbed my hand and led me to the table, "This is Bailey he is human to." she said as she smiled at him. "Hi Bailey." I said setting next to Xavier. He smiled at me as Cyndi set with him, "You know Piper if you marry X the vote would be a tie. It sucks to be the only girls in the Great House." she said with a lovely smile. "Marry Xavier?" I repeated. "Well yea he has waited for three hundred years on you." she said shaking her head at me. "We would most love to have you in the family Piper just don't break his heart." Regina said. "Ok girls that's enough come on Piper this is a good song." he said as he took my hand and led me to the dance floor. He held me softly pulling me close to him and I could feel his breathe on my neck. The smell of his cologne was captivating to me, "What kind of cologne are you wearing?" I asked. As he smiled at me making his eyes sparkle, "I'm not wearing anything, its just my scent. If you can smell it that means you are the one for me. You have a scent all your own even though you are wearing perfume I can still smell it, very addictive." he said with happiness. "Thank you I think. So Cyndi seems very exceptive of me still trying to figure out Regina." I said lightly. "She will come around just give her some time." he said as the song ended.

Regina came over to us, "Ok X you have to share her tonight we dance and you sit." she said holding my hand. He kissed me on the side of my neck and took his seat, "Look Piper I don't mean to sound like I don't like you cause I do, I just worry about X that's all. Cyndi is right he has waited on you for a very long time. Just be careful not all vampires play fair, he will fight for you so be careful who you let in your life. Sometimes its hard to tell vampire from human and Mike thinks it was a vampire who broke into your house. That's why Jon asked if you were coming to the house, you refused and Xavier stayed." she told me. "What would have happened if I made him leave?" I asked. "He would have stayed out of sight till you fell asleep and he would have watched you all night. We don't need to sleep like humans but we do rest a lot, I think the night he stayed with you was the first night he has had in years. Come on I need to get you back he is getting nervous." she said taking my hand. "Thanks Regina I was worried that you didn't approve of me." I told her. She laughed, "Not that at all I worry about others trying to move in on you he wont like that. You'll see someone will ask you to dance and he wont allow it." she told me. Shortly after we got back to the table he pulled me on his lap and we ordered drinks. A man came and asked me to dance, "No thanks I'm here with someone." I told the man quickly. "Its just a dance darlin that's all." he said. I could feel Xavier tighten up and I felt him growl at the man. "Look I'm here with him and I will always be here with him so no dance!!" I said quickly not wanting any fights. The man walked away in a huff, "Wow X she is a keeper, cant wait till someone asks you to dance she might scratch someone's eyes out." Jon said with a smile.

We talked and danced the night away, "Hey Piper you getting tired, you coming home with us?" Cyndi asked. "Yes I'm tired and I'm going home, Xavier can go home with you guys." I told her. "Yea right like he is going to come home, he's gonna be there without you knowing might as well let him in the house." Cyndi said. I looked at him and he put on his sly smile, "Hey that's not gonna work this time." I said laughing. "Oh yes it will." he said smiling even wider this time. "Fine you can have the guest room." I said as we started to leave. "Or we can sleep on the couch again, I love having you in my arms." he whispered to me. As we drove home he asked what Regina and I talked about. "She was just sharing that's all, am I going to be babysat from now on I have doubles to pull." I asked him. "Well maybe for just a few days." he said. "So the guy at the club he was a vamp to?' I asked him. "I'm shocked how did you know that?" he asked. "I don't know I just figured cause I felt you growl at him." I told him. "Sorry about that." he said lightly. "Was he the one in my house the other day?" I asked not looking at him. "Yes be careful of him he is dangerous, don't worry Sweetness I'll be watching always." he said with a smile as he took my hand. We got home grabbed my mail and checked my email. I opened a letter from my mom saying that she hadn't seen me for months asking when they could come up. I quickly typed back telling her that I had been very busy but I'll work something out soon. I even told her about Xavier and I finished a letter with I love you and dad, Always Piper. "Hey X go ahead and pick something out I'll be back in a few minutes." I called from my laptop. "Sure thing." he said whispering in my ear. I jumped out of my skin, "Don't do that." I said putting my hand on my chest. "Sorry I forget that I can be very quiet." he said whispering on my neck. "I have to lay out my clothes for work tomorrow." I said as I got my mind back from the way he smelled.

I laid out my Scooby scrubs and got into my sweats and tee shirt so I would be comfortable. "Hey what did you pick out?" I asked but got no answer. The front door was left open and no Xavier anywhere to be found. Not to sure what was going on I text the sisters and they told me that they would be right there. I had no time to text back before they showed up. "Wow that was fast." I said letting them in. "When you can move as fast as we can a few block isn't that hard." Regina said. "So this isn't very good huh?" I asked. "He called the brothers so I'm saying no it isn't. Come on Piper lets go and have a seat they will be back in a few minutes." Cyndi said. About a half an hour went by and Cyndi jumped up, "They are back." she said heading for the door. I held back as they came in looking at the torn clothes and bleeding faces of the three guys. "Oh my god what happened? Let me get some wet towels." I said heading to the kitchen. I gave each sister a towel so they could clean up the guys and I started on Xavier. "That's going to need stitches." I said as I pointed at the deep gashes on his perfect face. He reached up and took my hand to lead me to the kitchen, "There's no need for that Piper I'll be fine." he told me. "What happened?" I asked carefully. "You went upstairs and I picked up a scent that wasn't any of ours, so I went after him. He was outside your bedroom window he warned me that you wasn't marked and that made you fair game. Jarrod the one from the club tonight he made it clear that he wasn't going to leave you alone, I had to stop him." he told me softly. "Did you kill him Xavier?" I asked in almost a whisper. "Yes please don't be upset with me or my brothers we had no choice." he said with plea. "What did he mean that I wasn't marked?" I asked taking a seat. "It just means that I haven't bitten you so your fair game to others who don't abide by the rules. He knew you belonged to me but didn't care, I had to make it known that I wouldn't stand for it." he said taking my hand. "So what if I told you that I wanted you to bite me what would you say to that?" I asked. "No no you are perfect to me the way you are, I'm not going to do it! I would love for us to never grow old together but no!" he said getting up. "Oh I see you get to be a hot stud and I get to be your grandmother? I'm not going to let this go I want to be with you forever Xavier." I warned. "No Piper its . . . . Just no forget it." he said and walked out of the room. Mike and Jon looked up at me when I came to the doorway and all three were healed up just the clothes torn. "Come on guys they need time alone." Cyndi said getting up. I took a seat in the living room as Mike and Xavier talked about clean clothes for him, "Be right back." Mike said and was gone quickly. Before I knew it Mike returned with new clothes for Xavier and was gone again.

He leaned against the doorway, "You ok Sweetness?" he asked softly. "Yea you go and shower I'll be here putting things away." I said. I must have fallen asleep because I woke to the sound of the alarm clock in my room. I rolled over to find him laying on his side on top of the covers and his arm under his head, "Good morning Sweetness sleep well?" he asked smiling at me. "How did I get here?" I asked still half asleep. "You fell asleep on the couch so I brought you up here so that you could rest well. You are very beautiful when you sleep." he said. "I bet you say that to all the girls." I said laughing. "Come on Piper don't want to be late. You get dressed and I'll be down stairs waiting for you." he said as he left the room. I dressed and took a last look of myself in the mirror to find a necklace that read Forever on it around my neck. "Hey X where did this come from?" I asked as I came into the kitchen. "I got that for you do you like it?' he asked. "I love it thank you." I said as I kissed him on his juggler. He tightened up and his breathing became heavy, "Don't do that." he said as he smiled at me. "Why not?" I asked slyly. "Yes well . . . . I can be very convincing when I want something." he informed me. "Lets make a deal you give me what I want and in return I will give you what you want. How does that sound?" I asked looking slyly at him. "Forget it Piper we both will be waiting a very long time." he said shaking his head at me. "Fine but I'm not going to play fair now that I know your weakness!" I told him. "You are my weakness, I will give you anything you could ever ask for take you anywhere in this world you wish to go but not that. Even though I have a hard time telling you no for some reason." he said backing up from me. "Come on we are going to be late." I said taking his hand. He drove us to work and we walked in hand in hand with him kissing me lightly and leaving me to Michelle.

Days, weeks even months went by with it being the same work, home, and Xavier. Movies, dinner and the couch we never left each others side. Michelle and I were talking on our break, "Hey maybe we should have a cookout now that it is summer." I said. "I think that's great lets do it this weekend." Michelle said. "Ok I'll tell X maybe we can have it at his house his field is huge." I suggested. "Hey how are you and his family getting along?" she asked. "Its been great the girls and I hang out some but its mostly X and me, its been three months now." I told her as we walked back inside. Xavier walked up behind me sliding his arms around me and kissing my neck, "Hey Baby working hard?" I asked. "Nope just had to see you missed you that's all." he said. "Hey can we have a cookout at your house this weekend? We don't have much time with it being Thursday night now and I want to do it Friday." I asked. "Anything you want Sweets you know that. Lets get something to eat you guys." he said getting our hands and dragging us to the cafeteria. I had a salad, Michelle had chips and Xavier had a burger and fries. Michelle and X chatted back and forth about him inviting some of his single friends, and him agreeing. I text the sisters so they could get a jump on things for me. We made it back to the floor so we could go over our beds and make sure they had all they needed for the new docs to come on shift. Michelle and I walked out together with Xavier waiting on me at the car. We got home and I chucked my mail on the counter before I hit the shower quickly so Xavier could do the same. While he was in I checked my email and read the one from mom telling me that her and dad would be down Friday morning. "No need to send one back she will never get it." I thought to myself. I grabbed a soda and set in the floor putting in a movie knowing I would be asleep before the previews were over.

I sat in the floor drinking my soda thinking to myself about mom and dad coming, "What's up Sweetness?" he said with his hot breath on my neck and hand around my waist. "My parents are coming they will be here in the morning. We had this cookout planned and she gave me not even a days notice." I said. "That's great Sweets I want to meet your parents. They can come there will be plenty for everyone." he said as he laid on his back with a pair of shorts on and no shirt. "You wont be able to stay the night my parents are old fashion a bit." I said as I ran my fingers down his sleek chest. "I could sneak in your window after she goes to bed, I can be very quiet." he said smiling. "You don't know my mom she has spidey senses." I said with a laugh and pulling him to the couch. I waited for him to settle and then I laid down with him. As soon as he put his muscular arms around me I was asleep. The phone woke me with its ringing, "Hello?" I said still asleep some. "Hey Sweetie you awake?" my moms voice rang out. "I am now where are you guys?' I asked. "We are pretty close should be there in about thirty minutes, I love you." she said. "Love you to Momma see you soon." I said as I hung up. I kissed X on the neck, "Wake up Baby my parent will be here in about thirty." I told him. He tightened up on me and put his face in my neck and took a deep breath, "Mmmmm you smell delicious, sleep well?" he asked. "Yes as always and you?" I asked him. "I wont be able to sleep without you in my arms this weekend." he said. "I'm sorry." I told him. "I'll go home and check on the kids and let you get your parents settled." he said. "Hurry back to me they want to meet you." I told him. I watched him leave then I went to finish up in the house and get dressed since I only had about ten minutes before they got there.

My parents pulled up in front of the house and I went out to greet them, "Hi Momma, Daddy how was your trip?' I asked. "Fine I guess, you look good Piper." she said. We got inside and I took their bags to the guest room, "Hey Piper someone for you at the door." she called to me. I came down to find a flower delivery guy, "Flowers for Piper Danvers." he said. "That's me thank you." I said as I took the roses and read the card. Forever My Love, Xavier. "That's nice now where's the remote to the TV?" my Dad asked. "Here you go Dad." I said as I handed him the remote. "Purple roses Piper where did he find those?" Mom asked. "I don't know but he is full of little surprises like that. Oh we are invited to Xavier's house today for a cookout, so rest up we will go shortly." I told them. "When are we going to meet this guy Piper?" he asked looking up from the TV. "In about five seconds." I said hearing the Charger pulling up. He knocked on the door and I opened to him standing there wearing tight fitting jeans, blue button up shirt with sleeves rolled up and flip flops. He kissed me on the lips, "Hi Sweetness looking luscious as ever in your camo fitigs and tank." he said smiling. "Yea you to, come on in my parents are in the living room watching well fighting over the TV." I said taking his hand. My dad rose to his feet as we entered the room, "Hi sir I'm Xavier nice to meet you." X said shaking dads hand. My mom got up, "Wow he is very handsome Piper, I'm Pat and this is Ronnie very nice to meet you." she said shaking his hand as well. "You being good to my baby girl?" dad asked. "Yes Sir I give everything she wants." X told him. "Good good." Dad said as he sat.

Chapter 3

"Purple roses X where did you find those?" I asked. "Your favorite color right?' he asked. We headed to the kitchen so I could see them again, "Can I ask you something, why do you call me Sweetness?" I asked handing him a drink. He walked over trapping me between the counter and himself, "I told you that you have a scent right, well it smells so very sweet to me. That's why I love on your neck the way I do so I can breath you into me. I wont do it anymore if it makes you uncomfortable now that you know." he told me. "No I love it especially when you breath on my neck. I was just wondering that's all, I thought that maybe I smelled like Dr. Pepper to you since I drink so much of it." I said with a laugh. "Mmmmm your right Dr. Pepper." he said in a whisper on my neck. I kissed his juggler making my way kissing under his chin and up to his lips. I slowly ran my tongue over his lips before I kissed him. He began to breath heavily holding me close to his body. My mom cleared her throat, "We don't want to be late do we?" she asked with her arms crossed. He loosened his hold on me and opened his eyes, they were electric blue. "Wow how did you do that?' I whispered to him. "You do that to me always." he said. "You sure do love my baby don't you Xavier?" mom asked. "Yes very much so." he said as he looked at me. "You know that she lost her husband almost a year ago right?" my dad said as he came in. "Yes sir." Xavier said. "Good just don't rush anything!" my dad warned. "No sir I would never rush her in anything she will have my attention forever." X told my father. "Good now lets eat I'm starving Pat wouldn't let me eat before we got here. What's on the menu Xavier?" my dad asked. "Steaks, ribs, fruit just about anything

19

you want." Xavier said. My father was warming up, food had that effect on him.

We headed for the truck that has been parked since Brandon's death. It was roomy enough for all of us to ride in. Xavier helped my mom in and then me, kissing my hand when he did. "Mom X has two brothers and sisters that he cares for. His parents Kaleb and Charisma adopted them and shortly passed away when their plane went down." I told her as I turned around in my seat. "Wow he has a lot on his plate doesn't he, a doctor, a father figure where does he find the time?" she asked in one of her tones. "Mom be nice." I warned. "They are 16 and 17 so they care for themselves." Xavier chimed in. There was no way that we could tell her that they were all vampires she would flip her lid. Finally we arrived at the Great House with Jon coming to my door and helping me out, "You joining the army Piper?" Jon joked. "Maybe don't you like my pants?" I asked smiling at him. "I like em well enough just giving you a hard time that's all." he said as he laughed. Regina took my parents by the arm and led them into the house, "You look like you need a snack Ronnie." she said as my dad went willingly. "Food is the way to his heart." I said smiling and shaking my head. As soon as everyone was in the house Xavier took me in his arms, looked deeply in my eyes. I watched his eyes as they started to change from blue to electric blue. He kissed me with so much passion and let go giving me that irresistible smile, "I needed that." he said. "Your eyes how did you do that?" I asked. "That wasn't me that was you, I told you that your scent does that to me." he said. "That's amazing." I said still looking at his eyes. "Piper, X people will be showing up soon so shake a leg." Cyndi ordered.

We walked into the Great House together finding my dad with a plate of snacks and my mom with a drink. "You have a nice place Xavier, don't you think so Ron?" my mom asked. "Yea maybe we should get a TV like this one." my dad said looking up at her. Mom just shook her head disapprovingly, "I'll have you one sent to your house Ronnie if you like." Xavier offered. "Sure a big one like this." dad said with a laugh. "Dad!" I said. "That's ok Sweetness I will have it done by Monday." he said. People started to show up and there was dancing out in the field having a good time. Michelle finally showed up, "Hey nice turn out huh?" she asked. "Yea, come on I want you to meet my parents." I said putting my arm through hers. Xavier was talking to them as we got closer he walked off, "Mom, dad this is Michelle she has been my rock all this time." I said. "Nice to meet you Michelle its nice to know that my Piper has someone to count on." mom said. "I love Piper she is my best friend." she said. Xavier returned with a friend, "Ooooh who is that?" Michelle asked. "I don't know but he's hot." I said. "Michelle this is my friend Trevor." Xavier told her. "Hi you want to dance?' he asked her and she went willingly. "X sweetie he isn't well you know?" I asked. "No he is fine." he said laughing. "Have you hunted since we started dating?" I asked. "I don't need to go I eat my steaks very rare and I go to the blood bank and I have you so I don't need to go." he told me. I stepped into his arms, "Come on Sweetness lets dance." he said guiding me to the field. As we danced he pulled me close to his body and I lost myself in his breathing. The way he smelled took my mind over, "Are you having a good time Sweetness?" he asked. "Yes I am are you?" I asked. "Any time I'm with you I have a good time." he said looking at me. "Piper, I love you more than anyone could possibly love another." he said holding me close. "I love you the very same Xavier." I told him. "Will you become my bride to be with me forever?" he whispered. I just stopped dancing and looked at him with the music still loud in my ears. With his eyes glowing blue under the moonlight, he got down on one knee, pulled a little black box out of his pocket. "Piper will you marry me?' he asked as he opened the box. It was the most beautiful purple diamond ever made. "Xavier, its beautiful yes I will marry you!" I said with tears in my eyes. He slid the half caret diamond on my finger and slid his hands up my body as he stood up. He kissed a tear that escaped my eye off my cheek. "I love you Piper." he said. "I love you." I told him as the crowd of our friends clapped.

As the party started to close up I helped the sisters clean up, "Do you like your ring?" Regina asked. "Did you guys know about this?" I asked. "Oh yea we knew, we couldn't have told you X would have ripped us apart!" Cyndi said. After clean up was done Xavier drove us home and opened the front door for me, "You guys have a good night see you in the morning." Mom said. "I'll be leaving shortly Pat." he said. "Yea right like I said see you both in the morning." she said on her way up the steps. "Spidey senses." I said and laughed. He led me to the couch and put in a movie then laid down, "Come on Sweetness you look tired. Do you like the ring it can be returned and get another?" he asked. "I love the ring its perfect." I said. "Then what is it?' he asked touching me softly. "Its just when we get married and you give into me will I still have the same effect on your eyes?" I whispered to him. "Yes my Sweetness you will always have this effect on me, and you will just have to try harder to change my mind that's all." he said smiling widely. "Good." I said and settled back in his chest and fell asleep.

I woke up to the smell of moms famous pancakes and Xavier watching me, "Morning baby, mom is fixing pancakes." I said and kissed him on his chin. He pulled me close to him, "You smell so good this early in the day." he said and let me go. I kissed his face all over quickly and got up. "Good morning guys sleep well?" I asked. "Yes we did I can see that you two look comfortable on the couch." Mom said with a tone. "Patty." Dad said. "Yes Ronnie?" she asked. "Can I have more syrup?" he asked. That's was his way to make her hush. "Piper I think we are going to go home today so he can rest up for work." she said. "Awe mom I hate to see you go so soon." I said before I put more pancakes in my mouth. "Piper you aint gonna deny your mother a wedding are you?" Dad asked. "No daddy I was thinking a Halloween night wedding." I told him looking at Xavier. "Good Halloween or not just make sure its a wedding." Dad said. "You got it Dad." I said. After breakfast Xavier told my dad that the TV he wanted would be delivered to the house on Monday. "I thought you were just joking, you really don't have to do that." Dad told him. "If it makes my Piper happy I will do whatever so enjoy the new TV." X told him as he put the bags in their car. I gave hugs to the both of them, "You bring her to our house your welcome anytime." Dad said. "Yes sir I will thank you." Xavier said. I watched them drive off with Xavier holding me and my cell going off. "Hey you guys want to go swimming?" Cyndi asked. "Sure bring Xavier's trunks, see you guys in a few." I said and hung up. "Hey honey we are going to the pool hope that's ok." I said. "Anywhere you are than so shall I." he said as I went up the steps. I dressed in my purple camo bikini and tossed on some shorty shorts with a tank. I could hear them when they came in, "This is Julien he is from a neighboring coven." Regina told Xavier. "Julien." Xavier said. I came down stairs pulling my hair up in a ponytail, "Wow she has a scooby tat on her shoulder that's nice, you see that Xavier?" Julien asked. "I can see that she has a tattoo." Xavier said with a hiss and narrowing his eyes into thin slits. Regina stepped in between them, "Julien no comments on Piper he is very protective of her that is his bride to be." she warned. "I meant no harm I just thought it was cool that's all. No hard feeling X I'm sorry." he said in his defense.

"Sure." X half way said. I stepped in his arms and kissed him on the neck, "Lets go get wet." I said breaking up the tension.

We got to the pool and the guys hit the water with us girls taking our time. Cyndi had on a hot pink bikini, and Regina had on a black and hot pink bikini. I sat and watched them play and dive off the board having fun. Xavier looked like he glided into the air as he dove off. I slowly went to the water and inched my way in, before I knew it he grabbed my ankles and pulled me under to him. He kissed me on the way back to the top, "Hey that wasn't very nice." I told him. He pulled me to the deep part of the pool, "Don't let me go I swim like a rock." I said laughing. "Don't worry Sweetness I'm never letting you go." he said with his hot breath on my neck. We played all day like that and soon Regina came over, "Piper is hungry, lets get some snacks." she said. "You hungry Sweets you should have said something I don't want you to pass out again." X said. "I was having fun that's all." I said as he swam me back to the shallow part for me to get out. I put a towel around me as Xavier got some money for him and Regina to get snacks. "You coming Julien?' he asked. "Um sure." Julien said and got up quickly. I just looked at the guys, "He don't trust him right now after his comment on your body parts that's all." Mike said. "Its just a tattoo." I said. "Yes well its on you that means no looking, no touching and no speaking." Jon explained to me. "Don't worry you will get used to it Cyndi is the same way." Bailey said.

The trio returned with snacks for everyone and I leaned up for Xavier to slid down behind me. Bailey ate quickly and jumped up, "More swimming guys?" he asked. He was tall and chiseled like a model. "I think I'm going to set this one out just for a few minutes, you guys go on and have fun." I said. Xavier turned back, "You ok Sweetness?" he asked. "Oh yea just getting a little bit of sun that's all. Would you mind putting lotion on me first?" I asked. "Sure, I'll stay with you for a bit." he said as he put the lotion on. I was losing myself in his touch and the tingling feeling he gave me. "Ok you go on I'll be ok." I said to him smiling. He went on to the pool and I laid there watching them play, soon I had to flip so I tied up the suit and began to put lotion on my front. He was back out of the water in a flash, "I'll stay with you this time you look lonely." he said as he put lotion on me. "You don't have to I know you are having fun." I told him. "I wanted to tell you that I am sorry for growling at Julien like that. I don't ever want to scare you or think that I scare you. I don't trust other male vampires and I don't like them to look at you." he told me. "Its ok your brothers explained everything to me and you didn't scare me I trust you. Alright I know you want to get back in lets go." I told him. He smiled at me and got in the shallow side so I could follow him but I went to the deep side. He watched me intensely with his eyes glowing in the sunlight. He began to swim my way at a fast pace, I had never seen anyone swim that fast before. I jumped in and before my toes hit the bottom he had me around the waist and swimming me to the top. "That's was cruel." he said as I wrapped my legs around him. "I love you Xavier." I said as I let go of his neck and laid back to float. He lifted me up gently so he could kiss my tummy, then he slid his hands up my back so he could have me close. I quickly kissed his neck and bit him gently, then I moved under his chin kissing my way up to run my tongue over his lips. I kissed him putting my fingers through his silky wet hair. He pulled me so close that even water couldn't get in between us as his breathing got heavy and hot as he kissed me back. "Ok you guys the water is about to boil, X she has to breathe!" Mike said as he swam by knowing that Xavier may not be able to control himself this time. He loosened his grip on me and opened his eyes, they were glowing electric blue, "See what you do to me?" he said. "Mmmmm yes I do, would you like me to do it again?" I asked slyly.

He avoided my question by putting me on his back and taking me to the shallow end of the pool. He lifted me out of the water and set me on the side so we could talk with him still in the water. "Hey there what's your name?" a girl asked as she got closer to Xavier. He never looked at her, keeping his eyes on me. "You know you have the most amazing blue eyes?" she asked again trying to get him to talk to her. "He's with me so shooo." I told her. "I was talking to him not you!" she said in a smart ass tone. "How long can you hold your breath under the water? We are about to find out unless you go away!" I said so softly and mean that it had me worried I might hurt her. She swam off pissed that she didn't get what she wanted, "Keeper, she's dangerous Xavier she will fit perfectly!" Jon said as he swam up on us. "You are very mad Sweetness I can feel you. Come on lets go home." Xavier said as he pulled me back into his arms. The large group of us headed to the gate and split ways to go home.

As we pulled up I saw Michelle on the front porch waving to us, "Hey Piper since Michelle is here I'll go and shower be back soon." he said. "Sure you ok you look like you have something on your mind?" I asked. "I love you see you soon." he said as he kissed my neck. "I love you to, hurry back to me." I said. "Girl where have you been?" she said as I came up on the porch. "Swimming." I said smiling at her. "I just stopped by to see you and talk for a few minutes." she said as we went inside. "So how's things with Trevor?" I asked. "Oh yes he is great like your Xavier he brought me breakfast in bed and flowers, he's beautiful." she said smiling widely. "I'm so happy for you Michelle, X did good finding him for you." I told her. "Ok so tell me all that's been going on with you and Xavier." she said raising her eye brows. "Well I work, come home, chores, and wake up in Xavier's arms every morning. Michelle I have never been so comfortable with someone in my life, and he has never hinted he wanted to go any further than kissing even if I stress him up if you know what I mean. You should have seen the water at the pool we almost made it boil, what should I do?" I asked with a giggle. "If you are that comfortable with him and this is what you really want then talk to him, talking always makes it better." she said. "Oh I really want him to go further, maybe I can talk to him about it or I could just stress him and see how far he goes." I told her. "I want details all of em." she said laughing hard. "Hey a lady never kisses and tells well almost never tells that is. I love you girl you always make me feel better." I told her. "Love you to now I have to go Trevor is stopping by." she said getting to her feet. "Tell Trev hi for me." I said as she walked home. I headed for the shower so I could be ready for him when he returned.

I dressed and headed for my room that is where I found him holding a purple daisy. "So you gonna tell me what's on your mind or what?" I asked taking the flower from him. "Just a lot of things." he said lightly. "Is it me?" I asked quietly. "On no Sweetness, its just that I promised your father that I . . . ." he said before I interrupted. "You promised my father what?" I asked. He took my hand and pulled me to the bed, "I promised your father that I would never rush you that's all. But the things that you do to me makes me want you so bad. Please don't think that I and rushing you because if you say wait then I will forever if that is what it takes." he said looking at me. I rose to my feet so that I could sit across his lap, "Maybe I have been waiting on you to ask or attempt, did you ever think of that?" I asked as I kissed his neck. I could hear his breathing getting heavy as I pushed him back on the bed licking his neck and I bit him softly. "Mmmm." I breathed as I ran my tongue over his lips before I kissed him and his hands up the back of my shirt. "Really?' he asked. "Yes." I said taking his shirt off. We made love that night for the first time. "Are you sure there is no going back?" he asked in a whisper. "Yes Xavier I want you forever." I told him as he kissed my neck. While he made love to me he opened his mouth and put his teeth into my skin tasting me for the first time. "Mmmm so sweet." he whispered as he went back for more seeping his venom into me. I could feel him tasting me, feel his excitement as flashes of his memories raced through my mind. When he was finished he looked at me with a small amount of blood in his lips and kissed me. We laid there with him caressing my body next to his, "Are you alright Sweetness, I didn't hurt you did I?" he asked. "No you were wonderful." I said.

Chapter 4

I could hear him talking to me, "Piper wake up please, Piper can you hear me?" he asked with his voice full of worry. I could hear the sisters telling him things were going to be fine, "She's a fighter Xavier she wont let you down." Regina told him. "She has been asleep far to long, its been almost 24 hours. Her eyes should be my blue, they have yet to change. I should have never gave into my temptations, I should have never listened to either of you when it came to her!" he said with authority and worry. "Go get some rest Xavier we will stay with her, we have yet to be wrong so why question us now?" Cyndi said. The sisters laid with me when he left, I could feel his worry, his sadness. Cyndi played with my hair as they watched TV and talked back and forth. "Maybe we rushed him into this, he said he wasn't ready he said she wasn't ready." Regina said. "We told him that she would come and that she would understand when he told her the family secret. We were right about that she is just different that's all we saw that about her as well." Cyndi said. "For our sakes I hope your right, he will kill us if we are wrong even in the slightest." Regina reminded her. It seemed like minutes before I could feel Xavier near me, "How is she any change? Let me see her eyes." he said touching me softly. I could feel the sisters move from me and wait on how I was. "Still no change what if she never wakes up?" he said halfway to himself. "She is different X she wont let you down, she's a fighter. You know that no two are the same some scream and some don't." Cyndi and Regina both said. "Out the both of you." he demanded. "We will be downstairs if you need us." Cyndi said. "I need you Piper please wake up." he said in a whisper laying next to me. His scent intensified everything intensified my hearing, the things I felt, smelled.

Soon a small knock came to my door, "X, Michelle is downstairs wanting to talk to Piper what should I tell her?" Jon asked. "I'm coming I'll talk to her." he said as he got up. "That's it Piper get up you are worrying everyone in the house, Xavier is going to have a stroke." I thought to myself. I pulled myself out of bed and got my clothes for the shower that I needed badly. I could hear everyone downstairs like I was in the same room. He told Michelle that I was under the weather that I had got to much sun at the pool but I should be up soon. "Jon wont you go check on her and see if she is awake yet." he told him as Michelle and Trevor left. "Xavier Piper isn't in her room!" he called to X. I heard him running up the steps as they both headed for the bathroom, "Out Jon! Piper honey are you ok?" he asked carefully. "Yep never better." I said as I turned off the water. He had a towel in hand when I opened the shower curtain. He wrapped me up and helped me back to the bedroom and set me on the bed, "Do you have a thirst? You had me so worried I thought I may have taken to much from you, the way you tasted was amazing just like the way you smell. Your eyes are the most green I have ever seen, there is my blue on the outer parts most beautiful." he said from his knees. "No thirst just hungry all I want is a Dr. Pepper and you to kiss me starting at my collar bone." I said in a order. "As you wish my love." he said smiling widely. He started at my collar bone working up to my juggler then to my lips. "Wow when you get excited your eyes illuminate green they are wonderful." he said as he ran his fingers through my wet hair and pulling my head back so he could put his face in my neck. He smelled all the way up to my juggler, "Mmmm you smell the same." he said with his hot breath. He kissed me with electricity running through his body as we gave into the passion making love to each other. "Come the others are growing restless." I said after we finished enjoying one another.

I put on my camos and a tank and pulled my hair up, he dressed in jeans and a black silk shirt which he buttoned a few buttons and no shoes. Everyone came up to me when I came downstairs, "Piper you look great." the sister said with the guys agreeing. "What time is it?" I asked. "Almost noon, why?" Mike asked. "I've been asleep for days and I'm hungry, lets get something to eat." I suggested. "Pizza from the Hut?" Bailey said quickly. Xavier took me to the kitchen, "Dr. Pepper?"

he asked. "Hey will I need to feed now or what?" I asked as I drank the soda quickly. "Some do and some don't, you should have the blood to keep you balanced out. We could go camping I could teach you to hunt if you wish." he offered. "That's another thing I already know how you showed me." I said. "What do you mean I have already showed you?" he asked puzzled. "I got your memories, I thought you were the one to get mine." I said getting some chips. "I should have gotten yours not the other way around. What else did you get mine?" he asked reaching for chips. "Only that you were born a day walker, your mother was very beautiful and you look like your father. Kaleb was a very important man people called him their king and you their prince. Others came and asked Kaleb permission for many things and now with him gone it is up to you. Why didn't you tell me that you were royalty to vampires? Oh I got other things but I don't want to talk about that." I told him. He took a deep breath, "Yes my father was king and my mother was very beautiful, I never told you because I didn't want the crown. I always saw myself as an equal, but now that I have a queen I am very ready to be king over the vampires. Now as for the other part her name was Cora but I never loved her like I love you. You have my heart and soul and it will be like that forever. You must know that they will come to you as their queen for many things and you have to answer them as will I." he said getting me another drink. "Can I do that I mean I know nothing of the things they might need?" I asked. "We can do together, be warned your temper will be easy to set off now that you are vampire you must learn to control." he told me. "Yea Piper just like the pool the other day if you were a vampire that girl would have been dead trust me. Now that your and Xavier's love has come full circle he can calm you so let him. His blood runs through your veins and yours through his and you should be able to feel him and him you." Cyndi said as she came in carrying pizzas. "Thanks guys for helping me." I said. "Hey Cyn have faith." Bailey said shoving pizza in his mouth. Cyndi rolled her eyes at him, "I have lots of faith in her B." she said as she smiled at him.

Dinner and a movie was on the way, and I had worries of working tomorrow. Most of everyone fell asleep because they had stayed awake to find out what was going to happen with me. I tried to slip out of Xavier's arms so I could get myself another drink, "Sneaking out?" he asked as he took my hand. "Nope just getting a drink you want one? Oh we have to get B up he has school in the morning, he needs to get home." I said as I pulled him to me. He turned and woke Bailey and Cyndi so that she could get him home with the others going their own ways. I dressed for work and waited on him to get himself ready. "Hey stick with me today ok, I'm just worried if a bloody trauma comes in." I told him as we went into work. "Don't worry Sweetness I'll be there for you. Can you feel your eyes glisten?" he asked. "Yes it is a cool feeling." I told him. "When you feel your eyes glisten and your mouth water just hold your breathe and back away. If that happens then you must drink, the thirst can hurt if you don't get what you need." he told me as he kissed my head.

I walked on the floor hoping that I would have a peaceful day, "Hey how do you feel?" Michelle asked. "Better I think I just got way to much sun." I told her. "I came to see you but Xavier said that you were sick, man he was very worried about you." she told me. "I know I worried everyone in the house." I said. "Hey Trev and I want to go camping, you and the Matthews clan want to go? Oh yea he asked me to marry him." she said as she held up her hand for me to see. "What, when did that happen?" I asked. "This weekend, and I said yes." she told me. "I'm so happy for you Michelle, I'm sorry I was sick." I told her. "That's ok girl I'm telling you now." she said putting her arm through mine walking to the floor. "Hey Robert I'm early so if you want to take off that would be alright with me." I told him. "Thanks I think I will. Bed two needs IV fluids and bed three has a fever, that about covers it." he said as he handed me the charts and took his leave. Michelle took the charts from me, "I'll take the fever you can have the IV." she said. "Thanks pal your the greatest." I said as I took the paper work. "Good morning how are we today?" I asked the patient. "Alright I guess." she said. "Well we will get you fixed right up, I'm going to give you a IV so that you get the fluids you need." I told her as I started needle. I very carefully and nervously put the needle in her skin, I couldn't believe how I felt like a student again. "There you go no problem, can I get you anything?" I asked. "No thank you I'm fine for now." she said as I gathered my stuff and left. My phone rang out with a text from Cyndi reminding me that graduation was tomorrow not to be late. I text her back saying that I would be there.

Before to long my pager went off for an emergency on a gun shot victim. I didn't even think about it as I started to work on getting the bullet out of the leg as my mouth began to water. "Xavier was right the blood is very tempting and smells so good." I thought to myself. X seemed to appear out of no where telling me to step off. "I've got this!" I snapped. "Piper!" Michelle said to me. "I'm sorry I'm fine really." I said much softer this time. "There I got it, lets bandage him up." Xavier said. "Go on outside Piper get some air, I'll finish up here." Michelle said. I took her up on her offer stopping by the drink machine before hitting the outside. "I cant believe I let that happen, I'm stronger than that." I thought to myself. I looked up as they joined me outside, "Sorry about that guys, forgive me?" I asked. "Just as long as when we get to the mall you buy me a fruit smoothie." Michelle said with a smile. "You got it, hey X, Michelle has something to tell you." I said. She showed her ring to him, "Hey when did that happen?" he asked. "Just this weekend crazy huh?" she said. "I'm happy for you guys." he said. "Hey I'm going to go back you guys ready?" she asked. "Be there in a minute." I said drinking my soda. "You did very well Sweetness." he said breathing up my neck. "Well that was horrible I'm much stronger than that it will never happen again." I said. "I have to say the look in your eyes very scary." he said smiling at me. "You want to go to the mall with me tonight?' I asked him. "Yes and camping sounds fun." he said as I pulled him to his feet. "Come on the day is almost over and we can go home." I told him as we walked back in. I checked on my beds before I clocked out for the night, "Hey Michelle don't forget about graduation tomorrow the kids would be crushed." I told her as we walked out together. "I will be there swear." she said putting her arm over my shoulder.

Not much was said on the car ride home just the radio, "You putting things in the right folders?" X asked. "Yea long day I guess and I need to get the kids something for graduation." I said not paying attention. He pulled up at the Great House, "Hey I have to get home, I have to change." I told him. "Be right back." he said as he got out. I sat in the Charger waiting on him as I thought about how I almost lost my self control. Xavier came out of the house carrying two cups, "Here Sweetness try this it will help calm you." he said handing me one of the cups. I took a small sip of the warm blood, "Not bad." I said shrugging my shoulders. "All of it Sweets you need it." he said taking a drink of his. "Ok pushy I'm drinking." I said as I drank more. The more I drank the more I felt better inside myself, much calmer than before. I finished the blood cup as we pulled in the drive way at my house. I went in to rinse the cups out, "I want you." Xavier said trapping me between him and the sink

31

smelling of fresh blood. "Mmmm I need you." I said as I licked his neck smelling his blood run through his veins. He swiftly picked me up and headed for the bedroom never taking his blue eyes from me. The way he made love to me was electric touching my entire body with his hands. I nipped his neck and let his blood touch my tongue, "You are delicious." I whispered to him as I wrapped my leg around his body to have him closer to me. I could have laid there and have him make love to me for days but we both knew that Michelle and Trevor would be on their way soon. Both of us got dressed and hurried down the steps as soon as they knocked on the door. "You wanna take the truck?" X asked. "Sure that will be fine." I said as I got a soda from the fridge.

Michelle and I talked back and forth as Xavier drove to the mall, "Do you know what you are going to get the kids?" she asked. "No clue I guess it will jump out at me." I said as we pulled up. We walked around forever before I could find anything, soon I decided on necklaces' for the sisters and a nice bracelet for the guys. "Hey Sweets I found our wedding bands." Xavier said. The gentleman pulled them from the case, "They are amethyst, purple diamonds and white diamonds all across the top, very nice choice." he said as he handed us the rings. "Baby are you sure you want to wear purple forever?" I asked. "Yes you want them so we get them, size em up please." X said. "They should be ready in two weeks is that alright?" the man asked. Xavier took care of the bill while we waited, "Don't forget you promised me a fruit smoothie." Michelle said. "Come on lets get it now, I want one to." I told her. We headed for the front after the smoothie place to get something to eat, "Hey wait I'll be right back." I said in almost a whisper. Xavier jogged up behind me, "What's on your mind?" he said. "I think I found my wedding dress." I said going into the store. I went into the dressing room to try it on, "Well can we see or what Piper?'" Michelle asked. "Ok I'm coming out." I said. I walked out in a hunter green floor length dress showing my toes, and the top fit off the shoulders. "Well what do you think?" I asked when I heard Xavier gasp. "Damn girl that is beautiful." Michelle said. "Wow Piper that makes your eyes brighten up." Trevor told me. "You don't like it X?" I asked. "Completely breathe taking, lets get married tonight." he said standing up and giving me that smile I have a hard time saying no to. "Xavier now no we are waiting on Halloween." I said as I went back in to change.

Xavier paid for my dress and we headed out, "Where shall we eat?' he asked as we walked hand in hand. "Any where is good for me just as long as its food." Trevor said. We ended up at Logan's and I knew it was because Xavier thought I needed something with a blood taste although I didn't think so. I ordered ribs and he ordered his steak very rare, Michelle and Trevor had steak and shrimp. "Hey Piper try mine." he said as he offered me a bit. "No thanks I like mine more cooked." I said stopping his hand. "Just try how bad can it be?" he asked again. "Fine." I said as he put the bite in my mouth. "Yum that's pretty good." I said as he gave me another bite. "Feel better?" he asked in a whisper. I gave him love to let him know I was good until we got home, "Hey Xavier where did you get that ring?" Trevor asked. "It was my fathers I found it the other day. I also found my mothers matching ring." he said as he pulled out a small box. "Wow that is pretty." I said as I looked at the large garnet ring, almost the color of blood. "Fit for a princess." he said as he slid it on my finger. The stone was large to fit from knuckle to knuckle, "Shouldn't you give it to one of the sisters?' I asked touching it lightly. "No its yours, family crest and all." he said showing me the side where it had the same symbol as the Great House had. "Very pretty Piper." Michelle said.

After dinner we made our way home dropping Michelle and Trevor off, "See you tomorrow." I said. "You have been very quiet all day something bothering you?" he asked as we walked in the house. "Today when I tasted you I got more of your memories." I told him as I set on the couch. "I thought that was a one time thing." he said setting with me. "Me to." I said as I set back and shut my eyes. "What did you get?" he asked carefully. "I watched you morn the death of your parents, some of your childhood, the worry when you bit me. I saw you the night when you watched me, I even heard and saw you when you killed Jarrod. I heard you tell your brothers to never speak of that night to me ever, I could feel your anger as you killed him." I told him. "I'm sorry Sweetness I never wanted you to learn of that night and I made them swear to never tell you. I don't understand how you got to see them, are you angry with me?" he asked. "Never I just didn't expect to feel you like that. Just no more surprises now that we know that I can do this." I pleaded with him. "Sure just remember I have been alive for a very long time so lots of memories." he reminded me. "Sooo I wonder if I tasted blood of others if I would get things from them as well?" I asked. "Not sure we can try on the sisters if you wish." he said. "Maybe someday." I said getting my laptop to check my mail. Mom sent me pics of the cookout and telling me they missed me. I typed back telling her that I missed her and dad badly and thanks for the pictures they were great. I told her about our wedding bands and my dress and finished the letter with Always Piper. While X was getting drinks I went to change my clothes and lay out outfits for tomorrow. I opened the door to find him with drinks in one hand and chips in the other and movie in his mouth. "Hey come on in." I said taking the movie. "I just thought we could junk food it in bed tonight." he said. "Anything you wish." I said softly. I put in the movie while he dressed and waited on him in bed. "Why don't we go on a little trip this weekend Sweets?" he asked running his fingers up my arm. "That's fine I guess." I said not in the best mood. I missed my parents, saw his memories believe it or not I was very tired. "Would you like space tonight or would you like me to hold tight?" he asked. "Hold tight and don't let go." I said feeling he wanted to hold me. "As you wish my love." he said softly. "Hey I love you." I said. "I love you too." he said putting his face in my neck.

Chapter 5

The sunrise woke me and I slipped out of bed to take a shower to get ready. I came back into the bedroom to find him with his hands tucked under his head, "We have to work on this sneaking out thing Sweets." he said with a smile. "Get your lazy butt out of bed we are going to be late." I said and winked at him. "Feeling any better today?' he asked. "Some I guess." I said not looking at him and getting to my feet. I waited on him to get ready for the day and we headed to work. Michelle and I worked side by side and then we took lunch together outside because it was so nice. "Hey I'm leaving work a little early to get dressed, your coming to the Great House afterwards right?" I asked. "Be there with bells on." she said with a smile. Soon the hour came for me to leave and I did so without saying anything to Xavier, needing the time to walk and think. I grabbed me a cool shower and dressed in a light green sundress and flip flops. I gave myself a quick check and nod before I headed for the door. I opened up and found Xavier standing there with his arms crossed and not looking very happy. "Hi there Sweetness looking delicious as ever." he said. I knew that I was in trouble because of his tone. I stepped back to spin around so that he could see all of me, "Don't ever do that again, do you have any idea what it does to me when I cant find you?" he asked taking a step forward. "I'm sorry Baby I just thought that you would know, you know many other of my feelings." I said in my defense. "Not always Piper not when you have to put things away you shut me down so that I cant feel you. Do you have any idea what . . . . ?" he said and stopped short. "I had no idea really Xavier I'm sorry, I will be more careful." I told him as I put my arms around him and kissed him softly. His eyes began to get bright blue while he had a grip on me, "Hey we have to go we don't want to be late tonight." I told him knowing where this was leading. "Not fair Sweetness, you know you cant get this close to me and then pull away." he said. "The kids are going to be upset if we are late you know that." I said. "Fine." he said in a pout.

We took our seats that Jon had saved for us making it just in time for the music to start playing. We watched as Mike and Cyndi make their way across the stage followed by Bailey. After every hat from the class were tossed in the air we made way to the Great House for a party that the kids planned. "Dr Matthews we want to thank you for all that you have done for Bailey, he sure loves that sister of yours." Baileys father said as they shook hands. "Bailey is a good guy we love him hanging around. Have you met my soon to be bride Piper?" Xavier said touching my back. "Very nice to meet you, I have grown to love Bailey as well very sweet young man. If you will excuse me I have gifts for them." I said taking my leave. I gave the kids the gifts that I found for them with the sisters giving me hugs telling me that they love it and they will wear it always. When the party began to close for the night Xavier took my hand, "Come Sweets we have a long trip to make, your parents will be in bed when we get there," he said pulling me along, "How did you know that I missed my parents?" I asked once in the truck. "When you were sending your mom an email I walked passed you and I felt your sadness, so I called your mom and told her we would be down for the night. I know its a short stay but this will make you feel better I'm sure." he said as he drove along. Once at moms she had left the front porch light on and a note telling me to use the key and come on in.

She had left pillows and blankets on the couch for us to get comfortable with. Xavier put in a movie and we both went to sleep with him holding me tight. The smell of bacon filled the room and I could hear mom and dad in the kitchen talking, "I'm not sure Xavier called and said that she needed to get away and that they were coming that's all, I'm sure its nothing Piper has a strong spirit." mom told dad. "X wake up mom has bacon going this morning." I whispered to him. "Hold your horses I'm coming." he said as I got up. "Mom, Dad I missed you." I said as she gave my hug and then dad. "What's going on Piper why the quick visit?" dad asked. "Nothing is going on I just wanted to see you that's all." I said getting a slice of bacon. "Xavier I love the TV thanks again." dad told him. "Anytime Ron." X said setting beside me. After breakfast we went to my Aunt Barbs house and set around talking back and forth but soon it was time for me to leave. "I hate to go but we have a late night at work." I told them. "Don't worry Piper we will be down soon just you get busy on your wedding plans and time will fly by." mom said. I waved bye to them from the truck as we drove off, "What?" I asked when I noticed Xavier smiling at me. "You feel so good inside, told you this would make you feel better." he said. "I love you for this." I told him. "I love you." he said kissing my hand. "I'm going to run to the house and check on the kids, you want to go?" he asked. "Not this time I will get things done at the house while you are gone." I told him. "As you wish, see you soon." he told me when he dropped me off.

While he was gone I cleaned the whole house did the laundry, stripped the bed and went to the grocery store. "Sweetness?' he called as he opened the door. "I'm in here." I called to him. He walked into the living room with a not so happy face and a blood cup for me, "What took so long?" I asked looking at him from the computer. "Cyndi and Bailey." he said. "What's wrong with them?" I asked. "They are pressing me to let her turn him now that school is over." he said as he set with me. "What did you tell them?" I asked as I shut my computer. "I told them its not up to just me anymore. These are the things that you are going to have to answer for other people, Cyndi and Bailey are good practice." he said. "Tell them to come over and I will taste their blood and see what I get." I told him. He called Cyndi with a smile telling her to come on down. I drank my blood cup thinking about what I may get from her and Bailey since I had gotten so many things from Xavier. Cyndi and B showed up, "Piper you wanted to see us?" Cyndi said. "Yea X told me that you want to turn B. Are you willing to let me try something?" I asked. Bailey looked at Cyndi a little worried, "Its ok B she wont hurt you. Yes Piper anything you want." she said. "Let me taste your blood and see what your future holds. B are you sure you want to do this there is no going back?" I asked. "Yes I want this and have ever since I found out." he said with a smile. Cyndi stepped forward and bit her finger so that the blood would flow freely and offered it to me. I let the blood drip from her finger into my mouth and let the memories rush my mind. "Ok B your next Love." I told him. He stepped forward and gave me his finger. I took his hand and slowly bit down on his finger to let the blood come to the top as he jerked just a bit. I let his memories walk through my mind. "Well what did you get Sweetness?" Xavier asked. "That was the coolest thing I have ever seen. They will be fine the both of them I saw their future and his turning will be fine." I told them.

Cyndi smiled at me, "Thanks Piper this is great. We can turn you now B." she told him. "Whoa wait a minute, not right now we have a camping trip planned you can do it then." Xavier said. They both left very pleased that he would be vampire soon, "Can you imagine the power we can have with this gift of yours?" Xavier asked. "Power?" I asked. "Yes as you know my father was one of the very first day walkers so people looked upon him as their king. They came to him from different lands to ask for his permission on things. He had no way of knowing that some of the vampires he let into our peaceful community were human killers. Soon the lands were over ran with killers and he had to go to war with them and take back our lands for the humans to come back. Now that I have inherited his legacy they will look to me as their king and you as queen, its not the power its the elimination of surprise." he said happily. "So I taste and you decide?" I asked knowing talking about his father made him happy. "No we decide together just like with Cyn and B." he said smiling at me. "As you wish now lets have dinner before we go to work." I said getting to my feet. Grabbing something on the way out as we drove to work was much faster for us who now was running late. "So camping in two days huh are you excited?" Michelle asked. "You know I am girl." I said walking into work. The day was a good day with nothing for me to worry about although I had Bailey on mind most of the time. "What if I'm wrong about what I saw, what if he had a hard time?' I kept asking myself. "Hey Piper what's on your mind? You have been in deep thought all day." Michelle asked. "Oh you know just making sure that I have all I need to go camping that's all." I said lying to her. "I'm sure whatever you don't have I'll have so stop worrying." she said.

Finally the day came for us to let Cyndi turn Bailey. I came to the house putting my bag in the hallway and headed for a blood cup. I answered the door for Bailey who knocked as I passed. "Hey B how are you today?" I asked. "Ummm Piper can we talk privately?' he asked. "Sure hon what's on your mind?" I asked as we walked into the living room. "Will this hurt, I mean when she does it? She told me that some scream and some don't, you slept will that happen to me? Do you have any idea how embarrassing that would be if I cried or screamed the whole time?" he asked almost out of breath. "Bailey sweetie calm down now you are worried about something that I'm sure will be fine. Cyn loves you and would never hurt you, I'm sure that she has already seen your out come as I have. I'm not for sure how this gift of mine works so we both shall see. Please make sure that you go into this with a open mind other wise you may have a hard time with this. Talk with Cyndi about all your worries before you let this happen and feel free to come and talk with me about anything." I told him as I patted his leg. "Thanks Piper you helped me a lot." he said as he got up to make way to Cyndi. I sat and finished my blood cup, "Well done Sweetness, if I didn't know any better I could almost swear that you have been a vampire forever." he said as he made his way over to me. "Everyday I remember something new but it feels I have always known things like this." I told him as he sat with me. Before he could say anything to that Cyndi called down to him letting us know that Bailey was asleep. Xavier checked him over and making sure he was right on track. "How much venom did you give him Cyndi?" Xavier asked as Bailey began to wrench in pain. "I gave him a little just like you told me." she said in her defense. "Get some cool towels." I said as I looked him over. She came back and I placed the towels on his neck, legs and arms as he began to calm down.

X and I gave her instructions to keep the cool towels on him until this was over. "How did you know to do that for him?" Xavier asked. "I don't know like I said I just remembered." I told him. "Amazing." he said as we returned to the living room and waited on Bailey to wake up. After two long days he finally woke and asked for something to drink. Xavier asked Mike to bring Bailey a blood cup. Michelle and Trevor knocked on the door, "Hey guys are we ready or what?" she asked. "Yea just a few minutes to get the truck packed up." I told her trying to give Cyndi and B time to get settled. They were the last to get in the truck, "Bailey after the sun goes down you will hunt and stay clear of Michelle and Trevor they are human and I want to keep them that way." I told him. "I cant wait and I promise to stay clear." he said holding Cyndi's hand. Our camp sites were close together and the guys went for fire wood while us girls set up the food. Since the day was late when we got there we sat around the camp fire telling stories and laughing. "Ok I'm wore out so good night." Trevor said. "Hey night guys see you in the morning." I said. Xavier led the way for the hunt, "Are you going to go with me tonight?' he asked. "I think I'll just watch you much more fun for me to watch." I told him. "Ok then as you wish." he said pulling me on his back and hopping up into a tree. "I'll be fine Love go have fun." I said as I made myself comfortable. I could see him as he walked along until he found something that caught his eye. He darted off like lighting and glided when he got close enough to his prey and took it down drinking from it. He turned back towards me and in a blink of an eye he was in the tree with me, "So if you wont hunt with me will you take a late night swim with me?" he asked with eyes glowing in the moonlight. "That I can do." I said getting down from the tree.

The water felt good to my body as he pulled my legs around him and laid me back to float. "Your so beautiful in the moonlight." he said as he lift me to kiss my tummy. "Do you think so because there will be a full moon on Halloween." I told him. "Is this something that you want, I mean to marry me on Halloween night?" he asked as he lift me back up into his arms. "Yes of course do you want something else?' I asked. "I want you to be happy and have the things that you want as well. How is it that you knew I wanted a Halloween night wedding?" he asked. "I have a gift that tells me many things. This is something I want with a dozen candles to light my way to you." I told him smiling. "I would marry you anywhere anytime you so desire." he said as we swam around. "Come on Love lets get back and check on B." I said as I kissed him. We walked hand in hand back to the camp site to find the others setting around the fire, "Hey B how did it go?' Xavier asked. "Things went well, I had fun. How did you do Piper?" he asked. "Oh I just watched this time I like mine in a cup." I told him as I headed for my tent. Xavier put his strong arms around me and I could feel myself slipping into sleep, "Sleep well my Love." he said softly. "What are going to do the night before our wedding you know that you cant see me?" I said in a whisper. "Awe come on Piper traditions are kinda out the window here. We are vampires and we sleep together every night are you really going to make me suffer the night before the wedding?" he asked. "Ok ok let me think about it I may change my mind." I told him. "Good I have three months to change your mind I think I can do that." he said with a glimmer in his eyes.

Morning came through the tent waking me, "Hey X are you awake?" I asked. "Yes Love." he said pulling me close. "I have to have a cup this morning I hurt a little bit." I said. He jumped to his feet and rushing to get what I needed. I drank it down in two drinks, "Did you have a thirst last night?' he asked. "A small one but I made it through the night." I said knowing I was going to get yelled at. "Damn it Piper don't do that any more you could regret things if it gets the best of you." he said not happy with me at all. "Sorry I wont let it happen again." I said a bit taken by his tone. He walked out of the tent and I knew that he was mad as hell at me. I followed him out to have breakfast with the others. "Swimming this morning?" Michelle asked seeing Xavier's and my face. "Let me change be right there, you guys go on." I said hoping to walk alone to the beach. I came out of the tent to find him waiting on me. I turned to walk off leaving him standing, "Sweetness wait." he said catching up to me. "I know your pissed at me and I said I was sorry, what more do you want from me?' I asked hatefully. He pulled me to a stop, "Now it is my turn to say sorry, I should have never yelled at you like that. I love you deeply and I worry about your thirst because you don't hunt. Maybe this is the way you are made but still I worry." he said putting his arms around me. "I know what I need Xavier don't treat me like a child anymore." I told him. "Again I'm sorry can you find it in your lasting heart to forgive me?" he asked. I kissed him lightly, "Yes I can now lets go swimming." I said pulling him along. I watched him as he went to the diving area to meet with the other guys while Michelle and I laid on the beach. "You guys alright, I heard him raise his voice." she asked easily. "Things are alright and yes he did but that's ok we made up and he said he was sorry." I told her as we walked to the water. Xavier swam up to us grabbing our ankles pulling us under. I pushed him under the water as he came up, "Hey now." he said getting up. "Not nice to pull us under the water." I said laughing. Trevor and Michelle headed for shore with me following.

After lunch we came back for more laying on the beach and swimming and soon the sun started to go down. "We will catch up I have some mind changing to do." Xavier told them. "Mind changing huh?' I asked as he held onto me. He smiled at me but I wasn't going to let him win this one or at least not yet. He kissed my neck as he ran his fingers through my wet hair, "How am I doing so far?" he asked. "Sorry gonna have to work harder on this one." I said joking with him. He put his lips next to mine, "Ok as you wish." he said. The rest of the night we spent in the water making love under the moonlight. I bit him hard enough to make him tremble and hold me tightly. He bit me back so that he could have the taste of me in his mouth, "You are so what I desire everyday." he whispered to me. I put my finger nails into his skin just enough to excite him more, "Than you shall have all of me." I told him. The sun started to show the earth again as we came to a finish and headed back to the camp site. "Are you guys just getting back?" Michelle asked. I gave her a smile as I went into our tent. "Lets get a few minutes of sleep before Bailey wants to swim." X said laying down waiting for me. "That boy could be a fish if this vampire thing don't work out for him." I said laughing. "Your right about that." X said as I laid with him. This was the last day of our trip so we had a lot of fun before we had to pack up and get ready for work the next day.

Chapter 6

It was Monday again and I was deep into work getting better with the scent of human blood. I pulled a few doubles to make up for the camping trip that I owed Robert. Being a vampire had its advantages with the sleeping thing, and it was good since I pulled so many that week. I was on my third double and I had been asleep only a few hours before returning to work and trying to keep up with my blood intake. I sat at the desk to catch up on the paper work since this night was so busy and I fell fast asleep just going to close my eyes for a minute. I woke up in one of the beds in the ER with Xavier and Michelle at my side, "Sweets how do you feel?" he asked moving my hair from my face. "What happened?' I asked. "You tell us you set down and fell asleep, I tried to wake you and when I couldn't I called Xavier. "Sorry to worry you guys I'm fine just a bit tired that's all." I said setting up and Michelle handing me some water. "Come we are going home." Xavier said as he helped me to my feet. I sat in the passenger side of the car while he drove and him deep in thought. Once inside my house I went to the couch, "Wonder why I fell asleep like that, I know I have been working a lot but I shouldn't have been that tired." I asked him as he handed me a cup. "Well Sweets when I couldn't wake you I ran your blood thinking that you might be anemic." he said and stopped. "Well am I? I have been drinking as much as I can." I told him. "Your a little pregnant that's all." he said and took my hand. "WHAT!!??" I asked loudly. "Pregnant." he said a bit worried. I set there letting what he said sink in and not saying anything. "Let me take you upstairs so you can rest, I will get whatever you need." he said standing and offering his hand to me. I went in and

43

laid on the bed very shocked and him getting ready to let me to my thoughts. "Xavier." I said. "Yes?" he asked as he turned around. "Lay with me for a bit." I said. "As you wish." he said coming to me.

I laid there in his arms for about an hour before I said anything, "Are you ok with this, I mean we aren't even married yet and now you are going to be a daddy?" I asked. "A daddy." he whispered. I turned to look at him, "I think I can handle that." he said sounding like a happy child. "I guess you win this one." I told him. "You mean I don't have to suffer that I can have you the night before our wedding?" he asked. "Yes you win you can have me the night before our wedding." I said. He placed his hand on my tummy, "You know Piper you don't have to work those hours anymore we have everything we need for you not to worry. I have made you an appointment with a long time family friend, he will help with many things." he said. "Anything you wish." I told him. "Good you take the week off and rest I'll cover your shifts." he said. I gave into his request just laying around, drinking all the time and the sisters doing everything for me. "Wake up Sweetness we have a doctors appointment today." he said kissing my neck. I showered and dressed with Xavier treating my like glass helping me in the truck. "Who is this doctor again?" I asked. "Dorien Logan is a vampire that has been around for well ever I guess, he is a kind man." he said as he drove along. I sat back and kept to myself for the rest of the trip thinking about many things. "You know you have never told me how you feel about all of this?" he asked. "What do you mean?" I asked. "I'm excited as hell about being a father, but you have kept quiet all week." he said. "What if I don't know how to be a mother? All I know is how to take care of me and have for thirty years. This baby is going to be very special and I'm still learning everyday how to be." I said looking out the window. "Come on now I'm sure you are going to be a great mother, you take care of the others in the Great House they love you." he said pulling up.

We walked into the office and he told the check in nurse who we were. "Doc is waiting on you, come on back." she said smiling at Xavier. He had that effect on all the women that ever came near him. I glared at her letting her know that he was mine not to even look at him. "Awe Xavier how are you today?" Doctor Logan asked as we came in. "I'm fine thanks for asking, this is my Piper." X said showing me to him. "She is as breath taking as you have told me." he said as he shook my hand. I smiled at him as he guided me to the table and helped me up.

He took out the sonogram machine and ran the test on me and felt around my tummy, "Ok mom you are doing just fine and looks like you guys are going to have these babies in February. Keep up the blood intake it should become more as you get bigger and with two in there I'm sure it will be a lot. Rest as much as you can it is going to take a lot out of you since you are still half human, these babies will grow rapidly. Lets make another appointment soon and if ever you need I can make house calls." he said wiping the gel of my tummy. Xavier had a look of complete happiness on his face, "Whoa wait one minute, you said babies, two babies?" I asked swallowing hard. "Yes twins which is very rare for vampires even if you are still human or not." Doc said. I got to my feet and walked out now really freaking out getting into the truck.

Xavier got my next appointment and met me in the truck, "Did you hear that Xavier twins, what the hell am I going to do with twin vampire babies?' I asked with a shaky voice. "Its ok Sweets we will work things out I'm sure." he said softly. "Wait I'm going to have to tell my parents and Michelle!" I said loudly. "You don't want to tell them, are you not happy about this?" he asked. "How am I going to explain to them why I have gone only 7 months or what if they want to feed them? Am I to hand them a bottle with blood in it how will that look, oh lets not forget babies bite?" I asked. "You can tell whoever you want Love don't worry we can work this out." he said nervously. "To the other question yes I'm happy, its just a lot to absorb that's all. Just give me a day or two ok to work this out in my head." I told him. "Good, I'm glad your happy about being a mom. I cant believe that I have had to go my entire life without you." he told me touching me, making me feel better inside. "I love you Xavier no matter what comes our way." I told him. "I will always love you Sweetness forever and a day." he said as he walked into the house together. "I guess I should call the sisters." I said getting my phone. Regina beat me to it, "Go ahead Piper you are on speaker!" she said excitedly. "Twins due in February." I told her. "One for each of us Cyndi did you hear that! Get some rest Piper we will stop by later." she said and hung up. "I'll get you something to drink and let Michelle in." he said getting up. Michelle came in and set with me, "Well how are you feeling, Xavier said that you were just taking some time off." she asked. "Yea I feel fine just going to be a mom that's all." I said smiling at her. "What your kidding me?' she asked. "Yep and now X don't want me to work anymore, what do you think?" I asked her. "Piper maybe this isn't a bad idea I mean do you want someone else to raise your babies while you work those hours?" she asked. "Hell no I don't, man I guess he wins this one too." I said as he came back in with a smile. "Hey just don't forget about me alright." she said as she got up. "How could I you are my best friend?" I asked. "You better not." she said shaking her finger at me. Xavier handed me a plate of fruit, a blood cup and my laptop, "Here ya go and I'll put in a movie for you." he said. I made a few adjustments in the wedding file while I ate and drank.

The month flew by with me getting bigger and not going anywhere. Jon and Regina was making plans to go shopping for their school supplies when X got home. "Hey why don't we go now before he gets here so we can have dinner together?" I asked. "No way Piper if I take you out of this house Xavier will have my head." he said softly not wanting me upset. "Take me with you, I have been in this house forever and I'm about to go crazy." I told him. "Piper please." Jon said. "I'm going!" I said as I got up. "Ok but he's going to kill me for this." he said as we left the house. It was so nice to be out even for a few minutes although I knew deep in my heart I was going to be in trouble for this. I followed them around eating whatever I could find in the store while they shopped. "Hey guys I'm going to pay for my stuff and head to the truck." I told them. "Wait Piper we will come with you can you give us five minutes to check out?" Regina said. "Yea but I'm really tired and my feet are swollen." I said still eating the chips I pulled from the shelf. The car ride home was quiet but not for long as Jon's cell rang, "Shit its X." he said taking a deep breathe. "Hello? Yes she is with us and she is just fine. What was I to do X she made us bring her, I tried to tell her no but for some reason I couldn't." he said pleading his case. They talked back and forth as I worried about what he might do to them. "Just drop me off and you two go home, I'll take care of X." I said as we pulled up at the house. Xavier was waiting on the porch with narrowed eyes. Jon came around and let me out and returned to the truck. "Where are they going I told them to come see me?" he asked in a very mad tone. "I told them to go on I like their heads where they are." I told him as I climbed the steps. "Piper your feet are swollen why did you go out?" he asked as I laid on the couch. "I had to X I was going nuts here all day long, I had to see other people." I said.

He got me a drink, "I would have taken you out all you had to do was ask." he said not as mad at me. "You would have taken me to the porch and you know it." I said trying to make him smile some. "It would have been out. Without the swollen feet or anything else that could have happened." he said as he sat down. I set across his lap and put his hands on my tummy, "Can you feel them moving around?" I asked. "Yes I can." he said smiling widely. "You know we could find out the sex of them if you wish." I said winning this one. He laid me down keeping his hand on my tummy while he called Doc. "Come on he will see us now." X said helping me up. There was never any waiting when we went to Dorien's, "Come on in guys, how are we feeling?" Doc asked. "Fine I guess, how are you?" I asked him. "Very well Queen Piper thank you for asking." he said with me looking at Xavier. "Ummm I have a question or two, if that is alright." I said. Doc gave me a nod while he was looking to see the sex of my babies, "Should I put them in the same crib or one each, and is there any way to know what gifts they will have before they get here?" I asked. "I'm sure they are going to want to be in the same crib, and there has never been any way to foresee a gift although I'm sure they will have one." he told me. "That's great I was hoping to have a heads up." I said to him. "As far as I know there has never been a way to tell but I can research it if you wish. Ok mom looks like one boy and one girl." he said setting me up. "Thanks Doc for seeing us on such short notice." Xavier said. "Your very welcome as always." he said as we left. I got in the truck and text the sister and Michelle telling them about the babies.

Xavier got in and started the drive home, "Umm why did he call me Queen Piper like that?' I asked. "That is who you are his queen." X said as he drove along. "Well I don't like it, I'm just Piper." I said mostly to myself. "Not anymore you are his queen and to many others, not just Piper but Queen Piper." he said very satisfied. "Sooo when are you going to tell my father about the babies?" I asked smiling at him. "I have to tell them are you kidding?" he asked laughing. "I ain't, Dad is going to kill the both of us." I told him. He made a U turn and headed for my parents house picking up speed when he could, "Should we call and let them know we are coming?' he asked. "Na lets make it a complete sneak attack either way this isn't going to be good." I told him. I rested until we pulled up at Mom and Dads house. "Piper, Xavier is everything ok?" Mom asked when she opened the door. "Yep everything is good where is Dad?" I asked. "He is in the shower he should be down in a minute." she said leading us to the living room. "Hey guys I thought I heard you here, how long do we have you for?' Dad asked when he came in. "Just for the night, we just came to tell you both something." Xavier said looking very nervous. "Ok what is it?' Mom asked setting up in her seat. "Well Pat, Ron we came to tell you that Piper and I are going to have twins in February." he said with a smile that didn't last long. "WHAT, you haven't even married her yet!!!" Dad yelled. "Wait this is a surprise to us as it is to you, we are still getting married." I said quickly. "Damn right your getting married! Xavier how could you I told you not to rush her into anything, what do you call this?" my dad yelled again. "Ron I swear I never rushed her into anything we talk about everything before . . . ." X said before I interrupted. "You don't need to explain anything, we are leaving NOW!!!" I said screaming. "Piper how could you let this happen?" Mom asked. "Let this happen I knew what I was doing the whole time I'm not a child anymore Mother!! You both act like I'm 14 or something I'm 30 for god sakes!!" I said mad as hell and moving to the door. "Wait your not going anywhere young lady we are not finished here!" Dad said standing in front of the door. "Yes we are now step aside Dad or I will move you myself, we are leaving!!" I said still yelling. "Sweets step off right now." Xavier whispered in a small voice that only I could hear. "Please Piper stay and we will talk about this." Mom said trying to get in between Dad and me. She always hated it when we sparred like that because it could get bad sometimes.

I looked at X who motioned me into the living room and I took a seat. "Dad do you feel that? It is either your grandson or granddaughter." I said trying to calm down. Mom made her way over to feel the babies move, "When did you say they are due again?" she asked getting tears in her eyes. "Early February." Xavier said. "I'm sorry Piper I was hoping that you would have given the marriage some time to make sure children was a wise choice, not all marriages work out like you want them too." Dad said. "Trust me Xavier and I will be together forever no questions on that." I told him as X put his hands on me to calm me. X went into the kitchen to get me something to eat while we talked back and forth, "Sweets try this it will have to hold you over till morning." he said quietly. "I'll be fine." I said trying to convince myself. "Piper honey your feet are swelling why don't you get some rest and we can talk in the morning." Mom said as she moved Dad out of the room. "Are you alright, how is your thirst?" Xavier asked when I laid with him. "I have never been so mad before, I mean I have been mad but this time I felt myself losing it." I told him. "I told you that your temper is easily set off you must be very careful. You have no idea how quick and strong you are." he said holding me tight.

I woke up with the smell of Moms pancakes that I loved so much, "Hey how do we feel this morning, still mad?" X asked. "No not mad thirsty as hell though." I said as I stretched. "Thirsty thirsty?" he asked with wide eyes. "Yea what are we going to do, we cant go anywhere to get anything?" I asked. "You can take from me until we can get you something." he said helping me up. He guided me into the bathroom and shut the door, "I don't like to do it like this I would rather be making love to you while I drink from you." I told him. "So would I trust me. But you have to drink or you could attack someone." he said. "Is this going to be a problem for you?" I asked worried about him needing. "Don't worry about me I'll be just fine until we get home." he said as he put his hands around my waist. I pulled him close to near his neck, he smelled so good to me. I opened my mouth and pulled back my lips to show my teeth. I bit down on his juggler and sucked his blood until the thirst was no more. "Sweets careful or I will have to replace what you have taken." he said as he pulled away. I looked away from him feeling bad, "Forgive me." I said softly. "Hey no worries I will be just fine." he said wiping his ruby red blood from my lips. I kissed him softly and made my way to the door for breakfast. "Good morning Mom and Dad." I said coming in the kitchen. "What took you so long in there Piper are you alright?" Mom asked. "Just morning sickness that's all, I feel better now." I lied to her. "Crackers and water that always helps." Dad said. "I know and I do sometimes but this morning I want pancakes." I said smiling at him. "About last night." Dad started. "Not now Dad I really don't want to talk about it." I told him. "Just hear me out, I'm sorry about last night I should have kept my mouth shut. Your right you are grown up and very smart young lady and well sorry to the both of you." he said putting his hand on mine. "Just forget it Dad its over now we both said things that we shouldn't have so just let it go." I told him.

Xavier smiled at the both of us, "Thanks for not killing me last night Ron I'm sorry that we dropped this on you both like this." X told him. "Are there any other secrets that we should know?" Mom asked. "Like what?" I asked looking at her. "I'm not sure just anything." she said. "You guys are still having a wedding right?" Dad asked. "Nothing that either of you need to know and yes a wedding is still under way." I told getting to my feet. "Piper." Mom said quickly. "Look we have to go, we slipped out of town and X has to get back to work." I told her. "Please Piper I know and your temper do you really have to go?" she asked. Xavier put his hand on me, "I'm sorry that was a short stay but I really have to get back. We have a long trip and I want to make sure that Piper is settled before I go to work." he said to her. "Well then I guess we will see you guys next month, call me ok." Mom said. "Would you like me to help with the clean up before I go?" I asked feeling bad about this whole visit. "No I can do it this time you guys go and have a safe trip." she said with tears in her eyes. "Come on Mom don't be like that we will see each other soon, dry up those tears." I told her as I hugged her. "I'm ok Sweetie go on now and be safe." she said putting on a smile. "Shall we go Sweetness?' Xavier asked. "Yes Love we shall." I said taking him by the hand. He helped me in the truck and started the long drive home. He didn't say much on the drive home knowing I had a lot on my mind, "Hey how is your thirst?' I asked. "I can make it, I have had a long time to learn my thirst." he said. "Ok then I was thinking that since you like Bastian for your sons name maybe I could name our little girl Brielle." I said smiling at him. "How is it that you know what I wanted for a boys name?" he asked. "I saw it when I drank from you this morning. Your not upset with me are you, I mean if you want to pick the girls name that would be ok." I said quickly. "I'm never upset with you just you surprise me that's all. I would love to name our little girl Brielle. Bastian and Brielle Matthews I love it." he said kissing my hand.

Chapter 7

As September came to a close and October well set in motion I had things to get done. Xavier loosened his tight ban on me so I could do more and go if need be. The sisters worked on everything for me, getting things I needed. I had a seamstress come to the house so she could let out my dress, "Thank you so much for coming on such short notice." I told the elderly woman. "That's ok hon, now lets see what we have here." she said taking the dress out of the bag. "As you can see when I bought the dress I wasn't planning on being this big." I told her with a laugh. "I can see that." she said looking at the dress and then me. "Yea twins." I said rubbing my tummy. She measured me and then the dress writing down everything she needed. "Maybe you should make it a bit more loose just in case, I still a few days to go." I told her. She agreed as she gathered her stuff to leave as Xavier came in, "How long have you been on your feet, they are very swollen." he said bringing me a drink. "I haven't been on them to long she hasn't been here that long. But the thirst is getting worse everyday." I told him as I laid down. "I know only sometimes I can feel it." he said as he put my feet on his legs. "I had no idea that you could feel me like that." I told him. "Only sometimes that I can then other times I cant." he said. "So in a few days we will be married what you think about that?" I asked. "You know that I cant wait." he told me smiling. "Come on lets go to bed, that is unless you have something that you need to do." I told him really tired. "I'll get your favorite movie and another cup for you. Hey wait on me now don't fall asleep without me." he said as I made my way up the steps. As soon as he laid down with me I feel right to sleep. I stayed in bed and rested per his request until the wedding day when Mom and Dad showed up. "Where is Xavier, he's not working is he?" Mom asked. "Heavens no he is at the Great House waiting on us." I told her. "What do you need us to do for you?" Dad asked. "Just help me to the car and drive up to the house." I told him handing over my bag. Dad drove the truck up to the house where Regina and Cyndi was waiting on me. Mike came over and helped me out of the truck and up the steps. "Wow Piper how much bigger can you get?" Jon asked. "Thanks Jon not like I nervous as is," I said as I gave him a joking shove. "Come on I'm just picking on you, let me help you to your room that X had set up for you. By the way you look lovely Piper as always." he said smiling at me and taking my arm.

The girls help dress me and Cyndi wove leaves into my hair as she styled it loose around my shoulders just like he likes it. Michelle handed me a single purple rose, "Come on Xavier is about to jump out his skin waiting on you. I just talked to him and he said that it has been only hours but it felt like days since he has seen you. All the candles are lit and everyone is waiting on you." she said. "Thanks Michelle, I'm coming Dad will help me from here." I told her. Dad took my hand. "Well Piper the day has come are you sure you want this?" he asked. "Yes everyday I have wanted this. The first day I met him if he would have asked I would have said yes, we love each other deeply." I told him as we walked to the back door. I looked around and saw many of our friends and co workers with him standing up at the front. He was in light colored pants, button up shirt and no shoes with his eyes glowing under the candle light. I stepped out with my green dress and no shoes as well to walk to him. Once up front Dad gave me to him, "Take care of her and love her." Dad said. "Everyday forever." X told him. The preacher began his words, "Ummm make this quick she tires easily and her feet swells." Xavier whispered to him. After a short sermon he pronounced us Mr. & Mrs. Matthews.

I took a close seat while he made rounds and talked to our friends so they would come to me, "Piper I have to say that you make a lovely bride and we all miss you at the hospital." Robert said. "Thank you so much for coming and for your sweet comment. I miss all of you as well I hope I can make it by there soon." I told him. "Maybe you should wait until you have those babies your poor feet look like they are going to pop off." Robert said. I looked down and laughed, "They feel like it." I said as others came by. "Sweetness how about one dance with me?' X asked. "I can try." I told him offering my hand for him to take. I only got one dance in but I knew that I would have forever to dance with him. "Xavier get Piper its cake time." Regina said. We cut the cake and drank blood from our cups, "That was refreshing." I told him. "I thought you would need something a bit more than water." he said with a chuckle. "Mrs. Matthews?" X asked. "Yes Mr. Matthews." I said as I pulled him close. "Are you ready for your honeymoon?" he asked. "Yes Love take me away." I said. I slipped out to get on more comfortable clothes for our trip putting on flip flops and my sweats with a tee shirt, that way I didn't have to tie my shoes. Michelle was waiting on me at the bottom of the steps, "You looked so pretty tonight, I'm going to miss you." she said as she hugged me. "Thanks for everything and as always I will miss you to. Hey would you mind getting my parents settled at my house until they leave to go home?" I asked. "Sure thing don't worry about us we have it under control." she said. Xavier put the bags in the truck and helped me in, "Hey where are you taking me?" I asked. "Smokey Mountains, I have a cabin tucked away in the woods and I thought just the two of us all week in bed watching movies." he said. "That sounds like a winner to me." I told him. "Ok you sleep I drive." he said when he saw me yawn.

I must have slept the whole way because I found myself in a strange bed with rose petals all around. "Hey Xavier are you awake?" I asked rolling over to face him. He never woke up so I kissed him and still nothing. I kissed his face all over getting closed eyes and a smile on his face, "I'm sorry I wasn't awake to see everything." I told him. "That's alright I knew you were tired." he said putting his hand on my tummy. "You know when you get close to me or when you speak to me the babies hear and feel you. They move like crazy and sometimes they get a little carried away." I told him. "I hope they know how much I love them already." he said kissing my stomach. "They know trust me." I told him. "Are you hungry or anything?" he asked. "Not right now I thought we could lay here and watch a movie or something." I said. "Can we go for a small walk so I can hunt? If you are to tired I can wait awhile longer." he said. "If you get me a cup we can go." I said. He smiled at me as he got up, "Come on so we can get back." he said as I got up. The woods around the cabin were very pretty with the leaves so many colors and before to long Xavier's eyes lit up when he saw something to hunt. "I'll be right back you ok here?" he asked. "Yes go have fun." I said finding me a huge rock to sit on.

I waited on him to show back up as I was approached by two vampires and a human girl. "Stand back." I said without thinking. "Are you Princess Piper?" the man asked coming to a stop. "Yes I am who are you?" I asked as he moved closer to me. I stood up and backed away from him. "I am David this is my mate Rena and Tiffany. We have come to ask you for your permission." he said still getting close to me. I felt myself getting worried some looking for Xavier. "What is it that you need?" I asked looking at the three of them not liking what I saw. Xavier came through the trees at lighting speed sliding to a stop standing between me and the vampires, "Step away now if you value your lives!!" he said with anger running through his voice. "I'm sorry my Prince we have come along way to ask you for your permission. We didn't mean to make your mate uncomfortable." David said. "What is it that you ask of us?" X asked still mad that they were to close to me. I gave him a unhappy look then glanced back at the human girl. "We only asked that we can move into your little town and live a peaceful life." he said looking at me. Xavier stepped over to block his view, "What of the girl?" I asked. "She is no concern of yours Princess." David said hatefully. Xavier took a step forward, "Never forget your place, I will kill you where you stand if you speak to my wife like that again!" X said more mad than before. David shook his head and backed away a step or two while I kept looking at the young girl who seemed very timid and scared. "You will give Piper a few drops of your blood and she will give you an answer tomorrow." X said trying to get them gone. "Will you need the girls as well?" David asked. "Yes these are the rules that you must follow and if not you can leave from here." Xavier told him. "Fine we will give you what you ask for." he said.

He pulled out a pocket knife and slit his finger and then Rena's so I could have the blood taste. I took their blood and let it run through my mind as they took a step back. "The child's blood?" I asked. "Oh yes we almost forgot." he said with a evil smile. He took out his knife and stepped to her, "Give me you finger girl." he said hatefully. She tried not to give it to him but he grabbed her arm and she cried out in pain, "That's enough!" Xavier said as I placed my hand on his shoulder. David stopped hurting her and looked at Xavier, "Come to me child." Xavier said with silk lined words. She walked over to him without blinking and gave her hand to him, "I wont hurt you." he said as he bit down on her finger softly enough to break the skin without tasting. I stepped forward and tasted her blood that she offered to me and let it sink in. "You may go." X said with authority. David took his human girl and his mate leaving us alone in the woods. "I should have never left you are you alright?" he asked. "I'm fine can we go now?" I asked. "I swear this will never happen again." he said as we walked back to the cabin. I laid on the bed while he cut up some fruit, "I find it very sexy that tone you used back there, the way you protect me." I told him. "You really think so because I can be very protective over you and very demanding." he said as he laid with me. "I like demanding sometimes." I said as I touched his face. "Well then I demand that you love me forever and I demand that you bit my neck right here." he said pointing at his desired place. "Do you really demand me?" I asked. "Yes right now." he said with force in his tone and his hands up my shirt. "As you wish." I said putting my teeth on his neck. I bit him harder than I have ever bitten him as we started to make love as husband and wife.

The sun showed us the new day with him holding me, "Piper?" he asked softly. "Yes." I said. "What did you get yesterday when you tasted their blood?" he asked. "They cant move into the town, they bring bad things with them and their memories date back a long time." I told him. "Then it is settled they will not move into our town, what of the girl?" he asked. "She is their prisoner they killed her family and took her as a slave. They make her bring in humans for them to feed on how awful is that?" I asked sadly. "I will ask them for the girl if they refuse me I will kill them for her. I will not stand by and let this carry on anymore." he said setting up. "X be warned either way with or without the girl this is going to be a bad fight." I told him. "We have to go I will not fight without my brothers unless I'm forced to." he said. "If you say yes to them Hinton will die one soul at a time and if you say no we will lose that girl forever. You know I want her to be free from such horror." I said looking into his eyes. "Get ready to go they will be here soon, text the sisters and tell them to have the boys ready." he said getting dressed. As soon as we walked outside they were waiting on us, "My Prince we have come for your answer." David said. "We are going home you may follow to get the answers you seek." X said putting me in the truck. "You said that we could have our answer today that your Princess would have them." David said quickly. Xavier growled at him, "Your Queen will give you your answers when she sees fit do not question her for I have placed my warning." X said hatefully. "Sorry my King we shall follow you." David said. "The girl she comes as well." X said getting in the truck.

It took X some time to calm down on the ride home as I text the sisters telling them what was going on and to have the three boys ready for a possible fight. "Do you have the right to kill them for her?" I asked still learning his legacy. "Hell yes I have the right to do as I see fit. I'm am the king over these lands and what I say goes!" he said still very mad. "Don't jump my ass Xavier I'm still learning!" I yelled back at him. "It is up to me to keep peace and do what is right. If anyone enters this land I have complete say as do you. We both know that what they are making her do is very wrong and to set by to let this happen isn't right." he said calming down. "Your right that is a terrible life to live having to lure humans in to watch die as they feed. You know that they make her watch to keep her frightened just enough so that she wont try to run." I told him. "I'm sorry that you had to see that I guess this gift of yours isn't as great after all." he said knowing only some of what I saw in her blood. "What doesn't kill me makes me stronger I guess." I said looking out the window. "It will be up to you what happens to the girl after we set her free." he told me. "Me why me I know nothing to do with her. I guess we can keep her no need to send her to the streets at such a young age. The only fear I have is we are all vampires and she is human how will that go in the house all the time?" I asked. "She will be guarded to the fullest if you want her to be yours, the rest will never hurt her she will be family." X said softly. Xavier drove fast to reach home and maybe to get there before our strangers so he could run things down with the guys. "Stay away when we reach home I do not want you in the middle of this." he warned me. "As you wish." I said getting worried about all of my guys.

He pulled up at the house and as we went in the boys were waiting by the door, "Piper on the couch, girls stay with her. They are not to enter any further than the hallway." Xavier told them. The strangers knocked on the door and Jon let them in, "We want the girl she is not rightfully yours, set her free now!" X said in a raised voice. "The girl is ours she was given to us." David said quickly as he moved the young one behind him. "Bailey take the girl from them and give her to Piper." X ordered. Bailey did as he said with David and Rena trying to stop him, "As for your request to move in our town the answer is no. Your intentions are not as you said they were your Queen has seen all she needs." Xavier told him. "If you would let me talk with Queen Piper I'm sure I can change her mind so I can have the girl back." he said moving towards Xavier and the living room. Mike stepped in between David and Xavier putting his hand on his chest, "One more step to my Queen and you die now." Mike threatened. "Your Cora said that your heart was big enough to let us move here and live a peaceful life." David said. "A peaceful life you are human killers and you killed the girls parents and took her as a slave to lure food in for you and your mate. My Cora as you say has no right to tell you anything about me she has no right to even speak my name." X said getting mad as hell. "Where did you get these lies about us the girl was given to us and she chooses to bring us the food? Maybe your Queen was mistaken in what she saw." David asked. "You are a very brave man to stand there and call your Queen a liar after my fair warning. You will leave my lands and never return. You can tell Cora whatever you wish but stay away from my borders or your punishment will be harsh." Xavier said turning to leave them. David jumped at Xavier and the fight was on.

Screaming, hissing, growling, and tearing of skin. "She has seen enough take her upstairs the back way and stay with her until this is over." I said to Cyndi. Cyndi smiled at her and took her hand, "Come on there is no need to fear us here in the Great House we are kind." she said pulling the child along. I stood up and walked to the doorway with Regina behind me to see what was happening for myself. The boys fought brutally as did Xavier who took great pleasure in what he did. I stood there and watched him finish killing David, "Help me get this cleaned up so Piper don't have to see any of this." X asked of his brothers. "Too late X she is behind you." Bailey said quickly. Xavier spun around to face me, "How long have you been there? I told you to stay away." he asked me with anger in his voice. "Don't you dare speak to me like that, I have been here long enough to see all I needed. I warned you that this was going to turn out badly. As for your Cora I will kill her myself if she ever steps on my land do I make myself clear!!!" I said hatefully and full of warning as I walked off. I was very pissed that he spoke to me like that to think that I needed to be sheltered. I slammed myself into the bedroom slamming the door behind me knowing he was right on my heels. "Sweetness wait." he called to me before I slammed the door on him. He came in and shut the door behind him, "Stay away from me Xavier I'm pissed right now! You don't need to shelter me like that I'm a part of you and I will see it one day you know that. You said we are to do together and then you shut me out you are going to stop that understand." I said. "I'm sorry Sweetness I didn't mean to snap at you like that, I just worry about your fragile state right now. Will you ever find it in your lasting heart to forgive me?' he said touching me. "As for Cora I meant every word I will kill her if she gets close enough." I said still mad. "I know you speak the truth on her. Sweets your eyes are very dark green, the last time I saw them like that you and your dad went a few rounds. Can I help you calm down?' he said pulling me close so he could get to my neck. "That's cheating you don't play very fair. Come on we have to talk to the girl." I said pulling him along.

Chapter 8

We came back into the living room with everyone looking at us, "What?" I asked. "No one has ever spoken to Xavier like that and got away with it. Are you not afraid of him when he yells at you?" Regina asked with the others just as curious. "No I'm not it is good for him to have me stand up to him." I said with a smile walking over to the girl. "Still." Regina said lightly. "Tell me child what is your name and age?" I asked softly. "Tiffany and I'm 15." she said in a small meek voice. "There is no need to fear us we wont hurt you." Xavier said. 'Would you like something to eat?' I asked noticing that she was very thin. "No thank you my Queen I must wait on David to tell me when to eat." she said. "Please my name is Piper and this is Xavier. David will no longer tell you when to eat and when not to." I said wanting to touch her for comfort. "If you wish you may live with us and be free to eat, shower and have your own room. You must be warned that we have rules here that you will follow." X told her. "You mean I can leave or stay the choice is mine?" she asked. "Yes your choice." I told her. "What happens if I stay here?" she asked. "You will go to school, keep up with your homework and chores. You will never speak of us being vampires at any cost and we will care for you, teach you and love you like family." I said knowing that this is what she wanted. "I want to stay where I can have normal things." she said smiling. "Normal we can try for normal but we are vampires so it will take the both of us alright." I told her. "I just meant that I wont have to make friends just to watch them die." she said lightly. "You girls take her and get those torn, dirty clothes off of her. Put her in the shower and give her something to wear, we will go to the store to get what you need for the night." Xavier said smiling at her.

"Come Tiffany lets get you something out of my closet." Regina said. "Come I'll get you a cup." he said taking my hand. "Hey what did Regina mean about standing up to you?" I asked. "No one ever has stood up to me like you have. Most of the time they fear me even when I refused my birth right. Before you ask Cora never spoke out of turn to me but there is something about you that I fear." he said. "You fear me that is crazy." I told him. "I know but something about you tells me not to push you to hard. When I seen you go up on your dad like that and then the look in your eyes when you told me off fear went up my spine, that is something I have never had before." he told me. "I would never hurt you for any reason just like I know you would never hurt me." I said before I took a drink. Tiffany came back in the room looking fresh and clean, "Would you like something to eat now?" I asked. "Yes please." she said. "Help yourself, Piper and I will be in the living room so she can rest until you are done." X told her. I put my feet up while he sat with me, "When we get back I'm going to bed." I said. "You alright Sweets?" he asked rubbing my tummy. "Yea long day I guess." I told him still drinking from the extra large cup he gave me. When Tiffany was finished eating we took her to Wal-Mart for some personal items. "Get the things you need tonight and we can order off line the other stuff. Tooth brush, sleep clothes and a few other things. Feel free to get whatever you want and need." I told her. She shopped around getting a brush and comb, tooth brush, and a few other things that she needed. We took her home and showed her to her room, "Now you can fix it up over the next few days and if there is anything you need come to us." X told her. "Thank you for saving me." she said before we left her to her new things.

X guided me to the bedroom, "I'm sorry that we had to leave and come home. I will lay here with you while you rest." he said. "Just stay until I fall asleep, I know that you and your loyals have things to do." I said. "As you wish." he said. "Just hurry back to me that's all I ask." I told him falling asleep. As soon as sleep took me over I started to dream for the first time since being turned. "Wake up mommy, daddy is coming." a small voice said. "Who is this?" I asked in my own mind. "Brielle mommy you can hear me?" she said happily. "Where is Bastian?" I asked. "I'm here mommy." he said softly. I sat up in the bed and rubbed my tummy as Xavier walked in, "How long have you been awake?" he asked opening the door. I looked up at him, "What's wrong?" he asked moving faster to me. "I can hear the babies talk to me, they told me you were coming." I told him. He set the blood cup on the table and put his hands on my tummy, "That is amazing." he said. "Hi daddy can you hear us?" Bastian said. Xavier gasped, "I can hear you my son." he said excited. He looked at me with love in his eyes, "You are amazing." he told me. "Not me its all them I'm sure." I told him as I played with his hair. He kissed the spots where the babies moved touching softly with his lips. "Have you come to lay with me?" I asked. "Yes we can have the rest of the night together." he said as he laid down with me.

The days began to get busy at the Matthews house as we put Tiffany in school and getting ready for Thanksgiving. The door bell rang and Bailey went to answer it, "Hey Piper, Doc here to see you." he said. "Ok show him in." I said setting up. "Hi there Piper how do we feel today?" Doc asked when he came in. "Wore out." I said laughing. "You still have a lot of human in you that's why you are so tired. What are we doing for the holidays?' he asked checking me over. "Thought maybe going to see my parents." I told him. "I'm sorry Queen Piper but you should stay close to home." he said as he moved away from me. "So you think I should bring them here?" I asked. "Yes you are in a special state being pregnant with vampire twins. I told you that it is very rare to have twins." he said looking at me. "No one has ever had vampire twins before?" I asked. "Not anywhere I have seen or read about you are the first." he said. "Leave it to me." I said smiling. "So no trip out of town for a bit alright." he reminded me. "Yes sir you got it." I said as he rose to leave with a smile. Shortly after Doc left Xavier came home from the hospital, "Sweetness?" he called. "On the couch." I said watching a movie. "How are you feeling today?" he asked. "Let me ask you something. Before I showed up what did you guys do for the holidays?" I asked. "Just whatever we wanted nothing special, why?" he asked. "Well from now on we will. Family dinners every night and Thanksgiving together plus Christmas as a large family no exceptions. We are growing and I want us to be a family. The time has come for all of us to be as one." I said making sure he understood. "As you wish, I will talk to them tonight." he said. "Make them understand this is very important." I said. "It shall be done." he said as he laid with me. "I'm going to ask my parents here for the holidays since Doc said I cant leave town." I said getting close to him. "Doc stopped by today everything ok?" he asked. "Yea other than I have to be different and be the only vampire mother with twins." I told him as he kissed my neck. "Not different just very special." he said. "Yea yea you are just saying that so I will kiss you." I said turning to touch his stomach to mine. "Yes give us a kiss." he said smiling that smile I cant say no to.

Xavier called the brood in for them to have a meeting, "From now on we will do as your queen requested and have dinner together as a family, no exceptions." he said with his royal tones. "What if we have dinner plans with friends or girlfriends?" Mike asked. "You will change them and eat at home. Piper wants this and it shall be done, she said it is important for the family to become one." he said standing to make sure no one said anything else. Everyone parted ways and I called my Mom and Dad, "Hey I want you guys to come here for Thanksgiving. Doc says I cant leave town since my feet stay swollen and I'm very tired." I told her. "Well I guess we could." she said thinking about it. "Come on Mom my family is so big now and the Great House has plenty of room." I told her. "Alright we will be there." she said. I told her that I love her and we hung up as Tiffany came back into the room, "Could I get some help on my math?" she asked carefully. "Sure thing Cutie come on over here." X said. She sat beside him with a smile on her face as they worked together on her homework. "So how was your day at school?" he asked as she got her pencil. "Ok I guess." she said. "You guess what's that mean?" he asked. "I had this boy run into me today making me drop my stuff everywhere and he didn't even stop to help me pick it up." she said turning to the page. "Would you like Jon to walk you to your classes from now on?" X asked her. "Oh no I'm sure he's just being a jerk I will avoid him from now on." she said. "Go to Jon anytime you need he will take care of it." he told her and then started on her math while I rested. When Tiffany returned to school I was worried about her so I asked Jon to find out about this boy and what was going on before break. "Piper can I have a minute?" Jon asked. I motioned him in and he took a seat, "I did as you asked and this guy is bad news. He has been giving her a hard time for quite awhile now and he's vampire. I followed her to every class without her knowing and he saw me not very happy about that." he told me. "Oh well to bad if he gets near her take care of it." I told him. "As you wish." he said and taking his leave.

With it being the last day of school for the kids Mom and Dad showed up. "Piper honey how are you?" Mom said waking me up. "When did you get here?' I asked setting up. "Just a few minutes ago we went ahead and put our bags in the guest room." she said. "Xavier should be home any time are you guys hungry?' I asked. "I'm always hungry road trips does that to me." Dad said. "Well steaks on the grill today." I told him smiling. "To cold to grill Honey I can cook this time." Mom said. "Are you kidding me it is never to cold to grill out, X wont have it any other way." I told her as Regina came in with my cup. "Pat, Ron can I get you anything?" she asked. "You know since you are Xavier's sister you should call us Grams and Pops, I need to get used to it anyways." she told Regina with a smile. "Ok then can I get you anything Grams or Pops?" she asked again. "I can get me something to drink in a few minutes no need to wait on me I know my way around a kitchen." Mom told her. Regina spun out of the room to tell the others of the house the good news about Grams and Pops. Xavier came in the house, "Is Piper awake yet?" he asked Mike. "Yes she is in with Grams and Pops." Mike said. Xavier started to walk in the living room and looked back at Mike with a bewildered look on his face. Mike smiled and went on to do whatever he started to do. "Sweetness have you rested a lot today?" he asked as Mom rose to hug him. "Yep how was your day?" I asked. "Ron good to see you guys have a nice trip?" he asked as they shook hands. Dad gave him a nod as X came to me for a kiss, "The day was hell but I made it." he said and kissed me.

Mike and Jon started the grill so dinner would be on time while the three girls fixed everything else, "I feel bad that they are cooking I could go help." Mom said. "They are fine your turn comes tomorrow, Piper said you are great at Thanksgiving dinners." Xavier told her. "Well I have had some practice." she said smiling. "The girls can show you where everything is and maybe they can learn a few things from you." he said. "I can show them how to make pies and whatever they want to learn. Piper never had the time for that stuff she was busy saving the world one animal or kid at a time. She did learn how to make her favorite things like pancakes and bacon." Mom said. "Come on no need to tell everyone that I cant cook." I said laughing. Shortly after dinner I went to bed leaving the others up with Mom and Dad who followed suit shortly after me. "Hey did you have a talk with Jon?" X asked. "Yes and I told him that if the boy gets near her again to handle it. Jon told me that the boy is vampire and bad news so he followed her to every class." I told him. "Well done Sweets." he told me as I laid down. I only got through some of the movie before I feel asleep with Xavier beside me. "Wake up mommy someone is coming for Tiffany, wake up now!" Brielle's voice rang out. I set straight up in bed taking a deep breath, "Xavier wake up someone is here." I said shoving him awake. He jumped up looking around, "Get Tiffany bring her here." he said. I made my way down the hall to her room, "Tiffany wake up honey you have to come with me." I said softly so not to worry her. When we returned to our room Xavier was gone, "Just sit with me ok." I said. "What's going on did I do something?" she asked. "No no Honey just safety measure." I said.

Xavier swung himself back through the opened window, "You will tell me about this boy and now!" he said trembling with anger. "Back up some you are scaring her." I said getting to my feet. "He has been harassing me for a week or so. I have told him to leave me alone or I would tell my brothers and he said . . . ." she said with X interrupting. "I know what he said! Why haven't you told me this before we would have put a stop to this?" he asked getting calmer. "I didn't want to bother you and Piper. She is so tired all the time and you are very busy with work and with Piper I just thought I could handle this." she told him setting closer to me just in case he got mad at her. "Never let this happen again from now on you will tell one of us or the boys." he said. "Yes sir I understand, may I go?' she asked. "Yes he is gone for the night stay in the house tomorrow." he said as she left. "What did he say to you?" I asked. "I don't want to talk about it and don't push me on this." he said laying back down. I laid with him wondering what the hell was said out there to make him so mad, "Have you wondered why Mom and Dad hasn't asked about Tiffany yet?" I asked trying to get him to calm down. "Mike told her that she was homeless and that we took her in, she was fine with that." X told me as I laid my head on his chest. "You will tell me wont you?" I asked. "Never and stay away from my blood for a few days I don't want you to know." he said running his fingers up and down my arm. I said nothing else as I fell back to sleep hoping for a better day tomorrow. The sun came up waking me up and I rolled over to see Xavier watching me, "Hey have you been awake all night?' I asked. "Yes just watching." he said lightly. "Whatever is bothering you we talk about it or you let this go." I said touching his stomach. "Well we are not talking about anything, he will get his. Lets just get up and help your mom." he said as he began to get up.

Some how I knew not to push him on this he was mad as ever at whatever was said. "Good morning Mom need any help?" I asked coming in the room. "Nope we are doing just fine in here I have all the help I need. But you should eat something this morning." she said. I went to the fridge and found me a cold cup that was hidden and drank it down without heating it up like I liked it. Xavier stayed away from me for as long as he or I could stand it. Dinner was finally on its way and I was getting hungry. Dad and I set in the living room and talked while Xavier set by the window, "Something happen between you guys last night?" dad asked. "No he had a bad night last night. The hospital called and one of his patients passed away, he is upset about it that's all." I said lying once again to him. "Dinner is ready." Tiffany said when she came in. "Go on Dad I'm coming." I told him trying to wait on X. I got up and looked over at him, "You coming?" I asked. He never answered me, "Xavier Matthews answer me." I said with force in my tone. "Sorry Sweets what did you say?" he asked looking at me. "Are you coming to be with the family or what?" I asked again. "Yes my Queen I'm coming." he said. "He wont make the mistake he knows that you will make him suffer and I swear to be with one of the guys at all times." I said hoping to make him feel better. "Just give me some time to get it out of my head alright." he said. "As you wish." I told him. "Hey I love you." he said. "I love you always." I said with my arm around him. We ate and laughed as much as we could as a family no matter what we all were. Mike and Jon had their girlfriends Sharon and Amber over for dinner. "Thank you so much for dinner it was nice." Amber said. "Your very welcome I'm so glad that you come to be with us. Piper never had a large family and I'm sure this makes her happy." Mom said. I smiled at her, "I wanted a large family with brothers and sisters but Mom insisted on just me, that's why I'm so special." I said. "I was never blessed with anymore children." Mom told us. "That's because there is nothing like Piper in this world." Xavier said after a long silence from him.

"So I was thinking we will get ready to go home in the morning." Dad said. "So soon?" I asked. "Yea long trip and I have to get back to work." he said. "Alright then we can hang around the house since I cant go out." I told them. Everyone helped with the clean up as I took myself back to the living room to lay. "Movie time any requests?" Jon asked looking through the movie shelf. "Something funny." Mom said. "It don't matter to me movies put me asleep even the good ones." dad said with a chuckle. He was right anytime you put in a movie he was out like a light. "May I set with you this time?" X asked softly. "I waited on you last time, feel any better?' I asked. He didn't say anything he just set holding me tight through the movie. Mom went to wake Dad, "Ron come on lets go to bed." she said softly. He got up and told us all good night as he followed her to bed, "I guess I'm next see you guys in the morning." I told them all. I hated it that Mom and Dad were leaving today but I knew for some reason it was for the best. "I took your car and filled it up for you." Jon said as he handed Dad his keys. "Well thank you son you didn't have to do that." Dad said. "Really no problem let me know when you are ready and I can help with your bags as well." he said as he left us to say our goodbyes. "I want you both for Christmas, I know that Doc wont let me leave." I told them. "We will be back Sweetie don't you worry about that. Now you get some rest for those babies." Mom said. I waved to them as they drove off.

Chapter 9

The days flew by and soon school started back up again, "Come on Tiff we are going to be late!" Regina called to her. "You guys go on I'll catch up I have to get my notebook." Tiffany said. I watched as Jon and Regina walked slowly so that Tiff could catch up knowing I didn't want her alone. "See you after school." Tiffany said as she ran passed me. "Have a good day Honey." I said and returned to the living room. Xavier and I were talking back and forth with him in a better mood, "I'm so glad to have you back." I told him. "Sorry about the past few days." he said. "That's alright I know what you have been going through I have hurt inside this whole time." I said. "Let me get you something to drink, would you like it warmed up?" he asked. "Sure that would be great." I said. He returned with two cups in hand, when the door swung open and Jon carrying Tiffany, "Xavier help me!" he said as he laid her on the couch. "What the hell happened to her?" X asked. "She was attacked by Ryan, he ran off before I could get my hands on him." Jon said. Xavier looked her over well, "She hasn't been bitten, she should be ok." Xavier said. She began to wake up, "Tiffany Honey can you hear me?" Xavier asked her. "I'm ok, I'm ok just had a accident that's all, I can still make it to school." she said setting up trying to get to her feet. "No you stay down and rest I will take care of this once and for all." X said getting to his feet. Mike, Jon, and Bailey followed him as he moved to the door, "Stay inside Sweets." he said as he left. "This is my fault I should have been watching." she said. "This is not your fault Cutie, Xavier has to do this to keep you safe." I told her. "What if he gets hurt or one of my brothers?" she said putting her face in her hands. "I'm sure they are more skilled than you think so lets not worry, they should be back soon." I told her. "Come on Tiff lets me and you go hang out in your room for a bit." Cyndi said taking her hand.

I waited on the guys to return to the house and finally I could feel them getting close. They walked into the house and Xavier's clothes were torn and bloody. He walked past me and I followed him upstairs, "Start talking X or do I have to bite you to get the answers I desire?" I asked him as I shut the door behind us. "I found him and told him to stay away from my family all of you. He laughed in my face telling me that he would have her one way or another, that he knew her when she was a slave. Then it got worse when he spoke about you. He told me things that made my blood boil things that he would do to you if you were ever caught out alone. I told him to shut his mouth but he just kept talking about you and my babies. I flipped out and attacked him and killed him viciously, sorry Sweets." he said not looking at me. "What about his body what did you do with that?" I asked. "I burned him alive only after I ripped him to shreds. I should have never let him get the best of me like that but the things he said I hope you never find out." he said softly. "Come on lets shower maybe you can wash my legs for me since I cant see my feet." I said not wanting to hear anymore. "Sure Baby I'll wash your legs for you." he said gladly. I washed his hair using my fingernails just like he likes, and he in turn washed my legs and back. It felt good to have him rub my back because it hurt some being I was getting bigger everyday. He helped me out of the shower and dried me off, and I dressed in one of his shirts.

He laid with me while I rested all the while breathing on my neck, "Stop that you know what you are doing." I said. All I got was a seductive smile as he kissed down my neck and bit the buttons off the shirt and spit them on the bed. He made love to me with so much passion yet so soft. I felt his love for me run through his body into mine. I needed him, wanted him so badly at that moment, "Stay with me Piper, I need you to stay alive inside." he said. "Always." I told him as we finished to lay together for the night. A soft knock came to the door and Xavier got up to get dress while I put on what was left of my shirt. "Come in Cutie." he said when he opened the door. "How did everything go today, I haven't seen Mike, Jon, or Bailey?" she asked. "As you can see things are just fine and you don't have to worry about Ryan anymore." he told her. "Would you think about turning me, I mean I want to be able to take care of myself and I cant do that if I'm human." she said. "Tiff there are things that you must know, you will look 15 forever and the pain you could have while turning may be bad. There is no going back once it is done its done. There are many things that you haven't experienced yet like love and love loss. Tell you what you think about all I have said and when you come back to me I will give you an answer." Xavier told her. "I will think more about it but I have seen so many mean things in my life and I know that I'm ready. Thank you for hearing me out and thinking about it." she said as she skipped out of the room. "X are you going to do this for her, she is so young. It was different for me I was much older and I knew what I wanted the minute I met you." I told him. "Sweetness I'm not going to do this for her you are." he said. "Me I don't know what to do for her." I said getting worried. "You are the only female I desire to taste and I will be there every step of the way. You can get my memories that way you know how to bite her giving her just enough venom. This will be good for you both, she will be yours forever." he said laying with me again.

Sleep never came to me as I laid there and worried about turning Tiffany. I knew that Xavier would give me whatever memories I needed to make her safe yet I still worried. With everything else I now had to get the house ready for Christmas and start shopping. Deep in my heart I knew that no matter what we told Tiffany she wanted to be like the rest of her adopted family, she wanted to be vampire. I laid there until the sun gave me a new day and a reason to get up. "Xavier you need to hurry you are going to be late!" I called to him as he got out of the shower. "I'm coming be right out." he said with a chuckle. I went down to the kitchen where the kids were fixing breakfast, "Hey guys would you like to help me today?" I asked. "Anything you wish." Mike said. "Great we start after X leaves for the day." I said getting myself a blood cup. "Hey where's mine?" X asked as he came in the kitchen. "I will be more than happy to fix you one just lips off mine." I said laughing. "Hey now." he said. "What time you gonna be home today?" I asked. "My usual if I'm lucky, why did you need something?" he asked. "Oh no just wondering." I said as I kissed him. "Alright then if you don't need me I'm off." he said. "I always need you but I can let you go for now." I told him. I watched him drive off then headed back in the house. "Alright guys lets get started." I said. The whole house was busy decorating the house for Christmas. There were many things in the attic for me to choose from, that was where I found the crib. Kaleb built the crib for Charisma when they found out she was pregnant. I had Bailey pull it down for me so I could clean it up for my babies.

While some of the kids were working down stairs on what I had set in motion, the others were helping me in the twins room. Mike painted the room white for me as I cleaned up the crib, "Wow look at this nice huh?" I asked. "Very nice I cant believe you found it." he said as he made sure the walls were dry. Regina helped me with the painting on the ceiling mostly she told me where to put things and handed me the colors I needed. "Piper let me finish this your feet are swelling, you must go lay for a bit." Mike said. "I think I can finish." I said still painting. "No you go now if Xavier finds out he will be pissed." Mike said before he picked me up off the ladder and placed me on my feet. "Hey now I could have finished." I told him. "You and those babies are far to important go rest this will be done before dinner." he said. "Very well then." I said as I went on my way and fixed me a drink. I laid with my feet up for about an hour before X came home for the day. "Wow Sweetness the house looks great. Whose idea was it to make it look like this?" he asked as he looked around. I could feel sadness run through him as he walked the house. "I'm sorry we can take it all down, I didn't mean to upset you. I forgot that not all my memories are mine but yours as well." I told him. "No we leave it I love it, I just didn't expect things to look like my mother did it." he said. "I can move things around a bit if that will help." I said. "If you want it like this than so do I. It is nice to have it like it once was." he said holding me tight. "Ok maybe you would like to see what else was done." I suggested as I pulled him up the steps. I opened the twins room and stepped aside. "This is amazing Sweets did you do this all today?' he asked. "Yes well I had tons of help, everyone helped a lot." I told him. "The lake with the full moon, did you paint that?" he asked. "Mike helped me with Regina. I did find your crib by myself though." I told him. "My dad built this old thing three hundred years ago." he said as he touched the babies blankets. "You go shower and I will check on dinner." I told him as he put his hands on my tummy.

I found the kids fixing dinner with high spirits as they laughed back and forth. I looked out the window to see Tiffany under the willow tree, "Hey there you, feel like talking?" I asked as I walked out to her. "I have thought a lot about what Xavier told me and I know what I want. I was with those mean people for so long and then Ryan, I want to be able to care for myself. If I'm human I know that I will be a burden to the family and I don't want that." she said with tears. "Hey now there is no need for tears I'm sure X will listen to what you have to say. You will always be my daughter and a part of this family no matter what he decides. Come on lets get back to the house and have dinner you can talk to him afterwards." I told her as I got up. We walked back to the house together and took our seats. Everyone ate as the talked back and forth about the house and the way it looked, "I have missed it looking like this?" Cyndi said. "Why haven't you been decorating all this time you knew where everything was?" I asked. Cyndi looked at Xavier before she gave answers to anything, "Hey can you guys clean up so that Piper can rest?' he asked before she could answer. "Sure she has worked hard today." Jon said with a smile. "Lets have pizza tomorrow for dinner that way there is less to clean up." Regina said. "Xavier can we have a few minutes to talk?" Tiffany asked. "Sure right after dinner." he told her as he got up for a drink.

I made my way into the living room to wait on Tiffany and Xavier, "So what's on your mind?" he asked her. "I have thought a lot about the things that you told me and I still want to be like you and the rest of my family. I know that there are things that I wont get to experience as human but there are things that I can do being vampire. Please Xavier I wont disappoint you I just know it." she said with pleading eyes. "As you wish, Piper will do this for you when she is ready." he said as he patted her leg. "Really thank you both so much this is the best Christmas present you could give me." she said as she hugged us both and skipped out of the room. After movie and small talk I headed to bed. X laid with me smiling from ear to ear, "What?' I asked. "The kids haven't been this happy in a long time only you can make this happen." he said. "Come on now I just asked them for help." I told him. "You brought life back in this house. Now I think you should go ahead and bite me. I will think about biting you so you can have my memories." he said. "I still think I shouldn't do this." I said as he pulled the top of my shirt off my shoulder and began to kiss his way up. It was unfair how he used his seductiveness to get his way, but it worked very well. "You know I love you." he said as he stopped at my lips. I didn't say anything just let him make love to me with all the ease he possessed in his body. "I love you Xavier." I said just as I began to get close to his neck. I bit him with some pressure to make him tremble with pleasure as the memories of him biting me that night flow into me. I got his memories of when he first saw me at the hospital, and I could feel what he felt when thinks of me. The memory of our time at the lake where we conceived our babies. I pulled away from him as his memories rushed my mind as we finished making love. He laid there rubbing my tummy making the babies move, "Did you get everything you need?" he asked. "Yes and some good things." I told him.

I fell asleep in his arms like every night since we first met and slept the whole night through. I woke to start breakfast for the house and cleaned up after, "Piper I will put the dressers in the twins room for you today." Bailey said. "That would be great then it will be finished." I told him. "Oh by the way we have a baby shower planned for you tomorrow." Cyndi said with a smile. She loved to have parties and to put up streamers so I let her do as she wished. "That's great did you invite my parents and Michelle?' I asked her. "Michelle will be here but Grams and Pops will bring theirs at Christmas." she told me. Xavier came in and Cyn and B left to go to store, "Hey Sweets I got you a salad for lunch." he said. "Hey I have a lot to drink today wonder if we should call Doc?" I asked. "I know you are driving me crazy with thirst. We can call him when I get home if you wish." he said smiling. "I don't mean to make you crazy." I told him as we both drank a cold cup. "I'm going to get off a little early so I can start pulling doubles, that way when you have the babies I can have a few days with you." he said. I gave him a nod with a mouthful of salad. When Cyndi and Bailey returned Xavier got ready to leave, "Ok Sweets see you in about two hours." he said. "Hey you look sexy in those blue scrubs." I said as I kissed him on his neck. "Ok ok hold up now you know you cant do that and have me leave you, I'll die without you." he said backing away. "See you soon Love." I said taking my seat and smiling. I laid on the couch waiting on my brood to get home wishing I could go out.

I watched as the kids file in one by one seeing Tiffany walk past the door way and smile at me, "Mommy don't worry I have seen that she will be fine and so will you." Bastian's voice rang out in my head. "What if I give her to much or something its not like I have been a vampire that long and I'm still learning?" I asked him through my thoughts as Xavier came in. "You will just know how much to give her don't ask me how but you are stronger than you think." Bastian said. "Hey Sweets what's the serious look for?" Xavier asked as he sat down. "Just talking to Bastian for a few minutes that's all." I said. "I wish I could hear them all the time like you do." he said as he made them move under his touch. "I'm sure you will soon enough trust me loud and proud." I told him as I played with his dark soft hair. "Let me call Doc for you." he said as he reached for the phone. I sat there and listened to them talk back and forth until he hung up, "Well Doc said that you might have days like this not to worry." he said. "Oh ok then." I said softly. "You need out don't you?" he asked noticing that I wasn't happy. "Yes its been forever since I've seen what outside looks like." I told him giggling. "Come on lets go to Michelle's for a bit, I haven't seen Trev in forever." he said helping me up. "Hey hey where are you going? Piper needs her rest she has a party tomorrow." Regina said hold up her hands. "We will be back soon she needs this." X said softly. Regina moved so we could go. The crisp night air smelled so good to me as I rode with the window down. I could hardly wait to talk with Michelle when we pulled up.

Michelle opened the door, "Girl you look like your going to pop, come in guys." she said as I hugged her. X gave me a kissed and went to look for Trevor. "Hey can we sit on the porch and talk, it has been days since I have been out?" I asked. "I don't want you sick but come on lets go." she said grabbing a jacket. I told her about Tiffany and how she came to us even though it was the same lie that Mike told my parents. She filled me in about her and Trevor and work, "Hey the new nurse flirts with Xavier all the time, well she tries. He told her that he is very happily married but she don't seem to care. I told her that she better be very careful that if you found out she was dead." she told me laughing. "Your right about that." I said picking up a strange scent. "Xavier where are you?" I thought in my head. Within seconds X came out the door looking around, "What are you doing out here you should be inside." he said getting me up. As Michelle went inside to be with Trevor, X and I hung back, "What was that? I could hear you like you were right beside me." he whispered to me. "I don't know I just thought and you came, can I get another gift like that?' I asked. "Beats me but we can check it out." he told me with a smile. Usually we can talk like that when we are close but this time he was further than usual. We sat and talked for about another hour with me asking Michelle to come and stay at the Great House. "Come on that way we can hang out for a bit until the party starts." I pleaded. "Ok we will stay with you guys can we meet you there?" she asked. I agreed as we left all the while talking X into some ice-cream. I got what I wanted as we sat in and shared a banana split before we went home. "You know there isn't much time to sit and talk tonight with her." he said. "Oh I know but after I picked up that scent I was worried about them and you have to work in the morning for a bit so we can talk then." I told him as we pulled in the drive way.

Chapter 10

I was met at the front door by the sisters, "How was your time out?' Cyndi asked. "Great very needed. Tiff, Michelle and Trevor is coming to stay the night, they don't know about us just yet so just don't say anything." I told her. "I wont say anything to her." she said as I made my way to the couch. Tiffany let Michelle and Trevor in when they knocked, "Hey is Piper home?" Michelle asked. "She is in the living room resting come I'll show you the way." Tiffany said. "Maybe I should have said no Trev is wore out we could have stayed another night." she said. "Oh no that's alright if you guys want to go on to bed, I'll be right behind you." I told her as Trevor made way to his room. I could hardly wait on the morning I knew Michelle and I had a lot to talk about lots of missed stuff. The longer I laid there the more I got worked up about the new nurse who was flirting with Xavier, and trying not to bother him while he slept. I got up as the sun started to show up over the horizon and went down stairs getting myself a large warm cup hoping this would calm me. I waited and started breakfast, Xavier came in and stole a piece of bacon, "Hey you have to wait like the others." I said as I smacked his hand. "Ouch, you have had some already. Hey why did I wake to find you missing?" he asked. "Who is the girl that flirts with you?" I asked. "You mean that new nurse I don't even know her name, how did you know about that?" he asked. "I can feel her near you and I don't like it make it stop." I said getting upset. "I have told her many times that I'm married and very happy to be married." he said. "Take care of it Xavier or I will." I said now mad as hell. "Sweetness your eyes are darkening up just . . . ." he said as Regina stepped up on us. "Am I

75

interrupting?" she asked. "No I have it under control." I said trying to calm down. "No you don't Piper keep your distance she is human, just warn her and stay away." she said as she kissed my cheek.

I walked out of the room to step outside with X following me, "What did she say to you, do I need to remind her that you are not to be upset?" he asked. "Leave Regina alone its me that I'm upset with." I told him. "I have no interest in this girl she is my nurse I have no choice but to work with her." he said. "Get Michelle to work your rotation from now on and stay away from her. I don't want to feel her near you again do it today!" I said with force. "I will do whatever you wish of me, it will be done today." he said as he guided me back inside. "Sorry guys I needed some air." I said as I went back in. "You sick today Mom?' Tiffany asked. I looked at her with shock, "Did you call me mom?' I asked. "Yes I think of you and Xavier as my mom and dad I hope that you don't mind." she said. I hugged her as Xavier put his arms around both of us, "Yes you can call us Mom and Dad." he said. "Ok your are cutting off her air." I said laughing. I sent everyone on their way kissing all as they left for the day, "Don't be late today Love." I said as X went to the car. "See you soon Sweets." he said as he drove off. I showed Michelle the twins room, "Wow that's a cool painting on the ceiling." she said. "Thanks I did that well with help." I said. "Piper can I ask you something? You don't have to tell me but we are best friends and I hope that you can trust me." she said on the way back to the couch. "Well I can try to answer your questions." I said as I took a seat. I felt that we were going to have a deep conversation. "Ok lets have it." I told her.

She got settled and took my hand, "How is it that Xavier knows what you need and where you are all the time? Something about you is different like your skin and your temper." she said softly. "Michelle I'm not for sure that you are ready for this, what if I tell you and you never want to see me again that would break my heart?" I asked her. "I'm sure whatever it is I can take it." she said with a smile. I took a deep breath, "Xavier is a vampire and now so am I. You respond to that and I will tell you more." I said setting back. She looked at me like she had the wind knocked out of her, "Are you, I mean do vampires really exist? Did you let him bite you or did he just do it?" she asked. "Yes Love they really do exist and I was in love with him from day one so I asked him to make me like him." I told her. "Wait do you drink blood Piper?' she asked. "Yes I do, we don't feed on humans so don't worry. Xavier and I are connected by blood so what I feel he feels and vice versa. The twins that I'm carrying are like me half vampire and half human. Are you ok do you need some water or something?" I asked. Cyndi floated in with ice water, "Here ya go Michelle." she said and left. "I think I'm ok with this, does Trev know?" she asked. "No and I think we should leave it up to X to tell him when he is ready. You will see things that you might not understand so just ask." I told her. "Like what?" she asked. "Well we can talk through our minds and we can talk to the babies like that. If I worry or need him all I have to do is link up with him and he is with me in a flash. The babies move around so much when he gets near its neat, uncomfortable but neat. Michelle no one in this house will hurt you." I told her. "I know you would never hurt me and we are still very dear friends my best friend." she said as X came through the door.

"Sweetness you in here?" he asked. "In the living room." I called back to him. "You ok something bothering you?" he thought to me. "Just having a talk with Michelle about a few things that I wanted to tell her." I thought back. "Hey Xavier, Piper told me that the babies move when you are near, can I see?" she asked. "Sure, so how are we holding up with the information?" he asked her as he started to touch my belly. "Well to tell you the truth I cant believe I stayed in a house full of vampires." she said with a giggle. "Ok here we go." he said as the babies started to move to his touch. He moved his hand to a spot and they followed his hand, "Go ahead Michelle touch right there and lets see what happens." Xavier said knowing they would come to him. She put her hand on the side of my tummy and him on the other side. The babies quickly went to his hand, "Come on guys she wants to feel you to." Xavier said. Brielle made her way over to Michelle's hand with Bastian following her. "Wow that was the neatest thing I have ever seen." she said as they moved around for her. "That's my good babies." he said before he kissed me. "I missed you today." I thought to him. "Missed you too, your thirsty shall I get you something?" he asked. "Yes please make it a warm one this time." I said with a smile. "Be right back Sweetness." he said getting to his feet. "Why does he call you that?' Michelle asked me in a whisper. "Because her blood tastes sweet to me and it has the smell of sweet roses." X called from the kitchen. She looked at me with wide eyes, "He can hear even the smallest of whispers. Its very true about the blood everyone has a smell of its own. You have a unique smell as well that's how I know you are coming." I told her. "Here Sweets drink up we have company coming in about an hour." he said as we both drank.

Xavier decided to get Wendy's salads for us to have before the party guests started to arrive, "Hey Cutie lets have salads, come on down." X called to Tiffany as he came in. "Lets set by the fire place." I said getting up. "Hey Tiffany are you not scared to be in a house full of vampires?" Michelle asked. "Umm I don't . . . ." Tiff said as she looked at me for help. "Its alright Honey I told her." I said with a smile. "Well I love it here, I have two sisters and three brothers to call my own. I used to live with some really mean people and I have seen things that nightmares are made of. Now I live here with Xavier and Piper who are the greatest parents that I could ever ask for." she said as we ate. "Hey lets get this cleaned up Bradly is coming he is almost here." X said as him and Tiff picked up. "Help me Michelle I'm down and cant get up." I said laughing. I sat on the couch as Brad came in and him and Xavier talked back and forth. Another couple came in and made way over to me, "I am so pleased to finally meet you my Queen. I am Kassandra and this Justin and Joshua, if you like you may call me Kassi." she said. Kassi had a short hair cut that was blonde with lighter blonde running through it and bright blue eyes. "Nice to meet you Kassi, please call me Piper. This is my dear friend Michelle and Xavier and my daughter Tiffany, please make yourself a home." I told her getting a vibe from her that told me we would have words before to long. "Joshua is very cute don't you think so Mom?' Tiffany said not taking her eyes from him. "Yes he is but stay clear until I can talk to your Dad about him." I told her. "Umm why did she call you Queen?" Michelle asked. "Xavier's family is royalty and his father was king over the vampires and this land. Now that Kaleb is gone it falls to X so that makes me a queen, crazy huh?' I asked. "Wow that is a lot of new stuff for you to learn." she said. "Tell me about it." I told her.

Xavier smiled at me on his way over with someone, "Queen Piper I am Brad if there is ever anything you need please call on me night or day." he said kissing the back of my hand. "Thank you Brad that is very kind of you, please call me Piper." I said. "If you will allow me to stop by after the babies are born I would most love to see them." he said. "Yes well you can set up a time with Xavier you are welcome here anytime." I said as more people came in. "What do you know of Josh?" I thought to Xavier. "He is a good guy young comes from a good family, why you ask Sweets?" he thought back to me. I looked over at him and Tiffany talking to each other, "That's why." I said out loud this time. "She will be just fine with him." he said with a laugh. I was handed gifts from others when they came in and I opened them. My children was given many nice gifts. Some gifts were clothes and some were jewelry from an old time in this world. I thanked everyone who gave gifts as they started to depart making way over to me to say goodbye. Tiffany started to clean up with Josh helping her, "Hey girl I'm going home Trev should be home soon." Michelle said. "Thanks for today I'm so glad I could tell you things." I told her as I hugged her. "Don't worry it will be our little secret." she said with a smile. "I'm very tired so I'm going to go to bed." I said making my way up the steps. "Hey be right there wait on me." X said as I made it to the top. I laid down and was asleep before he even made it to the steps. I felt him lay with me and kissed my tummy, "I love you babies, Sweetness I love you always." he said as I snuggled closer to him.

I woke up the next morning or what I thought was morning to the sound of Xavier's voice, "She has slept all night and here it is 3pm." he told Doc. "Ok lets have a look in on her, I'm sure she is just tired that's all." he said making way into my room. I set up on the side of the bed when they came in, "Your awake Piper how do you feel today?" Doc asked. "Much better thank you, how are you?" I asked. "I'm fine but you have slept a lot is there something going on?" he asked as he looked me over. "No just had a few long days that's all, I must have been behind on my sleep." I said with a smile. "No more Piper you need this rest so do it often, these babies are not like any other." he said. "I promise I will rest more." I told him. Xavier walked him out and quickly returned to me, "Are you sure you are alright, fully rested?" he asked. "Yes much better after my shower, will you be joining me?" I asked. "I always have time for you, come on I'll wash your legs for you." he said. "Thank goodness I cant do it unless I set down and if I do I cant get back up." I said laughing. He washed my back and down my legs and it felt so good. I washed his hair with my finger nails and down his back before we got out. He dried me off, "I'm not helpless you know." I said. "I'm just making sure I cant have you asleep until these babies are born I would so miss you." he said as he helped me into one of his button up shirts. "So when are you going to do this for Tiffany?" he asked as he made me a large cup and some fruit. "I guess today there is no more school after today and Christmas is in a few days so I think its best." I told him. It wasn't long before the school kids came in the house, "Hey are you feeling better mom?" Tiff asked. "Yep, hey I thought if you are sure we can turn you when ever you are ready." I told her. "Right now I mean I can go change my clothes and be ready in just a minute." she said excited. "Very well you go on and I'll be right there." I told her and watched her skip out of the room.

I knocked on her door before I went in, "You ready in here?" I asked. "Yes and have been for a long time." she said setting on the bed. I sat with her and Xavier sat next to me, "Ok well lets get this over with." I said as I took her in my arms. I pushed her soft brown hair off her neck, parted my lips to show my teeth. I slowly put the sharp edges of my teeth into her skin and tasted her blood as I gave her venom to make her vampire. Her memories rushed me quickly as I pulled away from her sweet blood and laid her down, "Just sleep Love I'll wait for you." I told her softly. I felt bad for doing it but I also enjoyed it at the same time. I had my head down as X took my face in his hands, "You did just fine Sweets she will be alright. Lay with her and I'll wait right here with you." he suggested. I laid down and put my arm around her so I could have her close and help her if she needed it. She didn't sleep as long as me or Bailey she gave about 6 hours before she woke, "Wow I feel wonderful, I can hear the neighbors bird and smell many things." she said when she sat up. "That's was rather quick is she alright?" I asked. Xavier shrugged his shoulders at me, "Cutie you thirsty?' he asked so she would look at him. "Wow she has the same color eyes that you have Piper that's amazing." he said looking closer. "I'm a little thirsty." she said. "Good then we shall hunt." he said taking her hand. I went down and laid on the couch waiting on them to get back. She returned with smiles on her pretty face, "I take that as we had fun?" I asked. "Tons of fun." she said. "Now your grandparents will be here in a few days for Christmas and you need to keep yourself in check. They will smell very good to you so I want you to drink when you feel the need don't wait." I told her. "I will I promise." she said as she skipped out of my sight.

Mom and Dad was right on time like I knew she would be, "Hey Piper how are you? Poor thing you look so tired." Mom asked as she and Dad came in. "Very tired, if these babies get any bigger they are going to walk out." I said laughing. Dinner came and went as we all talked about our day with one another. I sat back and listened to everyone of the stories keeping to myself. Soon I was able to lay back down I only had one month and a few weeks left and then I would be able to get back on my feet and stay there. "Alright we need to get to bed so Christmas can come." Mom said. She was like a kid at heart and that made the older kids feel the same way. They grew to love it when Mom and Dad came to stay and her famous pancakes. Everyone hit the upper stairs as Xavier and I held back some. "Lets set out some of the stuff we got the kids this year, Mom and Dad did it for me and I loved it." I told him. "As you wish." he said getting everything ready. I showed him what I wanted and where while he did most of the work, then we went to bed. Early morning came quickly because I didn't want to leave his arms but the knocking at the door forced the issue, "Give us a minute to dress." X said as he kissed me. Everyone was at our door waiting on us, "When can we go?" Tiffany asked. "One minute let me set up the camcorder." Dad said as he went down the stairs. "Alright whose first?" he called. "Go on Cutie." Xavier said. She went on without waiting and was followed by the others. I could hear Tiffany and the sisters delight as they hit the living room. The boys were next but made no attempt to make any girly noise, although they were excited.

X and I set on the couch so we could watch them look over their stuff and what the others got. "Hey there is more under the tree if you want to hand them out?" I told Tiffany. She started to hand out the presents as she called the names. "Hey this one is for you Dad." she said as she handed him his gift. He looked at the large gift as he read the tag, "This is from you, how did you do this?" he asked. "I make due." I said with a smile. He slowly opened the paper to reveal a fully restored picture of his parents. "This is great Piper I thought this one was ruined." he said. "I made some calls and got the very best to fix it, I thought we could hang it above the fireplace." I told him. He smiled at me and handed me a gift, "You shouldn't have." I said taking the gift. I opened it and found a leather bound book. I opened it to find hand drawn pictures of many things that has taken place in my old and new life. Me walking in the rain, and us at the lake together. "This is beautiful Xavier, will you keep filling it in for me?" I asked. "Everyday that I can I will. It has everything that we have done together up until now." he said as I finished looking through the book. The front page had To My Everything, Love Forever Xavier. He handed me another small gift, "X what is this?" I asked taking the box. "Just open it." he said smiling. I opened the gift, it was a gold necklace with a heart locket that opened. "I thought you could put the babies in there along with us that way you can have them close to your heart forever." he said as he put it on me. I smiled at him and gave him another small gift, "Great minds think alike." I said as he opened it and found a matching heart locket. "You cheated I know you did." he said smiling. "I had mine way before you got yours." I said putting his necklace on him.

Chapter 11

Clean up was well on its way while Mom started dinner. Mike and Jon brought me and Tiffany a cold cup as X took Dad out of the room, "Did you guys like everything you got?" I asked as I drank. "Yes and we want to thank you for all you have done. You once asked Cyndi why we never did this before, well when Kaleb and Charisma passed on we all thought X would die. He shut down so hard and then there was the waiting on you." Mike started. "Mike maybe you shouldn't offer so much right now, X wants that stuff kept quiet." Jon said. "Well I can tell a little of it. He waited on you for so long and he thought you would never come so we didn't push him on things." Mike told me as Xavier came back in the room. "Everything ok here?" X asked. "Oh yes I was asking the guys if they got all they wanted." I said quickly. He gave me a look I knew he knew I was lying to him. "Dinner guys come on." Regina said. Dinner was very good and I got full as did Dad, "Well nap time." he said as he put his plate in the sink. "Me too." I said getting up. I waddled into the living room and took the couch giving Dad the recliner and put in a movie. Mom and the kids cleaned up the dinner mess before they came in to be with us. Xavier woke me when he put my feet on his lap, "Hey are you sure you are ok with a picture?" I asked. "Yes of course. When they passed away I stored all the pictures of them so I didn't have to look at them anymore. But now that I'm stronger I can have them out once again." he told me. "I never want to upset you at any measure, you know that right?" I asked. "I know Sweets." he said rubbing my tummy.

The days started to blend together when Mom and Dad went home with Xavier working all the time. On the couch or in bed for me so I never knew what day it was until I asked someone. I was so ready to be thin again to see my feet once again. "Piper we are going to have a birthday party for Regina is that ok?" Cyndi asked. "Sure do I need to be there?" I asked. "No its just a few friends and a human that she has invited over." Cyndi said. "You and Mike make sure all goes well." I told her. "As you wish. Doc is here to see you would you like him to come up?" she asked. I gave her a nod as I straightened myself up some. "Piper resting I see." Doc Logan said when he came in. "Its all I'm allowed to do." I told him. "Yes well soon I'm sure. Keep close to home these babies may come rather quick and you may have them in the house." he said. "Ok I'm here always so feel free to come and see me." I told him as he got up to leave. I kept in touch with the kids as the party went on and them having fun, with me falling asleep. Now that the new year was here I hoped that it would fly by so I could have these babies. Xavier worked all the time pulling many doubles leaving the older kids to tend to me. He would come in and lay with me for as long as he could then getting a shower to return to work. I had him for one night all to myself that he worked out knowing I hated him to be gone from me all the time. I rolled over and kissed him, "Hey you awake?" I asked. He rolled over and pulled me tight into his arms. I kissed him again all over his face with him looking at me through thin slits of his blue eyes. I sat up across him, "Ok if that is how you want it." I said as I brightened my eyes from playing to serious moving his way. He put his hands on my shoulders holding me off, "Hey I'm awake no need to get brutal on me." he said as I changed my mood back to playing. "How did you do that so quick." he asked. "I have learned a lot I can do that often." I said as I put out stomachs together. The babies moved around kind of hard to feel him, "That is amazing to feel." he said. "Come on I'm thirsty." I said pulling him up.

The kids went to school while Mike, Cyndi and Bailey took on the house and making sure that dinner was every night. "Hey Piper you awake?" Cyndi asked as she knocked. "Come in." I said very glad to see someone. "I have you a cup and some different movies, do you need anything else?" she asked. "Tell me who is the human that keeps getting near the house everyday and leaves?" I asked. "That would be Jovi he is Regina's friend. She tells him that we cant have company until you are better so he walks her home from school everyday and leaves." Cyndi told me. "I'm sure it wouldn't be a problem for him to come in once."

I said wanting to be a part of things. "Oh she knows but she worries about what Xavier might say if you are entertaining her company as of late." she said. I drank as she filled me in on the many things that I was missing and homework. "Thanks for helping out soon I hope I can get back into the family." I told her. "Just a few more days Piper hang in there." she said as she rose to leave. It felt like days since I have seen Xavier and I missed him enough for him to sneak home for a few minutes, "Hey Sweetness wake up." he said softly as he touched me. "Hey Love what are you doing home?" I asked. "I missed you badly, how do you feel?" he asked. "Fine, bored as hell but Doc comes to see me just about everyday." I told him as he laid with me. "Just a few more days and I can be home." he said. "How much longer do I have to be without you in my bed?" I asked playing with his fingers. "It shouldn't be much longer, I'm just waiting for the babies to get here so I can have a few days with you." he told me. "Tomorrow is February I wonder how long I will go?" I asked. "He said early February so maybe within the first week. Tell you what I'll be back tonight for a few minutes to see you can you wait till then?' he asked. "Do I have a choice?" I asked as he got up to leave me. "Get some rest Sweets see you soon." he said as he bent down to kiss me goodbye. "Hurry back to me." I told him as he went out.

I made my way to the shower and stood in there with the hot water running on me for as long as I could before getting out and dressing. I walked down stairs to look for something to eat and maybe to have some contact with anyone. "Piper what are you doing up?" Mike asked as he jumped up. "Just wanted something to eat anything good here?" I asked. "I can go get anything you wish of me." he said following me to the kitchen. "No that's ok I'll just find something here I guess." I told him. "Please Piper let me fix you something and bring it to you." he said. "No I needed to see the rest of the house I'm about to go nuts up in that room." I said with a laugh. I found some chips and a cold cup and set at the table, "Ok back upstairs you need to rest." he insisted. "Fine." I said unhappily. "I'm sorry Piper but like I have said before you and these babies are important to all of us." he said putting my arm through his. "I'm going I'm going." I said. He was very easy with me as he helped me back to bed. I was huge and my feet and ankles were so bad at this point that no matter what I did the swelling never went down. "Hey maybe if I jump up and down I can shake these babies out what do you think?" I asked as I laid down. "That's funny but don't even think about it." he said crossing his arms. "Who is out already?" I asked. "No one all is home, why?" he asked. "Oh I just wanted a salad but no special trip for me I'm fine." I said as he put in another movie. "It will be done." he said as he moved to the door. I napped while I waited on someone to come in to see me and bring me food. Mike returned with a salad and a extra large warm cup, "If there is anything else please call on me." he said as moved to the door. "Thanks Mike." I told him.

I ate alone, drank alone, slept alone and watched movies alone sadness was setting in on me. I could hear the Charger pull up and X came through the window, it was faster than the steps. "Hey how long do I have you for?" I asked. "Not long but I know you are sad what's up?" he asked. "Are you kidding Xavier?" I asked. "I made some adjustments at work and this is my last double, I will have days again." he said holding me tight. "Thank god I don't think I can handle anymore lonely nights." I told him. "I know I'm sorry about all this but we are down one good doctor and Robert needed some time off for family so I was all that was left." he said touching my tummy. "When are they getting a new Doc?" I asked. "Soon they have two new ones coming in. Listen Sweets I have to go its almost midnight." he said getting up. "Hurry home tomorrow." I told him. "I love you." he said as he stood up at the window. "Love you too." I said getting up to put in another movie. I could hear the Charger start up and him pulling off slowly when a horrible pain hit me in the stomach. I looked down to find the floor covered in blood. I screamed in my mind to Xavier and to the others to call Doc Logan. Mike and Jon busted into my room, "My god what is going on?" Mike asked. "The babies are coming!" I yelled as another pain hit me. I could hear Xavier lock up the breaks on the Charger and turn around. The guys helped me back in the bed as Xavier pulled up and coming back through the window with the Charger still running. "Jon went to call the doctor, she is in a lot of pain is that normal?" Mike asked. "Yea that's normal for vampire babies. Thanks man I got it just let the doc in when he gets here." X said coming to my side. "Piper are you alright, the pain is bad I can feel it." he said as I screamed out in pain again. I laid back when it eased up some, "Let me take a look." he said lifting up the covers. He looked and put the covers back down, "Well?" I asked. "Lets just hope Doc gets here or I may have to catch the first one." he said with a fake smile. "Its coming Xavier now!" I screamed as more pain hit me with force. "Ok Baby push." he said.

I pushed and pulled holes in the mattress with my hands. "One more make it count Piper." he said. I gave him all I had as the first baby came into the world. "Bastian." he said with pride. I let him know that Brielle was right behind him as Doc came in, "Piper, Xavier how are we doing in here?' Doc asked. "The pain is bad, she ripped the bed up and Brielle is right behind Bastian." X told him. "Ok well I can take over from here." Doc said taking a look. Xavier brought Bastian over for me to see, "No wait." I said as I ripped more holes in the bed, "Come on Piper push hard." Doc said. Finally I could set back and breath after she was born. "Let me see them." I said as I set up some. Xavier brought the babies over to me, "Hi my little babies I thought you were going to stay in there forever." I said as I kissed their heads. "We needed a full moon to see you." Bastian thought to me. I looked out the window to see the moon at its fullest and bright. "Ok Mom make sure you drink a lot and you should feed them. Just remember they will grow fast and so will their teeth and as for you in a few hours you wont even look like you had babies." he said. "Thanks Doc for all your help." Xavier said walking him out. "Your very welcome my King." he said with a smile. X returned to me cleaning up the floor and coming to my side. "Sweetness how are feeling?" he asked as he moved my hair out of my face. "I'm thirsty but other than that I'm good." I told him holding to my babies. "Let me get you something and a new bed then you can feed them and shower." he told me as he kissed my neck.

He opened the door to find all the kids waiting to see them, "Can someone get Piper a drink, and guys can you bring me the mattress out of the guest room?" X asked. Everyone went to do their parts and returned quickly. Cyndi brought in the crib, Regina gave me clothes for the babies, Mike and Jon brought in the mattress, Tiffany gave me a drink, and Bailey took the old one out. I went to shower while the room was changed out for me it felt so good to wash my own legs for a change. "Wow Sweetness you are ravishing, having babies has its way with you." Xavier said as the twins were passed around for all to see. "Think so I feel like a million bucks and I had forgot what my feet looked like." I told him laughing. "Ok all out she has to feed them and I have to call the hospital." X said. "I already did that for you Dad they said to bring them in when you can and have a good time off." Tiffany said. "Thanks Cutie." he said as everyone left. I fed the twins from the breast as Xavier began to draw in my book. "How was it bringing your son into the world?" I asked. "It was amazing." he said as he come to lay with us. "You look different to me now that you are thin again." he said. "I feel different inside and out its hard to explain but its a good different." I said. I laid there and watched them sleep before X and I fell asleep. The morning came through the window and they began to wake for another feeding and changing. I fed both at the same time and handed Brielle over to her daddy so he could take part in baby things. "Hey Michelle is coming do you want to go down stairs?' I asked. "How do you know she is coming I cant pick up on her yet?" he asked. "I can smell her she is getting close you will see." I told him as I gathered Brie and he took Bastian.

Michelle knocked on the door and Tiffany let her in, "I was told that babies were born last night?'" she asked coming in the room. "Michelle you heard right." I said. "Damn girl you don't even look like you had babies, you feelin good?' she asked. "Yes so good I can get up and walk instead of waddle." I said laughing. She took Brielle first and loved on her, "I'm going to miss you Xavier while you are off." she said. "Hang in there I'll be back in a week or so." he said looking up from the computer. "What are you shopping for?" she asked. "New mattress Piper ripped up the other one." he said as he finished up. She looked at me with wide eyes, "I'm just glad it was the bed and not X I could have ripped his arms off or something." I said handing her Bastian. "Are you really that strong?" she asked. "Yes and my sense of smell is at an all time high, I picked up on you before X did this time." I told her. "Man I have to go, gotta get to work. They are cute as pie and Trev and I will be back later." she said handing X a baby and me the other. X walked her out while I called Mom and Dad. "Hey Mom I have some news." I told her. "What kind of news?" she asked. "At midnight last night your grandbabies were born." I told her. "Piper really are you ok are they ok?" she asked excitedly. "We are all good X delivered Bastian himself before Doc could get here." I told her. "We are coming cant stay long but we are coming." she told me. "Drive safe Mom see you soon." I told her before I hung up. The twins became fussy and I breast fed them and burped them, "I'm going to get something to snack on you want something?" I asked. "I can get it for you." he said. "I have been waited on hand and foot its my turn to do for myself." I said getting up. I returned to the living room finding Xavier and the twins in front of the fireplace on a large blanket. "Let them rest Love." I said setting with them.

All of us fell asleep in the floor before I was woken up by the scent of my brood coming up the drive way. I set up and touched X on the face softly. "Hey the kids are coming home." I told him. I waited on them to come in and see the babies, "Who was with you guys today?' I asked. "Jovi and Josh." Tiffany said. "Who is Jovi?' Xavier asked quickly. "He is a human that was placed with Mr. and Mrs. Williams, I like him a lot he is real nice." Regina said. "Why haven't I heard about him before?' X asked setting up. "You have been very busy but Piper knew about him he was here in the Great House for my birthday party." she said stepping behind Mike. "Don't be upset with her its my fault I should have told you." I thought to him. "Maybe it is time we meet this Jovi if he is important to you." Xavier said softly. As Tiffany held Bastian he looked at her, "Don't worry Tiff you will get your gift very soon." he thought to her then turned to Regina. "Don't fight the visions that you are seeing, they are very true." he also thought to her. Regina looked at Xavier with wide eyes, "I thought they could only do that with you all." she said. "I guess not, what kind of visions have you been getting?" Xavier asked. "Can we talk about this when Grams and Pops leave so we can talk in private, please Xavier?" she asked. "That will be fine." he said with worry. "What's for dinner you guys?" I asked changing the subject. "What time is Grams and Pops coming today?' Tiffany asked. "They should be here for dinner so get homework done and you guys think of what you want for dinner and then someone can go get it." I told them. They went on while I fed the babies only this time I pumped so that Xavier could take part in the feeding. "Hey Mom and Dad are coming can you let them in until I can get buttoned up?" I asked X. "Are you sure I cant pick them up yet?" he asked. "Yes very sure. My sense is very sensitive right now, I kinda hope it stays like this ya know." I told him.

Jon let in my parents when they got to the front door, "How was your trip?' Jon asked. "Jon you are looking more handsome every time I see you. Now where are those babies?" Mom asked as she hugged him. "They are in the living room with Piper and Xavier, let me take your bags." he said. "Thank you Son." Dad said as he handed their bag over. "Oh my goodness look at those babies." Mom said with excitement. Xavier handed her Brielle and Dad was given Bastian. "Hey we are going to the Dairy Queen for dinner so tell me what you all want." Cyndi said. She took notes as the others came in to see Mom and Dad. "Maybe I could get Jon to get dinner if I let him use the Camaro." I thought to myself as everyone talked back and forth. "Really Piper? I will love you forever." he said out loud and very excited. "Just don't wreck my car ya hear." I said as he went for the keys. "I swear back in one piece." he said as he went out the door. "What did he mean he will love you forever did I miss something?" Mom asked as I looked at X. "No I just promised him that he could drive my car and today is the day I guess." I told her. "What the hell was that?" Xavier thought to me. "I don't know I was just thinking to myself and he heard me." I thought back. "Amazing." he whispered. It wasn't long before Jon got back with dinner, "Well how was it still in one piece?" I asked. "That was freaking awesome, yes in one piece." he said as he sat to have his meal. "Maybe I will let you race it, its all set up for that." I said. "Piper what happens if they get hurt?" Mom asked. "They are good kids I'm sure they will be careful and Jon knows if he wrecks that car Piper will get him good." Xavier said quickly.

Chapter 12

Soon after dinner was over the door bell rang, "Mom, Kassi and Josh are here to see the twins what should I tell them?" Tiffany asked. I looked at Xavier and told her to let them in, "Piper, I'm truly sorry about just popping in but we were in the area and I really wanted to see the babies. I hope that you are not upset with me." she said looking at both Xavier and me. "No this time is fine but next time give us a heads up. My parents are here on a very short stay and they are seeing their grandbabies for the first time." I said. She picked up on my pissed tone as Mom did, "Piper no need to be rude to your friends they want to see the babies as well." mom said. "That's alright Ma'am I really should have called." Kassi told my mother. "I'm sorry Kassi I don't mean to sound so harsh I guess I'm tired that's all." I told her. "No need to apologize you are her queen she will not make the same mistake." Xavier thought to me. I kissed him as the babies were passed around, "I'm sure she knows that." I thought back to him. After a short stay for Kassi and Josh she came over to me, "I'm sorry my Queen I shall never make the same mistake twice." she whispered to me where only I could here her. "I'm sure you wont, please allow Josh to stop by anytime. We will set up a date for everyone to see them I hope that you will return." I told her. "Stern yet forgiving I like that, I think you will make a great queen, well done Love." he thought to me. "Next time I may not be so nice." I thought. Jon finished his dinner quickly so he could search the internet for a place to race. "Hey Piper could I use the camaro to take Sharon to the movies?" Mike asked. "Sure just as I asked of Jon bring it back to me in one piece." I told him. "I am going to bed I worked all day and then drove so I'm wore out, sorry Piper Honey." dad said. "That's alright Dad I'm tired as well, we will still have a little bit in the morning." I told him with a smile. I waited for Mom and Dad gather their stuff and head to bed before I made my way up.

Most of the night Xavier and I laid there just holding each other while Bastian and Brielle slept in the crib together. "I wish Mom and Dad could stay a little longer but I know he has to get back to work." I told X. "I'm sure they would like to stay longer but it looks like we have business to tend to when they leave." he said as he began to fall asleep. "Yea I know it has bothered me." I told him. "Don't worry Sweets I'm sure it is nothing lets get some sleep." he said almost in a whisper. I laid there until the sun came up with no sleep coming to me as I did worry about what the sisters have seen. I got up to find Regina in the kitchen, "Hey how long have you been awake?" I asked. "Not long just needed a drink before the rest woke." she said as she handed me a cup. "Mom will be down in a few minutes so lets drink up. You want to start breakfast with me before I have to get the twins?" I asked her. "Sure is X awake yet?' she asked. "No but I'm sure he will be now that I'm not there." I said with a laugh. "What have I said about sneaking out Sweets?' he asked as he kissed my neck and breathing me in. I turned to him and watched his eyes glow blue, "Sorry Love I didn't want to wake you I just needed a drink that's all. Did you sleep well?' I asked. "Yes I did but you however did not, you want to tell me why?' he asked still holding me tight. "Just lots on my mind I guess haven't had much time to walk and clear my head out." I told him touching his satin skin. "Then we shall walk as soon as we can, you have to rest." he said as Mom and Dad came in.

Breakfast took off and soon Mom and Dad started their journey home, "I'm going to miss you and those babies. Make sure you bring them down soon alright?" Mom asked as she got in the car. "You bet as soon as we can." I told her with one last hug. I watched them drive off before I went back inside. I walked back in the living room to find my brood there waiting on me, "What's up guys, where are the twins?" I asked. "Napping we have to talk." Regina said. I came in and took a seat with Xavier, "Alright lets have it." I said. "The visions have been worrying us. At first we thought they were not true but we have had them more and more and when Bastian told me not to fight them I took a better look. The visions are of war and its coming to this little town. Word has gotten around of the new Queen the special babies not to mention that you have given her power of the covens as well. Cora is behind all this and her jealousy has driven into revenge upon you Xavier, she got tired of waiting on you to as her to marry you so she left. Now you are letting a mere half human half vampire make decisions. I'm sorry to tell you this now but we didn't want to stress Piper out before she had the babies." Regina said. "Xavier their numbers are great and we have about two months before it comes." Cyndi added. "Why now after all this time why is she doing this?" Xavier said as he stood up. "After your parents passed away that left you king but you didn't take any responsibility until you married Piper. Now you and her make all the decisions and Cora thought she should have been the one to be your queen." Regina said stepping away just in case he got more pissed than he already was.

He took a very deep breath, "Thanks girls let me know if anything else comes to you." he said standing in front of the window. I walked over to him and put my arms around him, "Don't worry yourself Sweets my father took care of this before and I know we can as well." he said touching my fingers. "What about the twins X, how can we take a stand and keep them safe? I warned you about this woman and I will kill her myself if she dares to show her face." I said letting go of him. He grabbed me and pulled me to him, "We will send the twins away with Michelle and never speak of where they go. I will need to get the other covens here to tell them of war." he said tighten up on me. "They wont be forced to fight, the ones who want to fight can and the ones who don't can make for safe way." I said as I let him comfort me. He called for the brothers to return to him, "We will make calls to have others join us and I want this Jovi checked out to the fullest. We will watch for any new comers and they are to be kept away from the babies no exceptions. Tiffany will need to be watched she is still newborn with no active gift right now, she will need training." he said. "Anything you want we shall do." Mike said. I sat back and let them make calls while I played and fed with the babies. Xavier would come over and kiss Bastian and Brielle loving on them as much as he could. I knew he was worried about them as was I. I was having a hard time dealing with the worry that I picked up from all of the guys, "I'm taking the babies to bed, you finish up and I'll see you soon." I told him as I kissed him and left. "Is she going to be alright?" Jon asked. "Yes, just fine she needs to walk or get out of the house I'm sure." Xavier told them. He was so right I needed something to rest my mind and body, I felt different everyday inside and I was still learning. Sadness had a way of creeping up in my heart that it hurt me to breath sometimes.

After Xavier came to bed and the both of us fell asleep a knock came to the door, "Come in." I said softly knowing Tiffany's scent. "Can I talk to you?" she said as she stuck her head in the room. I motioned for her to come sit on the bed with me as X sat up, "The past few nights I have seen things that I thought were dreams but after tonight I know they are not." she said softly. "Seen what?" I asked taking her hand. "Tonight Charisma came to me and told me to tell Dad to call in a special hunter by the name of Mikael but people call him Mik. Call Brad he might know how to get in touch of him and do this now. Make all the efforts you see fit to find him he can train all of us very well. He is human a different kind of human who comes with two female vampires. After she said that she disappeared." she said. "You have the gift of talking to the dead Cutie, many will come to you for things to tell you things that are going to be helpful." Xavier told her all the while having a look on his handsome face. "I will let you know if anything else happens." she said on her way out. I turned to X, "Say something are you alright?' I asked. "My mother, I cant believe it why not come to me?" he asked. "This isn't your gift it is Tiffany's." I told him as I set up behind him on my knees and rubbed his shoulders. "It is a shock to have my Mother in the Great House again that's all. I wish I could have seen her, maybe one day I will." he said lightly. "Your not planning on leaving me and making me a single mother are you?" I asked. "No Sweetness we will have forever together even after all of this." he said pulling me close.

Soon the sun rose for the twins to want breakfast and love from us and we gave it to them without making them wait. On the way to our breakfast a knock came to the door with Doc Logan on the other side, "Good morning Xavier how are we today?" Doc asked. "Piper and the babies are setting down to breakfast shall you join us?" X asked. "Oh no I just stopped by to check on Mom and twins." he said. "Maybe you should stay for awhile Dorien we need to have a talk." Xavier said with royal tones. "Anything you wish of me." he said as he came in. "How are the twins today and the feedings?" he asked me. "Things are well, I was wondering if I should be giving them something more?" I asked.

"Yes now would be a good time to start, they are going to need blood source to make them strong. Have you been out lately?" he asked. "No I have stayed in the house with them." I told him. "It will be good for you and Xavier to have some time out." he told me. "It will be done." X told him. "May I ask why you have asked me to stay?" Doc asked. "Dorien we have war coming, we are going to need you for any repairs to the fallen bodies are you up for that?" Xavier asked. "Yes my King I shall follow you to the very end, I will do whatever you ask of me." he said. I got up and handed Xavier Bastian and walked out of the room, I didn't want to hear "to the end" stuff. It tore me up inside to think that I could ever loose any of my family. "Piper." Cyndi said as I passed her. I took a seat in the living room alone hoping that I could pull myself together. I could hear the covens coming to the Great House as Xavier came in the room and shut the doors behind him, "Sweetness." he said. "I don't want to hear it, I know what has already been put in motion just let me put it in the right folders." I said to him. "We have to be one today, stand strong." he told me as he touched me. "I understand just so that you know many of them think this is because of me and maybe it is." I told him. "I don't give a damn what they think if they don't agree with the queen that has been given to them they can leave and never return." he said quickly. I kissed him softly, "Send Bailey to me." I thought to him. "As you wish my Queen." he thought back

Xavier let in the guest as I took the babies upstairs with Tiffany and the sisters, "They are to stay upstairs no exceptions girls I mean it." I told them. "With our lives they will be protected." Cyndi said knowing that I trusted no one when the twins were involved. I kissed all of them before I left the room, "Piper you wanted to see me?" Bailey asked. "Yes take one of your brothers and check Jovi out to the fullest I want to know what he is about and where he came from." I thought to him as I touched his face. "Yes my Queen it shall be done." he said as he turned from me. I walked back in the living room with many looking at me as I took Xavier's side. "Your queen has nothing to do with this, Cora started this with her jealousy. She wanted more that I was willing to give her therefore she made her decision. Piper was the only one for me and if you don't agree that she is the right person for the job then you may leave, just remember once you go there is no return for she is my Queen and yours." he said getting upset. Only one or two stood up, "What if we don't have the resources to fight?" a tall man asked. "Then by all means take your leave, you will not be forced into anything you have free will." I said softly. "Thank you my Queen, I have enjoyed meeting you even under these pressures maybe we can get to know one another at a later date.' he said as he shook my hand. "Yes I would like that, take care of yourself and family until this is over." I told him. Many of the men from the covens talked back and forth as I stood by and listened to everyone and their plans until I picked up on Bailey and Jon returning to the Great House. I met them at the door away from the others, "Well what have you found?" I asked. "He is as we were led to believe. He is a foster child and has been placed with Mr. and Mrs. Williams, but this is his third home. His father is dead and his mother in jail but all in all he seems to be a good kid works hard with school and a part time job." Bailey said. "Very well thanks so much and leave this to me don't tell Regina she would be crushed if she knew." I told him touching both of their faces. "As you wish." Jon said.

Many started to leave as the day grew late, "Are you hungry Sweetness?" Xavier asked as the last left the Great House. "Yes very." I said as he put his arm around my waist. "Let the girls tend to the babies and we go out it will do the both of us some good." he said. "What if they need to be fed?" I asked. "Go Mommy we will be fine here with the elders." Bastian's voice rang out in my head. "Yes we can have the bottles that Doc Logan spoke of." Brielle thought. "If you are sure my angles." I thought to them. "Yes go and clear your thoughts." Bastian said looking at me. I went to shower and dress in jeans and a V neck sweater while X dressed in holey jeans, button up shirt and timberland boots, "Wow you look amazing." he told me as he kissed the side of my neck. "Thanks Love, you look delicious." I told him with a smile. He opened the Charger car door for me then he got in, "Any where you wish to go?" he asked. "Any where you want as long we are together." I told him. After a very nice dinner we went by the store to get things for the house and headed home. "Bradly is at the house with his three sons." I told him looking out the window. "How is it that you know?" he asked. "I don't know just do." I told him. The boys helped carry in the many bags we brought home as I unpacked the bags. "I have the information you asked for, I can call Mik if you wish." Brad said. "No that's ok maybe I should do this but if I have any problems I will let you know. Thanks for getting this to me on such short notice old friend." Xavier told him. They shook hands and Brad tipped his hat to me before he left, "Piper you and X go on and spend time together I can finish this for you. If the babies wake I will cater to their every need tonight." Regina said. "Thanks if you need me please come and get me." I told her.

I took Xavier by the hand and led him upstairs to dress for bed. He laid on his back in a pair of shorts and no shirt with his hands behind his head, "I think today went well don't you?" he asked. "I don't want to talk about it tonight." I said as I set across him. I ran my hands up his sleek stomach and chest as I made my way to kiss him. He sat me back up so he could look into my eyes as they glowed green. With a smile he flipped me over to my back and kissed me from my shoulder to my juggler. When he got close enough I bit him and sucked his blood into my mouth so I could taste him. He pushed his hand up my shirt and ripped my panties off with a quick jerk as he bit me back, "Mmmmmm you are very delicious." he said as he kissed me. I could taste our blood mixing on my tongue, it was sweeter than before. We made love enjoying each others body until the day brought us noon. I started to get up to start what was left of the day, "We have enough time before we are needed." he said with his charming smile. I knew when he smiled like that there was no way of telling him no, he would take what he wanted and I would give it at free will. He put his fingers in my hair pulling my head back so that he could get to my neck better licking all the way up my juggler. I gave into him willingly and he made love to me until time came for dinner.

"I don't want to let go of you today Sweetness." he said. "Then don't." I told him. "See if you got the right memories from me last night as you drank, see if you can escape me." he said. "That's not fair you know that you are stronger than me. I did get your memories and your thoughts last night you are afraid of me your not sure of what I am capable of." I told him as I slipped out of his hold. "You want to talk fair I would have never told you that stuff. Not afraid for me just if you let your temper rule you. I let you go last time but not this time, you are going to have to be faster than I." he said getting me again. "As you wish." I said as I set across him again and brightened my eyes licking up his neck to his lips. When his breathing got heavy and he was under my spell I moved before he could get me again, "That's cheating I wasn't paying attention, lets try that again and no cheating." he said as I threw on some clothes. "You will have to catch me first." I said as I went out the door, "Piper get back here, you don't play fair!" he called to me as he got dressed. He came into the kitchen in a rush, "We will continue this at a later time I wont give up till I win now that I know you will cheat I will have to come up with something better." he said getting me and kissing me. We seemed perfect for each other, if I thought it he would make it happen as would I. Our love was a timeless love, no one could ever love as deeply or as passionately as we loved each other, I knew I would die without him. "Alright guys tomorrow I want you to invite your friends for dinner that way we can meet them." I said as I set down to dinner. "Are you sure I mean there is so much going on?" Mike asked. "Yes this is what I want and what we need. Just because there is war on the rise there is no need to stop living our lives." I told them. "Anything you wish we will have our friends over." Mike said looking at Xavier. "He is worried that we shouldn't let our guard down." I thought to X. "Are you sure that is what it is maybe it is something else?" he thought back. "No I can see into his mind this is something that he isn't used to and thinks if we let our guard down we will be taken by surprise." I thought to him as he came to sit by me. I could keep up with everyone in the room and their thoughts while I ate my dinner.

Chapter 13

I laid in bed with many thoughts going through my head, the thoughts of all the children and Xavier. Sometimes I could feel many feelings as they washed over me and never knowing why. I slipped out of bed to care for the twins before Xavier could wake up. When I finished with them I slipped back in bed touching X softly, "I wondered when you would come back to me." he said. "Come on Love we have company coming today we need to get ready." I said as I traced his abs. "Unless you are willing to spend the rest of the day in bed with me I suggest you don't touch me like that." he said smiling. "Up up going to the store you wanna go with me?" I asked. "I will go anywhere you ask of me." he said getting to his feet. After the store we came in and X started the grill as I cut up the salad. Sharon, Amber, and Josh came at the same time with Jovi showing last. "Welcome to the Great House, you must be Jovi." I said as I answered the door with Brie in my arms. "Thank you for the invitation Piper." he said coming in the house. "Your very welcome, come on you can meet my husband Xavier." I said as I led the way into the kitchen. X came over and shook his hand, "Regina and the others are out back if you would like to join them." he said. "How old are the babies?' he asked as he stopped and played with them. "Just a few days old now." I told him. "I'm so glad that you are feeling better Piper, the past few times I came by Regina said that you were under the weather." he told me. "Thank you Jovi that's very nice of you. I was some what under the weather just having the babies." I told him. He smiled at me and went outside to be with the others. "Well what do you think?" X asked. "I like him, he will be a part soon enough." I told him as I kissed him.

Both babies started to make a fuss at the same time, "Could someone like to help me for a minute?' I called out back. "I can help Piper if that is ok with you." Jovi said quickly. "Have you cared for a baby before?" I asked knowing Xavier was thinking the very same. "Sure I have helped with many babies when I was in different places." he said as I handed him Brie. He got her settled by bouncing her gently and giving her a bottle. "You seem to like Gina a lot by walking her home everyday." I said. "Yea she is very pretty and so sweet, there is something about her ya know? I miss her when we are apart it is strange but I do miss her." he said. "How long have you been at the Mr. and Mrs. Williams?' I asked. "About two months or so I have been bounced around so much all I ever want to be a part of something, a real family. This is a temp house though when I was placed here she already had so many kids that the social worker said I may be moved again." he said as he looked away towards Brie. "I'm sure before to long you will become a part of something alright." I said with a smile. "I hope that Regina and I can stay together until I can provide for her the way she deserves." he said and looked at me with shock. "Why wouldn't you be together?' I asked. "I just meant if I got moved I may never see her again. I'm sorry I never tell anyone things like this." he said. "You will get used to it I have that effect on everyone." I told him as Xavier came in with the steaks. "I can take her now so that you can eat dinner, thanks for helping Piper." he said as he took Brie. "Anytime I love babies." he said as he gave X his seat and going to Gina's side, kissing her cheek. Xavier cleared his throat, "Leave him alone that is what humans do when they are dating." I thought to him. "I don't have to like it." he thought back. "Yes you do they are fine." I thought once again. "See I need you." he said as he kissed me.

After dinner was over Xavier and I took the twins upstairs leaving the kids to hang out alone. "Goodnight guys don't stay up to late." I said with a wink. "Daddy, Gina will tell him tonight, he will panic she will need you for support." Bastian thought to him. "I will stay close to her." he thought back. We fed the babies and put them in bed so we could wait on Gina to tell her secret to Jovi. It wasn't long before we heard him freaking out, "Wait, what did you say?" he asked her almost screaming. "Sshhhh the babies are asleep if you wake them you will have to answer to Piper." she said trying to calm him down. X and I came down to see if we could help, "Xavier, Piper please help." she said. Jovi was heading for the front door quickly, "Jovi wait let me talk to you." I said rushing the door to stop him. "Is it true is she a vampire?" he asked backing away. "Yes we all are in the Great House." Xavier said. "Jovi you said that you wanted to be a part of something and well this is it. You are in no danger in this house trust me Jovi." I said making my eyes glisten for him to see. "Wow how did you do that?' he asked. "We all can even Gina. Are you willing to trust me now." I said so softly. "Yea I feel really comfortable, are you doing that?" he asked me. I smiled at him as Gina came closer. "Jovi I would never hurt you, would you like for someone to take you home?' she asked. "No I don't want to go home I want to see you do your eyes like Pipers." he said. She touched his arm and lit her eyes up bright blue and smiled at him, "See cool huh?" she asked. "Is it alright if I stay longer, I don't have to be home till midnight?" he asked. "Yes that is fine, Gina you know the rules he's out in time to get home at midnight." I said. "Now the babies are asleep so lets keep it quiet shall we." Xavier said as we went up the steps. I stopped by the twins room and looked in on them.

Xavier scooped me up and headed for the bedroom, "Now I have you in my grip dare you to get out." X said. "You know what, I don't want to get out. I think I will stay right here." I said as I got closer to him. "Awe come on Piper, you need the practice I want you to be ready." he said. "Then you should be showing how to fight. I don't think these people like me enough to hold me do you?" I asked with a smile. He laid there with this look on his face like he was gut punched. "Fine I will teach you to fight but I don't like this at all, I want you to stay away from the fighting." he said. "No worries Love I will be just fine." I said as I turned to face him. I kissed him from his stomach to his neck, "You smell scrumptious, I think I might have to have a taste." I said seductively. "You have a way with words don't you Sweetness?" he said never opening his eyes. I kissed around his throat to his juggler and bit him with a force that made him moan in pleasure. He flipped me over to my back so he could have a taste of me. It intensified the sexual pleasure for us to bite one another. He bit me with the same force I used on him, "Mmmm I love it when you taste me." I whispered to him as he drank my blood. His eyes were so blue and the electricity that ran through him into me felt so good. "Mmmm you are more sweet than before." he said going back for another taste while making love to me until sun rise. Every night that we spent together was magic to me like it was the first time every time. "I cant get enough of you." he said as he kissed my shoulder. Time came for the twins to need caring for even though neither one of us slept. I got up and dressed so I could get them, "Hey how did last night turn out for you?' I asked Gina when I ran into her in the hallway. "He had a lot of questions and he asked that I gave him some time to think things through, he wasn't even afraid to kiss me good night." she said with a smile. "Let him come to you don't push him and answer his questions truthfully without giving to much." I said as I made my way back with the babies.

We carried out the day as usual with the brood coming and going often. I worked with the babies a lot, "Hey X have you noticed the babies today, they seem bigger or something?" I asked looking over them. "Yes they do seem bigger now that you brought it up, would you like to call Dorien?" he asked. I nodded his way as I picked up Bastian and went for Brie, "Come on babies lets go in the living room while Daddy talks to Doc." I said carrying them both. I played with the babies waiting on any news from Doc. "Hey Sweetness Doc said that the vampire half is making them grow at record speed. They will be walking and eating whole food by the end of the month." he said proudly. "WHAT???? Are you kidding me, walking? That's just great how am I to send them away and explain how they are walking and only a few weeks old!?" I said with a touch of anger. "Sweetness lets not get upset I'm sure we can work this out maybe we can send them with Michelle and Trevor." X said making his way over to me. "How do you even know if she will do this for us? This means taking them could put her in danger she cant defend herself against vampires Xavier what the hell!" I said backing away from him because I was angry. I left the house walking fast and hard thinking about how I could get Michelle to do this and not get killed or my babies. I walked long and hard with anger pushing me. I wasn't angry at my very gifted and beautiful twins, I was angry at Cora and what she started. I was in thought and never noticed Xavier until he grabbed me by the arm. Without any thought I flipped Xavier over and put him on his back, "Damn it Piper what the hell are you thinking?" he asked from the ground. "I'm so sorry Baby I didn't know it was you." I told him as I offered him a hand. "That was quick, come on let me walk you home." he said taking my hand.

I walked back without any words between us, "Someone is making way to the house." I told him. He took off with me right behind him at top speed with him pinning the man up against the house and me stopping the two women from making way to the house. "Who are you and what do you want?" Xavier asked. "Whoa hold on there, I'm Mik you sent for me." Mik said holding his hands up. "I apologize we are on high guard here and for good reason." Xavier said backing off. "Yes I'm sure you are this new queen and babies have stirred up a mess haven't they?" Mik asked. "Watch yourself that queen is my wife and those are my babies." X said not very happy. "I meant no harm just stating a fact that's all." He said quickly. "Please lets take this inside shall we?" I asked softly touching X so he would calm himself. "I'm sorry to hear about Kaleb and Charisma they were my dear friends." he said as we started in the house. Mike, Jon and Bailey were waiting inside the door in attack stance. Xavier put his hand up to let them know it was fine and Bailey taking my by the arm, "The twins are upstairs with the three girls." he told me. "Thanks B." I said as we walked into the living room with Mik. I sat back and listened to everything that Mik had planned for the family. "Michelle and Trevor are on the way to the Great House I need to talk to her." I thought to X. He gave me a nod as I left the room all the while Mik kept his eye on me.

I met my friends on the porch, "Hey guys how are you today?" I asked as the came up on the porch. "Good, just wanted to see you and the babies." Michelle said as she hugged me. "They are upstairs come on I'll take you." I said moving them away from the living room. "Hey where's Xavier I wanted to speak to him?" Trevor said. "Umm he's a bit busy right now." I said quickly. "Alright Piper spill the beans what is wrong with you?" she asked learning to read me sometimes. "We have to talk." I told her as I guided her out of the room. "What is going on with you?" she asked. "We have a problem and I need your help. We are at war soon and I need you to take the twins away and keep them until this is over. I would send them to my parents but Bastian and Brie will be walking by the end of February and you already know the family secret. This will need to be done at the end of March please I will pay you for everything." I told her. "What about Trev he has no idea about you guys?" she asked. "I will tell him now so that he is ready for all he might have to see." I told her. "Right now?" she asked. I grabbed her by the hand and led the way back in the room, "Trev I need to talk to you its very important and I need you to understand alright?" I asked. "Sure Piper anything." he said holding Brie. I took his hand so that I could make him comfortable, "Trevor we are all vampires even the babies." I said and moved back. He shook his head back and forth, "I knew it, I knew there was something different about Xavier. I really had an idea when you came over and he just jumped up and came to you without any warning like he needed you or you called to him." he said. "Are you ok with this news?" I asked. "Yes have you always been a vampire? Why are you telling me this now?" he asked. "No Xavier turned me before I got pregnant with the twins. I'm telling you this because I need you both in the worst way. There is war on the rise for this Coven and I don't want my babies in the cross fire. If none of the Matthews family returns you both are young enough and strong to raise my children until they are old enough to take their crowns. Please I beg of you to do this for me." I pleaded to them both. "Piper we will do whatever you ask, Xavier is my friend and I'm sure he will make sure you all return." Trevor said smiling. "Oh thank you both for this you have no idea how much I love you both." I said hugging them tight. "Piper you are cutting off my air." Michelle said. "Please make yourself comfortable and play with the babies." I told them as I took a seat.

Michelle and Trevor stayed for a few minutes with me walking them out, "I'm sorry you didn't get a chance to see X maybe next time." I told Trevor. "You bet see you soon." he said as they left. I returned to Xavier's side as they were finishing up, "I will return so we can start the training. Will Piper need any training?" he asked. "No I will handle Piper but the youngest of us will need training." Xavier told him. "I will be here at sunrise if Piper wants to join in that will be fine." he said taking his leave. "Lets make it just after sunrise so Piper can care for the twins." Xavier said. Mik gave us a nod took his mates and left. "Wow his mates are very pretty don't you think? The one with black hair and blue eyes what was her name Celest and the other with red hair and golden eyes very pretty." I asked. "If you like that sort of thing. I like mine with burgundy hair, emerald green eyes and very powerful." he said making his way to my neck. I smiled and started for bed when he rushed me again and I put him down, "Stop that I'm going to hurt you." I told him. "You must be ready Cora has had many years of practice." he said holding me in his strong arms. "I'm not worried about Cora, I am learning many things when I drink from you. Now I need you to remember things about her."

I told him. "No I don't want to think of her at any measure. You are all I ever think about and will ever think about." he said walking off.

I followed him to the bedroom and set on the bed watching him think things over. I reached for him to come to me and pulled him down on the bed, "Please Love you must just this once." I said kissing his neck. "As you wish Sweetness." he said falling under my spell. He started up my neck and I waited for him to bite me first while he made love to me. "Mmmmm." he moaned as I bit him hard and sucked his blood. He tightened his hold on my body while I drank and getting his memories. Flashes came to me of him and his father and X learning how to fight well from Kaleb. Then the memories of Cora came to me, some were of her weakness and strengths. I bit harder when he remembered spending time with her, him smiling at her and them kissing. I put my fingernails into his back deep, almost ripping his skin. He began to think of our time together, our wedding, the lake, bringing Bastian into the world. I released my grip and turned it to more of a caress, "That's better Sweets." he said. I bit again to get more fighting skills from him. We made love for hours that night until I got what I needed from him. He laid there holding me, "You need to get some rest, we have a busy day tomorrow." I told him as I pulled him closer to my naked body. "Hey did you tell Trev, what did he say?" X asked softly. "He said he knew that something was different about you but he's fine with it. They will take our babies and take good care of them." I said. "What else was said I know you are hiding something I can feel you." he said. "I asked them to take our babies if none of us return to bring them into their crowns." I said sadly. "You asked them to raise our children?" he asked. I shook my head yes feeling sadness in my heart. "I swear nothing will happen to you even if I have to die to protect you." he said as he turned me to him. "Don't say anything else lets just sleep." I said. He held me with all his might as we both fell asleep.

I haven't dreamt about anything since I became vampire but tonight I did. Everything that Xavier gave me through his blood I replayed over in my dreams. I didn't rest well with me thrashing around in the bed, "Piper wake up." X said as he shook me lightly. "I cant sleep I'm going for a walk." I said as I set up in the bed. I got up and dressed quickly and out the door before he could say anything. He was at the front door before I could get there. His speed was like lighting when he needed it to be, "Wait Sweetness your not going alone." he said. "Do I have a choice?" I asked. He shook his head no and opened the door. I walked with him behind me a few steps trying to put things away in my head. It was a cold night and it felt good on my face as I walked through the woods. Finally I put my mind to rest, I stopped sudden with Xavier bumping into me. "Sorry Sweets." he said backing up. "I'm ready to go home now will you walk with me this time?" I asked. He took my hand and started home, "Piper this walking thing has made me work some things out. I have decided at the end of March you take twins and go I will come for you when this is over." he said. "Xavier Matthews how dare you say that to me! You know that if I don't go it will show weakness, I'm going and that's final. I know things will go our way don't ask me how I just know. I will take Cora down she is the fuel to the fire take her out and the flames die. We are one together not apart and we will raise our babies in peace." I told him. He didn't say anything for a few minutes, "I know you are right and I want you at my side but I need you safe cant you understand that?" he asked. "Yes Love I do understand." I said as I pulled him to come in home with me.

Chapter 14

Time came for us to take care of the babies before Mik showed up. We put Bastian and Brielle in the crib downstairs when the knock came. I opened the door to see Mik and his mates, "Good morning Piper how are we today?" Mik asked. "Fine, are you ready for today?" I asked him. "Question is are you?" Alea asked in a smart ass tone. "Ready as I'll ever be." I said using the same tone and giving her a evil smile. "Alea that's enough don't anger the lady, I know that look she is dangerous." Mik warned her. "Come Mik lets have something to eat before we get started." I said showing him the way. "We don't eat your kind of food." Celest said hatefully. "Don't eat then." I said just as hateful. "Piper be careful we need their help." X thought to me. "Yes we need his help not the women and if either of them speak to me like that I'll rip them to shreds." I thought back. "Celest I have already said my warning we are in their house and you will respect her. If you don't want to eat that is fine I will I'm hungry." he said giving her a look to shut up. "I'm sorry my Queen I didn't mean to disrespect. We hardly eat human food but if you wish us to try then we shall." Celest said. "I'm not your queen, you live a different life than the others. I know you don't like me or trust me for that matter. You are welcome in my home just don't over step, I cant be trusted and for good reason I am very dangerous. Now if you chose to eat fine if not then so be it." I told her. I handed Mik pancakes that I made and he ate while glaring at his mates.

After breakfast training started with me setting back watching to make sure no one got hurt. Tiffany got a lot of his attention and there were a couple of times that X had to put his hand on me so I would calm down with Tiff being flipped around. Xavier would join in on some of the training to show some of his teachings. Mik would show the girls many things to help them defend themselves. Mik walked over to me and took me by the hand, "Come on Piper lets show them how it is done." Mik said. Xavier stepped in front of him, "Mik look Piper is very tired, I really don't think this is a good idea." he told him. "Don't worry Xavier I wont hurt her she will be just fine." Mik said as he pulled me out onto the field. "Really Mik today is not the day." I said softly not really wanting to take part. Mik put me in a hold and held tight as he began to flip me over to put me on the ground. I let him flip me over, "Come on Piper you are going to have to do better than that." he said as he pulled me to my feet. "Mik." I said as he pulled a knife on me. "You better get away from me this time." he said hatefully as the others watched. "Maybe you should wait for another day Mik I'm warning you." Xavier told him making way over to get me from him. Mik put his knife to my throat before X could get to me, "Piper after I kill you I'm going after you babies." he whispered to me. Without any thought I took his knife, flipped him over and stabbed him in the shoulder. He screamed out in pain as his mates ran to protect him with my boys stopping them and Xavier pulling me off him. "What the hell Piper this is just practice!" X said as he took me inside. "It happened so fast, he said he was going to after Bastian and Brie I just reacted that's all." I told him. Mik came in the kitchen holding his shoulder, "Now that's what I'm talking about well done." he said. I walked over to him and looked at his shoulder, "I'm sorry Mik I did warn you." I said as Cyndi handed me the suture kit. "That's what I wanted from you." he said as I stitched him up. "Maybe you should refrain from using the twins as a push, she is very dangerous when they are involved." Xavier warned. "What about the newborn Tiffany?" he asked. "She is also my daughter." I said as I pulled tight on the needle. "I think we have had enough today. Piper may I make a suggestion?" he asked. "Sure go ahead." I said finishing up. "Get some rest and tomorrow Alea can help you place your anger." he said as he got up. "Very well." I said looking at her.

Xavier and Mike walked out guests out while I fed the babies. "He is right Mommy you are very dangerous. Your regards to all of us is what drives you to protect. Let the woman show you how to place your anger, you must beat Cora at her own game." Bastian thought to me. "He is right Mommy Cora wants the three of us dead so she can have Daddy for herself and be his queen, you must stop her." Brielle thought. "Don't worry my angles she will never get the chance to touch you, and as for your Daddy he is forever mine." I thought to her. Xavier wasn't included in this conversation this time as he tried to break in on what was said. We put the babies down for the night then went to bed ourselves, "What was so secretive that you wouldn't allow me to hear?" he asked as I laid with him. "Nothing really." I said not looking at him. "Is that so then why did I hear Cora's name?" he asked. "Why do you care anything about her!?" I snapped. "Hey that's not fair, you know I don't care anything about her. Most of the time I'm included that's all and I thought if it may be something you want to talk about." he said kissing my neck. "I'm sorry I'm just really tired that's all. They just told me that she wants the three of us out so she can have you all to herself. That I'm very dangerous when any of you are threatened." I said getting comfortable. "I will tell you this, she will never have me my heart belongs to only one and that's you. If anything ever happens to you or my babies I will not be here on this earth for long I shall join you in the after life. I love you more than my own life always and forever." he said as he put his arms around me. The month flew by with Mik at the Great House everyday and teaching many things. The girls and I worked with Alea and Celest on our mind control and me placing my temper. Mik taught Tiffany very well and she worked hard to learn everything he had to offer. Xavier worked at the hospital and then with Mik everyday so he could make up something for missing work when this fight broke out. We had about a week left of March and the time was coming for me to pack up the twins clothes so they could go with Michelle and Trevor. I sat in my room and wrote them a little letter just in case this was the last things I would ever get to say to them.

Dear Bastian and Brielle,

No matter what happens your Daddy and I will love you forever. You both made us so happy when you came into our lives. If your Daddy and I don't return please behave for your Aunt Michelle and Uncle Trevor. Remember you are the prince and princess of the covens and rule by a strong and loving hand. We will love you both always and watch over you.

Love Forever,
Mom and Dad.

I folded the letter and put it in the bag with the clothes that they needed and waited on Michelle and Trevor to come by.

Xavier came into the twins room as I was dressing Bastian and Brie. "You going to be able to do this?" he asked as he helped dress Bastian. "What choice do I have?" I said loving on Brie. "We don't have to do it like this you can still take them and go, I will come for you after this is over." he said softly. "I have already said my piece on this and we go together." I said taking Bastian in my arms. Michelle knocked on the door, "Piper are you in here?" she asked as she opened the door. "Yea I'm here." I said sadly. She came in and took a seat with us, "Are you sure you want to do this, you look like you are going to die or something?" she asked. "After you leave never call and never tell anyone where you are or going, talk to no one. Everything you need is in their bag. Look they may need to hunt so they can feed if so only at night and they are very fast you must go with them. Take them now love them well ya hear." I said with more sadness. "How will you know where we are?" she asked getting their bag. "We will open our minds to them when the time comes. Remember through the heart and burn the bodies if someone attacks, there will be nothing left." I told her. I called for the babies to come to me, "Remember my angels be good for your Aunt and Uncle they need to learn you so be patient. We will be with you soon I love you both with all of my heart." I said as I hugged and kissed them both. "I love you both so much we will be together soon. Do as your Mommy asked and don't talk to Michelle and Trevor through your bright minds, someone may pick up on your powers. See you soon my angels." Xavier told them as he loved and kissed them. I carried Brie out and X took Bastian to the truck and loved them once more before we put them in, "Take them far away Michelle, watch them closely talk to no one." I reminded her. "Don't worry Piper." she said as she hugged me and got in. Xavier put his arm around me as they drove off with the twins looking back at us. I waved to them as they drove out of sight and hearing far from us. "You ok Sweetness?" X asked. I didn't say anything I just walked off into the woods behind the house as he followed me.

Everyone at the house watched as we entered the woods as I cried for the first time since I was turned. I came to a stop and fell to my knees and cried hard, "Do you need me to hold you Love?" he asked. "No stay away I need this to clear my mind." I told him. As the tears fell they turned from sadness into anger tears burning my face as they streamed

110

down my cheeks. I stood up and walked over to a huge tree putting my fist through it and ripping it to pieces. Xavier stepped away from me as the group on the porch gasped in horror. I turned and walked out of the woods and to my room. I slammed the bedroom door so hard that it broke into splinters. I sat in the bathtub for about an hour before Xavier's voice rang out in my head, "Sweetness are you alright?" he asked. I didn't answer him as he slowly came into the room, I could hear him walking across the broken door. I stood up and reached for him as he came to hold me close. I cried on his shoulder, "This is the way it should be me holding and comforting you. I have never felt this much sadness from you before it is so deep, we will be with them again soon." he said as he stroked my hair. He lifted me from the tub and carried me to the bed, "I'm sorry X I never meant to frighten anyone." I said as he laid me down. "No one is frightened of you its just there has never been a female that strong before. The tears you shed is something vampires never do, where did they come from?" he asked. "I don't know the sadness took me over and the tears came to me. They felt so good to my heart but then they were so hot with anger. Please don't leave me stay." I said. "I'll be right here Sweets." he said as he moved my hair and put his face in my neck.

A knock came to the door as I woke up, "Come in Cutie." Xavier said softly. "Its time the war is in the next town over. I had someone come to me tonight and tell me it is coming fast and hard. Would you like me to inform the others?" she asked. "Yes get everyone together we will be there in a few minutes." Xavier said as he tightened up on me. I turned to X put my fingers through his silk hair and kissed him, "Make love to me." I said softly. He never said anything just complied with my request by making love to me so soft and gentle than ever before. "I love you." he said in a whisper. "I love you." I told him. We laid together for a few short minutes before we got dressed. I put on boots, camo pants and a tank top. Xavier dressed in jeans, boots and a tank then took me by the hand, "Lets get this over with." he said as we made way downstairs. "If we are ready, Tiffany stay close to your parents and the rest of you stay together don't split up. If we stay in groups we can win this. Remember don't rush anyone let them come to you that way you will have the upper hand." Mik said. We walked out together to get to our borders, meeting other covens that were in waiting. Their numbers were great but so was ours and the sight was horrid. Bodies were laying everywhere and the grass ran red with the blood of ours and theirs. "Bradly how long have you and your sons been here?" X asked. "Not long my King just arrived. Stay back let us take as many as we can before you and Queen Piper get involved." Brad said. "Shoulder to shoulder Brother." Xavier said standing up. Everyone was doing their parts as I watched them defend one another. Two vampires rushed Cyndi as Bailey went after her to get her back on her feet as he was taken down by two and then two more joined in. "Xavier, Bailey is down!!" I screamed as we both raced to help him. Mike was right behind us, I went for Bailey as Mike and Xavier took on the four that went for the attack. A week and a half of fighting went on night and day with only few of our coven friends down.

By the night fall of the second week came to a close Cora finally showed herself to me. She walked forward as I stood up from my kill. Xavier took my side mocking my every move, "Well well Queen Piper, you have done very well hiding your babies from me where are they?" she asked glaring at me. "Cora about time you show up." I said smiling at her. "Hello Xavier Love how are you?" she asked looking at him. "He is very well I assure you." I said stepping in her view of him. "Xavier how could you let a mere human cloud your judgment? You know it is I who should be at your side not her." she said trying to look at him. "I rule strong beside him as he does me, you will learn your place or I'll put you in it." I told her. "Shall I take that crown of yours now?" she asked stepping forward. Xavier took a step between us, "If you will allow me to show you something first then you can take my crown from my cold dead hands if you succeed." I said putting my hand on his shoulder. "Let me see what was so important." she said as she narrowed her eyes at me. I opened my mind to her and let the times Xavier and I shared with one another. I let the visions of us making love to each other. I knew I was getting to her as she let her true feelings run from her into me. She rushed me with all she had inside her. We fought hard with ripping and tearing on each other. She cut me deep with her sharp nails as she took me down, "Piper your babies she will find them and kill them." Mik shouted to me as she gave me a evil smile. I got to my feet and we began to fight once again. As soon as I had her in my grasp I made a lethal swing at her. She screamed out in pain as she went to her knees, and the others started to back off.

I sat beside her as she laid on the ground with the moon light shining down on her, "Cora, you know you didn't have to take this path." I told her as I held her. "Sorry my Queen I should have known this would happen." she said. "Sweetness we should go." he said as he bent down to get me. "She shouldn't die alone." I told him. "As you wish." he said. "Xavier I'm sorry, I know that you could never love me the way you love her please forgive me." she said dying slowly. "How could you put my children in this Cora and now you ask me to forgive you?" Xavier said with authority. "Please I beg of you to forgive me." she pleaded as she reached for him. He took a step back from her reach, "No Cora I cant forgive you for what you have done this time." he said with softness as he reached for me. She took her last few breaths and his words as she died in my arms. I laid her down softly as Xavier helped me to my feet, "You did well Sweetness." he said pulling me into his arms. "Lets finish this together." I told him. We rushed to meet the others and finish what was started. It took days to clean up the bodies so that we could hide our way from the humans. "Take your fallen and care for them as you wish, thank you for all you have done." Xavier said. I hugged Mik and his mates, "Please feel free to stop by the Great House any time you wish." I told them. "Thank you my Queen rule well here in this town, we will see one another again." Mik said. "Come on guys lets hunt to heal ourselves." Bailey said. "You go on Piper and I will have a cup see you back at the house." X told them. "Not this time Love I will hunt with you." I told him. He gave me a look like a kid in a candy store, "Really Sweets we don't have to we can go home." he said. "I want to do this with you, I have done everything else with you." I told him with love. I hunted for the very first time and I found it to be appealing to me, "You hunt very well Sweetness." he said as he drained his prey with me. "I was taught by the very best if I may say so myself." I told him when I finished. "Lets shower and get our babies." he said as he pulled me to my feet.

We raced back home and took our shower together. Tiffany was pleased with herself as she defended herself and the family. "Hey guys I just wanted to tell you that I'm very proud of everyone of you." I told them when we gathered in the living room. "I didn't do bad did I?" Tiffany asked. "No Cutie you did very well for such a young one." Xavier said. "Now I know not to pick on you." Jon said. "You better not Mik showed me a few extra things so look out Brother." she said trying to get him. "Hey now stay away." Jon said laughing and holding her off. "Alright we are going to connect with the twins and get them. I want you guys to rest and relax for a change." I told them. "As you wish, would you like one of us to go with you, it wouldn't be a problem." Mike asked. "No there shouldn't be any problems, we are going to bring them home everything is over." Xavier said. "Send for us the very minute you sense trouble." Mike said not wanting to let us go alone. Xavier took me by the hand and directed me to the door, "Wait Love just one minute." I said as I went back to Mike. "What do you know?" I asked. "Nothing my Queen I was just saying if there is any trouble then send for me, I would die to protect the twins." he said quickly. I put my hand on him and closed my eyes, "Make sure, you must have felt something to say that." I said in a whisper. "I swear to you my Queen I felt nothing I was making sure that you knew I would be ready for you to call on me." he said backing away from me. "We will return soon." I said sliding my hand from him.

Chapter 15

We opened our minds to our babies for the first time in many weeks, "Tell me where you are my angles." I said. "We are on the road Mommy we are in trouble hurry!" Bastian shouted in his mind to me. I looked at Xavier with panic, "Get on the bike we can move faster." he said as we ran to the garage. They had weeks on us I had no idea if we would ever catch up with them. I kept up with them as they moved around so much and fast then all of a sudden everything stopped. "Hurry X I can feel them they are in trouble." I said. He hit the throttle to speed up, "I can see the truck they are surrounded. Get ready for me to stop." he said. I put my hands on his shoulders so I could stand up on the back of the bike. "Piper there are six vamps around the truck." X shouted to me. They were scratching the windows and trying the doors, every time Trevor tired to move the truck one of the vampires would stop them. Xavier turned the bike to the side and brought it to a crashing stop as we dove off. I slid to a stop as he flew through the air and brought down three of the vampires. One took off at the sight of him coming at them and the other two started to fight with me. I put my hand through one of the males bodies ripping a hole in him. The other one tore at my skin making me bleed. Xavier fought with everything he had in him as the three took him down biting him and tearing deep gashes in his skin. I pushed the male that was fight me backwards so I could get to Xavier. I seen him run off with the other one as I ripped though one make that had Xavier down. The other two came towards me I backed up knowing that I could be in trouble. One rushed me and I put my hand through his chest ripping his heart out as he slumped to his death. The other one jumped on me and took me to the ground as he ripped my flesh on my face and neck. Just about the time he drew back to make his lethal swing he screamed out in pain as he slumped to the ground. I looked up as Xavier fell to his knees not being able to move anymore.

Trevor jumped out of the truck getting to X first. "My god Piper I think he's . . . ." Trevor started to say. "Keep them in the truck Michelle." I ordered as I went to my knees at Xavier's side. I looked him over and wiped the blood from his face. The bites were very bad and he was dying right in front on me, "Xavier drink." I said putting him near my neck. I couldn't get him to respond fast enough, I reached up and cut my neck some to make me bleed, "Do it now Xavier you are going to die!" I said as pulling him closer to my neck. He grabbed a hold of me and bit down on my neck with force. As he got more strength he flipped me over and drank harder. I grabbed him by his hair and pulled him off so he wouldn't bleed me dry. I got up slowly and he got to his feet, I felt very weak from my blood loss. The babies jumped in our arms, "Angles I have missed you." I said kissing them. "We knew you would come for us." Brie said softly. "Michelle, Trevor we never meant to put you in harms way will you ever forgive me?" I asked. "We are just shaken up that's all. Brie told us we needed to move before they had time to get us. How in the world did you heal like that so fast, I thought you were a goner?" Trevor said looking at X. "If Piper wasn't here I would have died for sure. Come on lets get home Piper needs to replenish her blood loss." he said taking Brie from me. Michelle and Trevor put my babies back in the truck as Xavier got the bike and we made way home.

I held tight to Xavier as he put his fingers through mine, "Thank god you are alive." I told him. "Thank god for you." he said as we pulled up at the house. Everyone of the young brood came out to see the twins, "Xavier, Piper why didn't you call for me?" Mike said as he helped me off the bike. "There would have been no time for you to get there Brother." Xavier said as the twins ran to us. "We have missed your touch so much." both said together. "I love you babies." Xavier said holding them. "Take them Mike and Jon, Xavier is very weak." I said as I helped him into the Great House. "Will you be staying for dinner tonight?" Regina asked. "No we will take rein check that way Piper and Xavier can do what is needed and you all can rest." Michelle said. We walked our friends out and watched them drive off, "Lets hunt so we can go to bed." Xavier said taking my hand. I stood back and made sure that

Xavier and the twins got what they needed before I hunted for myself. It was amazing how the children glided towards their prey like Xavier. We slowly walked back to the house as we enjoyed being home. I tucked the twins in so I could get to bed for the first time in weeks. Xavier was on his way out of the shower so I could get in because I was covered in blood from him and others not including my very own. By the time I got out he was fast asleep and I slipped in the bed. He was beautiful and his breathing was music to my ears with his emotions being high. He had done like his father and saved this town from being a ghost town. As I laid there I caught a glimpse of something out the corner of my eye. The figures of Kaleb and Charisma, "X wake up!" I said. He jumped up in a fighting stance and collected himself as he noticed who it was. Kaleb floated over to him, "My son you have done very well saving this town. You have grown into the man I always knew you would become. This queen you have chosen is very remarkable she completes you in every way. You are her strong side teach her well and together you will rule over many covens. Your mother and I truly love and miss you." his father said and floated away. X sat in the bed looking at me, "I told you my parents would have loved you." he said with a smile. I pulled him back down on the bed with me where he held me like I would disappear from him. The sunrise woke us up and for the first time in months we got out of bed without any worries. The whole house was buzzing with excitement as I started breakfast and X took on the twins. The twins blew through the kitchen with Xavier right on their heels and them laughing. Xavier was letting them win if he wanted to catch them he most certainly could without any problems. "Take a break your poor Daddy is getting tired." I told them. Mike took Brie and Jon got Bastian to put them in a seat for pancakes and bacon, "After we eat then you can play." Mike said. "Yes Unk Mike." Bastian said with a smile.

As the brood filed in the kitchen Cyndi and B was last, "Hey Bailey and I think it is time to get married now that the fighting is over." Cyndi said. "You will be staying in the Great House?" X asked as he sat. "Well we just thought that you guys might need the room if Gina invites Jovi to live here. Can we have your blessing?" she asked. My heart almost broke when she made it sound like she was moving out. "Of course you can have our blessing but you must stay within these walls. You seen what happened when someone left for just a few weeks we cant have that again." Xavier said looking at me. Cyndi came over to the stove and put her arm through mine, "Can I have a minute." she whispered. I led the way into the hall, "What's going on?" I asked picking up on her feelings. "Don't get mad I just couldn't tell you earlier." she said. "Tell me what, I would never get mad at you." I told her. "Ok here it is, I'm about two months pregnant and if X knew he wouldn't have let me go." she said stepping back. "Your right we would have never let you go, you could have went with the twins that would have been better. Does B know what does he think?" I asked being happy for her. "He knows and he is excited. Will you tell Xavier he is going to be pissed at me for this?" she pleaded. "No you can tell him and I'm sure he will be just fine." I said. "What is going on why cant I get through?" he thought to me. "We are coming just soft hands this time alright." I told him. I took her hand and went back in the kitchen where everyone was waiting to find out, "Xavier please don't be upset." Cyndi said trying to smile. "The suspense is killing me." he said with a smile. "I'm just a little pregnant, just about two months." she said and stepped behind me. He swallowed his drink hard and looked at Cyndi and Bailey, "Why didn't you tell us before we could have gotten through this while you were with the twins? You know what either way safe and sound now, shall I call Doc Logan?" he said giving her a hug. "Yes Doc Logan would be great." she said and returned to Baileys side. "Josh will be stopping by today for a few minutes." Tiff said as we ate breakfast. "Very well." X told her.

Everyone ate and cleaned up as the door bell rang, "That's Josh!" Tiff said as she ran off for the door. "Is Xavier and Piper busy?" Kassi asked. "They are in the kitchen." Tiffany said. Kassi came in, "I was wondering if I could have a few minutes of your time?" she asked. "How are you today?" I asked as X pulled a seat out for her. "Very well thank you." she said. "What is it that you need?" I asked. "Well Josh and I was wondering if Tiffany could come and join our coven. Josh loves her dearly and we would love to have her." she said. Xavier quickly put his arms around me just in case I planned on killing her for even asking. "Kassi I know that Josh loves our Tiff but there is no way that Piper is going to let her leave." Xavier said. "Yes I was sure that was going to be your answer but I was hoping to change your minds. She would taken very good care of and loved deeply." Kassi said. "I'm sure she would be Kassi, let me do this we will ask her what she wants. If she chooses to leave then so be it, if not then I will never hear of this again." I told her. "As you wish. I wanted to tell you that I thought what you did with Cora was amazing, anyone else would have let her die alone. I have never seen that kindness in any vampire." she said. "Yes well I am a different breed than most." I told her as Tiff came in. "You wanted to see me?" she asked. "Yes Kassi has come to ask you to live within her coven to be with Josh. What do you think would you like to do that?' I asked. "I'm sorry Josh I love you truly but I will not leave my parents." she said without thought. "You have your answer, I'm sorry Kassi this is her decision as it is ours." I told her.

She smiled at both of us, "Thank you both for your time." she said as the twins came skidding in. "Wow who are you?" Bastian asked. "My name is Kassi, you guys have gotten so big." she said as she gushed over them. "You are very pretty with your blonde hair and blue eyes." Brie said as she touched her hair. "Thank you but you are as lovely as ever." Kassi told her. Brie reached up and pushed her hair from her eyes as she talked to her through thoughts. Kassi smiled at Brie, "You are very gifted." she said. "I know you must go, it was very nice to see you." Bastian told her softly. "How is it that they can do that and how does he know I have to go?" she asked. "Like you said very gifted they both can do what Brie showed you and both know most of the future." Xavier said picking up Brie. "Amazing babies." she said on her way out. Cyndi and B came in, "How about some ice-cream?" she asked. "Ice-cream ice-cream!!" they both shouted. "Please watch them closely." I said on their way out. I walked back into the kitchen to find X smiling at me, "What?" I asked. "We have some time, what would you like to do?" he asked. "Well we need so many things so grocery shopping how about that?" I asked knowing exactly what he wanted from me. "Awe Sweetness I don't want to go shopping, I thought we could spend time together just me and you." he said giving me his seductive smile. I shook my head no at him playing, knowing I was going to lose this one. He sundered over and pinned me up against the sink, "You know I will win this one, I have a special talent for getting what I want." he whispered up my neck. "What is it that you want?" I asked falling under his spell. "All I ever want is you." he said with magic.

I couldn't tell him no even if I wanted to. I put my lips next to his and looked into his glowing eyes, "You can have me if you can catch me." I said right before I slipped out from his hold. I took off knowing he was faster than I would ever be, "I'm coming for you Sweetness." he said giving me a head start. I made it to the steps before he caught up to me. He scooped me up and carried me to bed laying me softly, "I love you my Sweetness." he said. "I love you deeply." I told him as I slid my hands up shirt and caress his naked back. We spent the next few hours worshiping each others bodies. I laid there in his arms feeling him breath on me, "What if I told you that Cyn wasn't the only one that was going to have a baby in this house?" I asked looking at him. He sat up in the bed, "What, this had better not be about Tiffany!" he said with authority. "No Love this has nothing to with Tiff, I was kinda talking about me." I said softly. "Are you sure, when did you know?" he asked. "Yes I'm very sure, I knew the day we left for the fight. I didn't tell you because I didn't want to cloud your judgment. Are you alright with me having another baby so soon, I mean I just gave you twins in February and here it is April?" I asked him. "Yes yes yes I want many babies with you." he said with his eyes getting brighter and brighter. "I am pleased to hear that from you. I feel very different this time much stronger than before." I told him with a kiss. "What do you mean stronger?" he asked. "I'm not sure what I mean just stronger that's all." I told him. "Hey Sweets are you going to give me twins again? I ask because I thought moving Doc in the Great House might be a good idea." he said as we got up to dress. "No just one special baby this time." I told him smiling. "Come on the twins will be home soon." he said taking my hand.

I met the gang at the door, "See extra room." Cyndi said as she came in. "Still you will stay." I told her as I put my arm around her. Gina came in with Jovi, Amber, and Sharon came in with Mike and Jon, "What's for dinner?" I asked. "Pizza works." Jovi said smiling at me. "You think that smile is going to win me over?" I asked him. "Yep." he said giving me a wider smile. "Your right, place the order Jovi. Should we have them deliver or carry out?" I asked. "That's crazy Piper, why would I want them to deliver to a house full of vampires when there is a shiny black camaro outside?" Jon asked with a smile of his own. "Well go on then it should be ready by the time you get there." I said shaking my head at him. "Your the greatest." he said hugging me before he grabbed Amber by the hand and hitting the door. "You are spoiling that boy, he will do anything you ask as long as you promise he can drive that car." X said with a sly grin. "I know but I love to make them all happy its what I do." I said putting my arms around him. "I called Doc he wants to see you both in the morning." X told Cyn and me. "You are going right?" I asked. "Yes but I have to go to work after so you can drop me off and pick me up." he told me. "As you wish." I told him. I heard Jon coming up the driveway and slide to a stop in front of the house, "What the hell was that?" I asked when he came in. "I'm sorry Piper it will never happen again." he said putting his head down. "We have humans that come here that cant move like we can. If you want to open it up find a place to race it." I said softly taking his face in my hands. "Yes it will never happen again I swear it." he said knowing I forgave him.

We ate dinner as a large family just like I always wanted and soon the day grew long. I put the twins up on their daddy for them to fall asleep with their sippy cups of blood. I carried Bastian to bed with X having Brie and soon we went to bed. I hardly slept any knowing I was going to see Doc in the morning, I was excited for myself and Cyndi. There was never no waiting when we went in as the nurse showed us to a room. "How are we today?" Doc asked. "Excited to know when our baby is due." Bailey said. Doc smiled at him as he looked Cyndi over and put his hands on her tummy, "Well you are right on schedule mom looks like we should see this one about early August. Lots of rest and plenty of blood the thirst can hurt badly." he told her. "Thanks Doc." she said as he helped her up. "Piper your turn please on the table." he said turning to me. I sat on the table as Xavier stood beside me while Doc gave me the once over. "Well this one is due September with no swollen feet. Xavier don't baby her this time she only has one and she will be more human acting. She is much stronger than when she was with the twins. Keep up with the blood and rest often alright. You and Cyndi can come together if you like." he said as X helped me up. We left and dropped Xavier off at work, "I have a double tonight so just think about me if you need me." he said as he kissed me. "Love you." I told him. "I love you." he said as he got out. Bailey drove us home with me and Cyndi getting us a cup. "What does everyone have planned for tonight?' I asked. "Mike and I have a date with Amber and Sharon." Jon said. "Tiff and I are going to the movies with Jovi and Josh." Gina said. "Well how bout it Momma you wanna go to the movies or something?" Bailey asked Cyndi. "Id love to, you going to be ok here alone Piper?" Cyn asked. "Sure will the twins and I are going to watch a movie and I have emails to do so I'm good go have fun." I told her. "Alright then send for us if you need us." Mike said making sure. "I'm good go have tons of fun." I said as I pushed them out.

Chapter 16

I catered to the twins playing games with them as I would hide and they always found me. I chased them around the house as they laughed that I couldn't catch them. "Ok Angels its getting late lets get our sippy cups and watch a movie how bout it?" I asked. "I get to pick it out tonight." Brie said. "Yes I know Sister better be a good one or I'm going to change it." Bastian said. "Hey now my Prince we don't speak like that to anyone. It is Brielle's turn and we watched what you wanted last time without any argument." I reminded him. "Sorry Brie we will watch whatever you pick out." he said much softer this time. She smiled at him, "If you want you can help me." she said giving him a evil look. "That's alright you pick on your own." he said. I put in the movie Brie happily picked out I worked on Emails that were sent from other covens to have simple questions answered. I did as many as I could without Xavier most were directed to him since many were still learning me. The twins fell asleep and I carried them up to bed. I still had a few things to do before the brood got home. I returned down the stairs and picked up a scent that wasn't any of ours, I quickly swept the upper floor knowing that my children could be target. With no luck upstairs I went back down the steps getting knocked unconscious. I soon woke to find myself in a different place and tied to a chair.

I looked around to make sure it was just myself and seeing a man sitting in a chair looking at me. "Well well Queen Piper, nice to have you in my home." he said glaring at me. "Who are you and what do you want?" I asked carefully. "My name is Cole and I want you to suffer just as I have." he said sitting up in his chair. "I'm not sure if I follow you suffer for what?' I asked looking at him picking up on his feelings. "Cora you killed her and therefore I'm going to kill you or maybe bring King Xavier here to kill him." Cole said. "Yes I see well she started a war with my family and she attacked me first I had to defend myself. I stayed with her while she passed I didn't leave her if that helps." I said softly. "YOU LIE!!!" he screamed as he hit me in the face. The force he used made my lip bust and bleed. He wiped my blood from my lip and tasted it, "Well I can see what attracts Xavier to you, everything a big bad vampire could want." he said with a smirk on his face. He walked out of the room and I gathered my thoughts zeroing in on Xavier, "I'm in trouble, I don't know where I'm at but he is going to kill me." I thought to X. Cole shortly returned to the room with me, "What are you going to do with me Cole?" I asked softly. "I haven't thought it out really, maybe I will contact your King and have him watch as I rip you from limb to limb. What do you think about that?" he asked. "Sounds like you thought it out nicely." I said with a smile trying to get to his feelings. "Hush yourself!!" he shouted as he hit me again. "If you call on Xavier you may not live long you do know that." I said lightly. "We will see about that maybe I will kill him and have you live without him just like I have to live without Cora. If you speak again I will spill your royal blood right here." he said with hatred and raising his hand to me again. I turned so that I faced him and licked the blood from my lips in front of him. He stormed out of the room hitting things as he went, and I took the chance to try Xavier again. "Xavier why haven't you answered me he is coming back and this time he means business!" I thought to him. Cole came back with a picture of Cora in one hand and a sword in the other, "I'm sorry Queen Piper I have to do this so my demons are at rest." he said with an intense look in his eyes.

He drew back his sword to kill me when Xavier busted down the door and Cole turned his attention to him. They fought long and hard with the same speed and strength of lighting. It was an unfair fight since Cole still had the sword in hand and Xavier had nothing, "On the desk another sword get it Xavier!!" I thought to him. Xavier turned and went for the sword as Cole made a swing at him. I watched as they fought back and forth, I had never seen Xavier move like that before as if it was second nature to him. They took on one another for a few more minutes, "I'm growing very tired of this, you should have never put your hands on my wife." X said with hatred as he flipped the sword around and cut Coles head off. After Xavier gathered himself he came to me, "My god Sweetness are you hurt?" he asked as he untied me. He pulled me to my feet and held me tight, "We are ok just a little bit of blood, I need to check on the twins." I said taking his phone. I dialed the number as he drove us home, "Piper where are you, I thought you were in bed?" Mike asked. "Go check on the twins now" I said in a small panic. He never said anything but I could hear him rushing the steps and into the room, "They are sound asleep everything is fine, what is going on?" he asked. "I'm on my way is everyone alright there and all accounted for?" I asked. "All accounted for tell me what is going on." he said with a touch of demand. "I was taken while you all were out but X is with me now and we are heading home." I told him. "See you soon." he said and hung up. "I'm sorry this should have never happened someone should have been home for you." he said gripping the steering wheel hard. "You have to work and the kids have the right to go as they please, they shouldn't have to carry the burden of my guardians. You should know that this is far from over." I told him as we pulled up in front of the house. He came around and helped me out kissing my hand.

I rushed in to view the children for myself touching them lightly. I returned to the living room, "Here Sweets drink up you will heal." X said handing me a fresh cup. "Piper are you alright you are a bloody mess." Regina said getting up to see me. "I'm fine just a busted lip nothing to worry about. No one goes anywhere alone, we either go in groups or we don't go. X has to work and you all will still come and go as you please, I will be more careful when I'm alone. You want to hunt do it in packs, its harder to take on two or more than one. Tiffany you will be escorted to and from school from now on, you don't like it to bad." I ordered. "We really don't need to be out Piper and you need not be alone either." Jon said. "No we will not give in to them with our fears we are a strong family and we rule strong, they will not break us in any way." I said with enough force that they didn't have a choice but to agree with me. I started to bed drinking my cup as Xavier led the way. I showered and dressed in one of his button up shirts and went to lay with him. He was waiting on me with a smile, "You look lovely Sweetness, I like the way you handled the brood. I was thinking maybe I should open my own practice and leave the hospital what do you think?" he asked. "I don't know I don't want you to give up anything you love, I can just be more careful when I'm alone." I told him. "The only things I would never give up are you, my children and my family. I will do this if you wish me to, I would love to work with you again." he said touching my fingers. "I wish you to do whatever makes you happy I will be at your right the whole way." I told him. "Then its settled we open our own practice here in town not far from the Great House." he said with a large smile.

I knew this made him happy to have his way on this one, I loved on him and settled down for the night. "You know that I love you deeply and all I could think about the whole time was what was he doing to you. Why wouldn't you show me or let me hear for that matter?' he asked. "X I love you more than my own life and I didn't want you to have judgment clouded. He was Cora's mate and he found out that she died at my hand, I tried to reason with him. He hit me and told me that if I spoke again he would spill all my royal blood. I called for you when he tasted my blood and told me that I was everything a big bad vampire could want. He said that he was going to call on you and make you watch him rip me from limb to limb." I said noticing him getting pissed at what was said to me. "Hey now all is done I'm home safe because of you, I didn't know you could fight with a sword like that. Your father was right you are a great man but you are great king as well." I told him with a smile. "I became a great king the minute you came into my life." he said. "No you were always a great king you just chose not to act on it." I said as I kissed him passionately. He kissed me back as I set up over him and moved my way to his juggler. "Please Sweetness I want you, I need you." he said breathing heavy. I pushed my hands up his shirt as I kissed him from his stomach to his chest. We made love to each other for hours with me needing him as much as he needed me. I ran my fingers through and grabbed a handful of his hair pulling his head to the side so I could bit him with enough force to make him moan in complete pleasure. I drank from him as he made love to me, "Please bite me back don't make me wait Love." I whispered to him. He did as I asked and I enjoyed the pleasure he gave me. "I love you my Sweetness you taste so delicious I have to make myself to stop, your blood calls my name." he said never taking his hands off me. "You are the only taste I want in my mouth." I told him.

He laid there caressing my tummy, "I hope this one reacts to me like the twins did." he said softly. "I'm sure this baby will." I said placing my hand on his. "Hey do you think Michelle would like to work with us, she is a great nurse who knows our little secret?" he asked. "Why don't you have her over for dinner and ask her." I told him. "I'll ask tomorrow at work." he said falling asleep. I laid there with hardly no rest coming to me as the sun rose for the new day. I slipped out of bed trying not to wake Xavier checking on the babies, Tiffany and Regina then I started breakfast. I could hear them getting ready for the day, "Good morning Piper, I'm going to be here all day with you and the babies. I will run any errands you need with you while X is at work today. It going to be just us Cyn and B have things to do today." Mike said when he came in. "You don't have to hang out here with me today I'll be just fine. What about Tiffany who will watch over her today at school?" I asked quickly. "I'll take her to class then Josh will be with her the rest of the day." Jon said coming in. I finished breakfast with the twins rushing the room and their daddy right behind them. "Morning Momma." both said in unison. "You are up and busy this morning, did you sleep at all?" he asked as he kissed me. "Some I guess lots of thoughts I need to put away, I hope I can find the time." I told him. "I can help you with that today Piper I don't have anything else to do." Mike said quickly. Xavier smiled to himself and I knew he was pleased to have Mike here with me. I sat as everyone ate their breakfast and started to get ready for school and work. I received love from all that left for the day with Xavier leaving last, "Don't forget Michelle today, I love you." I told him as I kissed him. "I love you Sweets." he said and left.

Bastian, Brielle, Mike and myself cleaned up the kitchen then I took myself to the attic to see if I could put away my thoughts. I knew this battle wasn't over, Cora dared to take the chance to stop Xavier's rule over the ones who wanted to feed on humans. There would be others and it was coming soon, I could feel it. After several hours of sitting the darkest part of the attic I returned to the lower floor, "Come on guys lets go to the store before the rest return home." I said as Mike looked at me wondering what took so long. "Is everything in order?" he asked softly as his phone rang. "Go ahead tell him I'm fine." I said knowing it was Xavier. Mike looked shocked that I knew as he text X back. The twins bounced around knowing we going to the store, "Lock your seatbelts." I told the children as I tossed the keys to the camaro to Mike. I was out of everything at home so shopping was a real chore, "Take them to the toys before their little heads pop off." I told Mike. He took each of their hands and led them away so I could get done. They soon returned with a toy each in hand as we headed to the check out. "Snow is coming can you smell it?" I asked as we pulled up at the house. "Yes I did pick up on a slight hint, Id say maybe a few inches. Please allow me to enter the house first to make sure it is safe." he said getting an armful of bags. I grabbed a few bags as Bastian made way into the house behind Mike with Brie staying with me, "Mommy when it snows can we play out in it?' she asked with her angel voice. "Sure thing Baby, hey how about a little hunt after Daddy gets home?" I asked her as we walked in. She didn't answer just jumped up and down and that was a yes to me. Mike returned to help with bags, "Please let me finish." he said trying to make it easier on me.

Soon the kids started to make way in the house and starting homework. The twins blew past me screaming that Daddy was home and I followed to greet him, "Hi my babies how was your day?" he asked as he was tackled and taken to the floor by the children and covered with kisses. "Our day was fine but I think Mommy had a bad day. She spent a lot of time in the attic and wouldn't let us see in. Unk Mike wouldn't let us go up to her either." Bastian told him, "Thank you Bastian for informing your Daddy." I said with a smile. "Daddy guess what Mommy said that it is going to snow and we can play out in it." Brie said. "I know all about you Mommy's day, she locks me out sometimes don't let that bother you. She needs to think and she cant do it when she has a lot of people in there with her. She is right about the snow we will have a great time playing in it." he told them both finally getting to his feet. The kids raced to be with the others out back, "Well Love how was your day before you got attacked at the doorway, what did Michelle say?" I asked while wrapping my arms around his strong body and breathing him in. "She said that they would be over about six and we could have Chinese. How about a hunt before we go Sweetness?" he asked. "I think a hunt might be just what I need." I told him. "Today was bad wasn't it Sweets, I text Mike to find out because you locked me out." he said. "Yea it was bad and this is far from over, everyone needs to be brushed up on their fighting skills even the twins. We will have another war with many losses but we will rein over this land. I don't know when this will happen but it is coming." I told him. "Lets just have a few days without the worry, come we hunt." he said pulling me along. Everyone went as a group and staying together per my request and me watching the children jump around after their prey. Xavier was trying to show them a little trick on how to catch quickly, but Bastian took off and scared it away. The look on Xavier's face cracked me up, "Bastian son you have to try like Daddy." he said with both of us laughing.

Both of them finished jumping around and finally got thirsty to hunt. After they found their mark we hunted for ourselves and headed home. Tiffany took them up to change since they made a small mess of themselves while playing. The fresh blood made them have so much energy that they played with everything that caught their beautiful eyes. Bastian's glistened just like his daddy's when he was excited and Brie's was green as ever. Amber, Sharon, Jovi and Josh all arrived around the same time and shortly after Michelle and Trevor showed up. The twins took off after their human aunt and uncle, "Hey kiddos take care they are made different then we are." I reminded them. They slowed as much as their excitement would allow. Brie went into Michelle's arms and began to talk to her through her thoughts and I could see that Michelle enjoyed it. Xavier gathered everyone together and moved us to the door. I let Bastian and Brie ride with Trevor and Michelle to the Chinese restaurant leaving X and myself alone. "You alright Sweets?" X asked as he drove along. "I guess." I said with him trying my feelings to make sure. The restaurant was not very busy so getting a table wasn't that hard. "Hey Michelle I wanted to tell you that we are planning on opening up our own practice very soon." X told her. "Really, why?" she asked. "So many things has happened as of late and I think it is best we do this before questions come up." he said. Michelle looks at me, "I was taken from the house the other night. It could have been bad being that I am pregnant again." I told her. "What your pregnant again when were you going to tell me?' she asked. "Girl when have I had the time?" I asked her smiling. "Michelle I want you to come and work with us, we need a top of the line RN and your it. Not to mention that you know our little secret." Xavier said. "When you say work with you guys how many vampires will I be helping with?" she asked in a whisper. "Many will come knowing that I'm opening and I will give you special books that will help you learn how we heal. There is no need to worry you will be protected at all costs just as you are now." he said. "What will be my hours, will they be normal hours?" she asked. "Yes very normal hours I want to keep it as simple as possible." he told her. "Then yes I will work with you guys. This will be great learn more about you and Piper and getting to see my twins more." she said smiling. "I love you Michelle." Brie thought to her.

After dinner we returned to the Great House so we could talk, "So what is going to happen now that you killed the man who took Piper?" Trevor asked. "There is going to be another war and this one will be bigger than the last. I'm sorry to call you guys once again but we may need you to take the children away." X told her. "We will no need to ask and the new baby as well." Trevor said. "I only hope that Piper has the baby before this takes off." Xavier told them as the twins climbed on him to fall asleep. They were wore out as was Bailey with the chasing around the house. Bailey ran the house many times before he fell out with Cyndi laughing at him. Michelle and Trevor stayed a little longer and soon they took their leave. "Xavier I looked on line and found a building close to home." Regina said. Xavier went to look at what she found while I cleaned up the house. My mind was full of everything my memories, Xavier's memories and when the twins dream something they would share with us. All this stress was taking a toll on me and I worried about the new baby coming. What was going to happen to the children if we didn't return, maybe I wasn't the right person for this job. Xavier had many years to get used to everything and I had only a year and still learning. "Don't ever let me hear that again you are the right person to be my queen. You were born to rule with me you just haven't seen it yet." he thought to me. I smiled at him before I started to bed.

Chapter 17

Morning came without much sleep to me and I could hear the children making way to the bedroom. They dove on the bed trying to wake their daddy but he never moved a muscle. "Wake up Daddy it is time for breakfast." Bastian said looking at me. "I don't know what to tell you try the wake up thing again we have to get him up to have breakfast with us." I told them. They shook him and tried wake up Daddy thing but still nothing from X. Brie looked at me for any help at all, "Try kissing him all over his face maybe that will work." I told them. Their eyes lit up hoping it would work as they held him down and kissed him all over his face. Xavier couldn't help himself as he grabbed and tickled them and they screeched in happiness. They hit the floor and made way to their aunts and uncles room, if they are up then so is everyone else. I put on today's clothes and started for the door, "Hey I don't get any love from you this morning?" X asked. I smiled as I walked over to him kissing him on the cheek. "I thought you may have enough love this morning." I told him getting up. "I don't think so my Queen lets try that again shall we." he said getting my hand. I gave him another quick kiss on the cheek and moved away smiling. "Awe come on Piper I always need you to love me I can never get enough from you. You could kiss me a hundred times a day and I would require more." he said looking inside me to see if I was hurting or upset. I gave in and kissed him with passion this time, "Now that's what I'm talkin about." he said getting up. I went down and helped with breakfast with Bastian running at top speed past me and Brie trying to catch up. "Let me catch you Bastian slow down." she said sadly. "You can never get me I'm as fast as

Daddy." he said picking on her and making her whine. "Not as fast as I am now slow yourself and teach her." I told him. "She will have to work at it." he said as he slowed up and Brie smiling that I helped her.

Breakfast finished up and clean up was well on the way, "Ok kiddos out the door." X said showing them out. We walked to the new building to look it over and meet with the man who was selling it. "Good morning Mr. Overstreet how are you today." Xavier said. "I'm good Dr. Xavier how are you and your family?" he asked. "Very well thank you." X said as we went in. We looked around the building and made the decision to take it. The guys talked back and forth about prices and I slowed the twins who forgot that they were in presents of a human. "Sweetness are you still with me?' Xavier asked as he moved his hand to bring me back to the room. "I'm sorry what did you say?" I asked. "Would you like to go by the bank and meet Mr. Overstreet back here in a hour?" he asked smiling at me. "Anything you wish of me." I told him. "Is an hour good for you Mrs. Matthews we can make it longer?" Mr. Overstreet asked. "No need an hour will be great." I told him. We walked home with the twins running and playing, "You know that was the first time I have ever been called Mrs. Matthews by anyone, it was nice but I still like Sweetness." I told him as we walked hand in hand. "You are called Queen Piper don't you like that?" he asked smiling at me. "No I'm just Piper." I told him getting in the car. I asked Mike to watch the children while I ran my errands and he took the challenge. I drove X to work then to the bank as the snow started to fall, and making way back to the building. Mr. Overstreet was right on time as I got out, "So here are the keys and paper work and I need you to put your name right here." he said. I scanned the paper then signed my name, "Thank you this will be a great office for us." I told him. "Yes Ma'am hope you all enjoy it." he said as we parted.

I drove by the hospital to see everyone before I went home, "Hey Lisa how are you today?" I asked as I came in. "Dr. Danvers I mean Dr. Matthews great to see you." she said. "Have you seen Xavier around?" I asked. "Sure he is in trauma one with Michelle and Jessica." she told me. "Thanks see you later." I said locking X down so I could see for myself. I neared to curtain looking inside his mind to see what he was doing. "Piper is in the hospital I can feel her." he whispered to Michelle. "What about Jessica?" she whispered back. "I'm not sure its hard to tell she has me on lock out. I cant tell what kind of mood she is in but Piper knows she is here with me." he told her. "Hi guys." I said coming in. "Sweetness everything alright?" he asked still working on the patient. "Yes Love just wanted to see the rest of the gang, where is Robert?" I asked. "He is on his lunch." Jessica said. I nodded her way as I stood back and let him finish what he was doing. When they finished Jessica walked over to Xavier and touched him on his arm, "Good job Doc as always." she said smiling. He never gave her a second notice as he walked over and picked me up in his arms. She huffed away mumbling under her breath as I growled under mine. "Now Sweetness behave." he said as he kissed me. "Do I have to I mean we are in a hospital someone can fix her right up!?" I asked. "You know you have to and by the way you feel there would be nothing left to fix." he said laughing. "As you wish but if I find that she touches you again I wont be able to help myself." I warned. "Come on lets have a bite to eat before you get back, how's Mike holding up?" he asked dragging me along. "I'm sure he will need a nap when I return to the Great House." I joked.

After a quick lunch I went home driving slowly because the roads we getting slick and I passed the kids as they walked home from school. "Hey guys do you want a ride?" I asked looking at poor Jovi who was a wet frozen mess. The brood crammed themselves on the camaro as best as they could, "To the Great House or your house?" I asked Jovi. "Yyyour house ppplease." he chattered. "You guys should have called he is nothing like us now look at him." I said unhappily. I called ahead and asked Mike to make a fire so Jovi could get warm. When we entered the house smelled of a fresh fire it was nice and had a great feeling of home. Gina went to get him some hot chocolate so he can warm from the inside as I looked him over. His face was pale and lips were a bit red, "Jovi how long have you felt like this?" I asked feeling his head. "I don't know a couple of days I guess. Mrs. Williams said that if I didn't go to school that I couldn't even talk to Gina on the phone." he told me as I handed him a blanket. I turned to call Mrs. Williams and his social worker, "Hi this is Piper Matthews I was wondering how do I get a child placed in my home?" I asked. "Well I would have to know your history and back ground." she said. "Kari I used to be Piper Danvers I worked at the hospital do you remember me?" I asked her. "Oh yea I sure do you married that handsome Dr. Matthews didn't you? Well I'm sure I can do something to help you guys out let me check on some things and call you back." she said. "Thanks Kari that is very kind of you." I said and we hung up. My next call was to his foster mother, "Mrs. Williams this is Piper Matthews I was wondering if I could keep Jovi for a few days he has a high fever and the roads have become slick." I asked her. "Sure I don't see any problem with that." she said. "Thank you I will have him call as soon as he is feeling better." I told her and hung up.

"I have to go don't I?" he asked. "No honey you get to stay here, now go with Jon and get out of those wet clothes. He came back dry and ready to lay down to get warm as Gina gave him something for his fever. "Thanks Piper for being so kind, I don't want to get you, Cyndi or the babies sick." he said. "No worries we don't get sick like that." I said checking his fever again. Dinner was well on its way when Xavier got home, "What's wrong with Jovi?" he asked rubbing my tummy. "He has a fever so we have him a few days." I told him with a smile. "Huh well I can check on him if you wish." he said. "Sure I've got chicken noodle soup going now." I told him. "Make sure you eat all this." Xavier told him. Jovi began to eat and we had our dinner before Xavier and I went out for extra fire wood. "X do you smell that someone is coming?" I asked. He took a deep breath, "Yes wonder who it is and what they want?" he inquired. "I'm not sure but they are coming fast." I told him. "Get back in the house Piper now!" X told me. I was making way back to the front porch when a male vampire rushed towards me. I put my hands up to defend myself and strong winds came from me and pushed him to the ground. I put my hands down and the winds stopped as X put himself in front of me and the visitor. Again the vampire took another chance and made way to us and I put my hands up again but this time making the winds stronger than before blowing him farther from us. He stood and left from the sight of us as we returned to the house. "What the hell was that?" X asked. "I don't know." I said looking at my hands. Mike, Jon and Bailey met us at the door, "What is going on out there, who was that?" Mike asked. "I'm not sure but I think Piper received a new power." X told them. "Call Dorien I want to see him as soon as possible." I said with demand.

I made my way to the bedroom while Xavier called the doctor asking him to join us tonight. "He will be here shortly." X said coming in the bedroom. It never took Dorien very long to make it to the Great House, "Piper is everything alright?" he asked as he came in. "I have received a new power, I want to know if it is mine or the babies. You keep telling me that I'm half human and half vampire what do you mean by that?" I asked setting on the bed. Dorien looked at Xavier then me, "Its hard to say, you got a gift from the twins and you kept it. You share mind connection with Xavier and feelings, so this maybe the babies power and you may keep it as well. I'm thinking that every time you conceive this will happen. The half and half well Xavier only poisoned your blood stream it will slowly kill the human part in time and then you will be full day walker. As for your children they will remain half human and half vampire, don't worry the vampire side is very strong and they can take a lot. If your body takes a hard enough hit the human part will die completely and you will remain vampire. Xavier's blood is true vampire and it is very powerful it runs through you all. If you chose to share these gifts with Xavier you can do so just by biting him. He was born royalty and you were born to rule by his side this is fore told so that human and vampire race can be saved." he said setting back. "Are you kidding me I cant handle this right now. So this is why we got to see his parents not long ago, this is Tiffs power." I said pacing the floor. "Yes well you bit her and took control over her power, don't you see Piper you can take or break the power as you see fit. There has never been a female vampire who has this kind of power." he said watching me walk the floor.

I walked the floor while they talked about whatever, "Sweets do you need anything else he has to get back?" Xavier asked. I shook my head no to them as Doc rose to leave. "You need to walk don't you?" X asked. "Yes in the worst way." I told him. "Let me get one of the boys to go with us." he said moving to the door. "No I cant have to many feelings or thoughts this time." I said. "No way in hell your going alone!" he said with raised tones. I took his hand and led him out the window, leading the way into our woods. I walked in the cold night putting things away as best as I could while Xavier mocked my movements. I stopped and put my hands up as the winds blew the trees, making them crack under the pressure I was using. I moved my hands in a sweeping motion and ripped a tree from the ground and laid it softly on the loose dirt. "Are you ready to go home Love?" I asked taking his hand. We walked back at a human pace hand in hand, "You know I have been alive along time and I have never seen anything like you before. You can make others give you what you want without even trying and the way you can change your mood from anger to seductiveness in just a snap. The way you control me is remarkable and you have helped me place my anger as it should be." he said. "I can control you because you allow me to, power has a way of making ruins of things. I swear X I'm not to sure I was made for all of this, yes to be with you and maybe be your queen but all of this?" I asked lowly. He stopped me and put my face in his hands, "Maybe my queen? I know you were made just for me and to be my queen no maybes about it. Your mind is a wonderful place I have seen it when you allow me, you put things away well when you walk. We are great together and we will rule great together, you make me strong in everyway. I never gave up anything for anyone before I met you, but I would have given up everything to be with you. If you asked me to give up my throne it would be done by sundown tomorrow, all I ever want is you and my family nothing else." he said as he kissed my cheek. "Xavier my love I am very happy to be with you forever and I would never ask you to give up anything for me, I know this is your destiny." I told him. "You are my destiny and nothing else." he said as we made way home.

We jumped through the bedroom window and I watched as he looked for a new set of clothes. I watched him as he took off his shirt showing his sleek stomach and chest, "You said that you would give up anything I ask?" I asked him. He turned to me, "Yes anything I swear it will be done." he said. "Will you be willing to give up a few hours to be with me?" I asked him smiling turning on my magic. He said nothing just took a attack stance and dove on the bed holding me down and kissing my face all over. I laughed at him playing with me making me feel better as he released his hold turning more into a caress. I moved my fingers across his back and up to his hair grabbing a handful pulling his head to one side and biting him. He moaned in complete pleasure and took his hands and pulled my shirt into pieces. His eyes glowed bright blue and his scent intensified as he kissed me from my stomach to my neck breathing his sweet breathe on me. His feelings were more powerful than usual he was calming me with every breathe he took. He began to make love to me and his naked body felt so good next to mine as we both trembled under the ecstasy of our love making. He looked into my eyes, "Will there be anything else I can give up for you my queen?" he asked never missing a beat. "Just more that's all I require." I told him. The sun rose the next morning with us still making love to one another with his skin feeling like silk next to mine. I knew whatever I was given I could handle with him next to me.

The moon came up over the hill side as we laid there together, "Would you like to hunt with me Love?" he asked. "I will do anything you ask of me." I told him. He helped me up and we dressed so we could get out and back. I always watched him hunt first he was beautiful as he hunted for his prey. I hunted after I found something that caught my senses, and we headed home going back in the front door. Jovi was looking better as Gina tended to his every need, Cyndi and Bailey we working on wedding plans, Mike and Jon were keeping the twins busy and Tiff on the phone with Josh. "Piper how are you, we were worried you were up there a long time?" Cyndi asked. "Yea I'm sorry guys had a lot to put away this time. Jovi you feeling better?" I asked. He shook his head yes as Mike walked over to us, "What's this new power Piper has?" he asked. "She can control the weather with her thoughts and hands, mostly it is the babies power but she will have full control. As she becomes more vampire she will receive each of your powers so be careful of her the change will be hard." he told them excitedly. They looked at me with surprise, "I can share with X if I desire, now tell me what you think." I asked. "I think you should let Gina turn me, I have thought about this for a long time now." Jovi said with a certain tone. "Now is not the time Jovi when Piper and Xavier has been upstairs this long don't push trust me." Gina said. He sat back and covered up, "Well I think it is great she is the one we go to with all of our problems." Jon said. "Your not just saying that so you can drive my camaro are you Love?" I asked throwing a lot of charm his way. "No Piper I swear." he said moving away from me and towards Xavier. "Stop that Sweetness your working up a scare in the boy." X said stepping in between us. "Wow she is more convincing than ever, I have never felt anything like that before." Jon said from behind Xavier. "Sorry Jon please forgive me." I said. "The twins have been fed and they have had a great time." Cyndi said. "Thanks for helping would you mind tending to them just a bit longer there is something I must do?" I asked.

Xavier smiled at me wondering what I had planned, I opened my mind to him and put my hand on his heart. He thought for a minute, "No Piper forget it, I'm not letting you do that!" he said loudly. I stepped up to him pressing my hand harder to his heart and walked around him never taking my hand from his body and thought to myself, "Yes Love I need to know who our visitor was you will go with me alright." I said into his mind. He stopped breathing, "No Sweetness I wont allow it." he thought back. I felt him fighting my magic so I put it on him thick, I wanted to win this one at all costs. I ran my fingers though his hair, "Yes Piper I will go with you." I made him say to me. "Good then its settled we will be back in a little bit." I told the brood. I led the way holding tight to Xavier's hand and when the fresh air hit him I released my hold on him, "Damn Piper that's not fair, you know that you could get hurt and we are not going!" he said now mad as hell at me. "X we need to know what he wanted so that we keep the children safe. He wont hurt me I'm sure he wants to talk, I'm sorry I pulled that on you but I knew you were dead set on not going. Please forgive me I wont do that again." I pleaded. "Don't do that again, you will be able to change my mind without your magic. Now I know what you are capable of I must be stronger." he said putting his hands around my waist. "So you forgive me then?" I asked. "Of course I do Sweetness, now lets go find our new friend." he said. I took a deep breath and picked up on him in no time, "He is west of here." I told him taking his hand.

Chapter 18

It wasn't long before we found our new friend and as soon as I could get close enough I put on my special charm to make him slow down his pace. I stepped forward while Xavier lingered in back a bit, "Hi my name is Piper, you came to my house the other night do you remember me?" I asked in a soft voice. "Yes I remember you all to well my Queen." he said staying a safe distance. "What was it that you needed from me that you felt like sneaking around?" I asked. "I wasn't sneaking I was being well . . . careful." he said. "Wont you come out and see me?' I asked. "Where is King Xavier, I know he is close?" he asked making way over to me. "He is here waiting would you like him to join us?" I asked. "Yes please have him join us." he said still moving to me. Xavier came out and stood between us as our friend stopped. "May we find the reason for your visit?" I asked. "My name is Thomas I have been sent to warn you." he said. "Who sent you and warn about what?" I asked standing beside Xavier. "We have a mutual friend Mik, yes he said to come and tell you things are getting bad to be on guard. This thing with Cora is not over she had backing from other covens that don't agree with your way." he said feeling very calm. "Our way what do you mean?" Xavier said. "Your queen for one she was human and you bit her to turn her but you don't allow others to feed on humans. I personally don't care either way, I have stood back and watched for sometime now your kindness is remarkable. I have heard some of the kind things you have done, the humans you let into your home and leave without a scratch. I seen your anger as well I was sneaking around the time you sent your twins away and I fled the area however the tree was not as lucky. Therefore I must warn you that one coven is trying to get five others to join them and they have yet to make decisions. One of the covens has the one I love there and I wish her not to fight I wish her to live what should I do my Queen?" Thomas asked. "Well I think if they trust you then you should have them come to the Great House and hear our side. I give you my word as Queen that no harm will come to them they can listen to our side and leave anytime they wish no matter which side they take. As for the one you love if you would allow me to meet her I will do my very best to keep her out of harms way." I told him. "May I be allowed to fight side by side with you and King Xavier?' he asked. "As long as you are on the up and up if I find that you are not as you seem I will kill you myself understand?" I said kindly. "I understand my Queen thank you for your time, I hope to see you soon." he said backing away. "Yes we will see each other very soon." I told him as I turned my back on him.

We made way back home to let the boys know what we found out. They were Xavier's personal guards and they were let in on all of everything. I slowed our pace and took his hand, "I've been thinking about something." I told him. "I know you have been in deep thought on the way home, what's up?" he asked. "As much as I hate it and deeply saddened, I think we should give Cyndi and Bailey the choice of leaving or staying I mean after this is all over." I said. "Hell no they are royalty and they stay within the Great House. This house is stronger if we stay together and besides I wont see you like the time you sent the twins away. When she has that baby you will love it as if it is your very own you will see." he said. I took a deep breathe to respond to what he said, "Mik he is at the house and he is hurt I can smell fresh blood." I said. Xavier took off like lighting with me two steps behind him.

Xavier hit the front door to see Mike bending over Mik covered in his blood, "What the hell is going on here?" X asked all of the boys. "I picked up his scent and went out to greet him, he was crawling up the steps tore all to pieces. We got him this far before you got here." Mike explained. "Hey Mik can you hear me!?" X shouted as he bent over him. With Mik not responding I went for Xavier's medical kit so he could fix him. "Has he been bitten?" I asked. "No not that I can tell, help me Piper." he said as he started to sew him up. I took the other side of Mik and began to stitch him up, "Mike you and Bailey look for his mates do not separate, search the grounds if they are here you will find them." I told them. "Jon help me get him on the couch." X said when we finished.

Tiff came in and looked sadly at him, "He will be alright wont he?" she asked. "Sure thing Cutie Dad is very good at this kind of stuff." I told her holding tight to her. "I'm sorry Piper nothing on the women if you wish we can keep searching." Bailey said. "No need until we wake Mik then we should know more." I told him. Hours went by as we waited then Mik woke in much pain grabbing Xavier's arm tightly, "Thomas did you speak to Thomas." he asked getting his mind together. "Yes we have spoken to Thomas he told us you sent him." X said helping him set up. I gave him something to eat and drink, "Mik you must eat so you can get your strength back." I said. "Thanks Piper." he said. "What happened to you out there?" X asked. "I was called to help one of our coven friends but by the time I got there the fight have broke out and it was bad. They are capturing vampires and draining their blood to sell it to humans. Its coming this way Xavier they have heard of the power you and your queen possess." Mik said. "What do you mean draining vampires?" X asked. "I mean the slit the throat and take it all, nothing to recover from. You don't have long, are you ready for this because it is leftover from Cora." he said as he ate his dinner.

Xavier looked at me and gave me heads up to call Michelle asking her to come right away. I was trying to keep up with any future visions that I was getting, the twins concerns would come to me, I wondered about Miks mates and I worried about the new baby and Cyndi I was frying my mind. Everyone gathered in the kitchen so we could talk about what was going to happen, "You know she wont go with Michelle." X thought to me while he washed his hands. "Oh yes she will one way or another." I thought back. "We have until June then they will come, if we attack in late April then we might have a chance. We have someone coming to talk with you, the numbers are large but they mean no harm right now just have to boys ready." Gina said. "When Michelle gets here the twins will be leaving with her and so are you Cyndi." I said softly. "Oh no I'm going you cant stop me!" she said with hands on her hips and tummy showing. "Don't you dare push me on this you will do what I say, you will be only two months until you deliver." I snapped at her. "Piper please I have to go so I can make sure Bailey is safe, X tell her change her mind I know you can I have seen you do it." she pleaded. "Sorry Cyn not this time she is dead set and so am I." Xavier said. "They are right Momma you know that, I need you to be safe with Michelle and I swear to you that I will return." Bailey said hugging her. "I know you want to go but you have to stay behind for the safety of your baby and ours. You will bring them into the crowns if we should not return." I thought to only her. "Yes my Queen I understand." she said as she left with everyone looking at me wondering.

On my way back to the living room I was stopped by the phone ringing, "Hello?" I said. "Piper this is Kari, Jovi's social worker." she said and paused. "How are you this evening?" I asked. "Very well thank you I'm sorry to call so late but I just got word that you will be allowed to have Jovi in your home." she said happily. "That is wonderful news thank you for calling." I said. "Yes I can stop by and let you sign papers is tomorrow good for you?" she asked. "Yes that will be great thanks again." I told her as we hung up. I went in the living room and took a seat, "Something wrong Sweetness who was on the phone?" Xavier asked as he leaned over me. "Jovi is ours now so we need to send him away with Michelle. I feel bad that I snapped at Cyndi I know she worries about B, plus this is a lot to put on Michelle and the twins leaving I should have a headache." I told him. I suddenly felt myself calming down getting swept up in the way he smelled to me, and my worries started to disappear. "Stop that Xavier you know that I need to worry it makes me stronger." I told him. "I know Sweets I just worry about you we cant walk right now and I just put on the new door from the last time we had to do this. Hey Regina will be pleased that Jovi is ours well hers." he said as he smiled and poured it on. "You told me no more magic on you so don't do it to me." I said as I had to kiss him.

Michelle knocked on the door and Tiff let her in, "What the hell?" she asked looking at me. "I'm sorry I forgot I was covered in blood, Mik had an accident and needed our help." I told her. "Piper you are scaring me a bit what's going on?" she asked. "I need you to take the twins again and this time Cyndi and Jovi has to go with you. I'm so sorry to put all this on you again and if it is to much we can make different arrangements." I told her. "It must be bad this time if you are sending Cyndi away, and Jovi I didn't know he was living here." she said. "Yes we found out he is ours and it is pretty bad she will be close to having her baby." I told her. "Lets get them packed so we can go, Trev has already made plans for different spots so the twins can hunt if they need to." she told me. "God I love you girl." I told her. "I love you to." she said as we walked up the steps. "Don't stay to long in one place, Cyn can see the future so listen to her. Trust no one Michelle I mean this." I told her. "I know we have it covered no worries we were caught of guard last time but not this time." she told me. I gave the bags to Trevor so I could hug my babies, "Here Brie take mommy's necklace and hold it tight to your heart. When you miss us just look inside and we will be here with you, don't connect with Mommy or Daddy you understand? Cyndi will need you to take care of her for a few days until her heart gets better from missing Bailey ok and listen to your aunt and uncles stay safe. We will come for you all when this is over just like last time." I told her in a positive tone. Xavier took his heart necklace off and put it on Bastian, "Take care of your sister and help Michelle out ok. Like your Mommy said we will come for you, go now and be safe." he told him as he loved on Brie and Bastian. I was having a hard time with my own feelings but Xavier's was worse this time. "Take them now and love them well be safe I love you both for this." I told them softly as I hugged them both. "Keep your mind clear Piper they will be safe I swear." Michelle said. I waited by the door as they filed out one by one, "Jovi when you get back we will have our little talk ok." I said as I kissed him on the cheek. He smiled and went out with Gina, "Cyn sorry I snapped at you, stay strong for your baby and ours. Just remember what I said you can and will bring them into their crowns when the time comes, Xavier has taught you well strong but loving hand and you will be great." I whispered to her.

She hugged everyone but Bailey she held the longest and he loved her tightly, "I love you Momma see you soon, go now and be safe." he said putting his hand on her tummy. I fell to the floor in great pain from Bailey, and Xavier rushing to my side. "Piper!?" he said. "Help me up." I said trying to get to my feet. Everyone was in the truck and I went out to say goodbye one last time watching them drive out of sight. As Bailey walked past me I hit the ground again, "Let me in to see Piper now!" Xavier demanded. "Get Bailey out of here make him hunt with the brothers!" I said trying to stand once again. "I'm sorry Piper what did I do?" Bailey asked trying to help out. "Just go Love I'll be alright you need to hunt." I told him fighting the feelings. "I'm ok I can wait till morning." he said. "Go now B if she says." X told him and the brothers taking him away. "Tell me why I just sent them out so late!" X demanded of me. "That was intense I haven't felt that since we sent the twins away." I told him from the floor. "Why wont you let me feel you when you are like this?" he asked. "Are you sure X it is nothing like you have felt before?" I asked. "Yes I want to know." he said holding me. "As

you wish sit flat on the floor." I told him. I placed my hand over his heart
and pushed my hand flat letting go all my fears and feelings that washed
over me. I watched as he winced in pain and held his hand over mine,
"There is more do you want it all?" I asked. "Yes everything." he said
lightly. I gave him what I said to Cyndi about the twins and her taking
over of need be, the pain Bailey felt, the worry from the babies about us
not returning, Jovi being ours and still human.

I could see that he was in horrible pain and as fast as I gave it I took
it all back leaving him on the floor breathing hard. "Are you alright
Love?' I asked not touching him. "How do you do it all day, how are
you coping?" he asked. "This is what I do I'm everyone's mother and I
feel what they feel it drives me to protect. Do you need a drink cause
I know I do?" I asked. "Would you like to hunt?" he asked. "No we
cant and leave Mik unattended we shall have a cup and hunt later." I
told him. "Sweetness you are remarkable the feelings you have must be
hurting yet you are still strong." he said fixing our cups. "Remarkable I
don't think so I'm just me this is who I was made to be. I lock you out to
keep you safe I can never lose you do you hear me." I said kissing him.
He put on his magic, "I know what you said but you are hurting let me
help you." he said as his sweet breath washed over me. "Xavier I cant." I
said. "Close your eyes Sweetness let me take you away make you forget
and just breath me in." he whispered up my neck as he held me tight. I
couldn't object to anything I just let him do whatever he wanted to me
as I fell deeper under his spell. I felt so good like nothing had happened
but deep in my mind I knew it was for a short while. We could hear Mik
waking and the boys talking to him as we made way to them, "Where
are your mates?" Jon asked. "They are fine the last I saw them they
were fighting they should be here soon. Thanks for the mending I feel
better." he told us. "Will you be up to talking to our visitors in a few
days?" Xavier asked. "Yes glad to help as always." Mik said. Bailey kept
away from me just in case of anything, "I'm alright now Bailey its just I
can feel what you all feel and it caused me great pain this time I wasn't
ready. Now I have to go and rest will someone stay with Mik?" I asked.
"Yes we will take turns and keep watch rest up Piper come and get us if
you need." Jon said. "Thanks guys see you in a little bit." I said heading
to the steps with X close behind me.

I put on the most comfy clothes I could find so I could maybe rest
and laid beside Xavier who was waiting on me. I could feel him and he

was calm and collected and I fell right into his feelings. He rubbed my belly with his satin hands and talking softly to me. I couldn't resist any longer I had to kiss him doing so under his chin. I needed to feel him close to me as possible and I held him tight without cutting off his air. "You alright Sweetness I have never felt you like this before, where you needed me so bad?" he asked. "I do need you badly, I hate this I'm not as strong as I pretend." I told him as he ran his hands up the back of my shirt. "You are very strong you are just a little down right now that's all. Come on lets hunt we can be back in a flash." he said getting my hand and leading me to the window. I waited for him to float down to the ground and I followed him into the woods out back. I slowly kept his pace hoping to think and put away many things as I watched him hunt. I finally found something for myself and took it down taking my time. Xavier leaned against the tree and waited for me to finish, "See I knew this would make you feel better." he said smiling. "Your right I do feel better, I know that we will help our visitors make the right choice they will join us in our fight. I want you to make me one promise." I told him. "I will if I can." he said. "Promise me that you will keep your mind on the objective at hand no matter what happens. You will finish this even if you have to do it alone." I said. "What have you seen tell me now!" he said full of demand. "I haven't seen anything I just want you to be ready that's all." I told him. "Piper I don't want to hear this and I wont make this promise to you!" he said walking off. I got ready to say something but he put his hand up, "No don't say anything else, we will finish this at a later date." he said walking in front of me. I picked up on his anger at me as I walked slightly behind him and him looking over his shoulder at me, "Your mad I can tell." I said softly. "Hell yes I'm mad you know I hate it when you talk like that. I have told you that if anything happens we go together, now at the risk of you getting mad at me I don't ever want to talk about this again." he said taking my hand and pulling me along. "Fine I wont say anything else." I told him.

We went in the house with him going into the living room and I went to my room. "Piper do you have a minute?" Gina asked through the door. "Sure Hon what's up?" I asked. "Things have changed we have company coming tonight, they are close I say about an hour." she informed me. "I'll let everyone know you and Tiff stay out of sight but close enough to hear, thanks for letting me know." I told her. "Umm Piper are you alright I know you and X had a fight?" she asked. "Yea he

is pissed at me nothing to worry about." I said with a smile. She turned
to leave and I followed her out making way to the living room. I entered
to find X sitting in the far corner and the guys talking to Mik. When he
seen me enter he rose to his feet, "We have company coming in about
an hour according to Gina so lets be ready shall we." I said as I turned to
leave the room. I made it to the hallway before Xavier grabbed me and
kissed me, "Don't stay away from me anymore I cant stand it." he said in
a soothing tone. "I'm sorry Xavier I just want you to be ready that's all."
I told him. "I'm sorry as well I know you mean well." he told me. "Maybe
next time turn your anger towards what is at hand and not me." I told
him. "Yes my Queen I shall try but I need you forever and I can never
lose you." he told me. I kissed him, "Lets get ready for our new friends
shall we." I told him. "Yes lets." he said.

Chapter 19

The hour seemed like only minutes to me while we waited. I picked up the scent of strangers and we greeted them with the brood standing behind us. "My King and Queen you said that if we came to talk to you that no harm would come to us." Thomas said as he took a step forward. "We mean you no harm we only wish for you to hear our side, you are free to leave anytime." Xavier told them. They followed us into our living room with the elders taking their seats and our boys taking our stance beside us. "We are the Dominick Coven and these our friends Vinski and Demetri Covens. Please say your piece so we can choose our sides and go." the tall dark man said. Xavier stepped forward, "No magic here as we speak we have come heavily guarded. We have heard of you and your queens magic the way she can control everyone's mood at the same time and your silk words." the elder from the Demetri Coven said. "There will be no magic worked on you however I forewarn you if you try she will stop you from doing so." Xavier told them with a certain tone. I set back and let Xavier tell them everything about Cora and her jealousy never saying anything. I knew they were having a hard time trusting me since I was once human. When Xavier finished they stood to take their leave, "We will give you an answer in two days time, we will send Thomas for he trusts you." the elder from the Vinski Coven said. "Thank you for coming and letting us have our chance to talk to you." I said sweetly as they left. Thomas turned and smiled at me letting me know things went well as the darkness swallowed them. I knew that the next two days were going to drag by with setting and waiting. Mik was back on his feet and eating well when his mates showed up and tried to rest. Our house was in a state of unrest as we waited on any news of the three covens choice. Mik would work with the boys as much as his body would allow with Xavier and I joining in some. "Hey B I just wanted to let you know that I checked on Cyn and she is just fine waiting on you to come for her." I told him. "Thanks Piper that makes me feel better." he said with a smile.

I went to lay down until Thomas come with our news just to see if I could rest. "Sweetness you alright you have been quiet all day, are the twins ok?" Xavier asked as he laid with me. "You know that you would have felt it if something had happened to the babies. Everything is just fine I hate to wait that's all." I told him. "You better get used to it, you are going to be alive a very long time and waiting is one thing we have to deal with." he said with a laugh. I flipped him over and kissed his face all over, "Still hate waitin that's all, now you give me a kiss or I'm gonna get you." I said joking. He flipped me back over without any trouble, "Nope gonna make you wait a long time." he said with a sly grin. I tried to get away from him but he just held me down tight, "I'm not going to let you up either." he said still giving me that sly grin. I play fought with him and giving up knowing that I would never over power him. "Come on Piper if you want a kiss you are going to have to take it." he told me still holding me. It felt good to toy with him, it helped take our minds off of things. "Awe come on Baby I really need you to kiss me." I told him. "Your not even trying Love, I'm not going to give you what you want you will have to take it." he said smiling. I gave him all I had and flipped him over to his back, with him trying to move so I couldn't get a kiss. Finally I held him down and made him kiss me.

As the moon shone down from the nights darkness we could pick up on Thomas' scent. "Come on lets get this over with." X said getting to his feet. "Hello Thomas glad to see you again, how are things?" I asked as he came up on the porch. "My Queen things are very well the other Covens have decided to join your cause. Now all we have to worry about is the other two that hates your way." he said as we showed him in the house. "Thomas you haven't come alone this time have you, who is lingering out in our trees?" I asked. He looked at me with surprise, "Yes it is Iceland and I wanted to ask King Xavier if we could get married." he said quickly. "Then shall we invite her inside?" I asked looking at the tree she was in. He gave her a quick motion to join us and she came up on the porch taking his hand. "My King and Queen my name is Iceland it is a pleasure to meet you." she said softly. She was lovely with her pale skin and almost water blue eyes. "Very nice to meet you as well please wont you come in?" I asked. "As you can see my King and Queen why I don't want her to fight, she is very young and frail I do worry about her so." Thomas said. "Please Thomas call us Xavier and Piper. I can see why you want to keep her safe she is young and lovely. As you know Piper will have to taste the blood of both of you, these rules have been set in motion and the ones from our own coven had to do the very same. If you don't agree with this you may leave." Xavier told them. They looked at one another and gave me their fingers to bite so I could taste. As I tasted the blood I quickly got flashes of the past and the future showing that if she fought she would fall quickly. I warned X on what I got so he could tell them whatever he wished. "Very well you may marry do so in the next few days. Hide her away from this fight she will not take any part in this." Xavier told them. "Thank you both for this, I will be back as soon as I can to help you out." he told us. Iceland's face glowed with happiness that she was going to marry him, "See I told you that they were very caring and understanding." he told her. They rose and disappeared into the moonlight.

When we turned to come in we faced Regina, "We don't have very long the fight is on the rise it is three cities over. The other Covens are holding back as long as they can we must be ready." she said. Xavier sent for the other Covens to be prepared as it was coming. I checked in our group that was hiding as Mike, Jon, and Bailey brushed up on a few things. Xavier came into the room where I was resting, "Sweetness I think we should hunt and go ahead meet this head on. If we get there and stop them before they reach Hinton it will be for the best." he said laying with me. "If you think this is best then lets get everyone together and get this over with." I told him. He took me in his arms and began to say something, "Whatever it is you can tell me when this is all over. Just remember I will always love you forever." I told him before he could get anything out. "I will always love you Sweetness." he said softly. We went down to meet the others, "Tonight we hunt and put this to rest." Xavier said. The boys got all together and we hunted for what might be our last time as a family.

When we finished we raced to our borders for the fight of our lives trying to stay together. When we entered the fight we could see vampires on the ground with all of their blood drained out of them. There were a few dead humans that had sadly became food for the ones who didn't think our way. Most of our covens were holding their own but the killers just seemed to keep coming. The boys took on many as soon as we came upon the fight. Xavier hung back to keep me out of harms way but as soon as we were seen they came for us. I knew they thought if they took out Xavier and me the fight was won. X was fighting as many as he could holding me behind him soon he had to let me join in the fight. I took on several at a time as they came to me. There in the clearing were a new set of newborns that were ready for the attack. I took my hands and put them in the air and pulled the winds down on them, this held them back for some time. This war took on a whole month night and day. Bodies of our fallen were on the ground under our feet, as well as the bodies of theirs. The ground ran red from the blood that flowed through the grass. Finally the month started to come to a close and I was wore out. Mike, Jon and Bailey stuck together watching each others backs. Xavier was bloody from his cuts and from the blood of others. As the other spread to try one last time I took the winds and gathered them together. I brought the rains and snow down on them, some tried to back out now that the numbers had grown in our favor. The men from our covens took on the remaining few that was left fighting.

Xavier and I stood on the mountain side holding hands looking down at the others, "Tell anyone who dare tries to take on my coven that they will be killed. This is over for the remaining of my rule here. If you don't like the way I have set you will leave or die. Your King and Queen has put up with for long enough, now take your dead and never return to this part of the world!!!" Xavier's voice boomed out across the land. It sent chills up my spine to see him with so much authority in his stance and voice, it was something that I have never heard before. I could feel that he was very tired and hoped that this was enough to keep others at bay. The remaining dozen bowed their heads in the presents of their powerful king and queen and backed away. Our Covens that was left standing took their bows to us as well, "Now go my friends take your fallen and bury them as you wish. Thank you for helping to keep our part of the world safe from this horror. Rest and rejoice that this is over." Xavier's voice had softened this time. Everyone departed and we gathered our family to return home. "Lets hunt to replenish what we have lost." X said. No one objected just complied as we all raced to find prey. The brood took off at top speed when they finished feeding to wash off the remains of the month. Xavier and I walked slowly in silence for awhile, "Now can I say what I wanted to say before we had to leave?" X asked. "Yes Love what was it that you had to say?" I asked. "I just wanted to tell you that I knew this was going to come out in our favor not to worry. Now that I said that I have to say I told you so." he said smiling.

I smacked him on his arm joking and raced off with him right on my heels, "I'm coming to get you my Sweetness and when I do I will never let you go." he said as I picked up speed when he did. I made it to the door and he caught me and carried my to the shower, "Lets hurry so I can have my family back together again, I will take one with you so it will be faster." he said with joy in his voice. "I was surprised at the royal tone back on the mountain, Kaleb would have been proud of you." I said with love in my voice. "Don't brag on me it makes me blush." he told me with a smile. We showered as fast as we could and met Bailey and Gina at the door. "Lets hurry its almost August and I want Cyn to have the baby in the Great House!" Bailey said with all of the excitement the could gather. I stood back and opened the door to find two young vampires approaching the house and quickly. The boys took fighting stance as they got closer just in case of any malice. When they got close Xavier noticed the hint of fresh blood, "Are you from the fight earlier?" he asked. "Yes we are here for your help, we know that you are a doctor. I'm Lee and this is my mate Kaylin, she is hurt badly isn't she?" Lee asked. "Lets move her inside so I can look her over." X told the boys. I went to get towels so we could see the damage on her body. I cleaned the bites and cuts as Xavier stitched up her juggler and the long cut across her neck. Mike went to get her a fresh cup of blood to help her heal. She began to rest with Lee staying away from us holding to her, "Now lets take a look at you." I said to Lee. "No thank you my Queen she is more important than I am I just need to rest." he said not wanting to take up any more our time than needed. "I know you are hiding something from me, you will tell me my friend." I said with magic in my voice. I watched his eyes glaze over becoming under my spell, "Its that I have been bitten and I don't feel very well." he said. Xavier cleaned up his cuts and bites while Mike went for him a fresh blood cup.

We waited for them to sleep and heal while Bailey paced the floor. "B either go hunt or sit we will leave as soon as we can she will wait on you." I told him. He huffed himself in a chair dying to get to Cyn while we waited for the results of our friends. On the second day of sleep from them Kaylin began to wake, "Where am I, Lee are you alright?" she asked in a panic. "Kaylin you are safe, I'm Xavier and this is Piper. Lee is just fine he needs his rest until his strength comes back to him." X told her. "I'm sorry my King I didn't know this was your home please forgive me." she said. "Forgive you for what?" X asked. "I have made a mess of your couch and you should be at rest not tending to us." she said quickly. "My heavens no you are fine please feel free to rest." Xavier said while she touched Lee. "I know you thirst allow me to get you something." I said. "How did you know I was thirsting my Queen?' she asked shocked. "I can feel you." I told her as I left the room. Xavier looked her over and removed many of her stitches as she was healing very well as she held tight to Lee. When Lee began to wake I warned X that I couldn't get a read on him to back off. Xavier did as I requested so Lee could see Kaylin for himself. He woke with fright in his eyes not remembering where he was. Just as soon as he saw her he calmed and hugged her like he hadn't seen her in months. "Thank you so much for your kindness how can we ever repay you?" Lee asked. "No need for that feel free to return if need be." X said. We watched them go into the darkness just as they came in.

Bailey was walking a hole in the floor, "Now can we go please?" Bailey asked. Xavier shook his head yes and led us out the door. It took us a day and a half to find our loved ones even when I opened up to the children. "Thank you both so much for doing this again, this mess is over and we can live in peace." I said hugging Michelle and Trevor. The twins didn't rush me as hard as they did with Xavier with my tummy being so big now. I did love on my babies with them being so big now as they touched my tummy. "If everyone is ready we can go and get something to eat." I said to everyone. We stopped by the nearest restaurant and for the first time we laughed and at as a family. "Are you alright Cyn you haven't touched your dinner?" I thought to only her. She looked at me and smiled, "Maybe we should get home." I whispered to Xavier. "As you wish." he said picking up on my tone. We rose to leave letting Michelle and Trevor go on home as we made way to the Great House. The sun brought us August the third as we entered the house. Cyndi grabbed Xavier by the arm, "Get the doctor X the baby is coming." she said slowly moving to the floor. Bailey rushed to her side, "Help her to her room." I told the guys. "Doc cant make it Sweetness, looks like

I'm going to have to do this." Xavier said not happy. "I can do this for her if you wish." I told him. I got a smile and a kiss, I knew he didn't want to deliver this baby with Cyndi being his sister. I walked into the room with her being uncomfortable, "How are we holding up?" I asked. "Where is the doc is he coming?" Bailey asked. "No he cant make it this time so I'm going to deliver the baby." I told him as I got things ready.

Poor B he looked like a mouse in a house with all cats, "Piper can do this she has done it many times." Cyndi said as she took a breather. "Ok Cyn give me a large push this time and it should be over." I told her. Bailey took her hand and moved her hair out of her face, "Deep breath Momma." he said. Xavier was waiting to grab the baby as soon as it was born. Cyndi gave it a large push as the baby was born. "Its a boy and he is very healthy." I told them both. "LaStat is his name, Xavier can I see him now?" Cyndi asked as she laid back and Bailey covered her with kisses. "I'm looking him over give me just a minute, I'll bring him to you just as soon as I get done." Xavier said smiling to himself. "Listen Momma he is crying." Bailey said with excitement. "Go to him he knows your voice and he will quiet down." she said now completely tired. He complied with her wishes as I finished with her. Xavier handed Bailey his son and he brought him over to Cyndi. "Hi there little man, we have waited on you forever LaStat." she cooed over him with love. Regina and Tiffany came in with a fresh large cup so she could get her blood back, "Ok everyone out she needs her rest we can see the baby tomorrow." I said moving all to the door. "Hey Jovi I have a few minutes if you would like talk now." Xavier said. Jovi about freaked out knowing what X was talking about, "Can I be turned now, I'm sure I would make a great vampire?" he asked holding Gina's hand. "I don't see why not lets get this done so we can rest." I told them. "Very well then take him and let us know when it is over." X told her.

Chapter 20

I tucked the twins in and went to our room where I found Xavier laying on the bed. I laid next to him for the first time in a month with his touching his soft skin next to mine. "Maybe we should wait before we fall asleep so we can check on Jovi and Cyn one last time." I said trying not to worry. "Anything you want as always.' Xavier said. It didn't take me long to find my way back down the hallway looking in on all the kids to make me feel better. I knocked on Gina's door, "How are we in here?" I asked as I opened up the door. "Yes he is fine just sleeping, I will lay with him till he wakes." she said. "Come get me if anything should become of him." I said. She shook her head as I shut the door behind me. Next door I knocked on was Cyndi and Baileys, "Do you need anything before I go to bed?" I asked. "I have fed him and I'm very thirsty, should I be?" Cyndi asked. "Yes if you are breast feeding or pumping then you will have to keep up you blood intake for yourself. Bailey keep her cup filled many times in the night and come get me for anything." I said touching LaStat softly. I made it back to my room hardly being able to wait to have Xavier breath on me, "Everything ok Sweetness?" he asked. "Oh yea just fine I cant wait till this one comes so we can see what it looks like?" I said. "Come let me put you asleep." he said softly. I laid with him and he kissed my neck as I got as close to him as I could, "You know its a girl this time, I think you should come up with a name for this one." I told him. "Jade I like Jade, I know she will have your eyes and the power she already has Jade will be perfect." he said without hesitating. "Been thinking about this for some time have we?" I asked. "Well yea I have and I hoped that you would like it." he said touching my tummy. "Then its settled Jade it is." I told him as I kissed him softly.

Sleep hit us both since it was the first real night in a long time. As soon as the sun hit the horizon the twins hit the bed, "Wake up Daddy and Momma the sun is bright." they said. Xavier grabbed them both and made them shriek with laughter as I rose to look in on Cyn. "Hey guys sleep any?" I asked. "I rested well how about you?" Cyndi asked. "Very well long over due." I said as I looked her over to make sure she was drinking. "Would you like to hold him?" she asked. "Love to." I said as I took LaStat from her. He had the day walker blue eyes and Baileys strong jaw bone and his hair was like both of his parents. I loved on LaStat and passed him to Xavier who was waiting to be next, "Love on him easy he is brand new." X told the twins as they touched his face. "He is to be my best friend forever isn't he?' Bastian asked. "Yes your right hand you must trust him." Xavier told Bastian. "We will let you rest call if you need me." I said moving the children out. Xavier stopped by Gina's room to look Jovi over making sure he was right on track with his turning. "It shouldn't be much longer maybe by the end of the day." X told her. I fixed breakfast for everyone as the rest made their way down, "No rest for the wicked huh?" Mike asked. "Not when the twins are around." Xavier said and laughed. "I'm so glad things are back to normal." Mike said as he hugged the twins tight. "That makes two of us." I said. "Whose normal?" Jon asked as he came in late. "We are of course." I said smiling. "Normal well yes we are just your everyday run of the mill vampires." Jon said laughing. "Tiffs turn Bastian come on." Brie said pulling him along.

With all in the kitchen we sat down for breakfast and talked back and forth, "I think today I will work on the new office anyone want to join me?" Xavier asked. "We will help you Daddy!" the twins said with excitement. The guys agreed to help with the big things in shifts so that someone would be home with Gina just in case she needed someone to help with Jovi. Mike and Jon put the tables in the rooms that Xavier told them, "I'm so glad that I ordered all this before we went to war. I hope to have this set up and get started by the beginning of the new week." X said happily. Our lives were turning out the way it should be. Michelle stopped by to see the progress and I invited her and Trevor to dinner, along with Sharon and Amber. "Jon will you pick up dinner and Josh for me?" I asked. "As you wish." Jon said heading to the house to get the keys. Xavier and I walked home with the twins so we could check on Jovi and Cyndi. Xavier went to look in on Jovi and I went to look in on LaStat and Cyndi. I kept up on Xavier and the feelings on Gina's room while I was in with Cyn. Jovi was waking when X entered the room, "Come Jovi lets hunt." Gina said softly. "Yes lets hunt I'm quiet thirsty, the feeling is wonderful." Jovi said with a smile. "Hold on Jovi don't get carried away." X said as he called for me. I walked in the room and I knew things were getting out of hand, "Piper keep his feelings at bay if he gives in I will have to stop him." he thought to me. I stepped forward and placed my hand on his heart, "Tell me what you are feeling Jovi." I asked with magic. "Yes Piper I will hunt and not give into those feelings." he said with glazed eyes. I smiled at him softly and took his hand leading him to the window.

We watched as Xavier hit the ground without moving a leaf, then Gina hit the ground softly. "Now Jovi it is your turn go hunt and return to me feeling much better. You are to follow Xavier and do as he wishes you understand me?" I said. He nodded his head to me and went out the window. I waited for about and hour before they returned to the Great House, "I can see that things went well." I said noticing that Jovi was feeling better. "What the hell did you say to him, he stayed glazed over till we got to the front door." Xavier said. "I just made him tell me what I wanted to hear that's all." I said as I kissed him. "Whatever you did it worked well." he said with a smile. "As long as you are pleased then I'm pleased." I told him. "I love this new power you have until you use it on me." X told me. "I swear to never use it on you until I really want something." I said laughing and taking off. "Sweetness you swore you wouldn't!" he called to me. I hid under the steps and waited for him to pick up on my scent. I jumped out and took him down to the floor, "Where did you come from?" he asked laughing. "Aha I got you Love, now what are you going to do?" I asked. "This!" he said as he flipped me over and kissed my face. "I needed that so bad." I told him. "Come Sweets are you interested in a movie or something?" he asked. "Unless you have something more important to do." I said from the floor. "What could be more important than you?" he asked as he helped me up.

I laid on the couch waiting on X to put in a movie of his choice as the door bell rang. "I'll get it!" Tiffany said as she sprinted across the floor. "Well Miss Tiffany looking lovely today." Doc said. "Thanks Doc you are so sweet." Tiff said as she showed him into the living room.

"Hey Dorien how are you today?" Xavier asked. "All is very well I just came by to check on my favorite moms. How did Miss Cyndi's birthing go?" he asked. "I delivered a healthy baby boy and he is very beautiful." I told him. "May I look in on them and then we can take a look at you?" he said. "Sure I will show you the way." Xavier said. Doc looked her and LaStat over, "You did very well and you should be up and running in no time." he told her. "Thank you Doc for stopping by." Bailey said. "Now Piper if you wouldn't mind." he said turning to me. Xavier led the way to our bedroom so I could lay. He listened to my belly and felt all around for a few minutes then he set back. "Umm well I'm not for sure how to say this, Xavier should I be worried?" he asked. "Tell us what?" X asked taking my hand. "I'm afraid that your body has taken a lot over the last few months and this will be your last baby." he said backing up. I rose to my feet quickly, "What are you telling me that I cant have any more babies, what about this one!?" I asked with a touch of meanness. Xavier put himself in between Doc and myself just in case I planned on freaking out. "Whoa Piper lets hear him out." Xavier said. "Yes my Queen this may very well be your last baby, and this one is doing just fine you know that. Your body is very tired from all the fighting and the powers you have gained. You are the only vampire ever reported to have this many powers at one time, there is no more power for you to receive. For some reason you haven't turned all day walker and you should have by now. Please my Queen forgive me for the information I am forced to give you." Doc said. "She will be fine Dorien, are you sure this is the path she has to follow?" X asked. "All I can say is I hope she proves me wrong." Doc said as they walked out.

Xavier came back to me while I set on the bed and cried real tears from the news, "Don't worry Sweetness we can try to prove him wrong." he said with sadness in his silk words. I soaked his shirt with hot tears, "I'm sorry I shouldn't let this get to me, I have had to accept things that I haven't agreed with why should this be any different?" I asked still crying. "I don't know Sweetness just cry you must need this or you wouldn't be doing it. Come I'll hold you until you don't need me any more." Xavier said softly. "I will always need you, your upset with me because I cant give you any more children I can feel it." I said. "Never with you its something you want and I cant do anything to fix it, I'm truly sorry." he said. He moved my hair from my neck and breathed relax up my neck. I fell right into his mood and started relax, I turned over lifted our shirts so our tummies touched. He laughed at the feeling of the baby moving around. "Lets go watch that movie that you wanted before all this." I said feeling better some. "Please can we wait I want to feel some more, I'm so far behind on this baby she wont even know who I am?" he asked. Jade made it known that she knew who he was by making the moon so bright, "See she knows you and your touch." I told him.

After a little bit he got to his feet and held out his hand, "Movie time come on." he said pulling me up. I followed him out meeting Cyndi with LaStat in the hallway, "Hey Piper how was your visit with Doc?" Cyndi asked. I looked at X for help not wanting anyone to know everything, "Things went well." Xavier said with a weak smile. "Good I'm glad." she said as she took LaStat down to watch a movie. All the family waited to hold the baby while I sat and rested my head on Xavier's shoulder still very heart broken. I could feel him he was as sad as I was and neither of us watched the movie. The twins settled themselves down on their daddy and fell asleep even though he was upset he was still able to comfort them to sleep. Mike and Jon took the children to bed while I slept very lightly on Xavier's shoulder, "Take Piper to bed she is very upset, what happened with the doctor today?" Gina asked. "The doctor said she cant have any more children after Jade comes. This hurt is so bad the last time she felt like this she tore down trees, I don't want her to tear the house down she is powerful enough." X said softly as he stroked my hair. "Take her and keep her in bed we will take care of the house for as long as you need." Gina told him. "Thanks I think I will." X told her.

He woke me to take me to bed, "Hey I was thinking if we cant have any more children no one will leave. When the others marry they will stay in the Great House, we will move to a larger home if need be. This house is stronger as one than apart even if you surprise me and ten more babies we will be together." he told me. "Anything you wish." I said looking at nothing really. "That's not an answer Piper if you will open to me you wont have to say anything." he said wanting to know what I felt. I opened my feelings to him holding nothing back and waited for him to gain his composer as the sadness washed over him. "I think I want everyone here, I know that making them stay isn't very wise but I would be happier. Maybe I should let them go so they can come back to me." I suggested. "This will happen, I hate that you feel like this not even wanting to hunt that is not healthy. You must hunt to keep up your strength for Jade if not anyone else." he said. I knew what he meant, "Xavier this is not your fault I'll be ok in a day or two just give me some time." I told him as I put my magic on so he would sleep. As soon as he was purring like a kitten I slipped out the window. I walked for hours in our woods behind the house and around town. The whole town was peace as I picked up on many dreams from different homes with the moonlight keeping my pace. I picked up on the scents of my very worried husband and the brood. I stopped and waited on them to join me at the swings on the nearby school house, "I'm safe I had to have this time and I knew you wouldn't let me go alone." I thought to him. "I'm coming Sweetness wait for me." he said with him running as fast as he could. "Yes I'll be here for you." I told him. Soon it was just his scent I got as he sent the brood back home so it would be just us.

Still running he entered the playground and I stood for him to get me in his arms. He held me tight, "I have asked you not to slip away from me, I about died when I woke to find you missing. I searched for you everywhere your scent was all over town and back woods." he said with a touch of demand. "I feel somewhat better." I told him. "Piper please never leave my side without telling me I cant stand it. I know you need the time but after the night we had I just don't want you to have any regrets." he said looking away from me. I placed my hand on his heart and looked inside him, "You think I regret asking you to turn me, meeting you falling deeply in love with you." I said putting distance between us. Now I was mad as hell as the rain poured on us, "Piper do you have any regrets?" he asked softly stepping forward. I put my hand up to keep him away until I could get my anger under control. He never hesitated, he put his arms around me. "Hell no I don't have any regrets I would have come looking for you. I love being your vampire queen and a mother to all of my eleven children you know that I was made for you only. Now I love you Xavier Matthews but never let this feeling pass you again do I make myself clear!" I said with just as much demand as he has used on me. "If you knew that I died a little inside when you are mad at me I'm sure you wouldn't be anymore." he said trying to make me cheer up. "Allow me to show you what I feel." I said putting my hand on his heart and letting him feel. I let the feelings run from me into him of what I felt when he loved on me, his every touch, his breathing up my neck. "Now here it comes." I said in a whisper.

I watched as the pain hit him as he took my hand with both of his hands on mine pulling us to the ground, "Please I cant handle anymore." he said as the rain poured with thunder and lighting. "No you must feel everything." I told him. When I knew he had enough I turned the feelings back to when he loves me making him breathe again. "Piper I had no idea that you had these kind of feelings." he said. "I'm sorry Xavier but you needed to know what I felt somewhat. I will never share that with you again I'm sure you will remember them vividly." I said sadly. "Wait please share with me just maybe not so hard. Just don't start shutting me out altogether I love the beginning of the journey." he said as the rain stopped. "Are you ready to go home? I'm sorry that I have burdened you with this." I told him. "This is what a marriage is sharing everything even the feelings just don't shut me out I want to feel you no matter what." he said as we walked back home. When we got home I laid him on the bed and set across him, "Do you love me and trust me?" I asked. "Of course I love and trust you completely, what do you have in mind?" he asked with glowing eyes. "Just trust me Love." I said as I seduced him into love making. I kissed him as we began with his silk hands on my naked body and I pulled his head to the side and bit him with force. I let the power of feeling slip from me into him as I felt his body tremble under mine. Then the sharing was over and I looked into his beautiful eyes, "Now you will be able to feel all that is near you, and you will be able to make them do as you wish with a touch of your hand." I told him. "I love you." he said as we laid together.

Chapter 21

The night began to let the sun be shone for the day and I rose to fix breakfast, "Sweetness you can stay in bed with me the sisters have the twins today, you should rest." he said helping me back to bed. "I have things to do today and it isn't fair to have the kids do them for me." I told him. "Well they did offer so I think we should take them up on it." he said with his convincing smile. "But I have to go to the store for groceries, household needs not to mention the things for the office." I protested. Xavier started to make his case once more to me when a knock came to the door, "Come in." he called. "Hey Jon and I are going to pick up the girls and go to the store, just wanted to know if you needed anything added before we go?" Mike asked. "Are you sure you want to do this I mean I can go and you can hang out with the girls today?" I asked. "No we have everything under control, dinner is planned and all has agreed to do their parts. You should rest today." Mike said. "Thank you all for this, you know I love you dearly." I told him. He smiled at me put his hand over his heart and bowed to me as he left. "Wow what an honor that was, he loves you as well." Xavier said taking my hand. "I know he loves me they all do but I still hate putting this on them. I have been away from the twins so much what kind of mother am I?" I asked looking away. "Sweetness you are a very tired mother that is getting ready to have another baby, you are entitled to rest." he said. "As you wish." I told him laying down with him. "Look we can do whatever you want tomorrow but today you rest. You know I have been getting Emails of when we open." he said with enthusiasm. "We can start anytime you like maybe before Jade gets here." I told him. I knew he was looking forward to getting back into work that he missed it some. "Tell me Sweets what else is bothering you?" he asked. "I'm going to have to pull strings to get the kids back in school, and my parents I haven't seen them is so long. You know my mother will surprise us like she has before and the twins are walking and talking and look at me." I said pointing at my tummy. "Well if she does I'm sure we can make her understand." he said touching my tummy softly. "Shut your eyes and focus on my parents, can you see them?" I asked. He shut his eyes and took a deep breathe, "Yes I can see them they are coming soon. That was awesome where did that come from?" he asked. "I shared a few things with you do you like it?" I asked. "You bet I do." he said pulling me to him. I laid with him and watched movies slipping in and out of naps with him never leaving my side. As the sun went down for the day I felt the need to hunt and before I could let X know he pulled me to my feet, "Come lets hunt before we go to bed." he said smiling. As always I watched him glide towards his prey and take it down so easily, then I hunted for myself. I knew Mom would show up soon and with the twins running and talking I was going to have to use magic on them. Then there were the kids who needed to graduate so I had that to face.

Xavier never stayed out of my mind when I didn't shut him down from my thoughts so he knew that I was thinking as we walk so he kept himself quiet. "Back in the window lets put all to rest shall we?" he said softly as we got close to the window. "I guess so." I said as I jumped the house and went inside. Days seemed to go by quickly as I got myself back into my usual busy self. LaStat was getting so big, he grew at vampire speed just like the twins. Bastian and LaStat stayed a handful as they both got into everything. August winded down and I was getting closer to my due date as Xavier's practice was on its way to opening. Mom and Dad were due today and I had to get the kids back into the right classes, "Hey Mom do you have a minute?" Tiffany asked. "Sure Cutie." I said. "I went to the school meeting and they said that I might not be going to the next grade and the others wont have the credits to graduate.' Tiffany told me. "We shall see about that." I told her walking out of the room. "Xavier I'm going to the school to have a talk with the principle." I said as I grabbed my keys. "Whoa wait a minute your not going alone you are way to angry, maybe you should have a cup first." he said getting up to stop me. I grabbed a cup and he drove us to the school. I was able to get in to see the principle and he told me that there was no possible way for the kids to move ahead to the next grade. There was no way that my kids were going to be held back because of this nonsense.

I tried to plead my case without to much information but he flatly refused to listen so I neared him placing my hand on his heart, "Yes Ma'am your children will be moved ahead this year with Regina and Jon getting the credits they need to graduate." I made him say to me. After he repeated what I wanted and I knew it was going to stick in his head I thanked him and left. "Piper shame on you, that was mean how you made him do that. Is that what you do to me when you want something?" he asked as he drove home. "One time I swear and that was when I wanted to find Thomas, the other times I just persuade you in my favor. Your disappointed in me aren't you?" I asked. "No I just worry about you using on humans like that they cant defend themselves like I can." he said with a smile. "Well I'm gonna use on my parents I don't have a answers for the way the children look so don't try to stop me, they are my parents." I told him as I crossed my arms. "I don't think I could even if I wanted to, just be careful that's all." he said taking my hand. We pulled up behind my parents as we pulled into the driveway with Xavier getting out quickly so he could help me out. "My goodness Piper why didn't you tell us that you were pregnant again, is that healthy for you so soon?" Mom asked. "How was your trip you guys?" I asked as I hugged them both and placing my hand over their hearts. "Mom, Dad the children have grown and you may not understand so you will just accept without any questions." I told them getting all the magic I had left in me for the day. They both nodded my way as I showed them into the house, "You feel bad about this don't you?" Xavier thought to me. "Yea I do but what am I to do, say "Hey Mom Dad we are vampires that's why they have grown" that would go over real well." I thought back. Xavier busted out laughing as we walked into the house with Mom looking at him with wonder.

Tiffany and the children ran to greet Mom and Dad with open arms, "Grams, Pops we have missed you so how have you been?" Brielle asked with Mom looking her over. "Wow my angels you have grown since the last time I saw you. Tell me who is this handsome young man?" Mom asked when LaStat came crawling in. "Grams this is my baby LaStat." Cyndi said with pride. "This is Jovi he moved in the Great House about a month ago when Piper and Xavier adopted him." Gina told her and dad. "What a houseful, how do you do it?" dad asked. "Everyone does their part so I get a lot of help. X is opening his practice on Monday and this baby is due in a few days I guess." I told them. "You stay busy don't you? You know you look like something is bothering you or you are very tired." Mom told me. "I'm just tired that's all, I have been helping X a lot with the office so we can get it opened." I told her as X took my hand. "So what's on the menu for the day?" Dad asked as he followed Xavier out of the room. "Grilling out today anything you like and tomorrow we can eat out." Xavier told him. "How long do we have you guys for?" I asked. "Till early Sunday morning." she told me. "Well good I have missed you both and I should have called but things have been so busy here. I delivered LaStat and that was exciting and school letting out just lots going on." I told her. "Well you are going to have to call more Piper I mean it." Mom told me. "I know and I will." I said making way to Xavier before she got into deeper questions.

Dinner took on quickly with all in the house helping out and then after clean up. I went to the living room so I could rest getting Brie on my lap, "Have you had a good day?" I asked as I kissed her softly. "Yes Momma I have what about you?" she asked as she breathed me into her. "Now that I have you in my arms I have had a great day." I told her. "I love the way you smell to me." she said in a whisper. "Go get your brother and behave." I said as she touched my hair. After we sat and talked for awhile the twins feel asleep and soon we all followed suit. "Mom just a fair warning the twins dive on the beds every morning, I will try to keep them from your room but they can be very sneaky." I told her as we went up the steps. "Thanks for the warning see you all in the morning." Dad said. I laid there in the bed with Xavier wrapped all around me as he slept just waiting on the sun to rise. Soon the footsteps of the twins came loudly with them always hitting our room first. I sat up so they could get to their daddy first and gave kisses to the both of us and started for the door. "Lets not forget that your Grams and Pops are not made like us they are made like Michelle and Trevor so maybe we should knock first." X told them. "We are going for Unk Mike next." Bastian said with an evil smile. "Guys hurry down for breakfast." I told them. "They are truly remarkable aren't they, we did well." I said without looking up. "You know we did, I think we make beautiful babies together I cant wait to see what Jade looks like. I bet she will look like you and Brie, burgundy hair and emerald green eyes, my most beautiful ladies." he said as he rubbed my belly. "I love you Xavier Matthews you know that?" I asked as I kissed him. "I love you more than one could possibly love another." he said. "Come Love lets have breakfast before the twins tear down the kitchen." I said getting to my feet.

Brie came in with Mike in hand and Bastian pushing him, "Come on Unk Mike we have others to wake." Bastian said moving Mike into the kitchen. "Hey wait one minute you guys, do not rush Cyndi and Baileys room." Mike said taking both of them in his arms. "Why not?" Bastian asked. "Cyndi is with the baby and you wouldn't want to scare LaStat and make him cry now would you?" he asked. They looked at him with wide eyes and shook their heads no at him, "Ok then go wake Jon." Mike told them. They took off with lighting speed to Jon's room, "They love you so much I think they would follow you to the end of the earth. You know they want to jump on every bed in the house but wont just because you said not to." I told him. "I love them as my own, I would take them to the end of the world if they wanted to go." he said looking a bit embarrassed. "Is it safe to say that you are staying with us then?" Xavier asked. "Yes I have been invited to live in Sharon's Coven but I want to stay here, so I was thinking that maybe you and Piper would talk to her parents." Mike said. Xavier looked at the both of us, "We can talk to them but Piper has to swear to keep her magic turned off." Xavier said smiling. I turned and gave him a mean look, "Magic what magic?" I asked. "Who has magic?" Mom asked as she came in. "Umm Piper can talk anyone into anything that's all, so we say that Piper has a special magic." Mike said quickly. "She was always like that helping the younger kids when she was in school. We always joked that she could talk down a grizzly bear." Mom said. "You could take down a grizzly with your touch." X thought to me with a smile. "Are we having your famous pancakes today Grams?" Jon asked as he hugged her. "Sure Sweetie if you want them I'll make them." she said.

Soon the rest started filling in the kitchen, "Hey do I smell Grams pancakes?" Gina asked. Mom smiled at Tiffany, Gina and Jovi as they made way over to her, "I thought her name was Pat?" Jovi asked in a low whisper. "We call her Grams because that is who she is and she likes it." Gina told him. "You can call me that if you like Jovi." Mom said. Mom liked it that she had grand kids no matter how they came to her, "You sure you don't mind? I really never had a grandmother or a real mom till I met Gina and Piper and Xavier treated me like one of their own." he said. I put my arm around Jovi while Mom looked like she just lost her best friend, "Well then it is settled you call me Grams. Piper likes everyone happy and you are very lucky when she was made they broke the mold." Mom said. "She makes everyone feel good inside even when she is down herself." Jovi said. I put my hand over his heart and perked his feelings right up, "I know you thirst but you must learn to control it understand, we hunt later." I thought to him. He smiled and put his hand on mine letting me know he agreed with me. I really didn't use any magic I just used my mother instincts to make him do what I wanted. "Yum Grams pancakes." Bailey said as he and Cyn came in. "That's it I'm not fixing pancakes for you guys anymore, you will have to wait till Grams shows back up." I said joking with them. "We love your pancakes Momma but we love bacon best." Bastian said. I kissed him on the forehead and took a seat next to Xavier.

Breakfast came and went as we sat around and talked back and forth. Mom and Dad played with the children as they talked to Tiffany about school. "Why don't you invite Michelle over for dinner today, I haven't seen her and I would like to." Mom said. I never waited on inviting Michelle over she was my dearest friend and the twins love her. When I called she agreed to meet us at the Great House so we can go together. We decided to skip lunch so we would be hungry at dinner but the twins needed to hunt I could feel thirst from them. "Would you and Jon mind taking Bastian and Brie on a little hunt?' I thought to Mike. "As you wish." Mike thought back. When they returned Tiffany rushed them up to change their clothes because they usually make a mess playing around. When Michelle and Trevor showed up we all gathered and headed for the restaurant. Dinner was nice to have everyone around and it was good to me for the first time in days, I mostly ate to keep up my strength. After dinner the large group of us returned to the Great House to talk, "You know, Dad and I will be leaving early in the morning?" Mom asked. "Yea I know one of the boys will take the car and gas it up for you." I told her. Soon bedtime came and I wondered if I would sleep tonight, "See you all in the morning love all you." Mom said. I laid in the bed with X next to me, "Hey Sweets can I ask a question?" he asked. "Sure Love you know you can." I told him. "How did you hold your parents all weekend and still talk to everyone through our thoughts?" he asked softly. "I don't know I just told them what I wanted and forgot about it." I told him. "Huh quite remarkable you are one for the ages." he said. "You really think so?" I asked smiling. He breathed the word yes up my neck making me feel good inside. "Tell me what you felt when you got near Sharon?" I asked. "She wants us to talk to her parents about her moving in." he told me. "I just wanted to know if you got the same thing I got." I told him. "Hey how about Monday after work we take Tiffany to get her school supplies." he said. "Sure that would be great I need to get out and do something else." I said as I rested.

The morning came with Mom making breakfast like every time she came to visit, "Morning Momma." I said. "Hey there how did you sleep?" she asked looking at me. "Fine I guess." I told her. "Piper I'm worried about you something is going on what is it?" she asked. "Nothing I'm just tired that's all." I told her. "Your lying to me I can tell you look depressed or something." she said setting with me. "Just tired that's all besides I really don't want to talk about it." I said getting up. "Ok well if you ever want to talk about it you know where I'm at." she said knowing not to push me on this. "I know thanks Mom." I told her as Xavier came in. "Morning Pat how are we?' he asked. I knew he felt what I was feeling about Mom asking her questions. "Fine I guess worried about Piper." she said. "Yes well I assure you she is fine, just after the baby gets here she will be able to rest." he told her with silk lined words. "Very well maybe I should come back and help out for a few days." she suggested. "You know that you are welcome here anytime but we have many to help Piper out." he said smiling at her. Breakfast went fast and soon her and Dad left with me waving from the porch.

Chapter 22

Monday morning came with me getting up and dressing the twins and telling Tiffany to stop by the office so we can get her school supplies. I came back to the bedroom to get myself dressed with Xavier in the shower already. I quickly ran around the house getting the things I needed to make it through the day, "Come on Piper I don't want to be late on my first day!" he called to me. "I'm coming I'm coming keep your pants on, your the boss you can be one minute late." I said coming down the steps. We made it there at the same time Michelle did, "Hey guys are you ready to get this started?' she asked just as excited as we were. "Yes very much so." Xavier said. Many humans and vampires showed up to get Xavier to look them over. Most of the day Xavier and I stayed in rooms with Michelle giving us charts and patients. Soon lunch time rolled around and I told Michelle to order and have them deliver it here. "You and Xavier not eating?" she asked. "We will get something later I'm sure we have to get everyone in and out today would you mind feeding the children for me?" I asked. "Of course not you know that." she said picking up Brie. "You know you wont be able to do that much longer, she will be a teenager very soon." I told her looking at Brie. "I know I have been reading the books Xavier gave me and I don't know how you do it." she said. "I have no choice in the matter now do I?" I asked as I went back to work. Michelle's lunch arrived and that got X out of the room for only a minute, "I smell fries who has em?" he asked. "I do and keep your hands off." Michelle said smiling. He stole fries from her anyway with her smacking his hands and he kissed the kids and back to work.

I came out of one of the rooms to make way to the desk, "Brad how are you today?" I asked. "Very well my Queen how are you?" Brad asked. "How many times do I have to ask you to please call me Piper?" I asked. "Please forgive me I'm trying to remember that you like the normal." he said smiling. "Yes I do now what can I do for you today?" I asked. "Oh I just stopped by to see how things are and I wanted to see what it takes to get in here for Xavier to see me and my boys." he said. "There will always be an opening for you and your family Brad never hesitate to stop by for anything. How many boys do you have now?" I asked. "I have three Bryce, Shaun and Timmy." he said proudly. "Well that is wonderful you must bring them by for me to meet." I told him. "Anytime you want us just send for me and we will be there never make you wait." he said. "Then we shall have dinner together sometime just let me have this baby and I'll have X call you." I told him. "Thank you Queen Piper I'm sorry Piper." he said a bit embarrassed. "See you later Brad have a nice day." I told him as he went out the door. The hour approached five and we were at the end of our patients when Tiffany showed up, "Hey Dad how was today?" she asked. "Busy busy just like I like it." he said smiling. We went on to Wal-Mart after we locked up for the night still dressed in scrubs with Tiff and the twins in street clothes. I let her shop for the things she needed while I shopped for the things the house needed then we headed home.

The first day of school finally came and the kids got ready to head out the same time we did. Mike kept Bastian and Brie for the day since they didn't want to go hang out at work. As September took off things fell more into routine which helped a lot. I always made it a rule to have everyone setting together for dinner and most of the hunting trips. It was hard to make it a family thing to hunt together since not all of us thirst at the same time. Many nights I laid there with things on my mind and different feelings filled up my insides, but some nights I fell asleep. Night enveloped the day and I went to lay on the bed while X showered but I feel asleep. I felt him slip softly in beside me getting so close to me. It wasn't long before I woke up to pain, "X wake up!" I said. "What's wrong Sweetness?" he asked as he jumped up. "Jade she is coming and fast." I said breathing hard. "Ok ok just breathe and push." he said. Just like Bastian he delivered Jade who came very quickly and under a bright full moon. "There all over, she is beautiful with my black hair and your amazing green eyes." he said as he handed her to me. When he was finished with me he took her back so he could clean her up. "Shall we get the guys to bring in the other mattress?" he asked while he bathed her. "Yes I want to stay in here." I said getting on clean clothes myself. "I have to say you did very well she is beautiful." he said as he handed Jade back to me. "We did well." I told him as I kissed him.

Xavier called for the boys to help him move the beds around and the girls brought me a large cup of fresh blood to drink. Everyone looked Jade over as the room was being put back together. "What is today?" Tiffany asked. "September the eleventh." Gina said. "Very pretty isn't she?" Mike asked as he looked her over. I laid back in the new bed as the brood went back to their rooms, "I'm taking tomorrow off." X told me as he laid with us. "No you have to work if you don't show up Michelle will kill you. I'll be fine with the others here I'm sure they will check on me." I told him. "Maybe I'll close half day I want to be here with you and Jade." he said. "Very well then come back to me about noon." I told him as I fed Jade for the first time. Sleep didn't wait this time I feel asleep as soon as she was finished feeding and six AM came quickly. I woke to find Xavier finishing his shower and putting on his blue scrubs, "You look very handsome today becoming a daddy again looks well on you." I told him. "You look amazing for just having a baby a few hours ago." he told me as he kissed me. "So you will be home about noon if you can get away?" I asked. "I'll be here one way or another, I'm so happy I'm not for sure if I can contain it all. By the way I need to know what you want to do for Halloween it will be our first anniversary so whatever you want I will do." he said. "It has been a hell of a year so far, I was thinking that maybe we could have me and you time alone in the woods somewhere." I suggested. "I think I can do that just me and you for a weekend, sounds great. I love you Sweetness see you soon as I can." he said. "Love you too." I told him as he went out the door.

The girls came in with Bastian and Brielle so they could see Jade for the first time with all the guys coming in after. "Piper I bought you a cold cup thought you might need it." Bailey said. "Thank you so much I didn't want to bother X with it this morning. Would someone mind watching her while I shower?" I asked. "Sure." everyone answered at the same time. I gave them a look knowing that they all were up to no good, "I'll be back in a few minutes." I said getting up. It felt so good to be thin again even though I knew that I would never have another baby. I felt a wave of sadness hit me while I let the warm water run over me,

"Don't think about it today Sweetness I'll be home soon, please don't be sad." Xavier's voice rang out in my head. I had forgotten that I shared with him and now he was able to pick up on me better. I got out of the shower and went back in the room to lay in the only spot they gave me, "Xavier didn't have anything to do with this did he?" I asked. "What are you talking about Mom?" Tiffany asked. "You all spending the day with me?" I asked. They all shook their heads no at me but I could tell that they were lying to me, "Very well then what's for lunch?" I asked. "Is X coming home early?" Cyndi asked. "He is going to try." I told her. "Well then I will get you a salad and whatever any one else wants." she said making a mental note of the order. Bailey and Cyn left LaStat with us when she went to get our food and Xavier making it home before she got back. "Hey Sweets have you eaten?" he asked coming in with Michelle. "Not yet, how was work?" I asked. "Xavier worked fast so he could get here." Michelle said taking Jade from me. "I'm sure I told her to get you something to eat." X said getting worked up some. "She went to get it she just hasn't made it back yet." I told him as I touched his hand. "She is very beautiful nice job guys." she told us as she gave Jade to X. "Thanks girl you staying for lunch?" I asked. "No I have to get home and make plans with Trev maybe something special." she said with a smile. "Have fun." I told her a she left. "You bet I will." she said. "I have to call Sharon and tell her not to come over today with her parents." Mike said getting to his feet. "No go ahead let them come I'm sure this wont take long." I told him. "But you must rest we can do it another day." he protested.

I smiled at him and he knew that I was planning on winning this one, "As you wish." Mike said as Cyndi came in with lunch. Most of the day I rested with Xavier beside me helping with Jade. Dinner came and I walked down the steps so I could be with the family, "Piper what are you doing out of bed?" Jovi asked. "Dinner is to be eaten together and I'm not as fragile as you may think." I told him. After dinner Sharon showed up with her parents as I set on the couch. "Phil nice to see you." Xavier said. "Very nice to see you King Xavier, your family has grown." Phil said. "Yes this is our newest addition Jade." X said with pride in his voice. "She is lovely, shall we get down to business so that Queen Piper can rest?" Phil asked. Xavier gave him a nod to go ahead and get started on his case, "Sharon has ask to move in the Great House with Mike, mostly I wondered why he cant join our coven?" Phil asked. "Mike is free to do as he wishes, you may asked if you like." X told him. I held my breath when Mike stood up to speak, "Sir I'm sorry but this family my family is royalty and we are stronger together than apart. I ask that Sharon move in here with me for this is the way it is." Mike said with honor in his voice. "Very well then it is fine with her mother and I if she chooses to live her remaining years with you love her well." Phil said shaking Mikes hand. "Thank you." Mike said. I started to rise to shake hands with them as well, "Please my Queen stay seated." he said offering to help me back down.

Days seem to pass quickly as I got back into work taking Jade with me so I could breast feed her when she needed it. I knew she would have to have a blood source before to long and she would grow like Bastian, Brie and LaStat. Tiffany was back in school having the time of her life and she would stop by the office with Josh and sometimes with girlfriends. By the end of the day I needed to hunt in the worst way, with me working and feeding Jade I wasn't eating well. I asked Tiffany to take Jade on home today and went to find Xavier. "I need to hunt I'm hurting so bad." I told him as he locked up. "I know I can feel your pain I have to hunt as well." he said. This time I didn't wait on him to hunt first I found my prey and drained it dry going for another. "Piper you must feed better than this you are going to attack someone if you don't keep satisfied." he said as I stood up. "I know and I promise I will do better." I told him as we walked home. Dinner was waiting on us when we came in and setting around felt good today. The boys talked about whatever they had in mind with Xavier and soon it was time to clean up, "I can help today." I said. "No you go on and rest we have it." Gina said. I went to rest and grabbed my laptop and surfed some sites for the kids to have fun with. Xavier came in the room, "What you doing Sweetness you look deep in thought?" he asked as he picked up my feet and put them on his lap. "Just thinking that's all." I said softly. The little ones came running in the room at top speed and X slowed them, "Guys Mommy is tired slow yourselves." he said holding his hand up. The three kids climbed up on my lap one at a time, "I have missed you Mommy." Brie said. "I have missed you all so I thought maybe you guys would like to have ice-cream." I said. "YES YES YES!!" they all said at the same time. "Ok well gather up the elders and see who wants to go." I said with a smile.

Ice-cream was what everyone needed and it felt good to do things as a family other than movies or just dinner. Home always felt good to me no matter how long we were gone. "Movie for anyone who wants to watch." I called up the steps. I walked back in the living room with X smiling at me, "What are you smiling at?" I asked. "You make me smile, I have noticed when the day is long and we come home to have dinner you feel good inside. I love the way you make me feel inside when you feel good. Only you have the power to make this happen, we never had dinner together or any family things before you came into my life." he told me as he pulled me on his lap. "Good I like to make you feel good inside. I like to have dinner together and I hope the kids like it as well." I told him as the kids filed in one by one. When the twins fell asleep on X it was time for me to go to bed as well. "I was thinking that maybe you should start giving Jade a bottle." he said carefully. "I'm fine really." I told him. "Its just think that with work, the kids, the powers, and the family maybe a bottle wouldn't be a bad idea. I worry you will wear yourself down like today." he said rubbing my back. "I know that I should its just she wont be little long and she is my last." I told him sadly. He took a deep breathe, "I didn't mean to upset you I just thought . . . ." he said drifting off. "I know what you meant I will try ok." I promised him. I laid my head on his shoulder and he would touch my tummy softly and I knew he was as sad as I was about no more babies.

I had to get past all this or I was going to shut down, "Lets go for a walk it may make us feel better." I suggested. Without saying anything he kissed my neck and out the window we went. I led the way to the darker side of town the darkness helped me when I had so much to put away. Not only that but it would look strange for us to be out without any shoes walking around town. Xavier would give me space as I thought and sometimes he would be floating around in my head. I began to put things in the needed folders as I walked, so much has happened over the past year. Two wars, new babies, new additions to the family, what Doc told me about the powers and babies. It all began to fall in place, I will fulfill my place as queen, Jade will drink from a bottle starting in the morning, I will be a mother figure to all in the house when they need me, and work will be squeezed in there because Xavier's happiness was very important to me. I stopped as he did, "You alright Sweets?" he asked. "Yes I'm ready to go home and get to bed if that's ok." I told him. He took my hand to lead me back to the Great House, "Umm I have a question, how come when I began to read your mind towards the last you shut me out? I didn't think you could do that anymore." he said. "I don't know I guess since I shared with you I still have full control, I didn't even know I did that. I just had so much to put away and there are a few that will linger for sometime but I will work on it." I told him. "Either way you feel amazing inside, lets get home are you tired?" he asked. "I'm not tired at all I feel great." I told him. "Good." he said smiling. "I'll race ya!" I said taking off. "Tag your it." he said as he tapped me on the shoulder and took off. I tried to keep up with him but there was no use he was much faster than I will ever be. "Where have you been Sweets I've been here almost two seconds?" he asked from a tree branch. I jumped through the window and landed softly near the bed, "I win I made it into the house before you." I said laughing. "Cheater." he said as he dove off the branch and on top of me growling. "Hey now that's cheating." I told him still laughing. "You never said inside the house just to the house." he said holding me down. "Maybe you should have been reading my mind." I said picking on him. It felt good to play even if it was just every once in a while. It took many things off both of our minds so we could get thing in the right order. "I should remember that you are sneaky, this is not the first time you have tricked me to win." he said smiling at me. "What can I say I love to win no matter what or how." I said kissing his soft lips. "Lets check on the house before we go to sleep I know you want to." he said pulling me up. "Ok that always makes me feel better to make sure everyone has what they need." I told him getting to my feet. "I'll wait for you." he said as he laid back in the bed. I made quick rounds to make sure all was tucked in bed and sleeping for those who chose to go to bed before I went back to Xavier.

Chapter 23

I laid down with Xavier and he kissed me, "Sleep well Sweetness." he said. I lit up my eyes to let him know sleeping was the last thing on my mind, "Are you sure your not to tired?" he asked. I pushed my hands up his shirt to feel his skin next to mine, "Yes I'm sure." I whispered to him. I watched his eyes glow bright blue as he smiled and kissed me. He put his hands on my back and ripped my shirt off as I took his off him. I kissed my way up his neck to his lips as he ripped my panties off my body. There was more passion this time than the others because I seemed to be pregnant most all of the time. Now we could share each other to the fullest with any worry of him hurting me. He held me close like he had missed me somehow, "Can you hear it? Your blood is screaming my name, I must have a drink or die without it." he said in a whisper with words like magic to me. I turned my neck his way so he could have what he wanted even though I had already seen what was about to happen, but there was nothing I could do about it with his magic voice. He bit me with more force than he ever had before as his body trembled holding me tight so I couldn't get away from him tasting me. His breathing changed as he made love to me while he drank from me, "Xavier." I whispered to him. He never stopped just held tighter. I grabbed a handful of his hair and pulled him off my neck before he bled me dry, "Are you alright Love?" I asked. He looked at me with fright in his eyes and turned his back to me, "Look at me Xavier." I said as I wiped the remaining blood from my neck.

He refused to look at me as I set up on the bed behind him. I put his face in my hands and turned him to face me, "Look at me Xavier right now, don't make me force you." I demanded. Finally he turned his blue eyes to meet mine, "I'm sorry I will never allow that to happen again I swear to you." he whispered. "What happened, you have never done anything like that before?" I asked. "Your blood always had a hold on me but after your walk it smells different to me." he said. "Different how?" I asked in surprise. "It is more powerful than before I could hear it calling to me. You have a stronger hold on me, I am at your mercy. Please Sweetness forgive me." he said as he put his arms around me. "Forgive you for what I wasn't complaining and I never said no did I, even though I foresaw what was going to happen." I told him. "Why did you allow me to bite you if you knew that was going to happen?" he asked backing away. "You have the same hold on me I would follow you to the fiery pits of hell if you said so. Your voice was like magic to me and I couldn't have told you no even if I wanted to. We just let our desires get the best of us this time and we will be more careful that's all." I told him. "There will never be a next time like this." he said in royal tones. "Oh yes it will happen again there is no need to punish ourselves for one mistake. I love it when you bite me during sex it heightens everything for the both of us I can feel you." I told him as I pulled him back down on the bed next to me. I put my fingers through his hair and rubbed down his chest making way to his stomach. His breathing changed like when he gets excited and he flipped me to my back and began to make love to me again. This time halfway through he changed course and it became more vigorous as I wrapped my legs around him tight putting my fingernails into his back. He was more in control of his emotions this time but stayed away from my neck. I however did not I bit down on his juggler and took what I wanted with him moaning in pleasure.

The sun brought us a new day as we finished sharing one another, "I love you Sweets." he simply said. "I love you." I told him. He hit the floor and took his shower as I fed Jade, and got dressed myself. He stayed away from me with no shower and he ate his breakfast on the move, it was just better to let him work this one out alone this time. Work came and the day seemed not as long as others, I had guessed that I could put my mind into work without worries of Jade. Michelle worked along the side of both of us when it called for it, "Hey your quiet today something bothering you?" she asked. "Not really X is just keeping his distance from me that's all." I told her. "Well whatever the reason he needs to fix it, I hate seeing you both like this. You know you have to feel each other or you will die." she said. "Still reading I see. Look he will come around when he is ready he is hurting right now best to let him alone he has a temper about this." I warned her. "Yea I have been reading I cant put them down. What happened for him to stay way, I know he can hear us but I don't care?" she asked. "He bit me last night and I had to pull him off before he drank to much now he has kept his distance. I need to touch him and soon but I want him to have the time he needs." I told her. "I have a temper you should see hers when she lets it go, and it isn't nice to talk behind someone's back either." he said as he came in the room. "I didn't think we were talking behind your back since you can hear everything anyway." Michelle said. "Still not polite." he said as he looked at her with surprise. "Now you two kiss and make up or I will make life hard for the both of you." she said. Xavier looked at both of us, "I knew working with two women who were best friends would bite me on the ass." he said with a laugh. He leaned over and kissed me on the cheek quickly while holding his breathe.

That was enough for me right now I could feel him needing more time. I patted him on his back and ran my hand over his chest, "Don't worry Love you take the time you need, I'll be here for you when you need me." I told him softly. Michelle was already on her way out of the room as he grabbed me hard by the arm and pulled me close, "Don't use your magic on me, I know the heart thing I have felt it before." he said hatefully. "Well then if you have felt it before than you know I didn't use on you I was being nice. You want to see temper, I can show you temper." I said as I jerked away from him and started for the door. He grabbed me again, "Piper wait." he said quickly. "What?" I asked. "Why should you get that tone with me?" he asked still mad. "Don't ever accuse me of using on you trust me when I do you wont forget it." I told him as I pulled away hard and left him standing. I worked the rest of the day with him trying to get in my mind and as soon as the last patient left I was out the door and him calling me. I made my way home quickly still pissed at him for how he man handled me and with his tone. I could hear the Charger pulling up behind me so I cut through the woods. He shut the car off and ran up behind me grabbing me. I flipped him over to his back and sat across him, "Look whatever happened last night you fix it or I'm not staying in the same room with you. You have never gave me a deadline and I planned not to give you one but the way you grabbed me and the tone you used I wont stand for." I told him and got to my feet. "Why wont you stay in the same room with me? I have never had someone hold this much power over me before and I'm trying to work it out." he said as he got up. "I wont stay where you wont allow me to touch you." I said crossing my arms. He passed me and walked home so I returned to the car and drove home.

I walked in the house with all the brood looking at me, "What's wrong with Dad he walked passed the twins without talking to them and slammed his door?" Tiffany asked. "Lets not worry ourselves he will be just fine. Now what's for dinner?" I asked. "Lets carry out if that is ok." Mike said. "That will be fine you know what we like from wherever you decide to go, I'll be back in a few minutes." I said as I loved on the four little ones. Xavier was laying in the bed when I entered, "Sweets." he said jumping up. "I'm not staying I'm changing and leaving." I told him as I put my hand up to stop him. I shut the bathroom door behind me, "By the way the kids are ordering out so if you want something come and get it." I called from behind the door. I dressed and opened the door and he had his hands on the door frame so I couldn't pass, "I'm sorry." he simply said. I shook my head to let him know it was all right still trying to pass. "Please don't go I have to touch you." he said as I tried to slip under his arm. "Then touch lets see if you can control yourself, I'm not afraid of you." I told him as I put my hands on my hips. He carefully slid his hands around my back and moved his face to my neck. I felt him tighten up as he smelled my blood running through my veins as he backed me up towards the bed, never moving from my neck.

I slid my hands over his shoulders and down his back softly, "Xavier you are stronger than you think. I don't fear you and you shouldn't fear me." I thought to him. I caressed his face as I began to kiss him as he kissed me back. When he opened his eyes they were a different kind of blue one that I had never seen before, this was a different kind of spell he was under. "Breath me in." I told him with my own kind of magic. He did as I asked and opened his eyes, grabbed me and put me to the bed with force. "I need you I will have you right now." he said with his royal tones. I didn't argue with him I just let him have me anyway he wanted. He pulled my clothes off with a quick jerk as I pulled at his and him grabbing me by the hair and biting me hard. I bit back needing to taste him just as bad as our bodies trembled as we drank from one another. He came up for air and his eyes were perfect blue like they were supposed to be. "Do you feel better?" I asked. "Yes much better now that I have you." he said with a smile. I got up and dressed in new clothes, "I think you are getting many emotions at one time and this power is new to you that's all." I told him as I watched him walk across the room naked. His body was perfect like it was made from a perfect mold. My body tingled as the sight of him moving to me, "You need to put your feelings in check Sweets or we shall never make it to dinner." he whispered up my neck. "You need to stop being so perfect and stop breathing your sweet breath up my neck." I said looking up at him. "Does it bother you with me doing this?" he whispered again. "What do you think? Now move your butt I'm hungry and the kids are trying to wait." I said as I put my hands on his shoulders and moved back.

I slipped out from his hold he had on me and went for the door with him right on my heels. I raced down the stairs before he jumped them and landed in front of me. "I win this time." he said with a smile. I jumped on top of him with a growl and knocked him over. I jumped to my feet and headed to the kitchen where the others waited, "To the kids remember so I win." I said as I laughed. "I'm gonna get you Sweetness you cheat so bad." he said as he came in the kitchen. I hid behind Bailey and Jovi for cover as the other boys took to their feet, "You cant get me I'm with my body guards they wont let you pass." I said smiling at him. Xavier came to a sliding stop at the sight of the boys protecting me. "Oh alright I surrender to you." I said as I moved to boys to the side and walked to X. "You have to be punished." he said as he kissed me. "My turn my turn!" Brie said jumping up and down. Xavier grabbed her up and kissed her little face all over as she giggled. "Lets eat and play later." Cyndi said as she handed out the plates. "Pizza, pizza, pizza!!!" Bastian yelled as he jumped around. I took my seat with Xavier as dinner was passed around, "So what do you all have planned for this weekend?" I asked. No one spoke up they just looked at me, "Good I have something planned for tomorrow." I said as I ate. "What do you have planned Sweets?" X asked. "I signed the boys up for a race this weekend, they each get to do a quarter mile if they wish." I said not looking up. Jon jumped to his feet, "Really Piper we can race the Camaro, how many times?" he asked with enthusiasm. "You each get to go once unless you make to top to race again." I said with a smile. Xavier just shook his head at me, "What I can do this for all the help they give me and then the girls turn." I said. "We do things for you Piper because we love you, not to be rewarded." Mike said. "Well this is my way of saying that I appreciate everything you all do for me." I said as I rose to clear the table. "We can do this Piper." Sharon offered. "Thanks I'll take Piper to the living room." X said. "I could have helped." I told him. "You are going to spoil them." he told me. "So what they are mine to spoil so hush and let me do it." I said with a smile as I took a seat on the couch.

The kids came in and picked out something to watch while the twins got up on their daddy and LaStat crawled up on Bailey to fall asleep. Mike and Sharon was talking over another movie selection with Jon and Amber waiting, "Just pick something out before I get old over here." Jon said from across the room. "Then you pick something out." Mike said as he shot Jon a look. "Just shut your eyes and put your finger on something." I said. Sharon did as I asked and picked up the first movie she touched and handed it to Mike. "Its a old movie Piper its Scream." Jon said. I looked over my shoulder at him, "But that's ok I love older horror movies, its great I haven't seen it." he said smiling at me. Amber gave him a jab in the ribs, "Ouch." he said pretending she hurt him. Soon the all the children were fast asleep. "Night guys see you in the morning. Cutie call Josh and see if he wants to go we wont wait on him he must be ready." I said as I headed for the steps. "I'll call now." she said as Jon laid the same rules on her about waiting.

I laid down and unlike many nights in the past I fell asleep in Xavier's arms. Before to long I heard a knock at the door. I woke and found the sun just starting up over the horizon and I pulled the covers up on myself and X. "Come in." I called softly knowing it was Jon. "Piper we need to get up so we can get ready to go, we still have to pick up Josh and Amber." Jon whispered as he came in. "Sure I'm getting up, do you want to start breakfast or grab something out?" I asked. "Either way is fine with me." he said stepping closer to me. "Well like I said today is about you guys so whatever you all want is fine. Wake the others and get them moving." I told him softly so not to wake Xavier. Jon smiled and kissed me on the cheek, "You are what this family needed, the greatest." he said as he moved to the door. I rubbed the night out of my eyes and took my finger and traced Xavier's perfect face. He laid there as still as possible while I traced his lips then without warning he tied to bite me. "Hey now you faker." I said poking him in his ribs. "Jon is right you are exactly what this family needed." he said with a smile. "I thought you were asleep." I told him. "I was until he got closer that would have woke me from the dead." he told me. "Get up lazy before he sends the children in on us." I said as I tried to get up. "I cant wait until Halloween just us in a cabin. It will be a year can you believe it?" he asked holding tight. "I know it has been exciting don't you think?" I asked as I looked over my naked shoulder at him. He hit the floor making his way to me in a flash, "Lets shower together." he said moving me along. We hurried and I dressed in blue jeans and a tank with a button up over top. X found him jeans and timberland boots with a shirt that contoured his every muscle. "I guess we are eating in." X said as the smell of bacon hit us. We walked in on everyone eating breakfast, "Come on guys hurry up and eat. Tiffany did you call Josh cause I'm not waiting on him." Jon said. "Jon honey you must calm down or your head is going to pop off." I told him with a smile. We had to take all the cars in the garage to get to the race track, Cyndi and Bailey took the Chrysler 300, Regina, Jovi and Tiffany in the Escalade, Mike and Sharon in the Charger, Jon in the Camaro, with Xavier and me with the kids in the Dodge truck. Xavier took the boys up to race as the girls and I took up the front row so we could see them race. Jon and Bailey were the first to race with Jon taking the finish line. Bailey came back to be with Cyndi, "That was fun." he said taking LaStat on his lap. Jovi and Mike was next and soon Jovi joined us on the stands, "Wow that was a rush!" Jovi said getting Gina's hand. "I know I can feel you all." I told him. Jon and Mike went head to head and Jon sent Mike back to the seats with us, "Man he is good." Mike said as the twins ran to him. "He is having the time of his life." Xavier said.

I sat back as the visions of what was going to happen next and I handed Jade to Gina standing up, "What?" X asked. "Come on Jon is going to need us." I said taking his hand. Just about that time Jon put the Camaro in the wall. Both of us hit the pavement running fast to get to him, "You cant pass here." the man said. "I'm the boys father and I'm a doctor." Xavier said. I jumped the wall not waiting to be told if I could or couldn't with X right behind me. When I got there he was holding his head, "Thank god Jon are you all right?" I asked. "I'm ok Piper sorry about your car." he said. Xavier took over the situation looking at Jon to make sure he was as he said. After we made arrangements to get the car home we headed that way ourselves, "What's going to happen to Jon when we get home Momma?" Bastian asked. "He will have to fix the car so he can race it again if he wants." I said looking out the window. "No this is the last time." X said quickly. "I'm not going to stop him from this." I told X. "Why do you put yourself through things like this?" Xavier asked looking at me. "What doesn't kill me makes me stronger and I'm not going to kill his happiness to make myself feel better." I told him as I took his hand. We made it home with all the little ones fast asleep, Jon and Mike took the twins up and Xavier took Jade while I waited on the couch. Jon came back down, "Before you say anything I want to say thank you for letting me do this and I will fix the car back to perfect shape." Jon said quickly. "You gave us a heart attack, you will fix Pipers car back to the way it was. You will keep racing if this is what you want to do but your family duties must come first. Just so that you understand Piper wants you to race if your heart desires but I'm not happy about this." Xavier told him. "Thank you and if I decide to race again I shall but I'm not sure I want to make a habit out of it. Your car will be back to perfect shape soon I swear it to be done." he said as he shook Xavier's hand and hugged me. I sat back on the couch and covered my face, "Jon isn't as breakable as you think he is very strong, I still don't know why you allow this to continue." X said as he sat with me. "They have been here catering to me and the babies and that's not fair." I told him. "Then kick them out on the weekends make them go and do things they want to do." he said as we started to bed once again. I pulled his arms around me as we laid there, "Then maybe we should have a family talk in the morning." I said. "Yes I will do this for you, I will make them do the young at heart things." he said falling asleep.

Chapter 24

I woke with the bed empty and the sun not even up yet. I rose and dressed to look for Xavier following his voice to the lower floor. I went into the kitchen and waited on him to finish while I drank a Dr. Pepper, "What's going on?" I asked not very happy with him. "Just having a talk with the kids I told you that I would fix this for you." he said as I nodded his way as I left to shower. "Spill it." he said as he opened the shower door. "When I said family meeting I meant the whole family and that meant me. I know you were doing this for me but I thought I would have been included that's all." I told him shutting the shower door. "Sorry I couldn't sleep and many were still awake so I told them what we talked about." he defended himself. "Next time it waits on all of us or nothing at all." I said. "Deal so I'm off the hook?" he asked. "Hell no you have to do Emails while I watch." I told him smiling to myself. He opened the shower door getting inside with clothes and all backing me up against the shower wall, "I don't want to do Emails right now." he said up my neck. "Well I'm very busy right now." I said smiling at him. That didn't stop him from what he wanted, "There you are no longer busy." he said as he shut the shower off. He guided me to the bed, "I love you." he said up my wet neck. "X I love you but we must do these Emails." I told him. "Don't care about mail right now all I can think about is you." he whispered to me. I gave into what he wanted without any question. "We have to get up don't we?" he asked. "Yep we have the day waiting on us." I told him as I got dressed.

I found the kids making plans for the weekend while LaStat came over and asked me if I would pick him up in a Greek language. I was taken back some when he spoke like that, and even more when I found myself answering him in the same language. Cyndi smiled at me when she heard him talking, "He can do any language even the dead forgotten ones." she said proudly. "That is amazing." I said kissing his face. He giggled and slipped out of my hands as I sat with X who was working on the Emails. "I've got a few done and you have a couple tasting's tomorrow." he said. "Thanks honey." I said shaking my head at him. I sat and ate dinner while everyone talked back and forth about many things. Many things ran through my mind and I really didn't want to taste the blood of others I had hoped that all I had to do was look inside them and get what I needed. The day rushed by and work approached me with a force. "Morning Michelle." X said. "Hey glad to see you guys made up." she said smiling. "You are with me today for the first five or so." I told her. "Alrighty let me get the charts." she said grabbing a pen. I walked in the room where two vampires waited on me, "Good morning how are we?" I asked. "Fine Queen Piper." the young man said. "Just Piper if you wouldn't mind." I said looking over the sheet Michelle gave me. "If you wish us to we shall." he said softly. I walked over and looked at them both, "Ok here we go, give me your finger." I said as I put my hand out. I tasted their blood and let the memories rush my mind, "You are both free to do as you wish be happy." I said as Michelle wrote down what she needed.

I went through two others with the same from them but the last was a surprise to me when I walked in the room. I walked in and backed myself up against the door, "Get Xavier." I said backing out of the room. She went for him, "Piper what's up?" he asked. "Human he's human I cant do this, I'm not ready." I thought to him. He walked into the room looking at them both, "Is there a problem my King?" the girl asked. "You should have said that he was human this posses a problem." Xavier told her. "What's the problem isn't your wife a ex human?" she asked. "My wife is no concern of yours or anyone else for that matter. There are rules and you should have warned us that your chosen mate is human." he said now very aggravated. He looked at me as I turned my glowing eyes up at him, "Step out Sweets I will take this one." he said helping me out. "Take your chosen and leave out the back door." he said as I went out for fresh air. "What happened in there?" Michelle asked. "He smelled so good to me if I would have tasted him I would have never stopped. This has never happened to me and I don't like it." I told her. "Come on Piper you are stronger than that." she said. "Michelle if I would have gotten close I would have killed that boy without blinking an eyelash and you would have never been able to stop me." I told her. "I'm sorry I didn't mean to make light of it." she said quietly. "It's alright I'll be ok in a few minutes." I told her as Xavier came out. "They are leaving out the back, I'm sorry you are upset." he said. I breathed him into me, "That's better." I said. "Will you be able to hold off for a hunt until after work?" he asked. "I hope so I'm going to try its bad." I told him. "I know I can feel you." he said putting his arm around me.

As soon as work was over I headed for the woods so I could kill the craving that lurked so hard in my soul. I caught the first thing that caught my eye and drained it dry. I gave Xavier an unhappy look, "This isn't helping, I have never felt like this before." I told him. "Come on I'll get you something else and this is the only time you will ever have this pass your beautiful lips." he said getting in the car. He made a quick stop and came back to the car, "This is a one time thing now get your mind ready and a fair warning the memories you may get might not be pleasant." he said handing me a bag of blood. I looked at it for a minute and then him, "Are you sure?" I asked. "Yes this is the path you must follow this time, careful it will take you places you have never seen." he said. The stuff we normally drank was man made but this is the real deal just cold. I took my first drink and the power of the human blood hit me. "Piper look at me." he said. I rolled my glowing eyes towards him, "Wow this is nice." I said. "Don't give into these feelings or I will have to stop you, please don't force my hand." he said with royal tones. I put his hand on my heart and he knew what I needed to help me even though he never used this power before. He pressed his hand on my heart and thought to me, "Piper look at me, you will do as I say you will not give in to these feelings and you will remember this always." he said. I sat there fighting the power the fresh blood had on me as he pushed harder, "Yes Xavier I will not give into these feelings, I will do as you wish of me and let this go." I told him.

He started the car and took me home putting me in the shower to break all ties with the blood that might have hold on me still. I looked up at him, "Don't ever give me that again and no more human surprises." I told him. "Thank god I was worried about you, what do you feel like?" he asked. "Same ol Piper." I said lying through my teeth. "Do you have any idea what would have happened if I had to stop you?" he asked lightly. "Yes you would have had to . . . ." I said as he interrupted. "STOP say nothing else." he said quickly. "This is never to escape your lips to no one." I told him. "Never." he said as we dressed. I sat at the dinner table and ate quietly, "Is everything ok Piper you look a little different today?" Mike asked as the others agreed. I looked at Xavier, "She is fine just a bad day that's all." he said as I got up and left the room. I was ashamed of what I let happen I'm supposed to be strong and never give in to my temptations like that. I could hear Xavier excuse himself from the table as Mike stopped him asking questions. "Like I said she had a bad day that's all she will come around so don't go asking her questions just be here for her if she needs." he told Mike. I took this opportunity to slip out the window even though I knew X was going to be pissed at me. I walked the back yard as the rain beat down on me with lighting and thunder until I made it to the willow tree. "Damn it Piper is missing we need to find her." I heard him call to the boys. "Dad she is under the willow and lighting is striking all around her." Tiffany called to him. I looked up at Xavier, Mike and Jon as they walked out in the rain to get me, "What are you doing out here Sweets you need to calm the weather and come inside." he said as I let tears fall down my face. "Just reach out to get her and make her come in before something happens to her." Jon said as he reached for me.

I held my hands up and forced easy winds to move Jon back so the lighting could strike where he stood. "Don't Jon she is very dangerous right now." X told them. "Is she controlling the weather like that?" Jon asked with shock in his voice. X shook his head at him as Mike bent down to face me better, "Back off Mike." Xavier warned. "Piper look at me." Mike said softly. I looked up at him with tears still streaming down my face. "You need to come inside, everyone is worried about you and Xavier is about to die can you feel him?" he asked. I looked at Jon and X as I felt the house and all the pain they had in them. It hurt in the pit of my stomach when it was grouped like that. I watched Xavier hit the ground as he picked up on my feelings so I shut him off so he couldn't feel any more of me. More lighting and thunder with hard rain pounded the ground, "Piper I'm serious now we need you, when you come home like this we worry that's all. None of us care what happened with you today just as long as you are home and safe. Please let me help you my Queen." he pleaded. I took the thunder away, "You don't care what happened to me today?" I asked. "That's is not what I meant I just meant that we would never think ill of you no matter what." he said still holding out his hand. "So if you were to find out what happened you would just over look it and say nothing?" I asked him again. "We would never judge you that is not our place, you would never judge any of us that we have learned from you. Now please allow me to take you inside." he said. I took Mikes hand as he helped me up and the rain slowed to a drizzle. He handed me off to Xavier, "Come Jon they will be in a minute." Mike told him.

Xavier took me in his arms and I cried from the human part that I was going to be left with so I could release the pain and sorrow I have. X carried me inside as Bailey opened the front door for us as Cyndi moved Bailey further back now that everyone knew what I was capable of. I was taken upstairs and undressed so I could be put to bed, "We leave on Thursday and you are to stay home the rest of the week." he said as he laid beside me, putting his face in my neck and soon I was fast asleep. Morning I woke to find Xavier gone and Mike in the corner who took to his feet as I set up, "Would you like something to eat or drink?" he asked quickly. "What time is it?" I asked. "Around 10:30 or so." he said. "Take me for a walk will you please I promise to behave?" I pleaded. "I'm sorry Piper I have specific instructions not to let you out of the house." Mike said backing up. I stood up and walked over to him, "You can take me of your own free will or I can make you either way I'm walking. Please Mike don't make me use on you." I said. "Xavier is going to kill me for this promise me that you will stay close to me?" he asked. "I swear I will just keep your feelings on total lock down so I can put things away in the right folders." I told him. I walked over to the window and floated down as Mike followed. I walked and he kept my pace staying a few steps behind me as I thought. I sat up in a tree as he stood and waited on me at the bottom, then I came down and walked until it was almost time for Xavier to come home. I knew I had to hurry so Mike didn't get in trouble.

I stopped sudden as I felt everything slipping into the right areas of my head with Mike almost falling over me, "Piper are you alright?" he asked. "Yes I say by the time I get home and shower I should be good as new. Thanks so much for this you have no idea how it has helped." I told him. We turned and headed home as I finished up all the left overs and erased all of the past day or so. I slowed so Mike would walk back with me, "If you wish I listen very well." he said. "I'm sure you do but I can put things away very well when I walk." I told him although I knew what he wanted from me. "Can I ask what happened that was so bad?" he asked. "Mike I really don't think I should right now maybe one day but not now." I told him softly. "Than may I tell you something?" he asked. "Sure I also listen very well." I told him. "Before I became a part of this family Jon and I was living on the streets feeding off of anything we could get our hands on. We were attacked by a vampire who either couldn't or wouldn't finish the job and we were left to figure out the rest. Humans were the favorites on the menu and we were attacking them night and day it was getting bad. That's when Xavier and Kaleb found us and talked us into going home with them. They showed us the new way the right way for us even though I have slipped a few times and X came and got me cleaning me up again. That's why I have a vampire as a mate and not a human I have never fully trusted myself. But over the years I have grown stronger and I have never seen anything like you in my life. You are the strongest female I have ever seen and the most head strong. Yet you are loving and caring you hold a strong hand if it calls for it. Your loyal subjects fear you and respect you at the same time. You are very important to Xavier and this family you have no idea. This thing that happened with Cora I was around the time of their courtship and he never loved her like he loves you. She wanted him to take her as his queen and he knew you were out there waiting for him so he refused her. I don't think anyone can love like X loves you. We tried to get him to go out and just find someone and he refused he just sat up in his room and drew in his books. The next time you are in the attic look for his old drawings you will see he has waited for you. All I'm saying is that we all have slipped one time or another so don't beat yourself up." he said.

"We have to hurry X is coming home." I said as we rushed back to the house. I jumped the window as Mike followed me. I took his hand and led him to the attic door, "Help me will you?" I asked. He opened the door for me as Xavier came in downstairs asking about me. "She and Mike has been in there all day." Gina lied to Xavier. Mike and I went through Xavier's old trunks until we found what we were looking for, "Piper here they are, see for yourself." Mike said as he handed me the books. I looked through the books with ease as Xavier came up the steps, "Mike you guys up here?" he called. "We are here she wanted to look through some things hope that is ok." Mike said. "Sure whatever she wants she gets, did she behave?" Xavier asked with a smile. "She was no trouble." Mike said as he rubbed my arm and left us. Xavier came and set behind me and put his arms around me, "So what are you looking for Sweetness?" he asked. I turned and kissed him on the cheek, "These books hope you don't mind." I said. He took the books and flipped through some pages. I put my hand on the page I wanted to see and slowly flipped through the pages. I found some hand drawn pictures of what looked like me and the further I went the more they did look like me, "See I told you that you were the only one for me, I knew the moment I saw you. There you were at the hospital laughing with Michelle and I thought to myself that is the girl from my pictures can it be true? I had myself put on your rounds so I could see if you were real. My heart skipped a beat when I really saw you and it took me weeks to even speak to you. I mostly watched you for a long time and when I touched you I felt like I was going to die when you left me that day. I followed you home many days without you knowing and then when the rain came I took my chance." he told me.

I became tearful up at the story and the beautiful pictures with him taking my face in his hands, "Why are you upset?" he asked. "I don't deserve you that's all." I simply said. He smiled and helped me down the steps, "You think you don't deserve me, I think it is the other way around and I don't deserve you." he said as we entered the bedroom. I wiped the tears from my face as I set on the bed, "You feel great inside Sweets have you been walking?" he asked with carefulness. "I made Mike go don't say anything to him." I said quickly. "Some how I knew you would make him go which one was it?" he asked smiling at me. "Well neither I just threatened that I would and he gave in after I promised I would stick close to him. I needed to walk I had to or I was going to go crazy and I hope the others can forgive me for the way I acted. Mike shared some things with me and I feel a bit better after hearing what he had to say. I hope Jon is ok but if I hadn't moved him back he would have been hit by the lighting. I have erased the memories from my mind all the way to before the third couple." I told him. His eyes got a bit bigger, "Since when can you erase memories from your mind?" he asked. I laid on the bed and he followed with his hand on my stomach, "Ever since I was a kid I guess." I said shrugging my shoulders.

I turned to face him and I traced his perfect face with my finger and down his neck. I worked my way down his chest and traced his abs with him laying there and enjoying the feeling I was giving him. "You shouldn't touch me like that Sweetness it is the most exciting magic you can do to me." he said never opening his eyes. I kissed him on his stomach and his chest working my way up to his neck and under his chin. I stopped right about his lips and he grabbed me and kissed me, "Why do you do that to me, you kill me when you start and stop like that." he said as his eyes met mine. "Sorry." I whispered up his neck. I took his shirt off and he removed mine laying there with our skin touching as I traced his abs making way to his chest. I kissed his neck and his lips tenderly, "I cant stand it anymore Sweetness." he said with excitement as he tore at my shorts. He kissed my stomach moving to my neck, "I love you." he whispered on my neck knowing what it does to me. I wrapped myself in our pleasure of each other as we made love. His hands never left my naked body as I ran my fingers through his hair. I kissed him for what felt like forever, it could have been forever I would have never cared. The day disappeared into night and we were still enjoying each other. When the moon was high we came to a wonderful finish, "Are you hungry or need to hunt?" he asked softly still touching me. "I haven't eaten all day maybe I should have something, maybe some chips." I told him. "Come on." he said. We dressed and went out the window heading for the car, "Lets take the motorcycle." I suggested.

He drove through town for awhile and stopped at the nearest convince store with people looking at us like we were crazy. It was late October and I was in shorty shorts and a tank with no shoes, him in jeans and tank. I heard him growl lightly at the stares I was receiving from a few men and I put myself in front of him and kissed him. He never took his hands from my skin either up the back of my shirt or my hand always touching. We paid for our snacks and headed for the bike. The three men who were looking at me was setting on the Honda, and I could feel X working up a anger. "Let me this time." I said knowing he would kill them. I walked over to the men, "Would you please move from our bike?" I asked sweetly reading the minds of them all. "If we don't what are you going to do about it little lady?" the biggest one said. "You really don't want to know trust me. I would step away of you value your lives all of you." I told him. Xavier moved to the bike and took a seat with one of them looking at him and he shook his head no at them. "You best move on man she will hurt you bad." he said with a laugh. "This little girl hurt me I don't think so." the man said as the others backed off from his fight. The guy tried to put his hands on me as I put my hand in his chest with lots of force putting him to the ground. I walked over to him and crouched down near him, "Leave me alone and other women or the next time you will be sorry understand?" I asked lowly and sweetly as I glowed my eyes for him to see. He shook his head yes and I helped him up and he jumped in his car taking off. "You have fun Sweetness, I sure had fun watching? The others took off before the show they missed a good one." he said as I got on the back of the bike.

Chapter 25

It was nice to have time together as he drove us to a near by park without all the worries and the Emails. I laid on the marry go round as he gave me a hard spin then joining me. We laid there watching the stars twirl by, "Where are you taking me Thursday Love?" I asked as we shared our chips. "Somewhere in a cabin tucked away just the two of us for a few days, how does that sound?" he asked. "Sounds great." I told him as the marry go round slowed. I climbed on the back of the bike and he drove us around town for a bit. The wind felt good on my face as he drove with me holding on to him. We made it back to the house, "Maybe we should see the brood." I said. He led me in the front door with Jon getting to his feet, "Piper how are you we have been worried about you?" he asked making way over to me. "I'm much better and I wanted to say that I'm very sorry about yesterday if I upset anyone. I had a very bad day and I had to fix myself before I could face any of you." I told them. "Yes but you spent the day with Mike and he wouldn't tell us anything about you only that you would be alright." Gina said. "Mike and I took a walk so I could think and put things in the right order." I told them. The twins rushed to my side and I picked them up to love them, "I have missed you my little angels have you been good for everyone?" I asked. "Yes Momma we have been good and so has Jade." Brie said. I loved on their faces and went to love on Jade and LaStat. Sharon sat beside me, "You should have seen everyone last night, after what we saw you do to the weather and then Jon we were so worried. I know it isn't my place to tell you these things but I'm compelled to. I knew Mike would be the one to get you inside he sat and looked out the window all night until Xavier asked him to watch over you. May I ask what the two of you talked about on your walk?" she asked. "I'm sorry Sharon if you want to know what he told me than you should ask him not me." I told her nicely. "I just thought maybe you could tell me because he hasn't." she said.

Xavier took the twins on his lap to fall asleep with Jade and LaStat following. Jovi and Josh kept their distance for awhile, "Jovi no need to be afraid of Piper she is much better." Gina told him. "Yea I know but I would rather stay over here for right now that's all." he said. I looked over at him and smiled, "That's alright I know what you are feeling and I would never hurt any of you. The weather is tied to my emotions and when I feel like I did it rains with thunder and lighting." I told him. "But what you did with Jon that was something that I have never seen before." he said quietly. "What I did with Jon was hold him back so he wouldn't get hit by the lighting I didn't do it to be mean to him. I hope you can learn to trust me again." I said with love in my voice. "You better get used to things you have never seen before Jovi, she is full of surprises and powerful. You never know what she can do or will do if ever pushed." Mike said as he walked out. I felt him struggling within himself so I followed him out, "Mike?" I asked. He shook his head as if nothing was bothering him, "I know you are dealing with things and I'm here for you if you need." I told him as I stopped him from walking off. "You are the only one I have told about my life and Sharon has asked and I don't want to tell her. You are different I have to tell things that I would never tell anyone that's why I stay clear of you." he said. "Well if you don't wish to share she will have to learn that. If you choose to stay away from me that's fine you will come around before to long. I never mean to make you uncomfortable or make you tell me anything it just happens." I told him. "Thanks Piper for understanding." he said.

Xavier came to my side wondering what was going on with Mike and myself. "Good night guys." Bailey said as he and Cyndi passed us. "Night." X said as I went to the kitchen to fix us a cold cup. I returned to the living room to find X laying on the couch, "Move your lazy butt over Mister." I said joking with him. He made room for me putting his arm around me just like when we were dating, "I have missed laying on the couch with you watching movies." Xavier said. "I have too." I told him. "Would you like to go to work and hang out with me tomorrow for a bit, I don't want you to work?" he asked. "Do you think it is safe for me to go around humans?" I asked. "I think after the storm you released you should be just fine. I have missed feeling you like this you feel so good inside." he said. I laid there as he fell asleep safe in his arms just listening to his breathing. It was relaxing and soothing to me and I felt like the world was at peace even though I didn't sleep that night. I could hear the world outside as it moved around to get ready for the sunrise. Xavier would every once in a while make some kind of noise as he slept that would make me laugh to myself. He would call out my name sometimes and I would answer him, "I love you." he would simply say. I finally was able to get up and make rounds the house having time to myself as I could hear LaStat making his wake up call to Cyndi. I was connected to the whole house and sometimes it was nice but when the tension was up it was hard to keep them out.

Jon was the first to hit the lower floor and to the kitchen, "I'm sorry Piper I can come back later." he said as he entered the kitchen. "Please stay I'm just looking out the window." I told him. He came over and stood there looking out, "I guess you and Mike had a long talk huh?" he asked. "I guess so he talked and I listened." I told him. "As long as it helped you. What did he tell you if I may ask?" he asked. "Just how he came to pass that's all." I said softly. He stood there looking out the window, "Did he tell you that I had a slip up as well?" he asked. I shook my head no at him and he never looked at me just at the willow, "Well I did and Xavier and Kaleb had a hard time with me, trying to keep me from hurting other humans. We didn't live here we had a different home at the time and I'm the reason we are here. Mike had his little slip up but mine was bad enough for us to move. I was unstoppable for a small time the human blood gave me pure speed I was faster than Xavier and sneakier than you. I was hiding out and when they found me I was almost gone with the desire of taste. I thought I would go crazy as they dried me out so to speak soon after his parents passed and we moved to Hinton. I have gotten better but sometimes I still crave the taste of human blood. Xavier forbidded me to date human girls because of scent, believe me there were a few I wanted to taste but Xavier is my king and in order for me to stay I had to abide by the rules. Look Piper its important that you know that no one is perfect and there will always be a human you have to taste. You have a very strong mind and soul I can tell, you will have to lock those feelings out. It isn't easy at all but I have complete faith in you as we all do so don't sweat the small stuff. Nobody will ever judge you for what happened or was about to happen or whatever. We all have asked Xavier and he refuses to share any details with us so I just thought you should know that." he said still never looking at me. "Thanks Jon you have helped me so much you have no idea." I told him as I put my arm around him. "Good now how about some breakfast lady?" he said laughing. "Sure I'll take whatever you are fixing." I said laughing back at him

He threw a towel at me, "Fine." he said as he grabbed the sink sprayer. "Hey you better not." I said hoping he wouldn't. It was to late he sprayed me with water and I chased him around the kitchen flipping over chairs to slow him. We came to a sliding stop at the sound of Xavier clearing his throat. As Jon stopped I slid on the water and we both went to the floor laughing, "Guys are we having fun or what?" X asked as we looked up at him from the floor. "Sorry Xavier we didn't mean to wake you." Jon said getting up and helping me to my feet. "You didn't Sweets did when she got up from the couch." Xavier said looking at me. "Morning Baby sleep well?" I asked. he shook his head yes at me, "You look like you have everything in order this morning." he said as he crossed his arms. "Jon started it I just flipped chairs over to slow him." I said and laughed. "I, X, she oh never mind I give up." Jon said as he took a seat. "Jon I know how she is she would have cheated to get you." X said putting his hands on Jon's shoulders. "I'll do the bacon but Jon has to finish the rest." I said starting breakfast. Xavier shook his head at me with a smile while I stole a piece or two of bacon. "Hey no eating of the bacon Piper that's for breakfast." Jon accused. "I'm not I swear." I said innocently. Xavier came over and kissed me softly, "Yes she did." he told Jon. "Wow you feel great today, I'm glad to have all of you back." X thought to me.

I kissed him under his chin, "Yep I feel so like myself today." I thought back as Mike and Sharon came in. "Good god Piper what happened your soaking wet?" he asked looking around. Jon and I busted out laughing, "They were playing making a mess in the floor its wet so careful." Xavier told them. Things got busy after breakfast with X and I heading out for a half day of work and I still needed to pack for our trip. When the work day closed we rushed home so dinner could be eaten together. "Will you take the little ones trick or treating while we are gone?" I asked. "There is no reason they cant have the same kind of childhood as the others in town." Xavier added. "That sounds like fun, it has been over a hundred years since I have been trick or treating" Mike said with a smile. "Good now don't eat all of their candy." I said smiling at him. "Have you packed yet Mom?" Tiff asked. "Not yet going after dishes." I told her. "Go on we will do the dishes." she offered. I thanked them and headed for the hall closet to get a bag so I could start packing. "Come on Sweetness lets get the little ones down so we can leave." Xavier called to me. "Ok ok I'm coming I have to get one more thing." I told him. I came in the living room to find Xavier covered in children, "My goodness where is your daddy I cant find him anywhere? Xavier where are you?" I called out. "Here he is Momma." Bastian said. "I found him for you Momma he was hiding right here the whole time." Brie said with her daddy's smile. "Thanks guys I'm so glad you found him for me." I said as I hugged them both. They shrieked in laugher that I couldn't find him as X took Jade, "She is getting bigger everyday, I bet when we get back she will be walking like LaStat." I told X. He looked up at me from the couch, "Sweets you knew she would grow like this she is just as special as the twins are. Please don't let this get you down I want you in good spirits when we leave." he said with a plea in his voice. "I know and I'm fine with it, I cant change it so I have to accept it." I said as I took a seat with him holding Jade.

It never took long for the children to fall asleep with Xavier's own kind of magic. We tucked them in and went to give the brood a few instructions before we left. "Take the kids out trick or treating watching them always. If you need us call but only if it is important, try to handle it on your own if possible." X told them. I hugged and kissed the entire brood and I could tell I was taking to long because X was about to bust with excitement holding the door open for me. "I hope you like this place it isn't the Smokey Mountains but I didn't think you would want to be far away from the Great House." he said pulling up at the cabin. "I love it already." I told him. He took my hand to lead me along so we could drop our bag off and go for a hunt before night left us. He laid on the bed and watched as I dressed in one of his button up shirts and then joining him. He slid his hands up the back of my shirt and his touch was magical to my body. We made love until the moon rose in the night bringing the end of the second day. "Happy Anniversary my Love." he said as I laid in his arms. "Happy Anniversary I love you." I told him. "What shall we do for the day?" he asked. "Its still night there is nothing to do Love but watch movies." I said with a smile. "We are vampire night and day are the very same for us. Either way I have your gift but I can wait to give it to you when the sun comes up." he said picking on me.

I sat up in the bed and clapped my hands, "No no you can give it to me now there is no need to make you wait is there?" I said with a evil smile. He laughed at the sight of me clapping my hands like a school girl, "I hope this pleases you." he said as he handed me a thin box. "If you had wrapped yourself in a ribbon that would please me to eternity." I said as I took the box. I opened to find bracelet with six diamonds and six amethyst stones that matched our rings, "One stone for every month you have been the best part of me." he said smiling. "Oh Xavier it is beautiful I love it. Now for your gift keep in mind that you are a three hundred year old vampire who has everything so getting you something was a chore. I can only hope you like it." I told him. "I'm sure whatever it is I will love it." he said laying on his back and putting his hands under his head. I handed him a tall box and watched him unwrap it. "Its called a Night Blooming Cereus. The flower only bloom by the moonlight." I said quickly as he looked the flower over not saying anything. "Umm I just thought since we got married, conceived our twins and had all three children under the full moon that you would like this." I said lightly thinking he didn't like it. "I love it Sweets I shall plant it in a planter in our bedroom so I can see it always." he said as he attacked me and kissed my face all over. "Ok ok I'm glad you like it." I said laughing. "I'm hungry are you Sweetness?" he asked. I shook my head yes and raced for the shower but he was faster and beat me there. "What would you like for dinner, eat in or go out?" he asked as he hogged all the water. I slid under his arm to steal some water, "Lets get something quick so we can come back here, unless you are more hungry than that." I said. He agreed as we play fought over the water and of course he won and was out before I could get finished.

I dressed and met him in the bedroom, "Finally, are you ready?" he asked laughing. "What are you laughing at you wouldn't share the water. Your lucky I didn't stay in there longer." I said as I jumped on him. He pushed my wet hair out of my face so he could kiss me, "Are we eating junk or real food?" he asked. I could feel that he wanted more hungry than he let on, "Lets go to Applebee's so you can have a steak." I said. He smiled at me, "If that is what you want then you shall have it." he said. "You don't have to give me everything you know, you could have said I want steak. I would have went wherever you took me like I've told you to the fiery pits of hell. Although I do love getting my way all the time." I said with a smile and pushed him from a setting position to a laying one. He rolled me over to my back and kissed my neck, "Lets go I'm really hungry and after we will get you junk for later." he said. "Your not playing very fair are you Love?" I asked. "Nope I'm not and you don't either so lets go and then we can come back to bed." he said as he released his grip on me. Dinner was nice with just the two of us and not many knowing who we were. Nothing was said aloud just our thoughts between one another. Things came to a halt when we returned to the cabin to find cop cars there. Xavier got out of the truck "Everything alright Officer?" he asked. "No sir we need to make sure everyone is accounted for. Some hiker was found dead in the woods and we are asking that no one goes into the woods at night." he tall cop said. "Dead from what exactly?" I asked putting my arm through Xavier's. "Not sure Ma'am, it looked like they had their neck chewed on so we are worried that we might have a rabid animal or something. So please stay away from any animals that might come around until we find out what's going on." he told me. "May I take a look at the body?" Xavier asked as I flipped on some magic so we were not told no. "Well I don't see why not." he said with glazed over eyes.

Xavier unzipped the body bag and opened it up, "Vampires!" I thought to him. He shook his head "Yes it could have been a animal of some kind we wont go into the woods officer." X said shaking his hand. We walked back to the cabin together, "We shall wait until they leave and find this vampire responsible for this." he said unhappily. We sat on the porch and waited until all the cars pulled out. "Lets go out the back I'm sure he is still here. See if you can get a scent on someone." he said with a touch of demand. I closed my eyes and took a deep breath to smell the air, "Up there to the left of the woods it is only one scent and its old blood I get. This one knows what they are doing so approach with ease." I told him as we started the run. Xavier ran at top speed with me right behind him, "Slow he knows we are coming and he is preparing." I told him. He slowed his pace as we neared the stranger, "We know you are out here, show yourself!" Xavier said with demand. The over sized stranger showed himself, "What do you want?" he asked keep his eye on both of us. "We want you to leave and never return to these parts!" Xavier said with force. "And who are you to make such a demand?" he asked. "I'm King Xavier Matthews and my Queen. We rule these parts and you are not allowed to kill humans here, if it is humans you want you will leave the states altogether." Xavier said getting pissed. "You think I fear you King? Your rules mean very little to me, I do what I wish when I wish." he said smugly. "You almost exposed our kind to the humans and that would interfere with our way of living. You will leave or you will die, your choice!!" Xavier said working up an anger. "Stay calm he is getting a kick out of you getting angry. Put yourself back together he is planning to attack one of us he hasn't made the choice yet." I thought to him. X put his hand on me and pushed me back some, "This one is well seasoned don't allow him near you." he thought to me.

I stepped back right about the time the stranger took out of the trees with lighting speed and straight for Xavier. They fought back and forth as I kept a read on the strangers mind and he was planning to kill Xavier. I kept Xavier informed with his every move so X could keep the upper hand. I could smell Xavier's blood as the stranger scratched his skin tearing it open, "X if you are going to kill him do it now. RIGHT NOW!!!" I screamed into his head. He never hesitated and killed the stranger quickly burning his body and any evidence that he was even there. He took my hand pulling me along, "You need to feed so that you heal." I said easily. He didn't answer me just kept walking fast. I pulled him to a stop, "Feed now or else, you need to heal." I demanded. He looked at me then took the nearest prey to feed on leaving his skin beautiful once again. "I hate killing good or bad, why wouldn't he just leave? This goes against everything I believe in I'm a doctor for god sakes I make people better." he said looking at the ground. I sat next to him, "Look you had no choice but to do this, he was a killer and had to be stopped. Kill one save many I know that don't make it right but this is your rightful duty." I told him. We made our way back to the cabin where he showered as I put in a movie and got dressed for bed. "Hey I'm sorry about tonight, it seems like every time we try to have a relaxing moment something goes crazy." he said as he laid on the bed. "Its fine you are king and this is something you must take care of for your people, human and vampire. Come on lets watch this movie we can still have a good time." I told him. We woke to the sounds of car doors shutting as the cops showed back up to look things over for the day, "Lets go for a walk this morning." he suggested as he rolled on his stomach. I agreed to his wishes knowing he wanted to make sure things were covered up from last night. After he searched the grounds we headed back to the cabin, "I'm not ready to go home, I feel like I owe you another day." he said. "You don't owe me anything I had a wonderful time. I'm sure Bastian and Brie wore out the house and they are looking forward to us coming home." I told him. "I bet Jade had the Great House on the move this weekend." he said smiling. He remained quiet on the drive home and I knew he felt bad about the stranger in the woods. It doesn't bother me that he had to fulfill his duties it was a part of our lives and I was always accepting of that. He took my hand while I was deep in thought, "Thanks Sweets for understanding me." he said kissing my hand. "Do you always read my mind?" I asked with a smile. "Yes when you let me in that is, I love to know what goes on up there always. I hate it when you lock me down from your mind and feelings." he told me. "I don't mean to sometimes but other times I do because they are feelings from others and they hurt. Then you ask me to share and I don't like doing that because I hate to put you through that." I told him.

Chapter 26

Home was right around the corner and I was feeling good about seeing everyone again. I was deep in thought about Jade knowing she would be walking and talking just like the other children. Wondering always what was new in the Great House and what they all have done over the weekend. "What?" I asked when I noticed X looking and smiling at me. "You always think about the kids?" he asked. "Do you know what I think about when we are apart?" I asked. "Sometimes I know and sometimes you shut me out." he said with a tone of wonder. "I'm always thinking about you and what you are doing. When I shut you out I can still see what you are thinking always. I always shut the kids out all the time never do I let them in." I told him. "All the kids all the time never slip?" he asked. "Even when I sleep they are on lock down and I can still read them even Mike." I said. "Mike has always been very hard for me to get a read on very hard headed I told him." he said laughing. "Now that I'm stronger I can pick up on him right now." I informed him. Xavier looked at me with surprise, "What is he thinking?" he asked. "Lets see he is happy today him and Sharon has had a good day. He is excited to have us come home although he will never show it. Oh yea he always has the little ones on his mind everyday all day." I said smiling. "That is amazing." he said. "Please don't tell him, if he knew he would be upset." I begged him. "Never would I tell him." he said taking my hand. I sat there still in thought knowing that anyone I chose to read I could and the store was the worst place for me to be when I was open like this.

We pulled up in front of the Great House with the whole family coming out to greet us. "Momma, Daddy you are home." Jade, Brie and Bastian said together. "My angels come let me see you." Xavier said bending down to pick them up. "Me too?" LaStat asked in Latin. "Yes you too Son." Xavier said holding out arms for him. I waited my turn for each to be let go from X so I could see them myself. "Look Momma I can run like the others, I have missed you." Jade said with her voice like mine when I used magic. "Jade you have grown so big over this weekend, have you been good for your elders?" I asked. "Oh yes Momma I have been very good. Aunt Cyndi wouldn't let me hunt with the others she said I had to wait until you and Daddy got back." she said sweetly. "Your Daddy would love to teach you how to hunt." I said smiling at her. All the others made way over to greet X and myself except Mike, he held back like always. I made way to the porch and hugged him first, "I think I have missed you the most ya know. If you and Sharon would like a night to yourselves that would be fine, I'm sure we can do dinner without you tonight." I said letting go and walking inside. "Mike man how was it?" X asked putting his arm around his shoulder. "Not bad Jade kept up well, Piper is glowing I take it you all had a good time?" Mike asked. "I know it I love it when she feels this good inside. We had a small problem with a human feeding vampire but we put a stop to him." X told him. "Did Piper get upset?" Mike asked. "Na she was very understanding as always, she would have been upset if we had to come home." X said.

I put our dirty clothes in the washer and went to put our bag away, "Hey Jade wants you to teach her to hunt she is ready." I told him as he walked up on me. "As you wish." he said looking for Jade. The twins blew past me with Xavier chasing Jade into the kitchen, "Are we all going or just the few us?" I asked. "I don't see why we all cant go together." X said in a tone that no one would object. I watched Xavier teach Jade as she jumped around playing with everything she could find. "Jade baby you have to look for something and catch it." X told her. I watched her glide towards her prey just like Xavier who was graceful in everything he done. She would show the family her power as she moved things around with her hands. "Are we fixing something at home tonight or getting something?" Bailey asked. "Lets have dinner here tonight." X suggested. Dinner took place with Mike staying like I knew he would and I was looking forward to my very own bed. I tucked the children in bed and met X in the hallway, "Come on." he said with a smile. "You are up to no good what is going on?" I asked. "You will have to wait and see Sweets I have a surprise for you." he said pulling me along. He opened the bedroom door and stepped aside for me to go in first, "When did you have time to put this in here?" I asked when I saw a large couch. "I ordered it and had the guys put it in here for you. You had said that you missed laying on the couch with me so I thought . . . ." he said. "Come on lets try it out." I said pulling him along.

I waited for him to lay and then I joined him, "So you are pleased then?" he asked as he tightened up on me. I kissed him and snuggled closer, "Yes very pleased." I said. I didn't get to sleep very long because of the feelings that overwhelmed me. I slipped out of Xavier's arms and walked the halls of the Great House to find my pain. Stopping by every room just to feel and then sneaking into the dreams of the children but still nothing came to me. I walked down the steps and found Mike by the picture window looking out, there is where the pain hit me the most. I took in a deep breath, "Mike?" I asked softly. "Don't come any closer." he said not looking at me. "As you wish." I said as I backed off. I stood there and waited for only a few minutes then turned to leave, "Damn it Piper I wished you wouldn't have came down here." he said harshly. "I'm sorry Mike I was looking for the . . . ." I said before he interrupted. "I know what you were looking for." he said and drifted off. "Yes it woke me and if you wish me to leave I will." I said knowing he was dangerous if he chose. I waited for him to make up his mind, "I'm sorry I shouldn't have jumped at you. I am just having a hard time with something and I wanted to work it out on my own. You know I don't like to share anything with anyone and now I have to." he said now looking at me. "Then I shall leave you and that feeling will pass in a minute." I told him turning to leave. He rushed the door so I couldn't leave him. I stepped back, "I could get Xavier for you if that is what you wish." I said and tried to pass him again. He moved to block me, "I know you don't fear me so just wait I'll tell you." he said. "Alright I'm waiting." I said softly.

He gave me a small chuckle, "I hate telling anyone anything but for some reason you are different. I have asked Sharon to give me children." he said and waited for my reaction. I wasn't sure what to say at this moment so I waited. "She said no, I don't want children we have plenty with Piper and Xavier's not to mention Cyndi and Baileys boy. I don't want the burden of being pregnant then dealing with all that comes with it not to mention the raising it. Can you believe that she told me no, no one has ever told me no and I don't like it!!!" he said yelling this time. I could feel Xavier's panic with me being gone form his side and Mike yelling downstairs. I didn't have time to inform X that things were fine before he and Sharon hit the living room door at the same time. "Get out of my sight, you will leave me be!!" Mike yelled at Sharon. Xavier came to my side, "Sharon I think it is best if you return to your room." X told her. She looked at all of us and did as she was instructed to, "What the hell is going on down here Mike, why are you yelling at Piper like that?" X asked in his protective voice. "I'm not yelling at Piper, Xavier I'm just yelling. Don't let her come back down here I don't want to see her at any measure!!" Mike said still yelling.

I stepped closer to Mike and he backed away, "I don't have to touch you to get what I wish, you know that. I was just coming to you for any comfort you may need." I told him in more of a motherly tone this time. "Wait just stay away." he said holding his hand up with me waiting. He dropped his hand and came to me putting his face in my shoulder, "Mike this is something that she may change her mind on later you mustn't give up so easily." I told him. "I'm so mad right now that I could die. When you and Xavier had the twins I knew I had to have a child of my very own. That's why I spend so much time with them, I wait for the chance for you to ask me to watch over them even if it is for a minute. When you had Jade and asked all of us to watch her I had her the whole time and put her back before you found out. I love Sharon but is she refuses me I will chose another mate, I will not spend the rest of my days on this earth without a child." he said with more sadness this time. "Listen Honey don't make up your mind just yet give her a chance to give her side. I bet after she said no you stormed out, am I right?" I asked. "Hell yes I did I didn't want to be around her any more. I don't like to be told no and I don't like that I'm not a father or soon to be. The last time I was told no they didn't have time to change their mind." he said. "Mike you must learn to control your temper and learn to talk a few things out." I told him. Xavier was setting there soaking in the way I handled him, "I cant believe this he would have ripped the house down by now. I have never seen this side of him before he don't deal well with things like this." X thought to me. "It is very deep this time." I thought back. I waited for Mike to finish needing me while I used very little magic on him, "Sweets don't use on him if he finds out he could hurt you when he feels like this." X thought to me. "Mike Honey listen I have to be very truthful, if she don't want children and this makes you unhappy you must let her go and find another." I told him softly.

He let go of me and stepped back, "I know you speak the truth but . . . ." he said and stopped. I showed him a seat next to Xavier on the couch as I took a seat across from them. "Why cant I have what you two have? I have the same heart as you both have, why cant I have the same love you share?" he asked much calmer. Xavier took a deep breath, "Mike maybe she isn't the one for you. I was lucky to find Piper but as you well know I waited on her forever and she was human." X told him. "What are you saying Xavier that I should find a human mate, you know I cant do that. I could never change her even if I wanted to I would be to weak, you know my past." Mike said with shock. "I'm not saying that exactly but if this don't work out with Sharon maybe you could think about it. Maybe if you wanted a human mate Piper can help you with that I know you don't like her using on you but she can help in many ways. Besides the past is the past you are much stronger now." X said with me agreeing. I stood up to stop Sharon from coming in, "Now is not a good time you must stay away." I said moving her backwards. "But Piper he said he was going to find another maybe a human please help me." she said quickly. "Sharon why don't you want children?" I asked. "Your not very shy are you?" she said. "I could tell you why you don't want children but I was giving you a chance." I said getting upset with her. "I like to do fun things when I wish and I have seen you and Xavier give up for your children. I don't want Mike to go looking for another mate even human one, he is very handsome and it wouldn't take him long." she said. "I know a few that would give their right arm to even speak to him and if you like to do as you wish on a whim then you must let him go and find you another. I would give up anything for any of my children and that includes Mike but this is something you both need to talk about together." I told her. "Who are the humans that want to meet him do I know them?" she asked. "He don't know therefore I wont tell you." I said harshly. With Mikes feelings and my own I was getting upset with her. "Come on Sweets I think he can talk to her now." Xavier thought to me when he came to the door. "No I'm not leaving." I thought back. "Sweetness don't make me come and get you to hold you down all night. This is between them only and you know that." he demanded. "Fine I'm coming." I said turning to him. I patted Mike on the shoulder as I passed him on my way back to bed, "You go on to sleep Love." I said as I laid down. "Wait, what your not sleeping?" he asked with surprise. "No and I'm really not that tired any more, most of the time I lay here and watch you sleep. I'm going to keep up with the things down stairs for a bit." I told him. "No you are going to lay here and try to sleep you need to rest or you will crash. This is between them and you are going to stay out of it, now Piper I mean it." he said with royal tones. "I'll lay but I'm not sleeping." I said. He gave in knowing he would lose this fight as he put his arms around me.

I laid there watching him and he watched me, "You know I think you are the most handsome man in the world." I told him. "You think so, I don't see anything special just me." he said. "You need to look harder, you are the best part of me." I said. "You are the very best part of me, you make me who I am. Can I tell you something without you thinking I'm crazy?" he asked. "Sure Love anything." I said putting my head on his chest. "Do you know why I have to touch you a little all day?" he asked. "If it is the same reason I do then yes." I told him. "I have to touch you so that I make sure you are real, my body aches when I cant touch you like my heart stops beating. Sometimes I lay here and watch you so that you don't disappear from my life. I love you like no other could forever." he told me. "I feel the same way when you are not near me like I was empty even when I was human." I said. "You will never feel empty again because I'm here forever." he said kissing my head and falling asleep. I laid there listening to him breath which made me very comfortable waiting on the sun to rise. I knew that if I tried to slip out X would be on me real quick. Morning came with Sharon's voice, "Xavier, Mike has left and I don't know where he went!" she said screaming. X hit the floor with both feet getting dressed quickly, "What happened last night?" he asked as she came in with a note that read . . .

> Xavier and Piper,
>
> I need to be alone for awhile, I have to do this to make sure my life is on the right path. Please don't try to find me, I have put my feelings on lock down so Piper wont be able to detect me. Give the little ones all of my love and tell them I will return to see them again.
>
> Love you all,
> Mike.

Xavier turned to me, "Piper I know you can call him make him come back." he said. "No not this time he will call me when he is ready." I said. Sharon looked at me with horror, "Piper what the hell is wrong with you call him?" she asked. "That's enough Sharon!" Xavier warned her. "If he told you what I think then he needs to come home please try?" X asked. "He will be fine I'm not going to bring him home right now he needs this time trust me." I said making way to the door. "Sweets wait." he called to me as I hit the front door. Bastian stopped him at the door, "Let her go she is having a hard time with Mike leaving." he told his father. "You already know about Mike?" X asked the kids. "We all do he is very sad right now." Jade told him. I walked for awhile and put my mind at ease with Mikes thoughts running through me. Some of his thoughts were very sad and some were of him thinking about a human mate. Mostly the child he wanted and Sharon thinking that maybe she wasn't the one for him after all. I knew that if I tried to connect with him that he would go further to get away from my power. I made way back to the Great House to have breakfast with the family. "Hi my angels did you rest well?" I asked the four children. Everyone looked at me for any answers but I gave nothing, "Um Piper do you think that maybe you should try and talk him home?" Gina asked when she pulled me aside. "What have you seen?" I asked knowing that she has seen. "This thing between him and Sharon has put him in a bad state of mind very conflicted. He is watching female humans and wanting to bite one of them but not stopping at the one. Very hard to pin point where he is because he is moving around a lot." she told me in a whisper. As she stepped off Xavier stepped up and pulled me out of the room, "That's it Piper I'm demanding that you call him home." he said as he had me by the arm. "You are what?" I asked with warning. "I heard what Gina told you and you know what I'm asking so do it now!" he said with a lot of power behind his tone. "I have told you that I'm not doing this he will call me before he does anything rash. Don't order me like I'm one of your subjects!" I said pushing his hand off of me. "Piper you don't know how hard it was to stop him the first time and if there is a female involved he will not give in so easily." he told me. "If I feel that he is going to do something I will intercept him trust me." I told him. "As you wish, I hope your right." he said as we went back into the kitchen. Xavier gave a nod to the others so they would get a move on for the day and focused on my mind, "Stop that Love I'm keeping up with

Mike right now, wait your turn." I told him with a smile. "I can see him through your mind I can feel him." X said with his powers getting stronger. "Conflicted isn't he? I swear he will return and if he gets into trouble I'll fix it." I told X.

Chapter 27

It has been a month and a half since Mike walked out to find himself, "Sweets do you still have Mike on your mind?" X asked. "Yes he is in Massachusetts right now in Salem. Don't worry he will be calling soon enough." I told him. Sharon stayed in the room most days but today she came out looking for me, "Piper I think I should go home for awhile." she said. "I think that is a fine idea, and if he returns you should let him come to you when he is ready." I told her. "I think your right I thought he would have been back by now." she said. "Well he hasn't and I don't know when he will be home." I said as Cyndi walked by. "Come Sharon I will help you pack and take you home." Cyndi said knowing I was still mad at her. Xavier and I went to our room, "You need to sleep tonight Sweets it has been months since your last rest." he told me as I laid with him. "I don't need to sleep right now and I don't want to sleep." I said loving on him. We shared each other for the first time in a while since we haven't had the time. "I love this couch." I told him as he looked at me with glowing blue eyes. He always made it special on the bed never the couch but tonight we tried something different and it was wonderful. "Sleep Love I'll be right here for the rest of the night." I told him as the night grew short. I played with his hair till he fell asleep and I could tune Mike in again. Just about sunrise I could hear Mike calling for me, "Mike I'm here are you alright?" I asked quickly. "I need you to meet me halfway, will you do this for me?" he asked. "Yes but you know Xavier wont allow me to come alone." I informed him. "X may come as well but when we talk I want just you." he said. "Yes I'm coming hang in there." I told him.

I woke Xavier, "Hey come on we can go get Mike today. When we get there he only wants to see me alright?" I said as I got up to tell Cyndi. When I made it to the lower floor X was waiting on me and we headed for the Charger. Finally we reached the halfway marker that Mike set up for us, "Keep me on I want to hear everything." X said as I left from him. "You bet we will be right back." I told him. I walked to the shadows to meet him, "Mike you alright?" I asked. "Where's Xavier?" he asked quickly looking over my shoulder. "He isn't here its just me like you asked." I told him dying to hug him. "I'm not coming home and I didn't want to tell you this over the phone or our thoughts. Don't come any closer Piper I'm warning you." he said hatefully. "The children miss you, why aren't you coming home?" I asked still moving close to him. "Piper I mean it I don't want to hurt you!" he demanded. I put my hand up to calm him, "I'm tired of this nonsense, get in the car before I make you! You will come home with me today!!" I said full of demand. "I'm not coming home I have found another and I'm staying." he said. "Mike she is not the one for you and you wont be able to stop at her. Either you come willingly or I will make you." I told him. "You cant make unless you touch me and I will never allow you near enough." he said smugly. "I have known all you have seen and done while you were gone and I could have made you come home weeks ago, I just chose not to and let you work this out on your own. If you try to leave me I will stop you and just to let you know Sharon has left the Great House. Now shall we?" I asked. "Fine I will come home for awhile I do miss the little ones." he said giving up.

We drove back to Xavier, "So if you had me this whole time why didn't you make me come home?" he asked. "Even though Xavier demanded me to make you come home I thought you should work this out yourself. I know you could have worked this out at home I don't see why you had to leave." I told him as we pulled up at Xavier. "Mike I'm so glad to see you again man, things better now?" X asked. "No but I thought it best to come along since Piper is making me." Mike said with a smile. "She has a way of getting what she wants even without her magic doesn't she?" X said. The drive wasn't as long this time since Mike was right behind us and I was feeling better already. "I thought you were going to lose him when you demanded him in the car." X said as he drove home. "It wouldn't have mattered he would have came my way I would have made sure of that." I told him as I took his hand.

When we returned home the Great House was waiting outside to greet us. The entire house was happy to see Mike and ran to greet him except Brielle, "Brie are you not coming to give me a hug?" Mike asked her. She put her hands on her hips, "No I'm not, you left me here without a goodbye hug or kiss and I am very mad at you." she said with a frown on her face. He got on his knees and put her face in his hands, "Brie I couldn't hug you because you were sleeping. However I did look in on all of you and touched your faces before I left. Please Brie I cant live very long knowing you are mad at me, please forgive me." he pleaded. That was all it took she was in his arms and the both of them on the ground laughing. I led the way back into the house with Brie and Mike being last, "Thanks." Mike simply said as I smiled at him.

Days went by with everyone doing whatever they wanted and Mike staying in his room. "Momma maybe Mike needs to walk like you do sometimes. I miss him and you said that we are all to have dinner together and you allow Mike to stay in his room." Brie said looking at me. "I know but he isn't better just yet and soon he will be down with us. Maybe I can go check on him would you like that?" I asked. She shook her head with delight knowing that I could make him join us. I went upstairs and knocked on his door, "Mike may I come in?" I asked. "I was wondering how long it was going to take you to get up here." he said as he showed me in. "I'm here in Brie's place she is so worried about you and she wants you to come down. You know it is just an invite that's all she will understand." I told him. "I've just had a lot on my mind over the past few days but I'm sure you already know that." he said. "No I have shut you down so I will stay out of this." I told him. He narrowed his eyes at me, "You think that I should talk to her?" he asked. "Do what you feel is necessary to feel better, I cant tell you what to do this time." I said setting down. "Thanks Piper you are no help this time, you have always have the right answers so why not now?" he asked. I took a deep breath, "Fine call her and have this talk. Don't demand anything of her you are a prince of this royal family and she will comply to you but neither of you will ever be happy." I told him as I stood up. "Thanks Piper I think I will talk to her." he said as he passed me to call her. I returned to the kitchen, "Mike wont be joining us today so we can go ahead." I said as I passed the helpings around.

We could hear the Charger start up and pull out with Brie jumping up and heading for the door, "Brie he will be back he has something to take care of so we will see him much later tonight." I told her as I went to bring her back to the table. Tiffany tried to change the subject by asking X to help her with her math homework and him agreeing. I kept up with Brie's thoughts as she worried about her most beloved uncle Mike. I gave her a wink as I started to clear the table, "Come on Brie lets find something to get into before Mom finds out." Bastian said trying to make her feel better. Mostly because when she hurt so did he, their ties to one another was like no other. After everybody cleaned up and went on doing what they wanted I offered the little ones some bath time fun. LaStat talk about many things with me and the twins in many many different languages. I was learning quickly as was the house the many languages that he would teach us. When ever he spoke them we just knew what he said and how to answer. Not many of our kind knew the dead languages that he taught us and that worked out for us. "Ok kiddos time for rest." I said getting them out of the water. LaStat ran to his mommy to tell her of bath time bubbles and the mess he help make. Soon the Great House became lazy as the evening grew long. "Maybe I should call Dorien about you not sleeping." Xavier said as he laid down waiting on me. "There is no need I will sleep when my body tells me to, its not like I force myself to stay awake. Besides I would rather keep this between us of you wouldn't mind there are things that I have to work out on my very own." I told him as I laid with him. "What kind of things, am I allowed to know?" he asked softly. "Sleep Love you are very worn tonight." I said brushing off his request.

He put his face in my neck and stated to breath in hopes that I slept as he did but still I lay there waiting for the new day. I hoped deeply that I didn't lie to my daughter about Mike returning she loved him as much as she loved her own daddy. He has a way with the children and he would play with them as if he too was a child sometimes. Finally I could feel Mike getting closer to the Great House and I rose to wait for him at the top of the stairs. He saw me when he entered and I smiled at him, "Are you coming??" he thought to me. I went down slowly as I could make myself go, I was ecstatic to have him invite me into his private life. I took a seat in the kitchen with him, "I talked to her telling what I truly wanted out of my eternal days on this earth and she didn't want to same. She said she had time to think about many things and that we shouldn't see each other anymore. For the first time I actually agreed with her not to say I didn't miss her while I was gone I did but I feel lighter about me if that makes any sense." he told me. "Yes I'm sorry that this had to happen and I'm very pleased that you are feeling better." I said getting to my feet so I would stay out of anything else he didn't want to tell me. "Where do you think you are going? I haven't felt this good in a long time and I thought we could go for a walk together." he said with a smile. I threw Xavier a little thought so he wouldn't worry and joined Mike on a midnight walk.

He was quiet for most of our walk together through the woods and town. "I was thinking that maybe if I came across a human female that I might try and talk to her. What do you think?" he asked. "Yes well I think you should take it slowly because of the trouble you had before. Now that you have many things in order and the strength you have gained over the years I'm sure you will be just fine. There is one thing that you must remember even though she is human she will want to know things about you like hopes, fears, dreams, trust me I wanted to know these things about X even after I found out he was a vampire." I informed him. He looked at me and smiled, "Were you afraid of him when he told you?" he asked. "To tell you the truth I thought he was just screwing with me knowing the love I had for scary movies, it didn't take me long to figure out he was telling the truth. You must understand that I was in love with him the very minute he spoke to me and I wouldn't have cared if he told me he was a zombie or something." I said with a laugh. Mike chuckled to himself, "How did X know you wouldn't run screaming?" he asked again. "Well I'm not sure but maybe the sisters had something to do with it, you will have to asked him." I told him as we made way back home. Many visions came to me as we walked and talked back and forth, "Hey you want to go to the store with us oh and the kids?" I asked. He gave he a smile and a nod knowing that he would get to take the kids to the toys and he could help pick out the most fun things. I slipped back in Xavier's arms trying not to wake him, "Sneaking out again Sweetness?" he whispered with his eyes closed. "Yes but Mike returned and wanted to go for a walk, your not upset with me are you?" I asked and kissed his lips. "Well not now." he said joking with me. I settled down in his arms and I got to rest never no sleep but rest will have to suffice for now. I knew that the things I had seen would come to pass for Mike even if he tried to fight it. I rose when the sun gave me a new day heading for the shower with X right behind me. I soon started breakfast as the small ones started hitting the bedrooms. The loudest screams came from Mikes room as the kids ran in to wake him and he jumped out from behind the door scaring them half to death. I felt a sense of relief that he was feeling better and now X and I could relax some. My feelings that I got from everyone was pure hell on Xavier sometimes for he has never felt so deep. The store was a crazy place for me and when I was with Xavier it got worse. Like him I didn't like others to look upon what was mine and I would do anything to keep him mine. "If you so dare to take them to the toys Mike you are a brave man." X told him as the four kids pulled him along. "If I'm not back in ten minutes send a search party will you?" Mike said smiling. Xavier smiled at him as we went to do the grocery shopping, "Nice to have him home he is my most trusted." X said halfway to himself.

It didn't take long before they returned with a toy for each of them, "Aunt Piper, Uncle Mike said we can have these toys." LaStat said. "Well then if your Uncle Mike said yes then yes it is." I told him as I ruffed up his sandy blonde hair. Many women watched Xavier as he was very graceful in everything he did even if it was just pushing a shopping cart. Few of the thoughts that I gathered were of Mike and who he was really since he didn't go out much. One young lady was watching Mike as if he was the only man left on this earth with him not noticing since he had the kids. She had her hands full a few things that she needed as I turned to her she went to walk off and bumped right into Mike sending her stuff flying. Mike without any thought caught her as she was about to hit the ground as well, "I'm so sorry." she said breathlessly. He gave her a crooked smile not knowing what to say as he stood her on her feet backing away some. She quickly started gathering her scattered items as he helped her, "Thanks for your help your very kind." she said with her very soft spoken voice. "Yes well you are welcome, here this is yours." Mike said almost speechless. "I'm Tesla by the way." she said offering her hand. "Mike I'm Mike." he said shaking her hand. Xavier came over and put his arm around me, "Sweets you didn't did you?" he asked. "No I would never besides I think she has him under her own kind of spell. Come Love he will be just fine, time for him to start trusting himself." I said pulling X along.

We paid for our things and headed for the car with Mike jogging up to us, "Hey sorry about that." Mike said. "Hey I know that feeling I've had that one before, when I saw Piper for the first time." Xavier said smiling. "Awe not you too, this isn't fair." he said putting bags in the truck. "Sorry Brother I can feel what Piper feels and most of what the others in the house feels." X told him. "Then I hope you don't mind that I invited her for pizza tonight." he said with a worried look on his face. "Dinner will be great, make sure you hunt before you go get her." I said. He smiled a smile that I haven't seen in a long time, "She is coming on her own thought that would be safer for right now." he said getting in the truck. We hurried home so we could get our affairs in order before Mikes human friend joined us for dinner. X gave a direct order for all to hunt before dinner that way there were no mistakes. Not that there ever has been but X wanted Mike to remain his loyal and stay happy. After a satisfying thirst quencher Mike went to shower as we could hear her pulling up. She slowly came up on the porch and knocked on the door softly, "Hi you must be Tesla? I'm Piper please come in and make yourself a home." I said with a smile. "Thank you for the invite to dinner." she said a bit unsure. "Your very welcome, Mike will be here shortly." I told her. She went into the living room where Tiffany introduced her to the family members as Mike come in, "Hey did you have any trouble finding the house?" he asked. "No trouble you give great directions." she said smiling at him. "What kind of pizza would you like we have to order so many here anyways so whatever you want is no trouble." he said quickly. "I'm sure whatever you like will be great." she said looking around the house. Mike was about to bust with excitement that she showed and now she was open to whatever he liked.

Chapter 28

Gina and Jovi went for pizza when we placed the order and Jon wasn't please that he didn't get to drive the Camaro. "Come on kids lets leave them alone we must wash up." I told them. Brie wasn't very happy about Tesla being there because it took up her time with Mike. After I finally convinced Brie that Tesla wasn't there to steal him away from her Gina and Jovi returned with dinner. "Come on guys I'm starvin." Jovi said on his way on the house. "My family sits around the table and talks about our day during dinner, hope that is alright." Mike told her as they walked in together. "I think that is really nice I wish we did things like that at my house. My dad isn't around anymore and well I don't think my mom really cares." Tesla said with a shrug. "Well its Pipers orders here." Mike said softly. Dinner went on as usual as we talked about most of the day with whatever was allowed since a human was in the house. We tried to leave Mike and Tesla alone as much as possible with Brie looking in on them as they walked out to the willow tree. "Hope to see you soon please come back any time." I told her as Mike walked her out.

She waved goodbye with a smile. "You have a great family, I had a nice time." she told him. "Yea the family thing came after Piper married Xavier, she is very demanding about the family getting together for dinner every night. It has been a long time since we had anything like this so ya know." he said and stopped. "What do you mean it has been a long time since you had the family thing?" she asked. "We used to be like this then Xavier's parents passed away and he went into a deep depression so we never pushed him, we just kinda did whatever. Hey enough about that I was thinking maybe you would like to come back for a movie. We set around in the back yard and watch movies on the back of the house like a drive in but at home, would you like that?" he asked changing the subject. "Sure I would like that maybe you can come and meet my mom not that she cares who I hang out with." Tesla said. "Sure now you be safe on your way home, see you soon." he said helping her in the car. We backed off from the window where X and I were watching him just in case he had trouble. "Well what do you think about her?" he asked when he came in. "Mike are you sure you want this, once you tell her there is no going back?" X asked him. I glared at Xavier to hush him because this was important to Mike, "I think she is nice and I hope you bring her back, have you decided yet?" I asked. "I thought it would be nice to have her back for movie night." he said smiling. "Well then shall we break out the blankets?" I asked. "Make sure she dresses well." X said not to sure if Mike could handle himself. Mike assured us that he would and went to play with the little ones. Soon it was bedtime and I laid there with X having a tight hold one me so getting up was not an option. Sometimes I couldn't wait to have the sun come up so I could get up instead of lay there although Xavier felt so good to me always.

Work started out well with folks in and out all day and Doc stopping by, "Dorien how are you today?" I asked when he came in. "Piper how have you been doing?" he asked. "I'm good busy as always. Are you looking for Xavier?" I asked smiling. "No I'm here for you today." he said now knowing that I didn't know. "Me what for I'm fine." I said. "You haven't been sleeping have you?" he asked swallowing hard. "No." I said crossing my arms and looking at Xavier coming in. "You didn't tell her I was stopping by did you?" Dorien asked Xavier. X shook his head no and smiled that seductive smile at me so I wouldn't kill him. "I'm not for sure why you haven't been sleeping Piper this isn't healthy." he said carefully. "Look I don't need to sleep I'm sure I will when my body says. Now if you will excuse me I have to get back to work." I said getting upset with both of them. "Sweets please don't get upset with me I just worry that you crash that's all." Xavier said stepping closer to me. I backed away from him as Michelle came into the room, "Fine you want to know then here it is. When I lay to sleep I can pick up on everyone in and around Hinton. When I say everyone I mean just that all the fears and tears that lay with them at their time of rest. The dreams that fill my body and what they feel as they sleep and dream. When Mike was on his little soul searching trip I was with him at all times and that took a lot out of me. Not including my children who share their dreams with me on a constant basis. Then there is Xavier who I feel the most, everything he feels. This is not bad it is just hard to stop all of it long enough to sleep that's all." I told them all.

The three of them just looked at me with wide eyes. "Are you telling me that when Mike was away you could still feel him, and the people near our borders?" Dorien asked. "Yes and I could have made him come home without any trouble." I told him. "This is amazing, I'm having a hard time believing this. Kaleb said that one day we would have a queen that could rule both humans and vampires with just emotion. I thought he was insane but look at our queen now Xavier." Dorien said with excitement. "Hey I don't know anything about that I have only tried it on just a few." I said quickly. "Yea she put a spell on her parents and went on about the weekend like nothing." X said with pride. "Your mind is a very powerful place but you still need to rest. Do you still cry real tears?" he asked. "Yea and when things gets real bad I can release a storm like no other has seen. Would you like to see what I can do Dorien?" I asked now very frustrated. "No thank you my Queen, you are a very special breed one that none has seen before." he said picking up on my tone. "So what do you think Dorien?" Xavier asked. "She will learn to deal in no time and she will sleep some I'm sure." he said getting ready to leave. I turned to Michelle, "We are having dinner and a movie would you and Trev like to come?" I asked. "Sure, are you and Xavier going to be ok your pissed right now?' she asked. "Oh he is in trouble but we ok." I told her walking out together.

With Xavier and Dorien still talking I took the time to walk home needing the time to think. I was mad as hell that X told Doc that I wasn't sleeping. I could hear Xavier walking close behind me and I could feel him, he knew I was mad at him. "Sweetness please wait for me." he called. "You should have told me that Dorien was stopping by today!" I said never stopping. He raced up and grabbed me by the arm to stop me, "Why didn't you tell me that you were dealing with all this?" he asked as he put his hands around my waist. "I didn't want you to know that's all. I knew that if you knew you would stay awake so I wouldn't feel you like I do when you sleep. Don't dare say anything to the kids and defiantly to the babies I like to see what they dream. I don't want to talk about this anymore." I told him as I started to walk on home. I knew he was working his special relax magic on me as he smiled and took my hand to walk home. We changed out of our scrubs and he went to start the grill with Michelle and Trevor showing up first. "Hey X can I use the Charger to pick up Tesla?" Mike asked coming in the kitchen. "Sure but make it a rush we have a movie to watch, hey you ok to do this?" X asked somewhat worried. "Sure I will hurry." he said looking at X then me. "Who is Tesla?" Michelle asked. "She is human who he is interested in he and Sharon broke up." I told her. "Awe that sucks." Michelle said. "Yea but it is for the best I guess." I told her as I munched on chips. Xavier came in the kitchen, "Hey stop eating chips." he said as he stole some for himself. "Hey now." I said smackin his hand. "Help!" Trevor said with the kids hanging off his legs. Xavier went to peel the kids off, "Come on guys you know he is not built like Daddy, you might break him somewhere." X said with a chuckle. "Sorry Uncle Trevor." they all said as they took off for their next victim.

Poor Bailey and Jovi they had to play hide and seek and chase me games. "Uncle Mike is back he is great at hide and seek." Bastian said. Mike was helping Tesla out of the car as the kids came running at vampire speed towards him, "Step back Tesla." Mike said putting her behind him. He picked them all up at the same time as they crashed into him, "Guys you know better than this, slow yourselves when Tesla is around." Mike told them with a warning tone. "Sorry Tesla we didn't mean to frighten you." Bastian said with his musical voice. "That's ok little one, you sure are fast on your feet." she said smiling at him. "Yea they can get like that when they see me coming." Mike said carrying them all. "I can take one if they will come to me." she offered. "I'll go to her Uncle Mike." Brie said. He turned and handed Brie to Tesla, "Uncle Mike is just as fast but he is best at hide and seek." Brie told her. "I like hide and seek, maybe we can play later." Tesla said smiling. "Brielle I will play later I want to get Tesla settled first, you go on and play." he told her giving her a look. "Awe that's ok Mike I can tell that they love you so if you will show me to wherever Piper is I can talk to her while you play with them." she told him. "If you are sure then Piper is in the kitchen, come on I'll take you." he said putting down LaStat, Bastian and Jade.

They came in the kitchen together, "This is Michelle she is Pipers best friend and she works with them at the office." he told her. "Nice to meet you." Michelle said. "Piper we need to have a talk with the kids, they came to me with vampire speed." he thought to me. "I know and

I will fix it, she is wondering how you knew they were coming you moved her back before she had them in sight." I thought back. "Think of something Sweetness before she asks." X thought to me. "Ok ok I'm getting to that." I thought back. "So Tesla hope you like steak." I said. "Sure rare if its not to much trouble. Is there anything I can help with dinner?" she asked. "Na we have it covered but thanks I can make Michelle help me." I said with a smile. "Hey now." Michelle said giving me a small shove. "Hey Love Tesla would like her steak rare." I told X as he came in. "Somehow I figured that." he thought to me with a kiss. "So what do you think about Mike you like him?" Michelle asked. "Yes he is handsome and very sweet to me and I like that he plays with the kids. Most guys don't do that kind of stuff these days." Tesla said with a smile. "Those kids are very important to him and he loves them dearly. Brie loves her Uncle Mike like crazy." Michelle said. "Yea I know he gave them a stern look outside but he loved on them anyway, it was so cute to see him do that. Most of the time he don't talk about the family so to see him interact with the kids makes me see a side that he is afraid to share I guess." Tesla said as Mike made way back over to her. "Mike has a hard time sharing personal things but give him some time I'm sure he will come around." I told her.

Xavier handed her a plate, "Hope this is what you wanted?" X said as I touched him. "I really like this setting around family thing it is nice." she told us as we sat to eat. "Sweetness likes it this way and she is very demanding that we give her what she wants." Xavier said smiling. "Why do you call her Sweetness?" Tesla asked him. "Well lets see she smells sweet to me like candy or sweet roses. She is my Sweets and I cant live without her or the way she smells when I get near her." he said touching me. "That is the sweetest thing I have ever heard." she said smiling at both of us. "Come on Tes lets get the blankets so we can start the movie." Mike said taking their plates. "You know it isn't hard to figure out if she can handle the news ya know." I thought to him. He smiled at me and gave me a nod, "I know." he said out loud. Movie time came and it didn't take the little ones long to fall asleep. Michelle and Trevor went on home after the scary movie was over and it was time for Tesla to be driven home. "Thank you guys for dinner and the movie, it was crazy fun to lay out here and watch scary movies. It is something I have never done before." she said as Mike walked her to the door. "You come back and see us you are welcome here anytime." I told her. "Are you ready for bed well rest?" Xavier asked me. "Sure I can lay until sunrise." I told him. "I'll stay awake with you tonight." he said. We laid on the couch together and I tried to put away many feelings as best as I could. "Do you know how soft you are to me?" he whispered to me. "No I sure don't." I said softly as he ran his fingers up and down my arm. "You feel like the softest satin in the world to me." he said still in a whisper. "Your sleepy Love you must sleep, I will be here all night long." I assured him.

He laid there fighting off my magic as I tried to make him sleep, "Lets go for a walk it may do you some good." he said setting up. "Alright then your it!" I said as I jumped up and out the window. I needed the head start because of his amazing speed, I knew he would catch me in no time. I headed for the highest ledge to wait for him, "Come find me." I thought to him. "I can smell you the sweetest you have ever been." he thought back as he looked up on the ledge. With a few quick jumps he had me in his arms, "You can always try but I would find you." he said with a smile. "Come on I want to show you something." I said pulling on him. I took him to the top of the hill side to a flat covered in lush grass. "Would you like to see?" I asked as I laid on my back with him joining me. "Most definitely." he said with a smile. I took my feeling of the times we have together and shared with him as the moon and stars brightened with every memory. "Well what do you think really?" I asked. "I think that you are amazing and I know that you belong to me." he said smiling. We laid there until the new day took the night away, "Come we have to get back." X said getting to his feet. "We have to hurry the children are stirring." I said heading to the shower and him right behind me. "You have to share the water Piper come on now." he said as I took up the water. Finally with him growing tired of waiting he picked me up and moved me out of his way, "That's cheating." I said. "You are a slow poke today." he said laughing. We just got finished dressing as the kids busted their way in our room, "Awe you are already up." LaStat said in French. "I'm sorry LaStat but I'm so glad that you come and seen me first." I told him in the same language he used.

I made my way through all the kids with kisses and hugs before they went for another. "Wait kiddos make sure you wait on Mike this morning, you must make him last." I warned. "Why did you make them wait on Mike?" Xavier asked as he put on his shirt. "He isn't alone, he is in his chair watching Tesla sleep and very content." I said as I opened my eyes. X looked at me and took my hand to lead me to Mikes room,

"This pisses me off he knows the trouble he had and allows her to stay the night." he said moving quickly down the hall. Xavier knocked on his door and waited on him to come out, "What the hell did you do?" X asked a bit to harsh I thought. "Nothing I swear, Tesla and her mother got in a huge fight and she asked to come back here. We watched movies until she fell asleep and I brought her up here while I sat in the chair. I thought you would know or at least feel what I was doing, I didn't mean to upset anyone." Mike said quickly backing away from X. "We went out for the night and just got back ourselves. Mike you could have hurt her you know the rules I placed for you and punishment if you fail me." X said. "That is enough he didn't hurt her and I'm sure he knows the rules." I told X stepping between them. "Wake her and bring her down." X demanded. Mike shook his head as we went down the steps, "Xavier Matthews don't speak to him like that he would never fail you for anything, he takes his loyalty to you to heart." I said stopping him on the steps. "Piper he had trouble with human blood many times and she is no different. If there happens to a difference she would allow him to do whatever he wished of her without even knowing what was going on." he told me. "Yes I know of the trouble he had and I know that he would die before he hurt her or you like that. He knows the damage would be to the family he loves so dearly if he would ever attack her." I told him. "I'm sure you are right but still he has rules he is to follow until I say other wise." he said moving down the steps.

Chapter 29

The smell of bacon filled the house like every morning with Bailey starting breakfast. "Good morning guys." Tesla said from behind Mike. The family looked at her and then Mike with wide eyes knowing that she was to go home last night. "Good morning Tesla sleep well?" I said breaking the silence. "Sure did I'm sorry about last night my mom is a hateful person. Hey did you guys see the moon last night it was so bright?" she said. Xavier put his arm around me and smiled, "Exactly what happened last night Tesla?" Xavier asked. "I went home and she had things to say she was drunk like always so I told her to shut up and she smacked me. She don't like it that I hang out with Mike she said that he was a bad guy that there were stories about this family. I told her whatever and I ran out and asked Mike to bring me back here. I know I should have asked you before I invited myself but you had already went to bed and I didn't want to disturb you." she said hoping not to get either of them in trouble. "Like I have said before you are welcome here anytime just a heads up would be nice not that we mind." I told her. "What kind of stories?" Gina asked with nasty thoughts running through her head. "I don't know I didn't want to hear them. I know what kind of people you are and you have been nothing but kind to me. Mike isn't a bad guy he is very sweet to me." she said holding things back some. Mike smiled at her. "Lets have breakfast I hate to have my cooking talents to go to waste." Bailey said breaking up and tension. "Will you be joining us for the Thanksgiving holiday?" Xavier asked. "Oh I don't know Mike and I haven't talked about it." she said shyly.

I knew she wanted to be invited and I knew Mike would be more worried asking her now her mom had said things about his family. "She will be fine if she hasn't asked you out right then she isn't going to. If you want her to meet Grams and Pops then invite her Mike by all means." Xavier thought to him. "Yes Tes I would most love to have you for Thanksgiving dinner, its your chance to meet Grams and Pops." he said. "Well then if you really don't mind I'll be here." she said with a large smile. Weeks winded down as the holiday approached with everyone running around getting ready. X and I worked everyday with Michelle who also would be there for dinner with Trevor. Mom and Dad were due tomorrow and I knew deep in my lasting heart Mike was wanting to tell Tesla the truth. "What am I to do at this point? She asks me questions weird ones sometimes and when we do things together she says things that make my mind wonder. I know that I cant live without her but she has to know the truth don't she?" he asked me while we had a warm cup together. "Yes she has to know the truth before this goes any further. Make sure the both of you are ready this is something that can ruin us if she freaks." I told him. "Then I shall tell her tonight." he said with a worried look. "Come and get me if you need anything." I said trying not to get into his business. "No wait I want you and Xavier there with me." he said. "Very well then I shall tell Xavier and we will be there." I told him as I went out the room.

I warned Xavier that Mike was going to tell Tesla tonight, "I thought this was going to happen long ago." he said. I asked the rest of the family to find something else to do while we talked to Mike and Tesla. None of them gave me any trouble and did as I asked. Mike came in with Tesla and they took a seat, "What's going on guys are we in trouble?" she asked. "No Tes it is I that want to talk to you for a minute." Mike said. "Ok is everything alright?" she asked nervously. "Yes but I have to tell you something and I need you to hear me out then you can say whatever you want." he said as she took his hand. "I'm sure whatever it is it will be ok." she said. He took a deep breath and stood up, "Tesla I'm very different than other guys that you know, we are all different here in the Great House." he said and stopped. "I know all I need to know Mike there is no need to go any further." she said stepping up to him. "We are different than say humans we are . . . ." he began. "Vampires right?" she asked. Xavier almost fell out of the chair we were setting in, "How, when did you know?" Mike asked. "I knew the second visit here at the Great

House. My mother told me some things and I started to pay attention so I just knew and I don't care I love you Mike no matter what you are." she said stepping up to him. "So you are alright with this then, me being a vampire?" he asked taking her hand. "Yes and I'm really glad that this is out in the open, I have asked many questions hoping that you would just tell me." she said smiling. "I feel so much better." he said.

"Well then if there isn't anything else we are turning in for the night." I said. "Good night." both said as we made way out of the room. "Do you think you may sleep some tonight Sweets?" X asked. "I don't know I try every night to put things out of my mind and body but it hasn't worked. My mind is so tired I think it is going to melt sometimes." I said laying with him. "I wish I could help you even in the smallest way." he said. "Don't worry yourself Love I will be just fine. The towns people are filling me up inside as we speak." I said looking away. He sat up and took my hand, "You walk and I will follow even if it takes all night." he said leading me to the window. I knew it was going to storm like crazy and soon but I needed to wait until my parents come and leave. Xavier tried to keep his feelings on lock down but I was so open that there was no way he could hide anything from me at this point. We made it back to the house as Mom and Dad was pulling up in front, "Hey Piper, Xavier been walking?" Mom asked. "Yep just getting some fresh air, how was your trip?" I asked as we hugged. "Wow we need to get inside there is a storm coming." Dad said getting their bags. X put his hand on my back and looked at me, "It is not all me Love the weather has a mind of its own." I thought to him as we walked inside. I ate very little this morning I was very tired at this point with all that has went on. Everyday there was a new feeling that I would get from someone who was worried or depressed. It was hard to tell the difference between the family or just the folks around town sometimes.

My mother who knew me very well was dying to ask me questions, "Mom you have something on your mind so lets have it shall we?" I asked. "You look like you haven't slept is everything alright?" she asked as she sat back and crossed her arms. That meant I was not to lie to her because if she found out there would be hell to pay. "Sure I sleep some, why do you ask do I look that bad?" I asked looking at the whole family. "You are beautiful as always." Xavier said quickly. "Its not that you look bad Piper I know you haven't slept in some time, this is not the first time for you. I am your mother you can talk to me about anything." she said.

"There is nothing to talk about I will sleep when time comes. Now if you will excuse me there is clean up that needs to be done." I said rising to my feet and cleaning up. "Xavier your turn." Mom said looking at me. "Don't drag him in this he has no idea what is going on right now and he wouldn't tell you anyways. Now is not the time to push me on this Mother. You know how I can get when I don't sleep and I'm sorry about that." I told her trying not to get pissed. She looked at Xavier who really didn't know what to say at this point, "Well Xavier what's going on?" Mom asked again. "I'm not sure Pat really she hasn't told me anything. This is better left up to Piper to talk to you about not me." he said softly. "Just drop it." I said walking out of the room. None of the children knew that I wasn't sleeping until Mom let the cat out of the bag. I didn't mean to be so hateful to my mom but there are things that I just couldn't tell her never. "Piper wait let me say something. You have a very powerful mind and you need to try to put things away as best as you can so you can rest. I know you Piper and I know your temper, you can be very loving but in the same token you can be very dangerous." she said with worry. "I know Mom and trust me I try every night but there are some things that just cant be put to rest right now. I lay and rest listening to Xavier breath and I relax to that some, and just to let you know he really don't know what is going on with me and I want it that way right now." I told her. "Ok then I guess I cant argue with that just promise you will come to me if need." she said. "I swear Mom." I told her. We decided to watch a movie since the rain was so bad today and the kids picked out something for everyone. Xavier held tight to me with Dad never making it through any movie. If you ever want him to sleep just pop in any movie and he was out like a light, instant sleeping pill. The kids would laugh at Dad and the way he snored while holding tight to the remote. "I'll be right back." I said getting up. Xavier gave me a feeling that let me know he was getting very worried at this point, "Just getting a drink be right back." I told him as he let go of my hand sliding his fingers off mine slowly.

I walked into the kitchen and got me a badly needed warm cup making my way out to the back yard. The willow was somewhat calling my name so I walked to where I felt like I needed to be. Many feelings washed over me as I walked through the yard and back woods. I found a tree, dug my nails in and sat on a branch. "Love I'm in the woods I need a few minutes so keep inside." I thought to him. "Wait I'm coming stay there." he thought to me. "Please stay in this is going to get very bad and please don't try to connect with me I beg of you." I thought to him. "As you wish just call on me if you need me I can be there before you finish the thought." he thought back to me. The winds almost didn't wait on me as it picked up with force. The clouds came in making the sky look like night as the rain pounded the earth as I shut my eyes and began shutting down my mind. I blocked the feelings as they come to me and I emptied my mind of all that has went on. With each crash of thunder and the strike of lighting my mind became lighter and lighter. My heart wasn't as full of worry and sadness that some were having, the dreams and disturbing visions that the dreams brought me. After about an hour and a half I finally began to feel like Piper again. I made way over to the nearest neighbor to see that if I chose to I could still feel and read minds. I opened up to the Great House and I could still feel all that I could ever desire. I felt Xavier pacing the floor with much worry searching for any sign of me, "I'm here and coming to you." I thought to him as I raced to the Great House and the arms I needed around me.

As soon as he saw me enter the clearing he came to me quickly putting his arms around me, "Where have you been, I have been worried about you. Did you get everything in order and why didn't you let me connect to you?" he asked. "I couldn't let you connect with me I needed to shut my mind completely down. I can still pick up on everyone that I dearly love so that is great." I told him. "I was coming to get you but Mike thought it best to leave you alone." he said. "Come on I have to change." I said leading him in the house. "Piper why are you soaking wet?" Mom asked. "Outside in the rain but I feel great inside." I told her. I was met at my bedroom door by all the kids, "Piper what went on out there, the power went out this time?" Mike asked since he was the oldest. "Everything is just fine much better so much that I think that I can sleep tonight. Now that I am better I can pick up on all of you so there is no hiding anything from me so don't try. Sorry Mike I know that you have a hard time with me knowing all you do this is something that I cant change." I told them. "That is alright Piper I have found its better to give you what you want." he said putting his hand on my shoulder. Bedtime followed shortly and I dreaded it to the fullest. "Whatever happens tonight you must sleep tonight." I told Xavier as I laid on the bed. "I will stay awake with you Sweetness." he said with silk words. "You have been awake far to long just to sit with me." I told him.

He pulled me close as I faced him, "Try not to force the sleep just let it come to you." he breathed up my neck. Xavier never took his silk hands off my body the entire night and before to long we both fell asleep, the first for me in months.

I finally woke to him watching me, "Good afternoon Sweetness." he said. "Is it really noon?" I asked as I stretched. "Yes and I told Tiff to inform your mom that you needed the rest and we would be down when you woke." he said smiling. "It felt so good to have at least one night even if it is the only night I get." I told him. "Well get up lazy we have dinner to eat." he said with a laugh. His voice and his laughter was complete bliss to me. Shower and dressed for the day before we went down to see the family, "Piper you look rested." Mom said with a smile. "Yes long over due, sorry I have slept so long on your last day here." I told her. "That's ok Honey you needed to rest, dinner is almost ready." she said. Tiffany told me that she learned how to make pies, that Grams showed them all how to make things for dinner. I was very happy for that Mom took the time to show them how to make dinner, learning from her would do them all good. "Piper how are you?" Jovi asked. "I'm good Jovi honey but what on earth are you wearing?" I asked smiling. "Grams gave me an apron so I didn't make a mess of my clothes and look I have a turkey baster and I know how to use it." Jovi said with a large smile. "That's great Jovi I'm very proud of you." I told him as I touched his young face.

Dinner was really good to me since I was in the right state of mind to enjoy it. "Hey I was thinking about something." I said as I ate. "What's on your beautiful mind Sweetness?" X asked. "I was thinking that maybe Mike and Jon could start taking on some of the Emails. We really don't have time to do them ourselves, and they can come to us before they make any severe decisions." I told Xavier. "That wouldn't be any trouble Xavier, it would take a lot off of you and Piper." Jon said. "I'm not sure if that is a good idea but if you think it is something we should try then we shall give it a trial run." Xavier said in an unsure tone. "That is what I wish." I said with a smile. "Then it will be done but they must come to us for any thing that they are unsure of." he said looking at them. "Thanks for allowing this Love, it will take some of the stress off." I said with a smile. He smiled that incredible smile that he has and kissed me. Just about then the coldest shiver went up my spine as I tightened up on Xavier's hand, "Something is going to happen, I can feel it." I thought to him. "What is it and when?' he whispered to me. "I don't know I can feel it deep inside the pain is killing me." I thought to him still holding so tight to him. We both excused ourselves from the table and he fixed me a very warm cup. "What do you feel exactly?' he whispered to me. "I don't know just something bad and I can feel what I'm going to feel like when it happens. Here you feel me and tell me what you think." I told him as I put my hand on his heart. The look on his sweet face was horrible as he felt what I was going through, "I'll get the boys in here." he said. "Please Xavier lets wait until dinner is over there is nothing to tell right now." I pleaded. "Promise me that you will tell me if it gets worse." he said as he put his silky hands on me to help relax me.

We came back to the table and took our seats at the table as I shut everyone down so only I was inside my head. Mike glared at me while trying to get in my head to find out what was going on. All the kids were wondering that very same knowing I would never leave the table unless it was bad. "Mike not right now Piper is working on something so stay out." X warned. "No I demand to know what is going on!" Mike thought to him. "I said not right now she is busy I will talk with you after dinner." Xavier said getting mad. The winds started to pick up and the rain poured hard on the house, "Sweets take a deep breathe and hold back, Mike and I are just speaking heatedly and we will stop." X thought to me. The rain pushed the clouds in to make the sky dark, the lighting and thunder was forceful this time. "Wow this is strange weather we are having." Tesla said without knowing my secrets. "Shhh Tes not right now, we will talk later." Mike whispered to her. She looked at me and figured that I wasn't doing so well. Out of no where a huge tree fell in the woods out back with a loud crash as I jumped to my feet. I headed to the back door so I could walk off the anger that ran through to me with the kids watching me along with Mom and Dad. Xavier was right behind me as I made way, "Back off!" I said kind of hatefully.

I was fighting the feelings inside myself as the winds tried to take down trees. I put my hands up trying to keep up many as they blew out of the ground I knew it was my emotions. I let out a painful scream as I fell to my knees and cried to release what was inside me. Xavier never moved a muscle as I finished crying myself better in the rain and lighting. As fast as it came on it stopped, "Lets go." I said somewhat harsh. As I hit the clearing I took my hand and swept the fallen tree back into the woods, "Sweets." X said. "What I didn't want that in my yard." I said taking his hand. "Well have you found out what is going to happen?" he asked. "Not yet but it will effect someone in the family I just know it. No one is to leave the Great House for any reason understand." I said with my royal tones. "I swear it to be done." he said walking with me. Everyone was inside the kitchen as I came in and I put my hand on my parents hearts, "I didn't see or hear anything." I said to them. "Now Mom and Dad do you have something to say?" I asked. "I didn't see or hear anything." they both repeated to me. I led the way for all to finish dinner with my poor parents glazed over. I looked at Mike who never took his eyes off me, "The very next time I shut you out stay out. If you and Xavier ever fight like that again both of you will feel my wrath understand me!" I said with demand. "Yes my Queen I understand never will that happen again." he said to me with his eyes down knowing I was disappointed in both of them. "Eyes on me Mike." I said standing up making a point. "I swear it to never happen again my Queen." he said looking me in the eyes. "Xavier." I said looking at him. "My apologies my Queen never shall it happen again." he said standing and looking me in the eyes as well. "I will take Tes home and hurry home." Mike said. "NO!!" both Xavier and myself said quickly.

Chapter 30

Both Mike and Tesla knew that I meant business this time, "Its not a problem I can stay the night." Tes said. "Good that makes me feel better." I said. When dinner came to a close I asked the boys to follow Michelle and Trevor home and then my parents. Mike grabbed my arm, "You had no choice in the magic you used on your parents." he said as I pulled away from him and went to my room. I slammed my door and laid on the bed to finish crying real tears for what I did to Mom and Dad. "Sweets you want me to leave or stay?" X asked as he came in. "Stay." I said softly. He laid on the bed and rubbed my back, "They are fine I checked on them for you like nothing ever happened." he said. "Still what I did was horrible." I said not looking at him. "I told Mike to never touch you like that. He is my brother and my loyal but to have him man handle you I wont stand for." he said. "He fears me and this is a test for the both of us. Each of the kids are drawn to me just like you are so this has to happen like this for awhile please understand. I belong to you and only you always." I told him. "Still I don't have to like it." he said as I looked up at him. "Your eyes have changed colors mixing the blue and green like sea water." he said looking deep into them. "They have many colors anger, sadness, and when you love on me. Your eyes change as well when your mad from blue to almost black." I told him. "Yes but this is one I have never seen before you never look me in my face when you hurt like this." he said. "Would it be to much trouble if we went for a cup?" I asked. He took my hand and led to the lower floor where all the kids were. Mike just glared at me and I could tell that he was angry at Xavier and me. He was angry at me for drawing him in like I do and at X for telling him not to touch me. He was also angry at himself because he was afraid that if he didn't touch me he would lose the connection we had.

I stared Mike back down trying not to lose my temper, "Whatever it is get a grip Piper." X said. "I don't like the way you are feeling Mike, you best get yourself under control. Don't you understand that I need you in this family and not to fear me? You are one of the strongest of the young ones, please keep yourself that way. I know that Xavier gets upset when you have to feel me under your hand but if this is what is needed so be it, I will handle X at all costs." I thought to him. "I hate giving you what you want and I don't know why. I love you deeply like a sister or even a mother but I have to feel you some and I fear the day Xavier grows tired of it for he may kill me. You are his everything and he has killed for you and will do it again. I know deep in my heart that I need this more than anything right now. You hold a magic spell over me without even trying and I would do anything you ask of me at all cost even die for you. I'm sorry I hope to grow from this need quickly." he thought to me as he looked at Xavier who heard everything that we both talked about. Mike touched me on the arm and removed himself out of the room as Xavier growled at him. Everyone stepped back at the sound X gave making the room echo with his deep growl.

I stepped in front Xavier as he started to follow Mike, "Let me go Piper." he said with anger and demand. "Not this time Love I need the both of you at your strongest. I need you to trust your brothers with everything even me. Whatever this thing is that's coming we need all of us together. There will be a time I need you to take control over me even when I say I don't need you." I told him always touching him for comfort to both of us. "Fine I will let this go for now but I will keep you even if it means the cost of my brother." he said hatefully. "This will pass soon enough, we are stronger together than apart and if we fall then we are doomed to whatever comes our way." I told him. "I'm sorry Sweets I will try to do as you wish but I will never loose you, we will be together loving one another forever." he thought to me as he put his hands around my waist. Bedtime was a blessing to me even though I may not sleep, "You are to sleep tonight Xavier." I said heading to the shower. "No way I'm sleeping after the night we had. I know you the very minute that I sleep you will sneak out." he said laying on the bed. I gave him a sly look over my shoulder as I went into the bathroom. I let the water run over me as long as I could to clear my thoughts before returning to bed. When I came out Xavier was asleep all stretched out on the bed. I did sneak out just to the tree outside our window for the fresh air. It didn't take long before he found me missing, "What are you doing out here alone?" he asked. "If you join me than I wont be alone will I?'" I asked. He gave me a handsome smile and jumped to the branch I was setting on.

I watched him get settled as I smiled, "What?" he asked. "Nothing." I said. "Come on now Sweetness I know you have something on your mind." he said. "Just that you are beautiful that's all." I said. "Awe come on Sweets your gonna embarrass me." he said. "Come on lets get some sleep." I said as I jumped back in the house. He dove off and pushed me on the bed covering my face in kisses. The sound of him laughing rang out in my ears and it felt so good to have someone laugh in the Great House again. He laid on the bed with his soft hands on me as he breathed up my neck, "You haven't been drinking much Dr. Pepper have you?" he whispered. I shook my head no as I nestled closer to him, "I didn't think so I cant smell it like I used to." he said with a smile. Before long his breathing put me to sleep and the things I had running through my mind was unbelievable. Brandon was running through my mind for the first time in over a year. I could see someone coming in the Great House and they were cloaked so never seeing their faces. The magic I used on my parents and the fighting between Xavier and Mike. This danced around in my mind most of the night over and over like a strange old movie. I could feel Xavier's hands on my face as I watched this movie, "Sweetness wake up, can you hear me?" he asked as he shook me lightly. "What is it!?" I said and jumped awake. "Nothing its sunrise and you were thrashing around. Would you like to talk about it, I tried to get in but you locked me out hard this time?" he asked as he moved my hair out of my face. "Its nothing just the day played over in my head that's all. Come on I smell bacon in the air, are you hungry Love?" I asked as I looked into his mind.

I got to my feet and dressed, "Not really." he said in a upset tone. He wondered why I spoke Brandon's name in my sleep and now that I avoided the question he was not happy with me. Breakfast went on as usual with most of us, the kids talked about hunting together as the little ones played at the table. Xavier hardly spoke to anyone including me and as soon as he finished he left the room. I knew he was upset with me with what I had said in my sleep and I let him work this out alone. I knew when he was ready he would come for me, "Look at me Momma I'm getting bigger." Bastian said with a smile. "Yes Love you are getting so tall and you are very handsome." I said as I kissed his face. "Ok my Prince let me have your Momma for a few minutes." Xavier said taking my hand. He led me into the living room hoping to get me to talk, "Wait Love Julien is on his way here." I said as I pulled him to a stop. I opened the door to let Julien in, "Piper, Xavier how are you, would you happen to have a few minutes for me?" he asked. "Sure Julien it has been a long time since we have seen you." Xavier said. "Yea and I have missed you all here at the Great House. How is Regina, I heard she is with another?" he asked as he took a seat. "Yes she is happy with Jovi is that why you have stopped by today?" I asked. "No not really my parents are planning a move as you well know and I don't want to leave Hinton. I was wondering if maybe I could crash here for a few days until I can make better plans for myself? I would be no trouble and I would take part in any family chores, I can serve the both of you well." he said quickly. "Julien what has brought this up, we haven't seen you and all of a sudden you pop in?' I asked making sure he was as he said. "Yes I know and I am sorry about that. I did what I thought was the best for Regina she wanted to be friends but I love her desperately so I stayed away. I wanted to come and visit the family but her happiness was top priority." he said somewhat sadly. "Tell you what Julien we will leave this one up to Gina and if she wants to have you here there is plenty room in the Great House. I'm sure the rest of the family will fill you in on the rules and you will abide by them understand." Xavier said as the children ran into the room. "Nice to see you Julien." Brie said smiling. Julien looked at all of us with shock, "How do you know my name and me not knowing yours?" he asked softly. "I am Princess Brie and I know many things." she said with magic. "Wow she is most lovely they all are." he said. "Thank you Julien now go on and see Gina." X said still wanting to talk to me. He stood up to go and turned as I called to him, "Julien, if you are up to no good you will pay dearly for it understand." I thought to him. "Never would I walk in the strongest coven under false pretenses." he said out loud and left us.

Xavier turned to me, "Now it is your turn Sweetness, tell me what you were dreaming before I go crazy. I have tried to figure out what you had on your beautiful mind but you locked me out all day. You may start with the most important, Brandon." he said trying not to demand. "I don't know I haven't thought of him since before we started dating and then all of a sudden he pops up, I don't know what it means." I said looking inside him. X turned away from me knowing I was reading him like a book, "Do you miss him, still love him?" he asked softly. "Look at me Love, I miss him little and we were married for five years so there is a special place in my heart for him. You are the only one I love and you have me completely forever. I'm sorry that I have caused you pain this is all my fault." I said getting up to leave the room. He rose and grabbed me tightly, "You swear that you don't love him like that anymore?" he asked. "I swear I only love you and with every breath I take I fall deeper in love with you. Brandon was a part of my life once but now I have chosen a different path and I wouldn't trade it for anything. You are my everything and forever will be." I said as I hugged him back. "I know you cant control what your mind brings you at night and I shouldn't have reacted that way." he said very much relieved.

With weeks running by like days and I was still having the same nervous feeling rush me. The guys were teaching Julien fighting skills that they had learned form Mik and showing him the best hunting places to hit. I was overwhelmed with all the house members having to touch me and the things they would let slip when they got near me I knew a storm was waiting for me to release. "Jovi, Julien come to me." I thought to both of them. They floated in as Jovi looked outside, "Awe Piper do I really have to this time?" he asked. "Have to what?" Julien asked nervously. "Yes you must trust again and this is the very best way for you to understand." I said as I led the way out to the willow tree. "Where are we going, understand what?" Julien whispered. "The storms she brings we have to endure them the both of us." Jovi told him. "Sit and relax there will be no leaving until I say, fear not no pain will come." I said setting in the rain. The rain came in as a drizzle and soon it pounded the ground with lighting and thunder. It felt good to have it rain on me once again and the feeling of Jovi's trust towards me was also nice. I moved things around with my mind as the storm made itself known to Hinton. I put things away as best as I could but that nervous feeling was lingering in my soul that I couldn't put away for some reason. The storm came and went while we sat there soaking wet, "Well what do you think?" I asked them both. "I was worried for nothing and I feel better around you." Jovi said smiling. "Julien what you think about your queen?" Xavier asked. "That was amazing lighting never hitting us. I cant believe the stories are true." he said with a smile. "I have to go lay and rest will you come with me?" I asked Xavier. "Yes anywhere you are I will be." he said as I took his hand.

Back to not sleeping very well and this nervous feeling took a lot out of me once again. I laid on the bed waiting on Xavier to join me so I could have some rest to my body. As soon as he put his face in my neck I feel to sleep as many things again took over my mind. I thrashed around in my sleep as Xavier tried to keep me calm knowing what I was going through. My feet hit the floor and then Xavier, "No children this time?" he asked as he got himself dressed. I looked at him and headed for Jades room first to wake her. Next I hit Bastian and Brielle's room, "Bastian where is your sister?" I asked. "I don't know she sleeps with Tiffany sometimes maybe she is in there." he said just waking up. I stepped out of Bastian's room and a cold wind went through me, "Mommy." I heard in the lowest of all whispers inside my head. I ran to Tiffany's room and swung the door open to find no one there. "XAVIER!!!" I screamed now knowing what was coming. He raced to Tiffany's room with Mike right behind him, "What is going on?" he asked with horror on his face. "Brie and Tiffany are gone they are no where and one of them called for me. "Check downstairs and I will hit every room up here." X said starting his search. Mike followed me as I ran the steps to again find no one in the house. "They are not here I'm heading outside to see if I can pick up on their trail." I thought to him. "No wait for me Piper, Mike keep her inside." he yelled as he came to the top of the steps. "Sorry Piper you must wait." Mike said stepping in front of me and the door. As soon as Xavier cleared the last step I moved Mike and went outside with Mike and the house behind us.

I tried so hard to pick up on the scent trail of my daughters but they had faded into the night. "Oh no everyone back up!" X warned them as massive winds came in without warning. I hit the trees with winds that came from my soul and few huge trees fell to my power. The clouds came in thick, black and heavy with rain, lighting and thunder harder and heavier than ever before. Golf ball size hail poured down on only me knowing the rest of my family was outside and soon it became out of control. I took winds and moved them all back to safety when the lighting struck where they all stood then I feel to my knees and cried all that I had left in me as the weather slowed. The girls took the children back inside as the boys waited on me and Xavier. I cried a long time and Xavier came to pick me up and carry me home, "Don't take me inside if we leave I'm sure I can find them." I told him. "No Piper you need to get yourself together and try to connect with them or at least with Brie." X said as he carried me through the yard. "I said right now Xavier don't make me force you! Tell him guys right now we have to go right now!" I demanded as I fought with X to put me down. "Come on Piper, Xavier is right lets just get you inside so you can calm down." Mike said as he touched me. "Put me down I will go by myself I don't need help from any of you." I demanded again. "I'm not letting you down don't say another word until I get you home!" he said full of demand and warning. Not many has ever heard X talk to me like that so everyone was very quiet, "Xavier I said put me down I'm going with or without you!" I demanded again. He set me to my feet with a touch of force and grabbed me by the arm, "That's it Piper I have heard enough don't say another word do I make myself clear?" he said more mad this time.

I could feel him having a hard time having to deal with me like that but this is what I needed. I feel to my knees and cried more that I allowed this to happen to my children. Xavier bent down and easily picked me back up in his arms to take me inside. He put me on the couch as he started to make plans, "Piper I will do whatever you ask of me to find the girls, what is it that you want me to do?" Mike asked as he sat with me. "Go bring me Michelle make her come to the Great House." I said not looking at anything. Mike gathered Jovi and Julien to make sure he brought me Michelle for whatever reason I needed. Jon stayed close to Xavier so that if I bolted he could help bring me back. "How could I let this happen, how could I be so blind that I didn't see it coming?" I asked. "Sweets please I want you to connect with Brie." he pleaded with me. "No I'm not going to try anything." I said looking into the air. "Why not?" he asked surprised. "What if I try and I cant connect with her? What if they are . . . . ?" I said as he interrupted. "Piper I'm warning you say nothing else!" he warned giving me a look that I knew not to say another word. The boys returned with Michelle, "Piper honey are you alright? The boys told me what happened and I just don't know what to say." she said as she hugged me. "I don't know if I can handle this. If anything happens to either of them I will kill everyone in my path." I said in a whisper and full of truth.

She sat back and took my hand, "You know that Xavier will find your girls. Hey did you do something different with your eyes Sweetie?" she asked as she looked at X. "Back up Michelle now, boys over here. Mike get Piper a large cup and hurry." Xavier said. "Xavier I cant she wont let me go." she said. Xavier came over and pulled Michelle free, "Here Piper I want you to drink this all of it." he said as he handed me a cup. I took the cup and sipped on the warm blood, "Now I want my favorite color back, close your eyes and take a deep breath when you open up again I want my green back. We need you Piper you are the strongest in the mind connection, I know you can do this." he said softly. I gave Xavier the color he asked for and searched inside myself as I drank. As I got closer I could see figures talking back and forth so I put everything inside me to look harder. "Roaman I don't think this was a good idea, you have heard the stories of that king and queen. When I went with you I didn't know we were going to steal their children." one of the guys said. "Shut up Justice you had a job to do and you do it that's it." Roaman said. Then a third figure stepped up just out of my sight, "Both of you shut up do as I say and things will go as planned." the man said as he stepped into my light. I dropped my cup and blood went everywhere, "What is it Piper what did you see?' Xavier asked as he held me up. "Brandon." I said in the lowest whisper I could find.

Chapter 31

I could feel the rage run through Xavier with extreme force, "What your dead husband Brandon!?" he yelled as took to his feet. I was still focused on what was a hand, "That Queen is rightfully mine and I will get her back. I was cheated out if a year and I will kill King Xavier to get her. As for the daughters he will come for them to please his Queen at all cost." Brandon said with hate. "My dad will kill you for this." Tiffany said. "Hush yourself little girl!" Roaman said as he smacked her. "Give me my sister and I will do as you say, she is no threat to you." Tiffany demanded. "You think I'm stupid if I give her to you and you do something rash I would have to kill you both no need for your daddy to come for you then." Brandon said looking at her. "I swear I would never I just want to soothe her that's all." Tiffany said, "Very good Tiff look him in his eyes they are the color of mine and he wont be able to resist you.' I thought to her out loud. I watched her make eye contact with him and he got ready to tell her no once again. "Please?" she asked again. "I said . . . ." he began as he looked her in the eyes. "You have the same eye color as your Queens, I have never seen that color on another." he told her as he turned to his men. "Bring in the small child without harm." he told the two guys.

I watched as they took Brielle to Tiffany, "If you try anything I swear the little one pays with her life." Brandon said as he gave Brie to her. Xavier paced the floor, "What is going on in there X read her mind, she has me on lock down." Mike said. "I cant she has me on lock out as well." X told them. "Are we talking about the same Brandon, the dead one?" Jon asked. "Yes a year ago his life was claimed by a car." X said. "Brie can you hear me?" I asked out loud. "Yes Momma I can." she thought back. "You must listen to me and do as he instructs you, stay quiet. He will be kind to you if you behave and don't sass him. Stay together if possible I will come for you very soon." I told her. "They are going to kill Daddy." she thought with sadness. "No they wont get the chance I will come alone to save you all. Now I need to get some things together and I will connect with you soon, I love you both." I told her. "You are not going anywhere alone understand me, tell me what is going on!" X demanded. "There are three Roaman, Justice, and Brandon, yes that Brandon don't ask me how but its him. You will not go this time you must stay behind I will go with the brood and take care of this. They took the girls so you would come for them and they can kill you." I said almost pleading. "Then I will die they are as much my daughters as they are yours." he yelled at me with the rest backing up at his temper. "Fine but we do this my way." I said in a tone that he wouldn't disagree. "Fine." he said unhappily. I told the guys what I wanted from them as we gathered up to get ready to go. As soon as Trevor showed up for Michelle we left in search of our daughters.

Days went by as we searched for them with the clues that they could send me. I wasn't doing very well with the thoughts that took my mind over, I knew Brandon was going to die again and I was going to watch. I would watch as Roaman poked fun at my girls telling them that they would watch us die and then suffer the same fate. Justice would try to make them comfortable when possible but when Roaman or Brandon would return his mood would change. After a few days of Brandon keeping watch over Tiffany he found a chance for them to be alone, "How is it that you share the same eye color as Queen Pipers small one?" he asked gently. "She is my mother they saved me from a horrible life and took me in." Tiffany said. "Is that so child so you are saying that you were once human and Piper turned you this way, by your choice or her demand?" he asked again kindly. "My choice always she would never demand this of no one. How is it that you know her?" Tiffany asked. "Careful you might upset him." I thought to her. "I know Piper very well and I'm sure she will conform to my way. I was married to her for five wonderful years and then Xavier stole her from me." Brandon told her. "Yes well she is very different now she is very much in control of everyone, she wont be the one changing trust me." Tiffany said. "Are you saying that she will control me?' he asked laughing out loud. "My mother will make you pay for this you will see. She has one of the kindest hearts ever seen in the vampire world and the most lethal. The wrath she will bring down on this town will be very satisfying to her." Tiff said. "That's enough Tiff we are getting close and he may move you, say no more." I thought to her. "What the hell is going on Piper, you wont let me see?" X asked as he drove.

I opened up to him and the others so they could hear and maybe see what was going on with the girls and Brandon. "Are you a human killer?" Brie asked in her captivating voice. Brandon looked at her with shock, "Never speak out loud again small one I'm giving you fair warning. You sound like Piper, you have her voice and her . . . ." he said drifting off as he jumped up hitting things as he stormed out of the room. We all could feel the panic of the girls as Xavier picked up speed, "Brie do as he asks and don't speak, you have the voice of an angel and he fears you truly." I thought to her as we stopped in a town for gas and snacks. "You need to eat Sweets you are growing weak." X said as we walked into the store. "I'll be fine." I said halfway knowing he was right. "I can feel you getting weak by the minute, you either eat or I will force you." he said. I pulled him to a stop as I took a deep breath, "They are here in this town!" I said. "We leave the cars and go on foot from here." he said taking my hand. "When we find them everyone stays back I will enter alone. This is not open for discussion, trust me things will go better if he sees me first." I told him as we raced the mountain sides. "You are my wife and I'm not letting him near you!" X shouted at me with fists clenched. "X you know she can handle the most vicious in this mind state." Mike said. "This has nothing to do with you." X said coldly. "If you go then I will be more worried about you and I wont be able to control what's around me." I told him softly.

Just up the hillside I picked up on them very well, "Stop we are close, stay and I will return shortly. No matter what you hear or see you must stay out of sight until I call for you. Mike I need you to keep Xavier back at all costs." I said as I loved on them all. I hugged Xavier like this was the last time I may ever get to touch him, "No matter what I will always love only you." I said and quickly left the safety of my brood. "Piper wait!" X called after me. "No X stay." Mike said getting a hold on him. I knew that Xavier had seen what I was hiding this whole time from him as I kissed him goodbye. I neared the door to the shack where my girls were held captive as Roaman jumped out and grabbed me by the arm. "Well Queen Piper it is an honor to have you here. Where is your King Xavier out there I assume?" Roaman asked. "I have come for my daughters alone, take me to Brandon now!" I said harshly. "So you already know about Brandon you are as amazing as we have heard." he said with a sly look. "I know many other things would you like to hear them?" I asked. He shook his head yes, "I know you put your hands on my eldest and for that I shall see your blood spilled on the ground by the end of the day." I said in a whisper. He jerked me by the arm and led me into the room where Brandon sat.

He rose to his feet and hugged me tight, "Piper you look amazing I have missed you deeply." he said as I pushed him off. I walked over to the girls, "Hi my angels has he been careful with you both?" I asked with my back to him. "Yes Momma he has been very kind but he wouldn't let me ask him if he was a human killer." Brie said as Brandon chuckled. "Yes Love he kills humans cant you smell the stench? He fears your voice that's why he wouldn't let you speak." I said as I untied them both. I stood up with my back to him still as I hugged my girls, "Go now I will see you at home later on, I love you both." I said ushering them to the door. "Wait we are not leaving without you." Tiffany said. "Yes you will and be safe, just up the mountain side you will see the road home." I told them and pushed them out the door. I turned to Brandon, "I hate you for this with all of me!" I shouted to him. He raised his hand to hit me with his fist, "Go ahead I have been hit before I fear you not!" I said in a smart ass tone. He put his hand down, "And your King has hit you?" he asked. "Never he loves me like you could never understand. Do you three have any idea what you have started?" I asked. "Where is your husband now?" he asked. "He is no concern of yours this is between the two of us. How is it that you become a vampire?" I asked. "Awe Piper lets talk about happier things, like us." he said with and uneasy smile. "There is no us and never will be. Again you becoming a vampire?" I asked laughing out loud. "Why don't you have a seat my Love and I will tell you everything." he said pulling out a seat for me next to him. "Don't ever call me that only Xavier has the right!" I warned.

Brandon cleared his throat and took a seat, "When the accident happened I didn't die as you can see. Someone came to me and turned me this way showing me the ropes if you will. She was lovely but never as beautiful as you. Cora allowed me to watch you with Xavier then took me away to show me what this life had to offer." he said as I interrupted.

"Wait Cora did this to you, that bitch!" I said crossing my arms. "Awe you know her a friend maybe?" he asked with a smile. "Hell no she was no friend of mine I killed her and rather enjoyed it." I said with a smile of my own. "This is way out of control, I want you back now that we can have forever together what do you say? Just remember you were mine way before you was ever his and I will stop at nothing to get you back." he said as he grabbed me by the arm. "Take your hands off of me Brandon you have no idea what I can do with a flick of my wrist. I have told you that I belong to Xavier now and forever, what you did wasn't right. I was made for Xavier to be his queen there is no changing that." I told him as I pulled away from him. He grabbed me tight and kissed me hard on the lips as I felt Xavier working up a anger. I pushed Brandon off of me, "Don't make me kill you Brandon I have the power." I said backing away from him. "You will be mine even if I have to force you. If I hold you long enough you will grow tired and give me what I desire. I don't fear the bedtime stories about you I'm sure they are just that stories." he said as he motioned the others to hold me down.

I took Xavier's anger and mixed it with mine and I pushed winds from my hands moving the boys back. "I will have no choice but to stop you Brandon you are out of control with the human blood you feast on. You touch me again and I will do just that." I said turning to Roaman and Justice as they fled the sight of my power. I watched as Mike and the others kill them quickly, "That is for my nieces and this is for Piper!" Mike said as he finished Roaman off. Brandon moved in front of the door so I couldn't leave, "Piper please I have missed you and we belong together. Xavier stole you away from me and I will fight to the death for you." he said as he took me in his arms again. "Brandon I have told you that I'm in love with Xavier this is the way things are to be." I said trying to get away from him. He held tight to me, "Then if I cant have you no one will. I am glad you told your daughters that you love them because it will be the last time you see them." he said moving closer to my neck with a handful of my hair. I put my hand on him to stop him, "At least I will get to taste you for the last time and I will be with you until you run dry, I love you Piper and always have." he whispered. "Brandon!" I said loudly as I put my hand on his heart to stop him. "Wait you don't know what you are doing." I said trying to make him stop and failing miserably. He shook his head brushing off my magic, "Shhhh Piper it will be over soon and I will be with gentle with you as possible." he said with his lips on my neck.

Xavier came through the door with anger in his eyes, "Take your hands off of my Queen!" Xavier ordered. "Well King Xavier about time you have come for your Queen, I have waited a long time for this. Stand back Love I will finish him quickly and we can have forever together." Brandon said as he moved me behind him. "Touch my wife again and I will rip your heart from your chest. you had your chance with her and she has forgotten all about you, Piper is mine!!" Xavier yelled at him as he put his hand out for me to join him. I started the walk towards Xavier and Brandon grabbed me. Xavier hit him without any thought running through his head with Brandon hitting the floor taking me with him. As Xavier helped me up three huge vampires walked in to take Brandon's side, "You see I will not lose this fight I will have what is mine." Brandon said with pleasure in his voice. Xavier smiled at him as Mike walked in followed by Jon, Bailey, Jovi and Julien standing behind X in fighting stance. "As you can see my Queen foresaw your plan all along and I have come prepared to save her." X said with just as much pleasure in his voice. I knew from the look on Brandon's face he know his demise was coming. Julien came and pulled me to him as the fight broke out, and I stood there against the wall and watch them take on the three huge vampires. Xavier went after Brandon most viciously with them fighting with everything they had in them. I could smell the difference in the blood as it spilled on the floor from the ripping and tearing of each other. My boys killed the three of Brandon's and came to me while X and Brandon continued. My heart was breaking at the sight of Xavier's blood on the floor as the winds and rains made it known to all how I felt. Then as Brandon took a lethal swing at X, I screamed Xavier's name as he killed Brandon. "Love are you alright?" I asked looking him over and kissed him.

Brandon put his hand on my leg, "Piper." he said dying. "Go ahead Sweets you need to do this." Xavier said backing up to be with his loyals. I sat in the floor with Brandon and cried just like that night over a year ago. "Please forgive me I should have known the love you share with him. I guess I did the many times I watched you but I just had to know for myself." he whispered. "Shh Brandon I forgive you, just stay still I will be here with you until there is no more I promise." I said as I brushed his hair out of his face. "Don't worry dying doesn't hurt its knowing that

I'm without you that is the pain." he said with his voice slipping away. "Don't go in hate that way you can have a peaceful after life." I said in a whisper. He reached up and touched my face one last time as I kissed him on his forehead just as he died in my arms. The brood walked out of the room while Xavier came to his knees to be with me, "I'm so sorry Sweetness that it had to end this way." he said as I cried like that night back in January. I rose to my feet and walked out never looking back, "Piper are you ok?' Julien asked. "She will be fine as soon as we get her home." X said. It was a quiet ride home but all that came to an end as soon as Bastian saw Brie. "I have missed you, alls well?" he asked as he hugged her tight. Michelle waited on me to get in, "I'm so glad you are all safe." she said as X left us alone. "I just don't know Michelle." I said looking away. "You don't know what Hun?" she asked. "What I'm doing here, I love Xavier and all of them but maybe I shouldn't be here." I said not looking at her. "Piper you shouldn't say things like that where he can hear you. What do you mean you shouldn't be here?" she asked in a whisper. "Ever since I married X I have brought nothing but trouble to this family. If I take the small ones the others can live in peace just as before without me." I said lowly. "He would hunt you until he dies you know that." she said as he walked in. "Everything ok in here you both are quiet?" he asked. "Yea but I should be going." Michelle said. "I will walk you out thanks again for all you have done." he said reading her like a book. I went to my room and laid across the bed not caring if he knew this about me this was how I felt.

Chapter 32

I must have fallen asleep because I woke to find Xavier asleep beside me. I slipped out of bed and sat in the hall way in front of the kids doors keeping watch. "What are you doing out here Sweets?" Xavier asked as he took a seat with me. I took a deep breath, "You know that I love you more than my own life right?" I asked not looking at him. "Yes and I love you the same, what's this about Sweetness?" he asked taking my hand. I pulled my hand away, "I'm leaving and taking Jade, Tiff and the twins with me." I said getting up. "THE HELL YOU ARE!!!" he yelled at me. He ran to stop me by pulling me into the bedroom and slammed the door. "You are not going any where do you hear me!? Michelle told me what you were thinking and I thought this would pass, you are never leaving my side!" he said still screaming at me. I didn't say anything I just sat on the bed never looking at him. He paced the floor in front of me, "What brought this on Piper, is it the fact that I killed Brandon?" he demanded. "You know that isn't true you did what you had to do. Brandon had it coming and this was his fate." I said still looking at the floor. "Would you at least look at me while I'm talking to you? What is it then?" he asked getting mad at me. "Its just that I have caused so much trouble ever since you married me that's all." I said looking at him. He put his arms around me as I stood up, "Sweetness this is crazy none of this is your fault." he said holding tight. "I just think that I were to leave you all would be able to live a peaceful life without all the fighting and stress." I said as the bedroom door swung open. "You cant leave us I wont allow it!" Mike yelled at me as the others followed him. "We will hold you down until you change your mind." Jon said as the others looked like they were dying inside. "I am truly sorry but I think this is best for awhile. I love you all forever and I will have you in thought always." I said leaving the room.

"Sweetness please cant we just walk for awhile and let you think this over?" he pleaded following me out. "Do you think this is what I really want? I want to be here be your wife and raise our babies to be great vampire leaders, but this is all I know right now." I said as he pulled me to the floor to sit with him. "Then don't leave we will work this out and that way we can have forever together. You know that the others will never stop looking for you as would I and if I gave into your demands and something happened to you I would die a slow, painful, lonely death without you. Please Sweets I'm begging you don't go." he pleaded with me. "Tell you what I'll stay but if anything else happens I'm out. I cant deal with the stress all the time and I have had to over come and accept many things in my new life. But the thought of someone hurting my family is very stressful to me, it isn't fair that they have had to see my trails I have went through. You all were just fine until I moved here and you met me now look at your lives stress, fights, not to mention the hell I put you through with my powers. Look at what I did to Mike, I made him leave for god sakes. Jovi is afraid of me, Mike don't like the way I make him feel, B stays clear of me, Jon seems to be ok, not to sure about Julien. Do you think I like to be feared and by my own family?" I asked laying down in the hallway. "They will over come their fears remember they haven't needed anyone in over a hundred years. The way you can control them with just your voice is hard for them to adjust to that's all." he said as the others gathered around to see what was going on. "So Sweets can I keep you?" he asked. "Yes you can keep me, I'm sorry I brought this up." I said as I got a group hug from all the kids.

I laid in the floor so that the day washed over me as everyone stepped over me, "We could have the ceiling painted so that you could have something to look at." Xavier said as he laid with me. "That's ok I'm getting up." I said as he moved his head next to mine. "What are you thinking about?" he asked. "Nothing I'm not thinking nothing for once. I guess we should get up and get the rest of the day started." I half way said. "Na we can just lay here and the kids can step over us." he said with a chuckle. Now with months streaming by without any problems and I was very happy. Xavier and I worked and the family gathered everyday for dinner. Mike and Tes were getting along better than ever with him learning to share with her. I was getting better at controlling the weather and my emotions. The small ones were no longer small they were as big as the others and just as smart. Xavier and I got them in school which took some of my charm to get them in with Tiffany. Dinner like any other day with ordering out so we can have movie night. We sat at the table and talked back and forth with Mike having a smile on his face. "What's the smile for Mike?" X asked. He sat straight up in the chair, "Tes and I are going to have a baby." he said proudly. The room went dead silent except the sound of Xavier's fork hitting his plate. "Is there something wrong with me being pregnant Xavier? Tesla asked carefully. "Well no its just a surprise that's all. I'm glad you both are going to be parents soon." X said not looking at her. "What's the problem guys?" Mike thought to us. "She is human and you are not. This baby is going to kill her as it grows from the vampire side." X thought back while still eating.

I looked at the sisters for any glimpse into Tesla's future and Gina giving me a no for a answer. "We will discuss this later just the few of us without Tesla present." I thought to both of them. Jovi and Julien talked about hunting later on as LaStat told us about his day in a different language every night. Tesla who hadn't learned as quickly as the rest of us would look to Mike who would whisper what he said so she could be included. I sat back and looked at all my children who were very beautiful. Bastian was a exact duplicate of Xavier, his build was muscular with amazing blue eyes and silky black hair. Brielle and I were on the same build and from behind it was hard to tell us apart. Her hair was burgundy and emerald green eyes with a touch of blue like mine. Jade who was soft at heart but built like Brie and myself slim and tall with emerald green eyes and Xavier's black hair. LaStat was on Baileys model frame well chiseled abs and blonde hair with lighter blonde streaks through it. After dinner we went out for a movie on blankets, "I love it when you are in good spirits the weather is so pleasant." X said as he pulled me close. "I'm very happy that I decided to stay I don't think I could have lived very long without your touch." I told him. "I know." he said giving me a sly smile. "What are you going to do about this Mike and Tesla thing?" I asked with a smile. "What me this is me and you I'm not going at this alone thank you." X said. "Very well then right after this movie we shall." I said with a giggle.

I wasn't ready for this conversation to take place because I knew the danger she was in and how Mike might take this. We waited in the living room for Mike to get Tesla settled so we could talk, "Hey what's going on?" Mike asked. "Mike what the hell where you thinking allowing her to get pregnant?" Xavier asked. I put my hand on X, "What he means is she is human and this baby is going to grow at vampire rate possibly killing her." I said softly. "Maybe you should give Doc Logan a call he might have the answers you seek." X said more calm this time. "Yes I will call Dorien but we want the baby to be born here in the Great House just like the others." Mike said with certainty. "Have you thought about turning her maybe that wouldn't be a bad idea?" I asked. "I'm not ready to turn her although she has asked and she said she is getting tired of not knowing what LaStat says not only that she don't like it when we mind read." he said. "You are strong enough to turn her you know that right? Not only that but it has been some time since I had to use my magic and I really miss using." I said smiling widely. "No need to use magic on me Piper but thanks anyways. I will call the doctor and then I will let you know." Mike said smiling at me.

Xavier looked like a caged lion until Mike returned to tell us that Doc would stop by tonight. "What is the problem X you look like your going to bust into flames? You know he will take care of her he is trust worthy." I said taking his hand. "Do you have any idea what will be said if she dies human with a vampire baby in her?" he asked. "Do you think for one minute that I would allow that to happen, I would turn her myself." I told him. "That's not what I want to hear Piper this is serious." X said trying to calm down. "Ok what would you like to hear, that is what I'll tell you. For heavens sakes calm down its not like anyone would know and what if they did it is nothing but a story that's all until otherwise said by one of us." I said. "Do you think he will turn her and what will happen I know you can see what will come to pass for her?" he asked. "Yes he will turn her as for what will come to pass we both shall see I'm sorry." I told him as Mike came back in. "Doc is on his way, I apologize for what I have allowed Xavier please forgive me." Mike said looking very hurt that X was mad at him. "Be nice this time he is truly sorry he let you down." I thought to Xavier quickly. "Mike man you are my very best right hand and I trust you to what is best for her and this family. Mistakes happen and it is up to us to correct them and I trust that you can make this happen no worries." X said putting his hand on

Mikes shoulder. "Thanks X nothing like this will ever happen again I swear it." Mike said relieved. "Now go to Tes and tell her what is going to happen she must understand everything." Xavier said. Waiting on Dorien to get finished with Tes seemed like an eternity, "Well?" X asked as Doc came out. "She is in grave danger he has to turn her and now. Even still if she is wore down from this vampire child she could still die from the turning. All we can do is hope that she is strong enough for this." Doc said on his way out. Xavier turned to me smiling, "Now Sweets lets not take this as bad news I'm sure she will fine." he said. "This is coming from Mr. I'm Freaking Out?" I asked with a giggle.

I guided Xavier to the bedroom so I could lay for the night, "Maybe we should wait on Mike to see if he needs any help." X said as he laid with me. "Na he is strong enough trust me, I can see inside him and he holds all the will power he needs." I said as I ran my hand up his chest. "Then he will come for us if he needs?" he asked. "I have missed you even though you have been by my side this whole time." I told him as I touched his silky skin. "I have missed feeling you as well. Do you sleep Sweets?" he asked liking my touching him. "No I mostly nap and besides I don't want to sleep. I lay here and listen to you breath, it is very comforting to me." I said. "I thought so I knew I wasn't dreaming when I would feel you touch my face." he said pulling me closer to him. "Sometimes you make funny noises when you sleep and that makes me laugh." I said with a giggle. "Oh I see I make funny noises huh?" he said as he sat across me and held me down. I shook my head yes, "Sometimes it is a different noise each night, very funny stuff." I said as I laughed. He kissed my face all over as I tried to get away from him. It has been such a long time since we played together and the feeling was nice. I got away from him and hit the window racing to where the moon touches the grass. "I'm going to get you my Sweetness." he called out to me as I took a different route. I stopped and took a deep breath so I could find where he was and back tracked myself. "Sweets?" I heard him whisper.

I never said anything knowing his tracking senses was a hundred times better than mine will ever be. I walked ever so softly not wanting him to find me but of course he was very good as he came out of no where taking me to the ground on top of him. "I have told you there is no hiding from me we are one." he said. "Lay with me so we can see the moon brighten." I said as I pulled him to me. "As you wish." he said putting his arms around me. I laid there and let all the good times I had run through my mind and his so that the moon would respond to me feelings. "I think I would rather watch you." he said as he rolled to his stomach. I ran my fingers through his hair and kissed him letting him know that I was more than ready to be with him again. He made love to me under the full moon until it was noon, "We should get back the kids are getting worried." I said as he held tight to me. We walked up on the porch to find Jon standing there with his arms crossed, "That's it I have had it either you tell someone that you are going out or leave a note. We have been worried sick and I had to get Bastian and Brielle to try to find you!" Jon said loudly. "Sorry Dad gees we wont do that again." I said as I put my arm around him and laughed. "I'm sorry Piper its just that after you said you might leave and we know X would go looking for you." he said and pulled himself together. "Its fine Jon she has decided to stay." X said with a smile. "You know Jon you could just connect with me just as the others do." I said as I patted him on the shoulder. "No thanks Piper." he said as he tuned and left.

I walked up the stairs looking for what was troubling me to find Tesla on the bed, "Tes honey you ok in here?" I asked knowing she was worried. "Well." she said softly. "You want to talk about it?" I asked walking in her room. "What is going to happen when he does this and don't tell me you don't know cause I have seen that you know a lot." she said. "Well it is hard to say everyone is different. Bailey was in pain, Tiffany slept, I slept and Jovi slept but you are very rare you are pregnant with by a very strong vampire so there is no way to know. I can see things only when I'm allowed as you well know and if I knew I would tell you. Look here Tes lets put it this way there will be no pain for you to endure while under my hand how's that?" I asked her. "What about this baby it is very important for this baby to be born." she asked quickly. "This baby will be very healthy and will comply to what I say." I told her as I patted her leg. "Thanks Piper I knew you could help me." she said. "Anytime now you rest up and Mike will be here in a few minutes." I said getting up. I walked out to face Xavier, "Something wrong up here you disappeared on me?" he asked. "Tes is worried but I'm sure she will find that it will be nice, I know I did." I said with a smile. Xavier laughed, "So you would do it again?" he asked. "Over and over as many times as it took." I said laughing. "You want something to eat?" he asked shaking his head.

I walked with him to the kitchen and had a sandwich until Mike needed us. "What is taking so long?" X asked. "Well maybe he is just taking his time I don't know I stay out of all that kinda creepy stuff." I said. "Come on no more waiting." X said as he pulled me to my feet. Just as soon as we topped the steps Mike came out of his room with a small amount of blood on his lips and not happy. Xavier looked at him and rushed to Tesla's side looking her over as I stopped him from leaving. "She is fine just let her sleep." X said with relief. "Can I go now?" Mike said not looking at me. "If you must." I said as X looked at him not believing he was wanting to leave. "Will you come with me?' Mike asked. I walked out with him to the back yard, "Are you alright?" I asked softly. "Hell no I'm not alright she had to tell me to stop and I didn't want to. It was like no other and I have had a few different tastes but she was well different. Do something Piper, fix me! I told you that I was much to weak for this." he pleaded with me. "Mike you did very well the most important thing is you did stop. Look I'll tell you something but you must never allow it to escape your lips." I said stopping him. "I would never betray your trust." he said very intrigued. I took a seat and he followed suit, "I had to make Xavier stop before. I had to pull him off my neck and with force before he bled me dry. He didn't look, touch, or even talk to me for the whole day." I told him. His eyes were wide with disbelief, "Are you for real I mean Xavier is the strongest of us all." he said with shock. "Didn't you once say that no one is perfect?" I said getting up. "Piper I need you now!" X thought to me. I looked at Mike who already knew and we both took off for the Great House.

Chapter 33

When we entered the bedroom we found Tes in great pain. I went to get some cool towels to put on her hot body. That only worked for a small amount of time with Mike pacing the floor. The hours went by and she moaned more and more, "Do something X she is in great pain." Mike said. "I'm doing all I know to do right now. Piper was the only one I have turned don't you remember it felt like forever?" X asked. "I'm only concerned about Tesla right now so fix her!" Mike said raising his voice. "That's quit enough either shut up or get out, I'll fix this!" I said getting up. I bent down near Tesla and put my hand on her heart and tummy whispering only where she could hear me, "Tesla listen to my voice you are calm just sleeping and when you wake you will be calm. There is no pain or panic here in your heart and Mike is here waiting for you." I told her. "Yes calm see you in the morning." she mumbled back. "There all fixed." I said casting a warning look at Mike. It took another day before she woke up, "Tesla how do you feel do you need anything?" Mike asked as he went to her side. "Maybe some water if you wouldn't mind." she said. "I'll go get you . . . ." he began as Brie walked in with a blood cup, "I just thought she might need something a bit stronger than water." Brie said as she kissed his cheek. He winked at her which delighted her to death because she was worried about him forgetting her now that he had Tes and soon a baby.

He took her hand as she turned to leave, "You will always be my only Brie and we will find time to hang out I promise." he said and smiled. "Love you Unk Mike." she said and danced out of the room with X and I behind her. "Tes turned out great huh?" I asked. "What did you say to her?" X asked. "Just what she needed to hear that's all. Mostly I worked on the baby who was causing the most trouble very thirsty one." I told him with a smile. "I really need to learn that one." he said as I took off for the bedroom. I laid on the couch and waited on him, "You have had it in you all along and soon you will use it to your advantage." I said as he laid with me. Laying on the couch was something I missed a lot since we hadn't had the time. "Hey lets go for a walk or a ride." I offered. "Sure thing Sweets shall we leave a note or something?" X said. "We don't want Jon to have a heart attack do we?" I asked. After Xavier told the kids where we were heading and we got on the bike and took off. He drove around town with the wind in our face. I slid my hands up his shirt, "Take me to the swings." I whispered to him. He flipped the bike around and drove to the park. I swung for a few minutes with Xavier pushing me, "Do you have everything in the right folders?" he asked as he pulled me to a stop. "Yes but mostly I was just wanting the fresh air. Thanks for the ride it was nice to have me and you." I told him. "You know you could ask me for anything and I would give it to you forever." he said getting back on the bike and heading home.

The nice bike ride came to a close as we got closer and we both picked up on the tension. Xavier picked up speed so we could find out what was going on at the Great House. Sharon and Mike were in the living room screaming at each other, "You said you didn't want to be with me and I don't want to be with you. We never agreed on anything while we were together so why are you here now!?" Mike screamed at Sharon. "What the hell were you thinking Mike you went and found you a human weak and frail. You should have checked with me to see if maybe I changed my mind!" she yelled back at him. "Tesla is none of your concern and I didn't want to be with you any more that's why I never called!" Mike said loudly. "You know she has something that belongs to me and I can take it back. You promised me the world and then you run off searching for yourself only to come home and get yourself a pet. That's all she is to you Mike a pet one you will grow tired of shortly." Sharon screamed. I watched as Mike tighten up all over at what she said, "Maybe you should leave Sharon before you say something that might get you hurt." Tes said sweetly. Sharon lunged at Tesla as Mike stepped in front of her. The sound of their bodies hitting was like a brick building falling, "Try that again Sharon and I will kill you." Mike said with a deep growl. Xavier started to make way to Mike, "No Love he has to do this on his own." I told him. "Awe I see you have turned her, now you have a pet forever don't you one that you can control." Sharon said with a evil smile. "Did you ever think that maybe you were his pet someone to keep entertained until something real came along?" Tesla asked standing beside Mike. He gently put his hand on Tesla's tummy and moved her back softly.

Sharon grew furious at his carefulness with her, "Please leave the Great House and never return you made your choice." Mike said and turned his back to Sharon. Sharon jumped over him and on top of Tesla without any thought. Xavier ran to stop any harm coming to Tesla or the baby. Mike reached for Sharon with force and without blinking he broke her neck and tossed her body to the side. "Tesla baby are you alright?" he asked so very softly. "Yes Love I'm fine just a bit shaken that's all." she said looking at Xavier who was helping her up. "Would you like to call Dorien?" X asked. "Maybe that's a good idea." Mike said as he helped Tes out of the room. "That's was intense did you feel him?" I asked. "Yes I told you that if a female was involved he would be more lethal. Now I have to call her parents and I have never liked this part." X said reaching for the phone. Bailey and Jovi came in the room, "What happened in here?" Jovi asked. "Lets just get this cleaned up please." I asked as Xavier talked to Sharon's father. I went to check on Tes after Doc looked her over, "Is it always going to be like this?" she asked. "What do you mean?" I asked. "Well I have never seen Mike so mad before." she said. "Mike is a very loving person but he is a fighter if need be. He did what he needed to protect you and nothing else." I told her with a smile.

Jovi and Julien came back with news that Sharon's father wasn't very happy he thought Mike would bring her body back. Xavier looked up Mike to have a talk with him and things became very loud between them, "There is no way I'm going over there to see him, I don't own him any explanation. She came over here not the other way around!" Mike yelled at X. "I didn't say you owed him anything he just wants to talk to you that's all." X yelled back. "I'm not going and this conversation is over." Mike yelled as he started out. I walked in the room and all fell quiet knowing I didn't like fighting, "Didn't I warn you both about fighting?" I asked. "Sorry Sweets we were just having a heated conversation that's all." Xavier said putting his arms around me. "Yes Piper but we are finished and I'm sorry we got loud." Mike said as he tried to pass me.

"So you are going to talk to her father?" I asked stepping in his way. "No I'm not." he said. "Well we will see about that. You have a royal duty to this house so you better get used to it." I said with compassion. "Piper I don't think I need to go she forced my hand." Mike said softly. "This is true but this is something that you must do. This house is ran under a kind but forceful hand and you will do your part. Now this conversation is over." I said with caress. "Fine I will do this but I don't have to like it." he said not happy with me. "Thank you." I said as I moved so he could pass. "You handled that nicely." X said. "Thank you now is the time that the boys start picking up on all their parts." I told him. "I don't know Sweets I have done everything and they have just followed." X said as he sat on the couch. "Well I trust them to do what is right and you gave me a lot to handle so you can trust them as you trusted me." I said rubbing his back and neck. "You are different you have an old spirit about you, there are things that I don't know and I was born a day walker. You are my queen and that's what you do." he said getting sleepy. "Now is the time for your trust in them all." I said. "Anything you want Sweetness Emails, research whatever you want." he said almost asleep.

I waited until he was sound asleep then I finished straitening up the house. I made rounds to make sure all the kids had everything they needed. Tiffany had a roomful of giggling girls, her sisters, Emily, Kirsten and SVannah. "Hey guys you need anything?" I asked. "Nope we have everything thanks for letting us stay over." Kirsten said. "You are very welcome now you girls need to be quiet your Dad and I might crash on the couch tonight since he is asleep already." I said to them all. "You know the rules no one outside for any reason understand." I thought to my girls. "We understand." Jade thought back. "Goodnight Ladies." I said as I shut the door. I hit all the rooms with Gina telling me that she was having a movie night in her room with the left over kids. Bastian and LaStat was last on my list of rooms to hit, "Hey guys how are you?" I asked. "We good Mom gonna hang out with Gina and the rest for a movie later. Maybe we can go and scare the girls a little before we hit the bed." Bastian said with a evil smile. "No way guys Tiff will have your heads and your father is asleep downstairs." I warned. "Fine maybe we will behave." Bastian said. "I'm warning you Bastian." I said pointing my finger at him before I left his room.

I ran into Mike on my way back down to be with Xavier, "Hey Mike the boys informed me that they want to scare the girls tonight so maybe if you get a hint you can stop them." I said. "Sure will hey are you really going to make me go to Phil's tomorrow?" he asked. "Yes but I shouldn't have to make you this is something that you should want to do. If anything should ever happen to Xavier or myself you will be able to handle things like this." I told him. "Don't say things like that you and Xavier will be here for the duration of forever. Fine I will go to Phil's and I'll take X with me happy now?" he asked with a smile. "You know I'm happy when I get my way and I don't have to break out the big guns on you." I said as I started down the steps. I slipped in Xavier's arms on the couch as easy as I could without waking him, "Everyone accounted for?" he whispered with his eyes still shut. "I thought you were asleep." I said softly. "I'm never asleep until you are in my arms. Everything alright on the second floor, what was the warning to the boys?" he asked. "Movies, scary stories, junk food so it should be great. Bastian and LaStat are wanting to scare the girls tonight and I told them no but I'm sure as we are setting here they will do it." I told him. "There will be hell to pay if they do." he said with a chuckle. "I love you now go back to sleep, I'm putting in a movie and go to sleep myself." I told him as I touched his face. "Don't lie to me Sweets I will watch a movie with you." he said getting comfortable. We didn't make it through the movie very far before the screams came from the second floor, "Come on lets get this over with." Xavier said getting up.

We topped the steps as the boys came running down and Tiff right behind them, "Hold it right there boys." X said putting his hand on them both. "Dad your awake. Umm we just, well, awe forget it, sorry girls." Bastian said. "Downstairs." X said calmly. Mike followed the boys while we made sure the human girls were ok, "Ladies are we alright?" X asked. "Sure Mr. Matthews we are fine, it was fun though." Kirsten said. "Well it will be the last time tonight and call me Xavier everyone else does." he said with velvet words. "Thanks Xavier and good night." she said as she fell under his spell. "Until tomorrow ladies." he said as he shut the door. Bailey and Mike had the boys shaking in their shoes when we came in, "LaStat what was you thinking two of those girls are human and you could have scared them to death. Your mother isn't very happy with you right now." Bailey said in his father tone. "Awe Dad we were having some fun they were already scared because of the stories and it was kinda easy for us." LaStat explained quickly. "They sure did didn't they?" Bastian said and started to laugh. Xavier cleared his throat and crossed his arms while glaring at Bastian, "What shall the punishment be?" X asked them both. "Maybe you should come up with something so Mom don't have to." Bastian said holding his breath. "Alright Tiffany's chores for the week both of you a week each." X said. "Maybe we should teach them a more valuable lesson." I said. "Awe Mom we were just having some fun and the chores is torture enough." Bastian pleaded his case. "The next time you pull a stunt like this big trouble understand?" I asked. "Yes my Queen we understand." Bastian said looking down.

They both rose to leave quickly so I wouldn't change my mind, "Look what you did Bastian now we have our own chores and now Tiffs." LaStat said. "I know but it was worth it, did you see their faces, awesome." Bastian said still laughing. "Shall we try for the movie again Sweetness?" X asked when we were left alone. "Sure why not." I said laying back down. X slept on and off while I laid there waiting on the sun to show us a new day. The kids started to make way for breakfast with Bastian and LaStat starting the bacon. "Hey Bastian nice scare last night." Kirsten said with a small smile. "Yea thanks Kirsten and I'm really sorry about that it wont happen again." Bastian said with a beautiful smile of his own. "Remind me the next time you want to do something not to help you. We would have got caught even if they hadn't screamed, you know Aunt Piper knows all and sees all in this house." LaStat said. "You shouldn't be afraid of Mom she is a kitten. I'm not scared of her just like Dad isn't." Bastian said. "So you don't fear me my son?" I whispered from behind him making him jump. "God Mom your like a ninja sneaking up on people." Bastian said gathering himself. The room of girls busted out laughing, "You should be afraid of me I could make you where an apron while you do the dishes." I said taking a seat. "Mom!!" he said looking at me with narrowed eyes. "Yes LaStat if Bastian wears one so do you." Cyndi said laughing hard. "I think Bastian would look cute in an apron." Kirsten said looking shy.

Xavier made his way over and kissed me good morning, "Lots of flirting is not something I need this early this morning." Xavier thought to me shaking his head. "Yea he likes Kirsten." I thought back to him. "Ladies how long do we have you for this weekend?" X asked everyone. "For the whole weekend till Sunday evening Mr. Matthews, I mean Xavier." Emily said still under his magic words. "Hey Tiff you guys want to watch a movie out back tonight that way we can be watched?"

Bastian asked. "Sure if you get my chores done." Tiff said with a large smile. Xavier listened to the plans as Mike came in the kitchen, "X are you ready to get this over with?" Mike said with hands in his pockets and not happy. "Please remember to be easy they just lost a daughter, answer his questions truthfully." I told him. "I know I know I promise." Mike said as X rose to join him. I secretly couldn't wait to watch the boys do the dishes as Tes came down for her cup. "Morning Aunt Tes." LaStat said softly. "Morning everyone." she said just as sweet. After a horrific mess with the dishes the guys went to blow off some steam on a good hunt. I stayed back with the girls with them talking about the next school dance that was coming up. "Hey Piper would you have asked Xavier out if he hadn't asked you first?" Kirsten asked. "Well to tell you the truth I know I would have, I was so taken by him the first day I saw him." I said thinking back to our first meeting. "He is a very handsome man." Kirsten said with a smile. "Yes very and he has a way with words, I love the sound of his voice." I said with a smile as he broke in on my thoughts telling me he loved me.

Chapter 34

I waited on X and Mike to return home so I could find out how things went. The girls were up to no good as usual and they were going to get the guys back for the scare last night. Tiffany, Jade and Brie told the human girls where to hide and when to jump out. The worse part was Jovi, Jon, Julien and Bailey were caught in the cross fire. As soon as the guys came back from their hunt the girls jumped out and scared them all. After that the running and screaming was on from the younger ones. The elders came back to me and took a seat, "Should always be on guard guys they had you from the get go and two of them are human." I said laughing at them. "We always have humans here so we just thought we were ok." Julien said also laughing. Mike and Xavier came home with them filling me in on what happened at Sharon's parents. "Hey Brie I have to run to the store would you like to join me? I thought maybe if you would like we can get some ice-cream or something." Mike asked her. She smiled and took his hand, "Sure thing Unk Mike lets go." Brie said. I watched her walk out with her long lost best friend with great emotions running through her. "So are we grilling or taking out?" I asked as X leaned over and kissed me. "Are you kidding me I'm not cooking for all these girls." he said with a smile. "Well maybe you should find out what they want." I said with a smile of my own. "Ladies, what's for dinner?" X asked with very silky words. "Pizza!" all the girls called at the same time. "Looks pizza wins." I said with my arms around him.

"I was really hoping for a fat, juicy burger and fries." he said with a pouty face. "Awe Sweetie we can still have burgers and fries if you really want." I told him. "Good its a date then, finally." he said pulling me along.

"Ok guys lets order before your poor Dad has a stroke or something." I said winking at Kirstin and Emily. Everyone placed their orders when Bastian and LaStat came in, "Two large with toenails and ears Mom, that sounds good." Bastian said laughing while the girls made faces. "Alright then as you wish." I said with a evil smile. "Hey Aunt Piper can I change it to just meat lovers?" LaStat asked. "You bet anything for my boys." I said make changes on the paper. "Mom I can make the order so you and Dad can leave." Bastian offered. "That's works for me." Xavier said picking me up and putting me over his shoulder. "I was coming Xavier put me down." I said laughing. "I know you there will be five minutes of rules that they already know. Now I have you and I'm not letting you down." he said opening the door. "She is going to get you for that!" Jade yelled to him. "I know I'm sure she is going to make me pay dearly." he said back. He sat me in the Charger and shut the door. I crossed my arms trying to make him think I was upset with him when he got in. "What?" he said with his seductive smile. "Are we in a hurry or something?" I asked. "Well sure we have lots of stuff going on later and I want us to have dinner without anyone calling." he said still smiling at me. "Sure sure has nothing to do with burger and fries calling your name?" I asked. "Never I'm in a hurry to have you all to myself." he said still smiling.

He pulled up at the restaurant and opened the door for me, "You still upset with me carrying you off?" he asked. I put my lips next to his as he slid his hands around my waist and whispered "I love you." He opened his eyes which were glowing bright blue, "Now that's what I'm talking about." he said back before he kissed me. After we placed our orders we found a seat, "By the way Tiff wants to tell the story about when her and Brie were taken tonight so maybe shut her down." X said carefully. "Why would she want to relive that moment from her life?" I asked. "I don't know Sweets she has a different kind of mind, she can talk to the dead. If you don't want this to happen I will tell her not this sleep over." he said. "No just let her have fun I'll shut her down I guess." I said taking a drink of shake. "I have told her that you can see and hear everything in the Great House that she needs to take heed." he said touching my hand. "Can you feel Brie like I can now?" I asked. "Not always but I know she is having a good time only because I can feel her through you. When I'm closer to her or anyone in the house I can pick up on their feelings." he said. "Just wondering how strong you are getting in your power of feel that's all. Yes she is really enjoying her time with Mike and someday they both will be to busy to spend time together. Sad in a way for me to see that come to pass before it happens." I told him. "That's enough Piper nothing else this is supposed to be a relaxed time." X said with a touch of demand. "Alright how's this, Bastian and LaStat has asked Kirsten and Emily to the dance." I said with a weak smile. "This I already know and I have to say its about time." he said before he put fries in his mouth. "Yes about time." I said finishing up my dinner.

I set back and let him finish his and my fries before we left to find out how Brie and Mikes time went. "I've been thinking that maybe it is time we share what you are all about with the children before they start coming into whatever you gave them." X said as he drove home. "No they are not ready and even if they were I don't want them to fear me. They know enough for right now as is." I told him quickly. "Sweets I don't think they will fear you and they will need to know how to control themselves as they get stronger." he suggested. "Bastian needs to see on his own he is very head strong and this will make him a better king when the time comes." I told him and looked out the window. "If this is the way you want it then so shall it be." he said knowing I didn't want to talk about it. I couldn't wait to get home and see what all was going on with my own eyes even though I already knew. We were greeted at the door with giggling girls, "Is it scary movie time ladies?" Xavier asked. "Come on Dad we have everything set up." Jade said pulling him along. Before to long I found my blanket and laid myself down waiting on the girls taking up time with X so Brie could make it back. I was glad we lived out in the woods that way when the girls screamed it wouldn't bring the cops. Those girls can really scream and when the boys were involved it was loud. They can be quiet as a mouse I guess you can say and with Xavier teaching them to climb the side of things it was much worse.

I laid there looking at the beautiful sky thinking how I wished X never taught them things like climbing up the side of the house. Xavier came and laid down with me, "Hey you have me on shut down what's going on up there in your beautiful mind?" he asked. "Just that I'm glad that the girls didn't ask how the guys got in the window like that. You should have never taught them things like this." I said as he got comfortable. "They have to learn things like that Sweets it will make them all great. Just think of them as your little monkeys how about that?" he said and laughed out loud. "Not funny Xavier I don't want another Mike and Jon nightmare with the boys, I like Hinton." I told him. "Mom you know we would never do anything like that we have had the scent of humans since before we were born. Please Mom don't worry we only play like that we never meant to upset you like this." Bastian thought in a comforting voice. "I know Bastian but its my place worry it keeps me on my toes. Its what I do best besides loving all of you." I thought back. He got up and came over laying beside me while watching the movie, "Mom you are the best mom in the world and I would never be able to live very long if you didn't love me anymore." Bastian said and hugged me. I could feel he was very sorry for what he and LaStat had done. "I love you Bastian all of you very much and never stop loving you all forever. If anything was to ever happen and I would leave this world I would leave behind all of me for you to remember." I told him. "Mom don't say anything like that, tell her Dad she will be here forever." Bastian said feeling very sad. "I'm sorry son, I just meant that all of you are my life. Lets just leave it at that and you go and have fun with your friends." I told him. "You alright Mom I feel very sad inside all of a sudden. I mean I felt bad but I feel even more sad now." he said with a worry look on his face. "Your mom is just fine no need to worry yourself Son." Xavier said with a smile. Bastian walked back over to his group of brothers, sisters and friends, "Everything alright Bastian?" Brie asked. "Sure I guess so." he simply said. "Come Sweets lets go." X said pulling me to my feet. "Where are we going? We cant go we have to many here for us to leave." I said. "Walking, if Bastian can feel you like I do you need to put things away." X said smiling so I would just follow along. I walked along placing many things in the needed folders with X walking with me, "Can I ask how Bastian felt you like that?" he asked as he took my hand in his. "I'm not sure I'm guessing that they are the very best parts of the both of us so it is only natural they get our magic." I told him. "The very best parts of you that is." he said. "Hey Bastian has your power to make the girlies melt by walking in a room just like his Daddy." I said play shoving him. "Sure I guess I made you melt huh?' he said laughing. "Whatever I think it was the other way around and you know it." I said picking up speed. "Right into my shoes." he said as we walked into the back yard.

All of the kids were waiting on us to return, "Is the movie over?" I asked. "No we waited, what going on Momma?" Jade asked with a worried look. "I just had a few things to put away that's all. You guys go on and have fun I'm great." I said with reassurance. They returned to the movie not really wanting to and all the human friends wondering what was going on. The movie went on its way with chips and drinks while LaStat hanging around me as much as possible. After the movie X helped the kids pick up some while I made rounds in the house so we can go to bed. "Is something wrong LaStat honey?" I asked when I noticed him following me room to room. "Did you have to walk because of what Bastian and I did?" he asked not looking at me. "Eyes on me LaStat." I said softly. He looked up at me and I could read him like a book when I looked into his blue eyes, "No it wasn't anything like that I just needed the walk. Yes I do worry about you and Bastian but like Xavier said you have to learn all you can so there is nothing to worry about." I said as I put my hand on him. "Are you sure because the look on Bastian's face and the pain I felt from him was horrible?" he asked never dropping his eyes. "LaStat you know I need to walk from time to time so I can think. Now I'm not happy with what you boys did and what would you have told them if they asked how you got up there?" I asked. "I don't know really we never thought about that we were just looking to scare the girls that's all. I'm sorry Aunt Piper I never want to upset you and if Mom and Dad found out that your walk was because of me I would never see sunlight again." he said with a light chuckle. "Don't worry about me or your parents everything is just fine. Now go and have a good time with your friends ok." I said. "Thanks I feel better already." he said as he turned and left me.

Xavier came in the room as LaStat made his exit giving him a pat on the back making way to me. "So now we are lying to the kids?" X asked as he put his hands around my waist. "Not lying just fibbing some to help him out he was feeling very guilty that's all." I said as I breathed him in. "Should we be doing that I mean they should know the truth." he said thoughtfully. "I'm sure deep down they do." I said pulling him to our room. I knew that I wouldn't sleep because Doc Logan said that he thought I was the kind of day walker that wouldn't sleep. I was different than any other vampire with the tears, the powers, and the kindness I had. The storms don't come as much anymore and sometimes I was thankful for that but on the other hand I wanted a storm to free my soul. Xavier had already feel asleep beside me and I tried to put myself in a safe place so I could at least rest. I played with his velvet hair and cried to make myself feel better inside. I thought I shut Xavier off from me but soon found out that wasn't true. "Sweets what's going on?" Xavier whispered up my neck. I couldn't answer him the tears took my voice. He sat up in the bed and caressed my face, "The kids have to learn these things and you know this Baby. One day Bastian will take over as king and he needs to know how to rule well." he said as he held me tight. "I'm sorry I have to do this, I have to cry." I said with tears streaming down my face.

He softly wiped the tears from my cheeks, "Would you like to walk or something, I will do whatever you wish of me." he said softly. "No I don't want to walk and I don't want to cry but this has to be tonight. Oh no Bastian is coming with his sisters, please do something I don't want them to see the weakness in me." I pleaded with him. He got out of bed and went to the door to stop Bastian from coming in, "What's up guys?" he asked holding the door halfway shut. "Can I see Mom please?" Bastian asked. "No not tonight sorry." Xavier said easily. "Dad I have never demanded anything of you before but I want to see Mom right now!" Bastian said in the same royal tones as his father. "Bastian now is not the time come back later alright." X said trying to make them go on. "No not this time I want to see her!" he said and pushed his way inside the room. Xavier stepped in front of him, "That's far enough take a look and go." X said warningly. "Mom what's going on? I know something is up I can feel you and Dad, please let us help you. Mom look at me." Bastian said. I wiped the tears that kept coming from my face and looked up at my very grown up son, "Nothing is going on Bastian honey. You will feel different in a few minutes you are going to have to learn to block these feelings so maybe start now." I told him.

He came to my side, "Mom I have never seen you like this only when things get so bad. When you came to bed you seemed fine what happened?" he asked taking my hand. "I have to do this for myself, I have to release it. When I hold things tight inside myself this is what I do." I told him trying to calm myself. "I will never forgive myself if I knew this had anything to do with me or LaStat. When Dad showed us how to climb up the side of the house we had to try it. I will never do anything like this again I swear." he said with worry. "This has nothing to do with you boys, yes I worry about you growing and learning new things but I have to except them for what they are. Now you go and rest I'll be fine in a minute and you will calm soon. I love you my Prince don't worry about me this will make me stronger you will see." I told him. "I love you too my Queen please sleep well. Remember I'm only down the hall or a thought a way if you need me." he said as he kissed my hand and left looking back. Xavier came to my side and wiped the tears from my face. His touch was like velvet to my skin and very relaxing. He pulled me close to his body and kept touching me knowing this time I was getting very sleepy. "Good morning Sweetness sleep well?" he asked as I began to move. "Very well and how did you sleep?" I asked looking up at him. "I rested well holding you all night." he said with magic in his voice. "Well I feel better inside." I said under his spell. The smell of bacon filled the room and I couldn't wait to have breakfast. We made our way down to the kitchen to see the kids playing around. "I just love bacon I never tire of it." Jade said happily. After breakfast Xavier and the boys went to hunt, "Where do the guys go every morning?" SVannah asked. "They go on a hike to keep up their strength and X puts them to a test everyday." I told her with the human girls listening.

Chapter 35

My life wasn't as busy now that the babies were all grown up but I tried to stay busy. I still had sadness that they were the only babies I would ever have in my long life time. My body would always be that of a thirty year old and still young enough to have another baby if I chose. Doc Logan thinks that I would never have anymore children because that baby would give me more power. He thinks that I wouldn't be able to handle any more power that it would become very dangerous. Poor Xavier would go nuts if he had to put up with me again. It hardly seemed unfair for me to want another baby because I already have so many to call my own. Michelle and Trevor were a large part of this coven even though they were not vampires they would have the protection of this house. I could feel everyone's eyes on me burning with questions, "What is everyone looking at me for?" I asked with a smile. No one said anything knowing that I was deep in thought and it could storm at any given time. "How about some ice-cream later or something?" I asked breaking the silence. "If that is what you wish Sweets than it shall be done." Xavier said trying my mind. I smiled and went to fix myself a cold cup and walked around the back yard. I saw Xavier walking towards me, "Sweetness you are very sad today would you like to talk about it?" he asked getting closer. "Not really I'm fine as always." I told him with a small smile. "I think if we talk about it you would feel better. I know you are not fine today I can feel you lying to me." he said trying to smile. "I know that you can tell and I know you can see only small clips of what's in my mind but I don't want to talk about it. Things will go away soon enough and it will be over." I said putting my arms around him so I didn't have to look him in the face.

"Please Sweets talk to me. I know some of what you are thinking and if Dorien said we cant have anymore babies does not mean we cant try. I will be here with you all the way not matter what happens." he pleaded. "I cant and we should never try understand." I said softly. "You are hiding something from me I know. You can handle anything that is given, you have a strong mind and spirit. You will tell me and now Piper." he said with ease. "You are mistaken Love I'm not hiding anything from you." I said and pulled away from him. "You must tell me now Sweetness. I knew you had many things on your mind for days now and I haven't pushed you to tell me in hopes you would. Is it that you don't want to have anymore children with me? "he said with worried eyes. "Xavier I would most love to have another baby with you but we must never." I told him still casting my eyes to the ground. "We will have a baby if this would please you, I will make sure this happens. I need you happy I need you." he said quickly. "No we cant and lets just leave it at that alright Love." I said trying to walk off. "No you will tell me what you have seen." he demanded as he stopped me from leaving. I stood there with my back to him, "If I tell you I need something from you." I said as the rain began to fall. He looked up and let the rain hit his face, "I will give you anything you wish." he said with a small panic.

The rain picked up and poured heavier as I gathered the strength to tell him, "Forgive me Xavier." I said with my eyes full of tears waiting to spill over. "Your forgiven I swear, just tell me." he said. "Xavier I love you more than my own life but if I would ever get pregnant again I would . . . . die. The baby would kill me slowly as it grew inside me. I'm so sorry that I cant give you what you want so badly." I told him crying. He just stood there and looked at me, "You have seen this and know it to be true?" he asked slowly. "Yes I have." I said backing away from him. I could feel him and I knew he was sad, the most sad I have ever felt from him. He sat on the ground getting soaked from the heavy rain, "I would give you anything you wished of me and I would be willing to have another baby with you. All you have to do is just ask me and it will be done." I said as I fell to my knees beside him. "No we will never try I will not lose you at any cost." he said yelling as he pulled me close to his chest. "We will never try." he said almost whispering stroking my hair as I cried. "Do you still forgive me?" I asked softly between sobs.

"This is not your fault we will get past this together." he said with care. We sat out in the pouring rain until I was able to calm the weather. Nothing was said as we walked back to the Great House and all the kids were waiting to find out what was going on. "What the hell is going on, last night you were sad and now things are much worse? You will tell me what is going on!" Bastian demanded holding his hand over his heart. "Don't push either of your parents right now Bastian." Mike said reading my mind the most. "I think I have a right to know, I can feel them both and it hurts!" Bastian said raising his voice.

Xavier narrowed his eyes towards Bastian, "She is very different Bastian, you only know half the power she holds inside her. You need to step off trust me on this." Jon said stepping between X and Bastian. I walked passed them heading to my room with Xavier right behind me. "Mom!" Bastian called. "Not now Son we will talk later." X said. Bastian growled at Xavier and stormed out of the house. I turned to go after him knowing he was hurting, "No Piper I'll go you stay and get better." LaStat said turning to run after Bastian. I sat on the bed and watched LaStat race after Bastian who was in lots of pain. Bastian knew LaStat was gaining on him so he slowed so he could catch up. I listened on their conversation as they took a seat, "Bastian you know your Mom is very dangerous when it rains, what's going on with you?" LaStat asked. "I don't know what is going on with me I have never felt like this before. I have never demanded anything from my father before and I went up against him last night and today. He is my father, my creator, my king and I should be thankful that he didn't strike me down." Bastian said. "Your Mom would never allow Xavier to do that and I don't think he would anyways. Can you feel them now what's going on at home?" LaStat asked. "Yes I can and they are both hurting and very worried about me. I should learn to control my temper around her. I wonder what Unk Jon meant when he said that I only know the half of it?" he asked. "I'm not sure Brother but I have heard Mom and Dad talking said she was a very rare breed and very dangerous. She don't even have to touch you to get what she wants. Her voice is magic enough and had the power to bring Unk Mike back, now that's power." LaStat said.

I winced at the thought of my son knowing what I was, "Sweets are they in trouble?" X asked. "No Bastian is learning about me and my magic I don't want him to fear me like the others." I said still listening. "I didn't know that Mom was like that, she has a way of keeping everyone on lock down. What about Dad what do you know of him?" he asked. "Your Dad has some of the same magic that of Piper. She shared with him so when the time was right he could use it, and everyday he gets stronger in that magic." LaStat told Bastian. "How did she share with him?" Bastian asked. "She bit him and passed it to him she has the power to share with whom ever she wants. She also has all the same powers of everyone in the Great House. Did you know that if she don't have a certain power that all she has to do is bite them and take it and harness it to the fullest." LaStat informed Bastian. "Come on lets get back before she sends a search party for us." Bastian said.

"Hey you know what else, Mike said that when she uses her magic it sends chills up his spine. She threatened Mike and X not to fight with each other. She should fear X but she don't even when he was growling angry. She turned her back on the one who took Brie and Tiffany even though she knew he was going to kill her, she went alone. She knows what she can do and what she can make you do. Your Grandparents were powerful because Kaleb was the very first day walker, but Piper makes Xavier the most powerful king ever in the vampire world. You do know that if either one of them should die the other would follow along within hours, right?" LaStat asked. "That's enough LaStat you have said far to much as it." I thought out loud to him. "Aunt Piper have you heard everything I have said?" LaStat asked. "You will come and see me upon your return to the Great House, understand me?" I thought to him. "Yes my Queen I'll be right there." he thought back knowing he was in trouble. I changed my clothes and waited on his return while Xavier looked through the pages in my mind. LaStat knocked on my door, "You wanted to see me my Queen?" he asked softly. "Yes come in please." I said back to him. "Aunt Piper before you say anything I want to say I'm very sorry about what was said to Bastian. I should have remembered my place but he is my Brother and I'm compelled to tell him everything inside me." he said very quickly. "Your right you should have known your place and never said anything without asking me first. You shouldn't know the things that you know about me right now and I'm not ready for the others to learn me. What should we do about this LaStat?" I asked. "Whatever you think is best I will comply to My Queen please forgive me." LaStat said with his eyes down. Bastian busted in the room, "LaStat out I want to talk to Mom and Dad!" he ordered. LaStat looked at me and I gave the go ahead to leave, "I want

LaStat left alone, you should have told me these things anyway. He did what he was supposed to as my loyal. If he knows something and I ask he will tell me without hesitation." he said with lots of demand in his voice.

Things began to fall all to hell and quickly. Xavier rose to his feet growling, and Bastian stepped back and growled back at Xavier. LaStat came back in the room taking his stand in front of Bastian. "Whoa wait one minute boys this is not going to happen. Both of you out I'll deal with you later, Xavier breath and step back." I said getting to my feet and getting in between them. Bastian pulled LaStat out of the room, "That boy ever forgets his place again and he will live to regret it to the fullest. He knows better than to speak to you like that after the day you had." X said as he began to calm down. "Love don't ever approach him like that again, he has the same mind set as the both of us. Maybe I should have told him about me and you know how I feel about any fighting between you and the boys." I said as I put his hands around me. "Fine you take care of this and warn him to never speak to you like that again. Don't try to shut me out because I will not stand for it, I want to hear everything understand!" he said with demand. "I understand." I said as I went out to the boys room. I knocked on the door, "Bastian may I come in?" I asked. He answered the door and stepped back, "Mom I am very sorry I shouldn't have acted like that." he said looking down. "You know better Bastian, after the day I had and then you go and act like this. LaStat you know better and Bastian you know how your father gets when you speak to me like that. He is very pissed right now and I'm warning you to never do this again. If you have a problem calm yourself and then come to me. There are things that I don't want anyone to know and that is my business and now you know some of it. As with what LaStat told you every word is true and I am very powerful and dangerous if I chose. I can make humans and vampires do whatever I wish and I can see, hear and feel all of everyone at all times. It looks like you are going to have some of the power your father and I have so you will learn to adjust quickly. Bastian you will take over as king and you will rule the way your father and I have set forth understand." I said with force.

"What's going to happen to LaStat now that he defended me against Dad?" Bastian asked lowly. "He is your Bother in arms and he did what he was born to do and that is take your right hand when it is needed. Now I am in control of what is felt in the house and I hope you have enjoyed yourself because it comes to an end right now." I said with harshness. "Mom please don't shut me off I want to feel you, I will behave from now on." he pleaded. "No Bastian this is the end and that's final. Now you are to come and apologize to your father and never push me again like this." I said with demand. "Um Aunt Piper will you be talking to my parents about this?" LaStat asked. "No it is up to you to tell them if you wish. By the way well done my Son I'm very proud of you." I told LaStat as I left the room. Xavier was pacing the floor when I came in, "That's it a stern talking to!?" he asked raising his voice. I knew he thought I let them off way to easy that I should have really given it to them both but I felt this was good enough. "Yes that's it. Now Bastian will be here in a few minutes to talk to you so behave." I told him as I took a seat on the couch in our room.

Bastian came to the bedroom along with LaStat, "Dad I am truly sorry for talking to you like that. You are my father and I have the most respect for you and Mom. This thing I have inside me is new and I felt your and Moms pain, all I wanted to do was make it stop but I only made things worse. I only hope that you can forgive me and LaStat for our actions tonight." he said with sadness. Xavier stood up and both boys took a step back with LaStat standing in front of Bastian. He walked over and put them in a playful head lock, "Don't ever and I mean ever put your mother through this again. Next time she will not be able to stop me and neither will you LaStat. I am very proud of the way you defended my son but when it comes to Piper neither will be able to over power me I promise you that. Now go and let your Mom rest see you both in the morning." he said letting them go. I listened to them as they left, "My God Bastian I warned you, from now on you are going to have to learn to listen to me. We both got lucky do you have any idea what your father could have done to us?" LaStat said shaking his head. "I'm sorry and now that I know I will be very careful." Bastian said. I gave Xavier a look crossing my arms, "That's it a stern warning?" I asked as I raised my eyebrow. "Come on now Sweets I could have been much worse I chose to be nice." he said.

Mike and Jon knocked on the door. "Is there anything that we can do for you this evening?" Jon asked. "No thanks guys everything is just fine." X said taking a seat with me. "Should we have a talk with the boys?" Mike asked. "If they come to you and ask questions about me then you can fill them in unless it should be answered by one of us." I said. "As you wish my Queen." Mike said softly. Jon and Xavier talked back and forth about a few things for the house and Mike gave me a look, "May I see you out in the hall please?" he asked with ease. "Tes alright?" I asked out in the hall. "She is fine but it is you I want to talk about." he said in a whisper. "Alright what is it?" I asked. "I read your mind when you and X came back and I saw some of what you talked about." he said with his eyes on the floor. "You did well what did you see exactly?" I asked crossing my arms. "I saw that you and very sad because you cant have any more children with Xavier. I don't see the problem you are young and strong enough to have many more. I just want you happiest you can be so you wont leave like you had said." he said this time looking at me. "Yes well that's true I cant have any more children, you don't understand . . ." I said before he cut me off. "Then make me understand, you not want to have more with Xavier?" he asked. "Mike this isn't very fair and if I tell you never breath one word or I will make you pay for the rest of your very long life." I warned. "I'm sorry Piper I don't mean to push but I have shared with you and now it is your turn. I would never crush the trust you have in me, I would take whatever you say to the grave I swear." he said with worry in his soft voice.

I tried to hold back the tears that was forming in my eyes, "Piper what is it I will help if I can, please don't cry." he said sadly. "If I were to have another baby the power it held would kill me. Now if you breath one word I will kill you myself this is my cross to bear and I shall do it alone." I told him. He hugged me close, "Piper I'm so sorry I know that having a large family was important to the both of you. Please allow Xavier to help you it is not only your cross to bear but his as well, let him help you heal inside." he said. "Not one word to the others, I'm sure Bastian has heard most of it so if he comes to you." I said as I wiped my face. "Yes anything you ask of me." he said as Jon came out. "Whoa I didn't mean to interrupt, you look like you have been crying again Piper everything alright?" he asked. "All is well Jon no worry." Mike said quickly. "Be careful Brother Xavier is not in the best of spirits and if he knew that Piper was out here crying and you had anything to do with it there will be hell to pay." Jon said. "Go on and talk to the boys for me." I said turning to my door.

They walked down the hallway with Mike looking over his shoulder at me with pity on his strong face. I opened the door to see Xavier making way out, "There you are Sweets I wondered where you got off to, Tes alright?" he asked with a fake smile on his face. "Yes Love she is fine and you don't have to try to put on good spirits for me." I said laying on the bed. "Alright then what did Mike want and remember I know when you are lying to me?" he asked as he laid with me. "Are you really going to make me tell you, I know you were listening?' I asked with plea. "No I guess not and yea I was listening to every word. I'm pissed at him for making you do that right now." he said. "Don't be he only thought I was unhappy and he was making sure I wasn't leaving that's all. Lets just sleep or something please." I said. "Would you like something to drink I will get it for you?' he asked. "Yes please." I said with a smile. He got up and headed for the door, "Xavier." I called. "Yes Sweets?" he asked as he turned to me. "I do love you truly." I said. "And I love you truly." he said with a smile. I laid there on the bed trying to make light of all that had happened. I hated myself because my body couldn't do what it was made for and give Xavier more children. Somehow he would find a way to make me feel better inside he always did. I love him more than anything in this world and I had a small fear that maybe he wouldn't be able to forgive me. I could hear him talking with the others downstairs telling them that all was well. "Your Mom will be alright she just had some things to work out and it was painful. All I ask is that however long it takes her to heal just be there if she needs you and don't ask why she is upset. If there is any problems you are to go to Mike, Jon or Bailey please don't disturb your Mom right now she needs some time." he told the girls. "Daddy tell her that we love her." Jade said with some worry. "Don't worry Jade you can tell her in a little bit ok." Brie said trying to make her feel better. "Yes girls I will tell her and I'm very sure she loves you all." X said trying to make it back to me.

Chapter 36

I laid there looking at nothing really just trying to get my thoughts together as Bastian stepped into my room, "Mom?" he whispered. "Yes my son?" I asked never looking at him. "Is it true what I seen you and Mike talking about in the hallway?" he asked softly. "Bastian please this isn't a good time right now." I said as I looked over at him. He was standing there with his hands in his pockets and his face reminded me when he was little. "I'm sorry maybe we can talk about this later. You will talk to me later wont you?" he asked. "Come over here and lay with me for a minute." I said as I patted the bed. He slowly walked over and laid beside me as I played with his soft hair. "Yes it is true what you seen us talking about. I'm sure your sisters know by now?" I asked. "No they have no idea I wont let them in my mind and haven't for a few days. Are we not enough for you to be happy with?" he asked as he put his arm over me. "Are you kidding me, you three are my very best work I have ever done in my whole life. You three and your father are my life, I could never imagine it any other way. I was an only child so Xavier and I wanted many children. You know he delivered you right here in this room and he was so proud. You know he is very proud of you in every way, you just caught him in a bad time that's why all the growling. I was never trying to replace any of you by wanting another baby and I want you to know this. I have had this bottled up ever since before Jade was born and then after what I saw and knew it to be true I had to tell your dad. We share an amazing bond and he would have seen it before to long then he would have been furious with me that I couldn't stand." I told him holding him close to me. "Is it true that you flipped Dad on

274

his back a few times, and stabbing Mik?" he asked. "Yes and just about everything you will learn about me will be very true." I told him.

He took a deep breathe, "Did you stay with Cora while she died and turning your back when you knew Brandon was going to kill you?" he asked. "Yes there was no reason for her to be alone that is where my kind heart comes in. Brandon I knew he was going to try and kill me but I also know your dad was so angry for him kissing me that I would return. Look Mike and Jon can answer your questions and if there is anything they think I should answer they will send you to me. Share with your sisters just leave out the baby thing this is between your dad and me and I want it kept closed in your heart ok? Now I want you to go and rest don't worry about me I'll be stronger when this is over." I told him. "Stronger how is that possible?" he asked. "Every time your Mom goes through something very hard and over comes it she is stronger. You must be careful one day she wont be able to keep herself in check and she could hurt someone. Most of the time it is the male that bears the strength but not this Queen she holds me at bay. I would do anything she wishes of me without any thought of the danger, all she has to do is speak when she wants something bad enough and you will comply at all cost. You will see it will happen to you one day and after it is over you wont be able to believe it happened to you. The physical strength she has when she is angry is unbelievable, so be on guard when she is having a bad day. I can only control her some but if she chooses for me not to look out. I fear the day she is angry enough for me not to stop her." Xavier said as he walked over to the bed and sat with us. He handed me a cup and patted Bastian on the leg, "Now Son you go and let your mom rest things will get better soon." X told him. Bastian got up to leave and turned around, "Did you threaten to leave the Great House?" he asked. "I never threaten I meant it. Now I love you my Prince." I told him with a smile. "I love you both." he said and went out the door.

Morning came through the window with me still not sleeping. X was in the shower and the whole house was wondering what was going on. Word had gotten around that the boys went up against Xavier and no one was for sure why. I laid in bed until X finished his shower, "You stay home today Sweetness and rest. I will inform the others not to disturb you today that way you can stay in bed." he said as he dressed for work. "I really don't want to lay in the bed but I guess I can hang out here. Maybe I can come by for lunch today." I told him. He laid with me putting his face in my neck breathing me in, "Mmmmm I would love to have you for lunch any day." he said looking at me with glowing eyes. "Behave X your gonna be late." I said with a fake giggle. He kissed me and headed for the door, "Check in with me later, I sure do love you." he said. "Love you too." I said as he went out the door. The kids got ready and went to school and the others went to do whatever they needed to do. Now I was left in this huge house with nothing to do so a shower seemed like something to take up time. I went to get lunch from Wendy's and stopped by work. "Hey how you feel today?" Michelle asked. "Alright I guess, haven't been sleeping again." I told her softly. "Hey Sweets I was wondering when you were going to get here, still not feeling well I see." Xavier said as he kissed me softly. "That house is lonely when all is gone cant stand to be there." I told him putting out the salads. "Sorry Love but you are going to have to get used to it you are staying home for a while until you heal." he said as he took his seat. "Xavier I . . . ." I started. "Nope this isn't open for discussion." he interrupted. "Fine if this is what you want." I said not very happy with him. "This is what I want." he said with royal tones.

I sat back and gave in to his demands knowing I wasn't going to win with him anyways. I said nothing as I ate while Michelle and X talked back and forth about work trying to get me included. "I'm going home see you later." I said as I threw my trash away. "Hey Piper are you upset with Xavier for making you stay home for awhile?" Michelle asked as she caught up with me. "Not really like I said that house is huge when no one is home, and I hate to be alone." I told her. "Maybe this is for the best Honey maybe you can get better and get back to work." she said smiling. "See you later Michelle call me or stop by and see me." I said as I went out the door and walked home. I hoped that the kids were home when I got there but I soon found out that wasn't the fact. I went to my room and laid in the bed until it was time for dinner. I walked down the stairs and into the kitchen, "Piper how are you?" LaStat asked. "Fine I guess hey let me know when X gets home I'll be in my room." I said getting a slice of bacon and leaving. "Let her go Jade she will be fine." I heard Mike say. X came home asking questions about everyone's day, "Daddy what is going on with Mom?" Brie asked. "She just needs her rest so lets leave her be for a few days she will be back to herself soon." he told her. I waited on him to make his way to me, "Hey Baby how are you?" he asked. "Fine." I said not looking at him as he laid with me. "Maybe we can walk if you wish." he said quietly. "No I don't want to walk but thanks. You go and have dinner with the kids I'll be there in a few minutes." I told him. He looked at me with worry and did as I requested.

Days went by making a full two weeks in bed not leaving my room or hunting. Every once in a while the girls would come up and lay with me never saying anything and Jovi would hang outside my door. The guys would come in and set on the bed or in a chair but never stayed to long. None of them knew what to do or say. I knew I was killing the house and myself up there but I was so depressed that I really didn't care this time. Mike came in at the end of the very long two weeks with lunch and a cold cup, "I brought your favorite today." he said and set the plate on the bed. "Thanks Mike but I'm not hungry." I told him and turned my back to the plate. "That's it Piper I have had enough, get up and get in the shower. You need to come down for dinner everyone is waiting on you and Xavier is going out of his mind." he said with a touch of demand. "Thanks for lunch Mike." I said again. Mike walked over and picked me up taking me to the shower clothes and all. He sprayed me with water, "Shower Piper and we will walk just the two of us. You walk and think I'll follow until you are ready. You have ten minutes then I'm coming back in here to get you." he said as he shut the shower curtain. I knew he was good at his word so I showered quickly getting out so I could go back to bed when I heard Mike and X screaming at each other. I came out of the bathroom in clean clothes and the stepped away from one another, "Are you alright Piper?" X asked breathing heavy. "I'm fine, what's going on out here?" I asked looking at Mike who was at the window with his arms crossed. "Nothing is going on, I have told Mike to keep his hands to himself and I have had enough." he said trying to touch me. "She needed to be woken up or something Xavier and you wasn't doing anything about it, she was dying up here!" Mike yelled at him. "She would have came around before to long. You know not the push her its bad this time just leave her to me from now on!" Xavier shouted back. "Both of you shut up I cant stand it anymore!" I screamed as the winds blew the windows open breaking the glass. "Sweetness . . ." Xavier started. "Get out both of you right now!" I shouted and put my hands up. The winds moved them both backwards and out the door then I flipped my hand shutting the door. The winds were so loud and forceful holding the door shut, "Sweetness please let me in. Mike help me with the door help me get it opened!" X called over the wind. The rest of the boys came up to help with the door, "Mom open the door." Bastian pleaded. "No the door stays shut!!" I yelled in my mind.

Xavier came through the window behind me, "Xavier if you know anything about me you should just leave." I said softly without looking at him. "No I'm not leaving, Mike was right you were going to die up here. Please let me talk to you." he pleaded knowing I was pissed at him. "Fine I'll leave." I said as I made my way to the window. The winds released the door when I turned away letting the boys come crashing in the room. Xavier grabbed and stopped me from going out the window and I flipped him on his back. I sat across him and held him down, "Let me work this out alone this time!" I demanded. He flipped me over on my back as the kids watched us fight back and forth. "You are not going anywhere, this is our problem and we will work this out together." he said as he held me down tight. "Dad your hurting her back off some." Bastian said. "Stay out of this Bastian!" Xavier yelled. LaStat pushed Bastian back, "Calm down he wont hurt her." he said. "Get off of me Xavier before I hurt you!" I said hatefully. "Go ahead and see if you can hurt me, my pain is deep from the way you feel." he said still holding tight. "Please don't force me you know I can and I will." I said. He stood and pulled me to my feet hard, "Go then if you really want to, I dare you to leave!" he shouted at me.

He stood aside and motioned his hand towards the door. I walked passed him knowing he was pissed at me now, "Xavier what are you doing, don't let her leave?" Jovi said as he followed me out. When I made it to the front door I found Xavier standing there with his arms crossed, "I'm so going to be in your face, you wont be able to get rid of me." he said. I turned around and faced the boys who was waiting for me to bolt. The storm was just over the hillside and moving fast, "Damn it you are impossible, why aren't you at work?" I asked. "You needed me that's why and I know what you are thinking go ahead call the clouds let it rain for days I don't care." he said putting his hands on my skin softly. He felt so good next to me, it had been days since he touched me like that. I could feel that I was calming and quickly. I turned and glared at the kids so they would leave us alone, "Everyone back inside now." Mike said as he ushered them back. "Come Sweets lets walk for a bit." he said with love his voice. "Will you sit and hold me?" I asked. "I will give you anything you wish of me Sweets you know that." he said as he pulled me on his lap. "I'm truly sorry for the weeks I have wasted and the way I acted." I told him as he touched me. "I knew this was going to be very hard. I knew what you were thinking and then all of a sudden I couldn't get a read on you at all." he said understanding. "Why did you come home today, I mean what brought you here?" I asked. "I could feel Mike touching and putting you in the shower. It was kinda neat I just shut my eyes and I was here in the house seeing everything. I know he did what was best for you but that don't mean that I have to like it, so I came as fast as I could." he said with a smile.

We sat on the porch waiting on the sun to take the day away, "Come Sweets you haven't eaten in days." he said as he pulled me to my feet. I walked inside with the kids making a path for me to enter, "I'm better guys really." I said as I picked up on the panic from them. "Does that mean you will back down here for dinners from now on?" Julien asked. "Yes and I'm sorry that you all had to see Xavier and I fight like that." I said. "I almost lost her this time she has never used the weather against me like that. She has never talked to me like that before." he said sliding his hand up my shirt. Every time he touched me I would feel better he would make me forget the sad things. I knew bedtime was coming my way and the kids decided to let us have the house to ourselves. We laid there watching TV with Xavier holding tight and sleeping on and off while I rested. As the sun rose to bring in a new day I picked up Miks scent, "Love wake up Mik is coming and he is in a hurry." I said softly. He jumped up and slid in his shirt, "Is he hurt?" he asked quickly. "He is fine he is in a hurry for some reason." I said as I put on my shoes. Both of us waited on the porch for him to show up, "Mik nice to see you again." Xavier said. "King and Queen so glad to see you all is well I hope." he said as he came up on the porch. "Would you like something to eat?" I asked avoiding the question. "No thank you Piper maybe a rein check? I was kinda needing your help with something." he said. "Anything after all you have helped us with." X said leading him in the house. "I'm sorry to just drop by like this and hand you this problem but I cant take care of this in my line of work." he said. "I'm sure whatever it is we can help." I said.

He turned and pulled his hook sack from his back, "This is the problem, his name is Ely. His parents have perished and he has no where to go. I just thought that Piper is a great mother and I thought maybe . . . ." he said and stopped short looking at my face. I stood up and took the baby out of the pack and looked him over, "Should I have called first Xavier?" Mik asked. "I'm not sure at this point Mik." X said picking up on my feelings. "He is beautiful isn't he Xavier?" I asked holding him. He was very tiny with soft blonde hair and very red eyes due to the human blood. "Sweets be careful if you get attached and his family comes back for him we will have to give him back you know that." he warned. "He has no one Xavier he is all alone in his world. I have seen all I need to know the truth about this baby." I told Xavier. "She is right X he has no one. I'm sorry for this what do you need me to do?" he asked now worried that he made a mistake. "There is no way you are going to get that baby away from her trust me. Are you sure that he has no one?" X asked. "I'm very sure I have searched everywhere. You need to know that his parents were human killers and he has had the taste of human blood before. He is going to need a lot of work." Mik said. "There is no need to worry Mik you did the right thing bringing him to me." I said with lots of magic in my voice. "Cover your ears Mik don't listen to her." X said standing up. "We can keep him right Love?" I said with more magic than before. "Don't say anything else until I look him over, bring the baby to me." X said trying to block my strong magic.

I gave him a warning look, "Sweets I just want to see him that's all you can have him right back." he said as Mik covered his ears. I handed him Ely and waited on X to look him over and use his magic of foresight on him. "Give him back you got what you needed." I said holding my hands out. Xavier stood up and handed me back the baby, "Come on Mik we can talk out here so you can hear me." X said. I loved on Ely while they talked out in the hall, "We have no choice in keeping him now she would burn hell down if you tried to take him back" X told him. "Why did I have to cover my ears?" Mik asked. "She would have made you say whatever she wanted with the amount of magic she was using on us both." he told him. "So you think I shouldn't try to take him back?" Mik asked. "She would tear you alive without a single thought." X said with a chuckle. "As long as your sure I should be getting back." Mik told him. "You sure you wont stay for something to eat?" X asked. "No thanks old friend maybe next time." Mik said on his way out. "Take care of yourself and see you soon." X said before returning to me. "Can we keep him please?" I pleaded. "I guess so Sweets if you think this is best, I don't want you hurt." he said taking a deep breathe. "Yes this is the best thing we can make him a great vampire under our rule." I said still loving on Ely. "Alright Piper you win this one, we will keep and teach him the right way to survive." he said softly as the kids came home. "Stay on your best behavior around Piper she is very protective right now." he warned.

They came in the living room and saw me with the baby, "Is this a good idea Dad?" Bastian asked. "We have no choice at this point but if you are willing to try go ahead." X said laughing. Bastian shook his head knowing if his dad offered like that is was no good for him to try. Jovi brought me a bottle of blood for Ely to have, "See what he does with this?" he suggested. I gave the bottle to him and he spit it out with it not tasting anything like what he was used to. "Piper he will not be given anything else, human food and plasma that's it." X warned. I placed my hand over Ely's tiny heart, "You will drink this and nothing else do you understand me little one. Human blood will never cross your lips again while in this house." I told him where all could hear me. I gave him the bottle again and he gave in taking it this time. There was something that troubled me about this baby but I was strong enough to work with him. If he ever attacked humans Xavier would go through the roof but still something had me worried. X watched me for days with Ely to make sure I was doing well and helped me make him a room. I was back to sleeping some at night and staying home with the baby. Dinner was back to being nice now that I could face myself and the family. I would sit back and soak in what they had to talk about and it felt good. "I was thinking that I would get back into work if that is ok with everyone." I said as I ate. All I got was looks even Xavier was speechless, "What you don't think I should get back to work?" I asked. "No Sweetness that's not it at all I just thought you would hang around until Tesla had the baby that's all." he said quickly. "If that is what you wish then it shall be done." I said getting up. "Lets talk about this later maybe we can go to the flat and talk." X suggested as I kissed him and started cleaning up.

Chapter 37

I waited on the walk that I really needed so badly and as soon as dishes were done Xavier came to get me. I walked with him following me then I slowed so we could walk together, "You know I miss you when I'm gone and I want you back to work with me but I think Tes needs you more." he said. "I miss you as well but I will do as you ask of me and wait." I said. He narrowed his blue eyes at me and looked inside my feelings, "You feel different today, something on your mind? You have never given in to me so easily without saying something." he asked. "Is there any reason to argue my side you are going to win this one? I feel really calm inside very different that's all Love." I told him as I took his hand. We made way back to the house and finished the day out on the couch. The kids were off doing things with their friends and I felt better that they were not sitting home worried about me. Mike and Tes stayed in their room mostly because she was so tired these days. Her body has went through a massive change being turned so that the vampire baby wouldn't kill her as it grew. Over the next few days it was the very same Xavier working and teaching Ely many things. X would take the boys and train with them letting them learn everything he could teach them. I worked in the house and with Ely so I could keep his craving under control which made me have cravings for the once tasted human blood. "Come Bastian lets take Ely out for a while and show him a few things." X said as he flipped the TV off. Bastian was always eager to see what his dad had for him and LaStat to learn.

I waved at the girls as they passed me on their way to the bedroom for some girl chat. "Piper!!" Mike yelled to me. I raced up to his room and found Tesla screaming in pain. "Send Jon to find X and hurry." I told him as he paced the floor. He went out the room calling Jon's name and telling him to get Xavier home. "He is going, are you alright to take this until X gets back?" Mike asked nervously. "Tes honey just relax and breath everything will be alright." I told her as I checked her over. "I cant do this the pain is horrible!" she screamed out. Mike came to her side and gently touched her face, "I'm sorry Love. Do something Piper!" he said with worry. I took a deep breath, "As you wish." I said not wanting to feel this since I had put it away. I placed my hands on her and took her labor pains giving them to myself. She fell silent and relaxed, "What the hell happened to her?" Mike asked. "I have her pain inside me she will be just fine from here on out." I said softly not looking at him. I felt Xavier panic when he felt my pain and before he could get to me Mike and Tesla's baby was born. "Its a boy and he is beautiful." I said as I handed him to Mike. "We will call him Lucian. Do you like that Tes baby?" he asked as he showed her the baby. "I think Lucian will be a great name for our son." she said as Mike laid him in her arms. Xavier came in the room with the pain I felt on his face, "I see things are alright up here." he said looking at me. "Look X, Lucian is his name." Mike said handing the baby to Xavier. "He will fit just fine in this family a great vampire just like his daddy." X said as he checked Lucian over.

I made sure she was comfortable and went to clean myself up, "Now Tes make sure he nurses from you and you will have to keep up your blood intake. If you need anything please come and get me." I said as Brie came in with a warn cup for her. "Can we see him now?" the rest of the house asked. "I'm sure Mike wont mind but only for a few minutes Tes needs her rest." X said as we went to our room. I waited on Xavier to get undressed for bed and I could hardly wait for him to near me. "What?" X asked with a smile. "I just love the way you make me feel when you walk in to the room. You smell very delicious tonight." I said as I laid on the bed. He slowly came to the bed and sat on the edge, "So you can hardly wait huh?" he asked with a sly smile. I grabbed him and pulled him to me, "Not safe to make me wait Love." I said as I kissed him. He turned so he could get a hold on me, "And what if I think you should wait?" he asked still smiling slyly. "You would be very wrong." I said as I sat across him. He ran his hands up the back of my shirt touching my skin. That was enough for me to live on for days. I opened my eyes and looked into his glowing blue eyes, "Maybe you should just give me what I want that way everyone wins this one." I said with a smile of my own. He finished taking my shirt off and his hands never left my skin. We spent the whole night loving each other with the way he made love to me was like no other. I bit him softly so that I could have a taste and him biting me back. "You taste very scrumptious tonight Sweetness." he whispered up my neck before he went back for another taste. I would have gave him anything he wanted from me at that moment. I ran my fingers through his silk hair and down his back, "You shouldn't touch me like that or we will never get to sleep." he whispered. "I don't want to sleep all I ever want is you forever." I said looking at him. "As you wish. I could have you like this forever and a day." he said.

He loved me until the sun showed us a new day through the still broken windows. I laid there in his arms never leaving his touch. I felt bad for all the things I have put him through especially after the night we just shared. He would do anything for me even if it meant that it would drive him crazy. "Stop thinking no more sad stuff right now Sweetness." he said softly. "I was just wondering something." I said. He pulled me closer to his body, "What is that?" he asked. "You said that you waited on me forever, did you ever think it would be like this, I mean us?" I asked. "I'm not sure I understand. Yes I have waited on you forever and would have never stopped looking for you. I didn't know that we would be the most powerful couple ever, if that is what your asking." he said looking at me. "Well yea I guess. Did you ever think you would have this much trouble with me and the children thing?" I asked. "Everything you have learned I have learned. I never thought you would be this powerful or have this much trouble, if I had I would have never turned you this way." he said softly. "So you regret turning me this way sometimes?" I asked. "Hell no I don't regret anything. I just meant that I never wanted you in so much pain. I am in this for the long haul I love you more than anything in this world. I would kill, fight and die for you at any cost. As for the children thing you have given me three great, powerful children. I never thought I could love anything as head strong as our three. I could never think of myself alone ever again." he said as he kissed my neck. "Good cause I would never leave even though I have threatened. Now get up lazy we have sleepover to shop for." I said trying to get him out of bed. He grabbed me tight, "Not ready to let you go today, lets get someone else to go." he said shutting his eyes. "Xavier I have to get out of this house so please go with me. If you would rather

I could ask Bastian or LaStat or maybe Jon to take me." I said giggling knowing that would get him moving. He opened his eyes, "No no I'm getting up right now Sweets." he said rolling over me and hitting the floor with his feet.

We dressed and hit the lower floor so we could see what everyone wanted or needed. "I could go with her if you rather." Jon said to Xavier. "Thanks man but she has put her foot down on this one." X said smiling. "She loves to get her way, did she charm you or ask?" Jon asked. "All she ever has to do is look at me and I'm charmed." X said as he snacked on bacon. "There better be some bacon left for me." I said as Ely and I entered the room. "Sure I saved you some Piper. Hey have you checked on Tes today is she doing well?" Julien asked. "Not yet I'll go now and see if they need anything from the store." I said as I grabbed a slice of bacon. "Good morning Tes how are things?" I asked when Mike let me in. "Fine just tired and very thirsty. I have drank all night and still I thirst." she said as I looked Lucian over. "Maybe you should hunt if you like, I could watch Lucian for you until you get back." I said. "Sure that would be great and maybe I can get Mike to take me to the store or just out, I've been locked up in this room for days now. Hey can I ask you something?" she asked. "Tes please don't not now." Mike pleaded. I looked at both of them, "Sure what you got for me?" I asked smiling. "How is it that the pain stopped all of a sudden last night?" she asked as Mike gave her a careful look. "As you well know I can take the pain or make the pain so I just took it. It wasn't as bad for me as it was for you I have a different kind of mind and pain tolerance." I said with a smile. "That's not true Piper don't lie to her. I saw inside you mind and I saw Xavier's face when he got here, I know you had to hurt." Mike thought to me. I patted his arm with a smile, "Go on now and hunt I'll take Lucian downstairs with me." I told them as I was handed Lucian.

I returned to the kitchen, "Sweets did you steal Mikes baby?" he asked laughing. "No I just have him until Mike takes her to hunt. I'll give him back just as soon as they return." I said with a evil smile so they couldn't tell if I was lying or not. "Piper you didn't?" Jovi asked. "Now do you think Mike would let me out of the room with this baby if I wouldn't give him back?" I asked loving on Lucian. "YES!" they all said at the same time. "Come on guys I'm not that bad am I?" I asked looking at them. "We know how you can get what you want without even trying." Jovi offered. "Well not this time I was well behaved." I told him as Mike and Tes came back. She was feeling better now that she got to hunt, "Piper thanks for everything." she said as she kissed me on the cheek. "Your very welcome." I told her as I gave Lucian back. "Come on Love we have to go and get back before Bastian and LaStat gets home." I said tugging on him. He took a deep breath "I'm coming Sweets." he said moving slowly. It was nice to be out without all the stress of the last few days. I held on to Xavier's arm while he pushed the buggy loading it down with chips and dip. I would pick up on the feelings and thoughts of other women when they looked at X. I had to bite my tongue on a few thoughts and keep my hands on Xavier. "Come on lets get out of here before you hurt someone. You have become more protective the last few days since your last storm. I bet Bastian is getting a kick out what your feeling right now." he said as we moved to the front. "He is on lock down now and forever, he isn't happy with it but he will have to deal." I told him. "When did this happen, I thought when you talked to him you would let him figure it out on his own?" he asked. "No after you both almost went a few rounds I told him that I was done letting him feel me and you." I told him as I put things on the counter.

We walked to the car and loaded it with many bags, "Sweetness I have to know something." X said as he got in. "Please don't ask me." I pleaded. "Why would you do that to yourself and take her birthing pain knowing that it would hurt your mind and soul like that?" he asked anyway. "My soul is old and more powerful than hers, no need to worry I'm fine." I told him looking out the window. "The last time you said you were fine you stayed in bed for many days and I watched you die slowly. I beg of you to never do that to me again I was dying along with you." he said as he took my hand. "I missed that kind of pain I know that is strange to hear but it is the truth." I said not looking at him. He pulled the car over and pulled me into his arms, "This isn't over maybe the future will change and we can try once again. I hate to see you so unhappy and I know that you are I can see it in your green eyes when you hold Lucian." he said with sadness. "Xavier it will never change for me it will stay the very same until the end of time. Now we have to get passed this somehow I cant live like this where you are unhappy." I told him. He sat back in the seat with horror on his face, "Never?" he asked lightly. I shook my head no at him with tears in my eyes, "I will get passed this I swear just give me some time to put it in a place where it will never show back up." I told him. He started the car and we drove home in silence.

LaStat came out to help with the bags, "Where is Bastian he should be out here helping?" I asked. "He is in his room and has been for some time." LaStat said carefully. "You mean he skipped the rest of the day?" X asked. LaStat shook his head yes while I searched Bastian's feelings. I headed for his room to find him laying on the bed, "Bastian what's is going on with you? You shouldn't have skipped school ya know." I said as I came in. "I really don't want to talk about it right now Mom please." he said never looking at me. "Come on Bastian you can tell me and maybe I can help you." I said touching his back. "I cant take Kirsten to the dance this weekend. It is the way she smells to me I thought I have over come that but she kissed me on the cheek and man I couldn't stand it. I almost bit her, I felt my eyes glow and I stopped breathing the worst part was I had her in my arms and if LaStat hadn't been there I would have done it. I know I would have I really wanted to you have no idea." he said now pacing in front of me and his fist clenched. "Ok well maybe I should get your father." I said softly. "No and don't tell him!" he said quickly. "Bastian he can help you I had the same effect on him many times before he turned me." I told him taking his hand. "How do you know this did he tell you?" he asked sitting with me. "When we were dating he would stay at the house with me. When I got close to him or at night when I slept he would fight with himself not to bite me even though I had asked him to do it. You see I can get memories from him only the ones he is thinking of at the time." I told him. "How can you get his memories? You said if I wanted to know all I had to do was ask." he said with a smile. I took a deep breathe and shook my head, "When I bite him I can get his memories. That is how I learned how to fight, hunt, turn Tiffany and anything else I have learned was from his memories. I can do this with anyone's blood I taste along with seeing their past and future." I told him looking a the floor. "That is the coolest thing I have ever heard, wonder if I can do that?' he asked.

I gave him a serious look, "Bastian you must not try this power just yet and don't think you can taste Kirsten's and stop you are far to gone with her scent. Swear to me as Prince of this house you will never try. If I find out and I will I swear things will get bad for you here." I said raising my voice with some panic. That feeling never took Xavier long to find me. "Mom I swear as Prince of the Great House I will never try." he said holding my hand. "What's all the panic up here?" X asked as he came in. "Now I will leave you two so you can talk and both of you behave cause I'll know." I said as I kissed them both and left. They were upstairs a long time and I had some time to order dinner for everyone with Jovi and Julien going to get it. The girls descended the steps and I was hit with questions from Kirsten, "Hey Piper is Bastian sick or something? He skipped out of a few classes and LaStat said he wasn't feeling well." she asked. "Yes well I checked on him and he was feeling pretty bad his dad is with him now so we shall see." I told her. "Aunt Piper is was such a close call, you don't know just how close." LaStat thought to me. I smiled at him and put my arm through his, "Take me to the kitchen kind Sir." I said letting him know I understood him. "Well he might be down later he still don't feel to good." Xavier said as he came in. "Did he tell you and you help him?" I thought to him. "Yes Sweets he has the same problem that I had before you were turned. At night while you slept you would radiate that sweet smell that has a hold on me." he thought back as I ran my fingers through his hair and kissed him softly. His eyes glistened bright blue as he slid his hands up the back of my shirt and breathing on my neck, "X stop that right now we have to keep an eye on Bastian tonight." I whispered to him. "You started this." he said with his seductive smile. "I love you Xavier Matthews." I told him. "Not as much as I love you Sweets." he told me with the girls under his spell.

When Jovi and Julien came back with dinner Bastian came down for dinner, "Glad to see you Bastian feel better?" Kirsten said. "Just a bit but a growing boy needs to eat." he said and smiled lightly to her. "I saved you a seat next to me." she said. "I think I'm going to stand just in case I'm coming down with something, don't want you sick." he said and moved next to me. "Why don't you and LaStat take dinner to your room tonight." I told him. LaStat grabbed his dinner and made way for Bastian to follow him. Friday night started to come to a close since most of the day was taken up by school and work. Ely came in sliding to a stop and taking in a deep breathe, "Who are you?" he asked with a evil smile. "I'm Kirsten and this is Emily and SVannah." she said with a smile. "You smell very nice." he said moving closer to them slowly. "Ely out of the kitchen now!" Xavier said with authority. He ushered Ely out of the room and I followed so I could use magic on him. "Ely you must never say things like that to human girls that is in the Great House." I said as I put my hands on him to make sure the magic took.

"Only two of them are very human." he said still looking in the kitchen. "I know what you were thinking little one and you will never have that taste again while in this house. You know the punishment if you were to even attempt don't you?" I asked. "Yes death is my punishment." he said crossing his arms. "That's right death will be handed to you, now off to bed." I said.

Chapter 38

I watched as Ely made his way to his room looking over his shoulder at me, "You better get a hold on that boy Piper I wont stand for this and you know it. If he does anything like this again he will be punished understand me?" Xavier said not very happy. "I have seen his future and I know what he will do until that time comes." I told him very sad. Not long after that Bastian came down the steps, "Did you use your magic on me Mother?" he asked in raised tones. "You may lower your voice Bastian and yes I did." I said looking at him. Xavier was laughing as hard as he could, "I told you that it would happen to you one day." he told Bastian. "You feel better don't you Love?" I asked. "Yes but that's not the issue that wasn't very fair." he said raising his voice again. "Bastian you will learn to control this in time." I said. He turned and stomped up the steps and slammed his door. Xavier was still laughing with his arm across himself, "I warned him." he said when he could stop laughing. "Not funny X he is very pissed at me right now." I said crossing my arms. "He will talk about this with you later Baby don't worry." he said trying to regain his composer. With bed time coming I made rounds to make sure all was well and see if they needed anything before I went to lay. "Why didn't you stop by Bastian's room?" X asked as he laid on the bed. "I thought it would be best if he came to me this time." I said as I laid with him. I waited on him to breath his sweet breathe on me so I could at least rest, "I hope you don't think I'm going to sleep while you are up worrying. We could take a walk if you wish maybe it would feel good to get out and go to the flat." he said softly. I thought about it for a minute and before I could agree or disagree he took my hand and pulled me to the window. He drifted down and waited on me, "Come on Sweets I'll race ya lets see if you can trick me this time." he called from the ground. I smiled at him and floated down next to him so I could kiss him and take off.

I went many different directions hoping to out smart him, I even back tracked myself then took to the trees. I picked up on his scent and I knew he was going to get me so I went to take off but he was on the side of the tree grabbing me before I even had a chance. "That's cheating you don't play fair and I think I should get another run at this." I said laughing. "No way I'm giving you a chance to make it there before me. You always cheat and this was my turn." he said as he pulled me on top of him. "Fine why don't we finish the trip together then?" I suggested. "As you wish but I'm holding tight to you so you cant ditch me. It wouldn't matter I would beat you there anyways." he said setting up. "If that is what you think." I said getting to my feet. It was nice to walk the hill side and hold hands with him while I kept up with Bastian and LaStat. "If your dad could be with your mom every night for months and never give into his temptations than I know you can. Have you smelled your mom, she is like cotton candy or something? He cant stand to be without her scent now so can you imagine what it was like for him every night?" LaStat asked. "I love Moms scent and after a good rain she is unbelievable. Sometimes Kirsten smells like that well just sweet and I cant stand it. Dad said it is hard to turn someone that you love that he had a hard time with Mom because she tasted the same as she smelled. He wanted her to be his vampire bride but he didn't want to hurt her so he held off for as long as he could." Bastian said. "Now that's will power. Hey did she find out or did he tell her?" LaStat asked. "Oh he had to tell her. Come on we better get to bed." Bastian suggested.

LaStat and Bastian put in a movie and got themselves settled, "Did you know that he saw her in the parking lot at work and he wanted to tell her that he was vampire even before he knew her name. He just called her Sweetness that's how she got her name, did you know that?" Bastian asked. "That is amazing I hope that I can have a love like that one day ya know like what they have." LaStat said smiling. "Yea right they have sucked up all that only they can love like that. There isn't any kind of love like what they share ya know timeless. If one should die the other would follow in hours. She threatened to leave the Great House and take us kids, Dad almost died inside. He told her hell no she wasn't leaving him now or never." Bastian told him. "I cant believe X is still standing after talking to her like that." LaStat said laughing. "Hey Mom may have everyone else scared but not Dad. He can stand up against her and all he has to do is just touch her or breath on her neck and she is butter in his hands." he informed LaStat. I thought they have learned enough so I broke in on them telling them good night as we made it to the flat. We laid on the ground and watched the moon brighten up every time he touched me. "Ya know Sweets I love to watch the moon do that when you feel good inside." he whispered. "I don't do that you make me do that with every touch. It makes me melt and the bad things just disappear from inside me and I feel like I can do anything." I told him.

He pulled me close to him and I felt safe inside myself near him. "Hey why didn't you tell me that every night we spent together you had a hard time trying not to turn me?" I asked softly. "Can I not have any secrets?" he laughed. "Nope." I said and kissed him under his chin. "What was I supposed to say? I wanted you to be with me forever to be by my side and to taste you every night but I just . . . ." he said and drifted off. "You just what? I had already asked you to turn me and if you would have brought it back up I would have give in to you without any thought." I said quickly. "I know Sweets but I was just afraid that if I did I wouldn't have been able to stop. You don't know what your scent does to me even now. At night you would radiate that sweet smell and it would call to me so loudly. When we first met and you got in my car wet I had to hold my breathe until we got to the restaurant. Even then I had to hold my breathe I was just afraid of hurting you. When you are wet you are screamingly incredible and I can be convincing when I want something bad enough therefore I wouldn't have been sure if you really wanted to or me making you want to, so I kept it to myself." he said scanning my mind. "I just wished you would have talked to me about this we could have figured out something. I hate to think you were in so much pain all that time it breaks my heart." I told him. "You would have made me go home or refused to be with me on the couch so I did what was best for the both of us. I needed you in my arms every night and now I have you." he said holding me tight. "Still I hate that you suffered." I said. He kissed me up my neck, "Xavier Matthews you know we should be getting home." I said falling under his spell. We made love under the full moon with him taking my mind away with every touch.

"I love you." I said with my fingers in his hair. "I love you too Baby." he breathed on my neck.

As the moon started to go down we made our way back to the Great House. Jon met us at the door with his arms crossed, "Sorry Jon we should have told you where we were going, I promise it wont happen again." I said. "Your mom called and I went to get you so call her when you get a chance." he said trying not to be upset with me. "Again I'm sorry that I had you all locked out next time I will leave a channel open for you." I said as I went to call mom. "Hey Mom how is everything?" I asked when she answered. "Piper honey your dad is in the hospital because of his heart. He is doing just fine as of right now so I came home to get him some of his things." she said with worry in her voice. "I'm coming Mom I'll be there in about two hours. I cant stay long but I'm coming." I said as I hung up with her. I called for my brood to join me in the living room where X was waiting on me, "I have to go to Virginia my father is in the hospital so would you mind watching over the remaining few? I will take Bastian and LaStat with me but you have to watch Ely around the human girls." I instructed. "What is wrong with Pops?" Bailey asked. "Something about his heart but I want to make sure for myself." I explained. "Leave the boys with us they will be fine and you need to have a clear head." Bailey said. "I know but I will feel better if I took Bastian with me there for LaStat will want to follow along. Thanks anyway you guys but I think they need to get out for a bit." I said with a smile. "Then go and give Grams all of our love." Jon said as the others agreed. I went to get Bastian and LaStat gathered up before I went to change clothes, "Boys get ready we are leaving in five minutes. If you get ready I will explain everything in the car." I told them and exited the room quickly.

Xavier was waiting on me in the bedroom, "Would you like me to look over his chart when we get there?" X asked as we changed our clothes. "Yes that would be great and don't hold anything back on me I want to truth all of it." I said giving him a look. "As you wish I'm sure he will be fine." he said knowing what I meant. "This could be bad I don't want him to well you know." I said as I walked into his opened arms. "Sweetness you are freaking out people get sick all the time and they turn out fine." he said as he held tight to me. "Come on lets go we have a long drive ahead of us." I said as I looked up at him. Bastian and LaStat was waiting on us in the truck, "Now can we find out what's going on?" Bastian said. "Dad is sick and in the hospital so we can look him over ourselves. So therefore if there is anything on your mind get it off your chest so I can have my mind straight while I'm with Mom." I told them. "Alright do you always listen to our conversations or everyone's?" Bastian asked. "Bastian I can everyone all the time it isn't something that I focus on it just comes to me. As for the magic I used on you that was a little selfish of me I wanted to spend time with your father and have no worries, for that I'm sorry. Kirsten's scent would have brought you to her room and not even LaStat would have been able to stop you. You are going to have to learn to control your emotions all of them even the human ones." I told him.

Bastian set back and took a deep breathe before he sat back up, "Have you ever had this problem ya know with a human scent?" he asked. Xavier looked up in the rear view mirror at Bastian, "Maybe we should talk about something else shall we." he said. I took his hand and held tight, "Yes I have and there are only a few things that I can remember. I went to do a tasting and there was a human male with his vampire girlfriend and his scent about drove me crazy so your dad had to finish with that one. There was a huge storm that night that I brought down but that is all I can remember so please don't push me on this." I told them both now with LaStat setting up in the seat. I turned and looked out the window so that no more questions would be given to me while X and the boys talked back and forth. It seemed like no time that we reached the hospital where my father was staying and the night nurse was with him when we went in. "Can we see my father?" I asked softly. "I'm sorry but visiting hours are over you can come back in the morning." he said as he tried to walk away. I put my hand up and X put his hands around my waist, "I know the hour is late but I have driven for hours to see him and my mother so please allow me in." I said using magic on him.

The boys covered their ears and Xavier tightened up on me from the power I used, "Alright maybe I could let you in few minutes but please try not to stay long." he said completely under my magic. He showed us in and then left the room, "Mom how are you holding up?" I asked as Xavier looked over Dads chart. "I'm fine but you need to look your dad over." she said as she handed out hugs to everyone. I went to Dad and hugged him tight, "Dad why haven't you been keeping up with this?" I asked. "Come on now Piper." Dad pleaded with me. "Why hasn't his glucose been checked yet?" I asked the nurse as he came back in to give him water. "I'm not sure but let me get a meter and we can check it now." he said. "Cant we run labs on him they are more accurate?" I asked looking over Xavier's shoulder at his chart. "I have to get the doctor before I can order anything." he said. "Then wake him." I said getting upset. It wasn't long before the night doctor came in, he was a round little man with glasses, "How are we tonight Ron?" he asked. "His glucose is up and I would like labs ran." I said. "And you are?" the doctor asked. "I'm his daughter." I told him crossing my arms. "Piper is a doctor in West Virginia and she can be very hard to say no to sometimes." Dad said with a smile. "Well as you know when we get sick our sugar levels can raise a bit." he said in a hateful tone. I took a step forward and Xavier got in between us, "Either you run the test or I take over from this point on." he demanded. The doctor gave in with Xavier's tone and called in the lab techs so they could run his levels as I paced the floor with many thoughts. If I could only get a taste of his blood that way I could read his future but there was no way I could ask him for that.

I looked up after a few minutes to see LaStat setting with his arm around Mom and his mouth wide open, "LaStat honey sit up straight." I thought to him. "Aunt Piper please tell me that you are not going to taste his blood. How are you going to do that without anyone knowing?" he thought back. I noticed Bastian and Xavier looking at me with worry in their eyes, "Do we all listen to my thoughts?" I asked with a smile as the doctor came in. "Good morning Ron how do you feel today?" a thin young man asked. "Just fine Doctor Champe how about you?" Dad asked. "Well I'm pretty good I guess but I see that your daughter made us run labs on you. Nice call your sugar is rather high in the six hundreds." Doctor Champe said with a smile. "Yes Piper can be hard to say no to sometimes." Dad said taking my hand. "Come on Dad lets get Grams something to eat." Bastian said. Xavier kissed me and took his leave with Bastian while the doctor and Mom talked. I was reading Dads chart over the doctors shoulder as fast as I could, "Would you like to read it?' he asked with a warm smile. "Yes please." I said holding out my hand. "I hope you can read the scribbles I have made on there." he said as he softly touched my hand. "I'm sure it cant be any worse than Xavier's when he is in a hurry with his patients." I said as I backed away.

LaStat took to his feet and made his way over to me with the look of a good fight coming on, "I'm alright Son." I said softly as I put my hand on his heart. "Don't allow him to touch you again, Xavier will kill him if I don't get to him first." LaStat thought to me. "You are much to young to have a son this age." Doctor Champe said. "I'm her nephew but she has three around my age. Bastian has a twin and then a younger sister." LaStat said offering his hand. "Very nice to meet you LaStat is that right?" the doctor asked. "That's right LaStat please have a seat with Mom until I get this looked over." I said softly. LaStat turned slowly and took a seat with Mom as the doctor moved closer to me, "As you can see I'm thinking a bypass might do him some good and a healthy diet for his sugar." Doctor Champe said with him so close I could feel him breathing on my neck. Xavier seemed to come back from no where and place his hands on my skin as he pulled me to his body, "Everything alright in here?" he asked glaring at the doctor. I handed X Dads chart, "A possible bypass." I said as X kissed my neck. "These things happen all the time and we are going to take good care of your dad." Doctor Champe said. "Damn right you are." I said without thinking. "Piper be nice." Mom said. "Sorry Doc she has a temper on her sometimes to." Dad said. "Forgive me." I said. "That's ok Piper no harm done." he said. "When can he come home?" Mom asked. "Well he can go when we get his sugar down a bit. Ron you have to follow the diet I set up for you or I'm going to call your beautiful daughter and tell her to make you behave." Doctor Champe said with a chuckle. "No don't do that she is mean when I don't listen to her and she will feed me everything that has no taste." Dad said laughing.

Chapter 39

After the doctor took his leave I paced the floor while all the others talked back and forth still wishing I could taste dads blood just to see for myself. Bastian gave LaStat a solid look wondering where he was when the doctor got that close to me. "What she took care of it and I made my presents known to him. She put her hand on me and asked that I care for Grams." LaStat thought to Bastian. "She is your queen you are to keep her safe at all cost LaStat you should know that." Bastian thought back. "That's enough we will deal with this later." Xavier thought giving both a look. "Maybe you should go down and get a drink Mom, would you like for me to take you?" Bastian asked. I was so deep in thought that I bumped into Xavier when he stepped closer to me. "I'm sorry Love I didn't see you there." I said as he put his hands on my hips. "Take her Bastian make her have something to eat." he said as he seen the worries in my eyes. "I don't want to leave the room X please." I pleaded my case. "I will be here if anything should happen and I will keep you informed the whole time, now go and get some fresh air." he said as he kissed me.

Bastian came and pulled me out of the room and LaStat followed. "Hey Aunt Piper are you really going to taste Pops blood in front of Grams?" LaStat asked. "Come on Mom you cant do this you will have to tell her what you are and I thought we are to keep that close to heart." Bastian said. "I haven't made up my mind just yet guys please allow me to think for a minute alright. It doesn't matter any how your father will never allow me to do that so you can stop the worry." I said. "So you mean to say that if Xavier said no than that would be that?" LaStat

asked. "Yes that would be that I cant go against his order he is my king."
I said getting a drink. LaStat and Bastian couldn't believe that I said
that, "What, its the truth I cant go against him he would be extremely
pissed, you both know that." I said as I quickly drank my drink. "Come
on I know its not the woods but we can walk and maybe you can think."
Bastian said. "No thank you we should be getting back." I said getting
to my feet. "No we walk that's final." he said with his own royal tones.
"Bastian maybe you should be careful how you speak to her right now
she under a lot of pressure." LaStat said. I knew that if I didn't give in
to his wishes we would be fighting so I went along and walked with so
many thoughts in my head. I would listen in on the conversation that
Mom, Dad and Xavier had while I was gone. Mom would ask about
me and all the children how they were getting along in school. I knew
she was trying to get him to give any clues on our secret life, Mom had
that way about her. "Come on guys the doctor is making way back to
the room and I want to be there." I said getting their hands. I came in
with the doctor watching my every move. "Well Piper you made it just
in time. Your father is going to need a bypass." Doctor Champe said.
Mom stood up with Bastian helping her, "A bypass what are the risks to
a bypass?" she asked.

LaStat got up and put his arm around her, "As with any surgery there
are risks but this is done everyday and he is in good hands." Doctor
Champe said. "He better be in good hands." I said hatefully taking a step
forward and Xavier getting in between us. "Piper mind your manners."
Mom said. "She is just worried Doc she means no harm." Xavier said
holding tight to me. "Its alright I have had worse said to me before."
Doctor Champe said touching my arm. Xavier was working up a growl
and LaStat was waiting for a fight. "When can I go home?" Dad asked.
"Well lets see what we can do about getting your sugar down and then
we can let you go home until your surgery date. I'm going to give a diet
to follow to keep your sugar down." he said as he scribbled on the chart.
"Piper maybe you should go on home and get the kids settled so you
can come back for the surgery." Mom suggested. "Are you sure I can stay
longer if you need me?" I asked. "We will be fine Piper honey you have
a long drive so go ahead and I will call you." she said. "Alright Ron let
me know if you need anything. Piper, Xavier nice to meet you hope to
see you soon." Doctor Champe said with a smile. "I'll be back for sure."
I said holding Dads hands. After the doctor left I gave all my love and

we headed home. Bastian and LaStat took turns driving home since we were all tired for no sleep. Xavier and I rode in the back with my head on his shoulder while I kept up with Mom and Dad. I also couldn't wait until I got home so I could check on the house and all the kids. "Piper we are home." Xavier said softly. The whole house was waiting on us when we pulled in the driveway asking questions about my father. I gave them all loves and the brush up on what was going on as we walked inside, then Mike and Jon gave me all the house news.

Xavier took me by the hand, "Piper should lay and rest." he said as he guided me to the steps. "I should be back down for dinner if not come and get me." I said and quickly shot Bastian a warning glance. "Yea maybe I should go rest myself I'm pretty tired." he said knowing what I wanted. Xavier shut the door behind us, "Now I have to know what you have done." he said smiling. "What are you talking about?" I asked. "You smell different like Dr. Pepper but there is a hint of something else that I cant put my finger on tell me what it is." he said moving closer to me. "I'm not sure what your talking about Love is it awful or something?" I asked. "No you are amazing right now, I have to have you." he said putting his face in my neck taking a deep breath. "Oh I drank a cherry Dr. Pepper at the hospital. Would you like a sample?" I offered as I pushed him down on the bed. He kissed me softly and flipped me over on my back never taking his hands off my skin. I couldn't wait for him to make love to me, I needed to feel him close to my body. The way he made love to me was incredible his emotions were never the same twice it was something new. He bit me with extreme force which made my body tremble as I put my fingernails into his back. "I love you Xavier." I said softly. "I love you Sweetness, you are the most delicious thing I have ever tasted in my entire life. I have never wanted anything more than what I have in my arms right now." he said with magic as he went to the other side and bit me again.

I knew he was deeply taken by the taste of my blood, "Look in my eyes and tell me you love me." I said as I grabbed a handful of his silk hair. His eyes we glowing electric blue when he looked up, "I truly love you." he said as he began to come back to me. I kissed his blood covered lips, "I truly love you Xavier." I said with a smile. "Please forgive me my Queen." he said when he saw what he did. "There is nothing to forgive my King you did nothing wrong." I said as we got up to dress. Jade knocked on the door as we finished, "Come in Jade." X said. "Dinner will be here in a few minutes." she said quietly as she and her sisters came in. "Thanks Baby Girl how are things with you? I feel like I haven't been around much to check on you." I said. "I guess I have been avoiding you and Dad some, I have learned a great deal about the both of you." she said not looking at either of us. I took her face in my hands and turned her to look at me, "Jade the things that you have learned about your father and myself are very true. Bastian would never lie to you when it came to us and it is fine that you have learned. I had a hard time with you all learning about me I was afraid that maybe you would fear me because sometimes I fear me and I never wanted that. The time has come for you all to learn some things about me if not all. One day your brother will take over the Great House and all of you need to know the truth." I said as I loved on the three of them. "Are you sure because I have tried not to listen to Bastian and LaStat as they talked but you are very interesting to learn. I always wondered how you could cry the real tears with you being a vampire." Brie said. "Never be afraid to come to me about anything that's what I'm here for. You may ask your elders anything you desire and if there is something they think we should answer they will send you to us." I said with a smile.

"Ok Ladies we will be right behind you for dinner." Xavier said as he kissed them all. "Are my very own children afraid to come to me?" I asked with tears in my eyes. "No they don't fear you Sweets they are just worried that it might upset you that's all." X said as he led the way to dinner. "Make them understand that I can handle what ever is handed to me. I don't want them to fear me in any way." I said as I pulled him to a stop. "As you wish I will speak to them later." he said flipping through mind quickly. My mind was very tired as the events of the past few days caught up with me. What was going to happen to my dad and if by some chance something did what would become of my mother. I was pretty sure she wouldn't be happy living with us because of the many secrets we hold. Xavier walked the floor while looking through my thoughts and dealing with the anger that I felt when I couldn't see into Dads future. I walked the lower floor before dinner as X talked to the kids trying to figure out what I could do for Mom and Dad. "Hey Sweets you should eat and then why don't you walk alone this time." Xavier said with a warm smile. "Are you sure I can go alone this time?" I asked as I put my hands around him. "Yes all I ask is that you hurry back to me." he said as we walked in to have dinner.

I tried to listen to the kids tell about many things during dinner but for the life of me all I could think about was Dad. Xavier gave me the heads up to go on and fix myself so I maybe could rest. I rose from the table giving him a kiss and exiting quickly. I made it halfway through the back yard before I heard Bastian, "Mom wait up." he called to me. "Yes my son?" I asked as I kept walking. "I thought maybe I could walk with you this time." he said as he caught up to me. "Very well just stay out of my mind I wont allow you in this time." I told him. We walked the woods behind our house while I thought about many things and him doing the very same. About an hour of walking I came to the conclusion that I would have to except whatever fate my father was to face. My mother was a strong woman who would be better off in the same town as her sister. Dad would have to do as the doctor laid before him and take better care of himself. Then there was Ely who was preying on my mind. It didn't take long for his very red eyes to change to the blue that they were to be but he still craved the human blood that called to him. I held tight to what the future held for Ely I knew that if Xavier ever found out there would be hell to pay for me and Ely.

I slowed for Bastian to walk with me, "Well did you find some release on this walk?" I asked. "Yes and I knew I would because we are a lot alike in our own heads." he said as I put my arm around him. "So what are you saying that maybe you will get close to Kirsten and see what happens?" I asked. "Sure I guess so but what happens if I cant control myself?" he asked a bit worried. "Talk with your father I'm sure he can help you. I had the same effect on him every night and I didn't make it very easy on him trust me." I said with a smile. "Wasn't you scared that he might hurt you or what might happen?" he asked softly. "Nope and to tell you the truth I wanted to be with him so I didn't care if it did hurt. I knew in my heart that he would be very easy with me and take care of me. When he told me and I had time to think about it, I knew what I wanted and that was him forever. Then I was stalked by another vampire who told Xavier that I wasn't marked and I was fair game I asked him to turn me. Man he flatly refused me on that until I found his weakness and I used it every chance I got." I said with a self satisfied smile. "That wasn't very nice." Bastian said with a laugh. "Yes well I have never played very fair and I still don't." I said as I laid my head on his shoulder. We made our way back to the house with Xavier waiting on the back porch with a smile, "She really likes to cheat in every thing, I can never win with her." he said with a chuckle. "You have had your hands full since day one haven't you?" Bastian asked. "I would have never gave into anyone else this easily but your mom has her way with me and I wouldn't have it any other way." Xavier said as he rose to his feet to greet me. "Hey your father has his own way of winning things he wants, don't let that handsome face fool you." I said.

Bastian smiled and went inside to find LaStat so he could have back up when he neared Kirsten. Jade was on her way out with everything she needed for a movie outside with smiles on her pretty face, "How about a movie?" she said. Xavier shook his head at her with a smile as he helped her with the armful of stuff. Brie was right behind her with all the snacks we had left in the house, "So what did he say Jade?' she asked with a bag a chips in her mouth. I took the chips, "He said sure of course did you have a doubt?" I asked. She giggled and took the stuff to the picnic table. I walked inside and stood at the fridge while I checked in on Moms thoughts for the evening. "Piper are you alright?" Mike asked. "Oh sure I guess so." I said as I took Lucian from him. "I can tell that you have had a lot on your mind lately and if there is anything I can help with I would hope that you would come to me." Mike said. "Thanks Mike but there is nothing to do but wait I'm afraid. Besides you have Tes and Lucian to watch over and I feel bad enough asking to watch over the younger ones as is." I told him as we walked out back. "Piper I will do anything you ask of me you know that. Tesla is getting stronger and Lucian is growing as you can see and soon he will not need me as much." Mike said as I loved on Lucian as much as I could. "He will always need you for many things, needing your guidance through out his life. Your strength is one of the many things he will ask for in his time of need and you will be there for him." I said. "What have you seen my Queen?" he asked in a panic. "Go on Lucian baby and play, your daddy will be along shortly." I said as he put his nose next to mine. I put my arm through Mikes as we walked the back yard, "Your Queen what's that about?" I asked. "I'm sorry but you are my queen and always will be. Please tell me that I will get to keep my Lucian." he said. "Well I may be a queen but here in the Great House I'm Piper. As for Lucian yes you will keep him forever its just like all the others here he will have problems with the scent of human blood and you will guide him the right way." I told him as we met up with the others. "Which one of the children has you on edge, I could help with that at the least." he said. "If it wouldn't be to much trouble just keep an eye on Ely that would be great." I said with a smile. "As you wish my Queen it shall be done." he said with a smile as he handed me to Xavier. I made myself comfortable as the kids finished moving around making connections with their dad and me telling us good night just in case. They knew that if my body decided to allow sleep to pass that it would come quickly without warning even to me. With Xavier's soft hands on me and his sweet breath next to my neck I felt safe and with no worry. I knew he put his magic on me because he was worried that I might slip by him and taste my own fathers blood just to read his future. "I love you Sweetness." he whispered. "I love you always." was the last thing I ever remembered.

Chapter 40

I woke up in my own bed this time with Xavier wrapped all around me. His arms and legs were thrown over my body and he was sound asleep. Usually when I move he tightens up on me but not this time. I turned to face him and watched him sleep forever before he woke, "Good morning Sweetness, I'm so glad you slept some hope it was peaceful." he said as he woke all the way up. "Yes Love hope you did as well." I said. "Very well with no dreams." he said with a smile. "Dreams?" I asked looking him over. "Yes never have I dreamt until you shared your magic with me. Three hundred years I have lived and the only thing I have ever seen that was a vision was you. Tell me Sweets how are you feeling today?" he asked getting up. "I feel better today and I hope it stays that way. Mike said he would help out with Ely some and that takes a lot off of my shoulders." I said getting up and dressing. "I heard that conversation how did it feel having him call you his queen?" he asked with a sly smile. "I didn't like it I'm just Piper here in the Great House that's it." I told him. He slid his hands up the back of my shirt, "I know but you are their queen above all else and they know that." he said making me forget everything. "You should have seen LaStat when that Doctor was flirting with me and when he touched me man I thought it was going to be on right there. LaStat has a tone all his own when he is rather pissed ya know made me think twice." I said. "I need to tell him that I am proud of him then don't I?" he asked. "Yes and make sure you do it today please. He has a lot on him right now and this would mean the world to him." I said. "As you wish my Queen." he said with a huge smile. "Lets get to the store so we can get back." I said shaking my head at him.

Xavier would rather do most anything else than go to the grocery store but letting me go alone was something that hell would have to freeze over for. We walked every isle on the store filling the cart up with all the yummy stuff for sleep overs and many friends. "Can we go now we have everything that the store has to offer?" Xavier said making way to the front door. "Yes we can go I think I have everything I need." I said knowing he really disliked the store. After the truck was loaded down we headed home, "When are you going to talk to LaStat?" I asked reminding him. "The very first minute I get I swear it to be done." he said as we pulled into the driveway. Most of the house was waiting on us to help with the unloading the truck. "LaStat we need to talk just as soon as we get done here alright." Xavier said to him. "As you wish." LaStat said looking at me then Bastian. I put the many groceries away when LaStat came in, "You wanted to see me?" he asked nervously. "Sure wont you come out and help me with dinner for a few minutes." Xavier said with a smile. "Get to it Love you are scaring him to death." I thought to him. "Your Aunt Piper told me how you handled the doctor while I was out." he said with a smile. "Yes sir I didn't like the way he looked at her or even talked to her. That smile made me angry inside and all I could think about was how you might kill him, I know I did." LaStat said. "Well son I'm very proud of you, it took a lot of guts to stand up and take control over something like that. I know that if I ever had to leave someone with my girls I could trust you to do the right thing. I'm sure you will grow into a great man you have a good head start." Xavier said and shook his hand. "Thanks Xavier that means a lot to me." LaStat said with a relieved smile.

Xavier finished cooking on the grill while the boys were throwing the football around. I gave Mom a call to see how coming home was for Dad. "He hates everything I give him, what am I to do?" she asked. "Mom he has to follow what the doctor said or he wont be able to have his bypass. Make him eat what you give him or I'm coming to make him eat it." I said getting worked up some over this. "Ok Piper don't worry I'll behave." Dad said with a chuckle. "Ok then call me for anything." I said. "Sure will Honey we love you." she said. "Love you too Momma." I said and hung up. "Things alright Piper you look a bit upset?" Mike asked. "Yea fine just Dad not wanting to eat the things he should that's all." I said as I picked up Lucian. I loved on Lucian while we walked to the kitchen together. "He knows that you will make him right?" Mike asked. "Oh yea I told him and he swears that he will be good. Its just I really dislike to wait that's all." I said as Lucian touched his nose to mine. "Shall we eat?" X asked worried that loving on Lucian might push me over the edge. I took my seat with Xavier and slowly ate my dinner while listening to the others talk back and forth about their day. After dinner I told everyone to go on and I would clean the dinner table. Bastian offered to give me a hand which was something he never did so I knew he had something on his mind. "Bastian you alright?" I asked as I took up the dishes. "Oh sure just wanted to spend some time with you that's all." he said not looking at me. "Ok then maybe a walk or just set under the willow how about that?" I asked. "Just hang out nothing else right?" he asked. "Anything you wish as always." I said as I finished up the dish washer.

We walked out to the willow together and took a seat as he put his head on my shoulder. "Could you make it rain for me?" he asked lowly. I said nothing as I let the rain start. "Come on Mom I know you can better than that." he said with a small smile. I gave into his taunt and let the thunder and lighting come with forceful rain. After about a hour of rain and us just setting there I had to know. "Bastian honey are you going to tell me what is going on?" I asked carefully. "Nothing I just like the way you smell when it rains that's all." he said as he put his head on my lap. I played with his silk hair not wanting to push him. "Hey Mom do you think I will be as great as Dad when I become king?" he asked. "You are your fathers son I am very sure you will be great." I said looking at him. "Are you sure that I can make the right decisions when the right time comes?" he asked. "Son listen to me you will be great. You will have to listen to your queen when you choose her. There is so many to choose from human and vampire and take your time in making up your mind." I told him still playing with his hair. "How could I ever choose when I have set such high standards?" he asked softly. "Don't worry she will come along, what kind of queen would you like at your side?" I asked. "Someone like you, someone who will love me unconditionally for the rest of my days. Powerful and loving who can get everyone's attention just by walking into the room." he said.

I thought things over while we both were getting soaking wet, "Well I'm not for sure if there is anyone else like me out there. Lets not forget the hell I put your father through and I'm sure that I get others respect because I bear your fathers name nothing more. Now as for your queen she is out there waiting and you will find her." I told him. Xavier was walking the floor with us out there soaking wet and me not letting him in on our conversation. "I don't know sometimes, I want what you and Dad have, hell we all want that. The things you share and the love you have for one another is incredible." he said as he sat up. "You will have it I'm sure, your future is going to be great. I have seen flashes of it and you will be great, happy and strong." I told him. "Why cant I see my own future?" he asked. "I don't know maybe because its yours. I cant get a read on Dads maybe because he is so close to me." I said. "That cant be because you seen your future about the baby, so why cant I?" he asked. I shook my head, "I don't know why Love but when you are to know then you shall see it I'm sure." I said letting Xavier in on some of our talk. "Lets make our way back but will you let it rain and lighting till we get back?" he asked. "As you wish." I said as we walked back with my head on his shoulder.

Once back inside Xavier, Mike, Jon and Bailey were waiting on us. Bastian hugged me tight, "Thanks Mom for doing this, I love you very much." he said. "Love you too my prince." I said with a smile. He walked off to change clothes leaving me with questions, "Alright Sweets spill it, what's going on?" Xavier asked. "Nothing to worry about this time just raining that's all." I said trying to get away. "There was lighting this time and you let it strike near you both as you walked back." Jon said. "Yea Piper we have seen many great things but never have we seen you allow Bastian out there in the lighting like that." Bailey said. "That was his choice he wanted to hang out that's all." I said. Xavier was searching my mind just in case I had made promises to Bastian. "So there is nothing to worry about then. I thought this may have something to do with Lucian." Mike said. "Absolutely not I am fine loving on Lucian and him loving on me. This trip was for Bastian only and so was the rain." I told them as I got a drink out of the fridge. I made my way to change my clothes with Xavier right on my heels. He shut the door behind us when we made it to the bedroom, "Sweetness I love the way you smell after a good rain and now that you have that cherry drink in your hand." he said smelling up my neck and holding me tight. "Xavier what are you doing?" I asked with a smile and running my hands up the back of his shirt. "Don't touch me like that unless you are willing to give me what I want." he said with silk words never moving from my neck. He walked me backwards to the bed as he breathed his way into what he wanted. "You are the most desirable woman in this world and here you are in my arms." he whispered.

He laid me on the bed gently and his eyes glowing electric blue, I knew there was no going back from that not that I ever wanted to. He never gave into his temptations to bite me first but I however could never wait. I bit him with a little force and without even thinking he bit me back. We made love and worshiped each others bodies with every touch. I kissed him from his neck to his soft lips as I ran my fingers through his hair and down his back. I felt him tingle as I made my way down his back with my hands and he would tighten up on me. "You have the touch of an angel, your hands are like silk to my skin." he said looking into my eyes. "You think so Love, so you love the way I do this?" I asked as I ran my fingers up his naked back. "God yes the way you touch me gives me complete ecstasy." he said with his eyes shut enjoying the way I made him feel. "Then by all means I shall touch you always." I said with a smile. "Why is it that you feel less than what you are?" he asked as we laid together. "What makes you ask that?" I asked. "I over heard some of the conversation with Bastian. You said you are respected only because you bear my name, you are more than just my name. You are their queen and they know what you can do not to say the wrath I'll bring to protect you." he said. I got up to dress and he pulled me back to him, "You are so important to all and you are so mine." he said as he kissed my face all over. "I love you with every breath I take." I told him. "You are the reason I live and breathe." he said as we both got up and dressed.

I was met by LaStat with worry in his eyes, "Is there anything I can help with today Aunt Piper?" he asked softly. "Everything is just fine why do you ask?" I asked him. "The rain means you are upset and then Bastian has me on lock out I cant read him. Please if there is anything I can do let me know I'm sure I can make you proud." LaStat said. "Thank you my son but the rain was for Bastian this time and as for you making me proud it is done everyday." I said with a kiss to his cheek. Bastian looked up at Xavier and myself to let us know he was fine and I knew he would be. There are things in Bastian's future that I cant tell him that he must find out on his very own and this made me sad inside. "Please Sweets try to think of something else I don't want you upset today." X thought to me. I took Xavier by the hand to lead him into the kitchen, "I think it is time you give Bastian and LaStat your fathers old books. Tell them to read every page that Kaleb wrote and when you get home I want you to teach them everything you know. All the boys I want them all taught and refreshed." I said in a whisper. "Anything you wish but why am I doing this we will be here for him always right?" he asked as I was hit by another vision of Bastian's future. "At all cost he needs to be taught." I whispered. "Sweets answer me!" X said in very loud tones. After the vision played its entirety I looked up at him, "It isn't what you think when Bastian takes your seat we will be gone on a long trip and not here for him when he needs." I told him. With Xavier's raised tones and the rain it didn't take Jovi and Julien long before they came to check on me. "There is nothing to see here boys, Piper and I were just having a loud conversation." X said. "If that is true then why is it we only heard you with raised tones and not her?" Jovi asked. Xavier turned and started towards them both, "You know I never raise my voice unless I'm very angry. I'm fine thank you both for checking on me." I said softly as I stepped in between them. They nodded to me and took leave as I turned Xavier to face me. "You have everyone of those boys wrapped around you little finger you know that?" he said with a smile. "Yes I know." I said with a smile. "I'm not sure if this coven would last if anything would happen to you. I'm sure we would all follow you in death. This house is alive because of you and everyone in it." he said. "That isn't true you all did very well before I came along." I told him. "This was just a house we came alive the minute you walked in. We are a family now not just a coven." he said and kissed me.

Chapter 41

As the movie played on Xavier was walking all over my mind just to make sure I was telling the truth. He never took his eyes off of me, "What is it Love you are staring a hole right through me?" I asked lowly. "I think your not telling me the truth, I know you well enough to know you would keep such things from me." he said in a whisper. "That isn't true Love I would most definitely tell you so that we could make the most out of our last days. Please feel free to use your magic on me, see for yourself." I told him softly. He took me by the hand and led me upstairs, "Please Sweetness have a seat." he said with ease. He walked back and forth a few times then he took a seat with me, "Will you let me see what you have seen?" he asked carefully. "Do you trust me enough to let this happen?" I asked. "Yes but don't alter it in any way I want to see it all." he said with warning. "As you wish just sit back and open your mind to me." I said as I set across his lap. He sat back and held tight to me as I put my lips next to his neck and bit him. His hands slid up my shirt to touch my skin as he tightened up on me as I shared the visions with him. I bit harder as we finished our journey through time with his breathing changing. I released my bite on him to that he could have room but he never opened his eyes or let go of me, "Xavier baby are you ok?" I asked carefully. He took a deep breath and opened his eyes and they were so blue, "That was amazing, Bastian is beautiful isn't he? He has all that you and I possess in him." he said lightly. "Yes Love beautiful and very powerful. Did you see everything that you needed to see?" I asked. "Yes and I will do as you asked me and maybe if you like we can have Mik back for a visit." he said as I stood up. "I feel very light headed

I think I'm going to lay down for a minute." I said moving slowly to the bed.

Xavier jumped up to help me to the bed and I feel asleep as soon as my head hit the pillow. When I woke Xavier was waiting for me, "Hey Sweets there you are, did you sleep well?" he asked. "How long have I been asleep?" I asked stretching. "About a day and a half." he said handing me a cup. "Wow that was a long time." I said as I set up. "I was thinking that maybe we should see Dorian just in case." he said with a light smile. "I'm sure I'm fine no need to bring Doc into this. You know I sleep when its time." I said not wanting to see the doctor. "Well your going and that's final so get a shower and get dressed." he demanded. "Xavier." I pleaded. "No Piper I mean it get a shower and dress right now!" he said with more demand. I got up and went to shower knowing it wouldn't do any good to say anything more. I took my time in the shower hoping that Doc would be to busy to see me. I slowly got out and got dressed then I took my time putting on my shoes. "Doc will be waiting on you no matter what time we get there, so go ahead and take all the time you need." he said with an unhappy look on his face and his arms crossed. "Fine lets go." I said as I walked out ahead of him.

Doc was waiting on us when we arrived, "Xavier and Piper how have things been?" he asked. "Well X thinks something is wrong with me so we are here." I said dryly with my arms crossed. "I will take a look at you and then we shall see if something is wrong with you Queen Piper." he said. I took a seat and let him take a look while Xavier sat in the chair and when Dorien took blood from me it hit me. Xavier was worried that since I slept so long that he thought I was pregnant. I sat in the room as they both looked over the blood test. I stood up and got ready to leave mostly because they were taking to long and I didn't even want to be there. When I opened the door Xavier was standing there, "Where do you think you are going?" he asked. "Home." I said as I tried to pass him. He put his hands on my hips and moved me back into the room, "No Doc wants to talk to us so have a seat." he said. "Well it looks like you are fine. Xavier told me some things about you sharing with him and then you slept. I think if you share with him more than you maybe you might sleep normal hours." Doc said. "So I'm fine I'm not pregnant then?" I asked. "You are fine, not pregnant and wont be sorry Piper." Doc said. "Can I go now?" I asked as I pushed my way out. I walked home with all kinds of thoughts running through my mind now and I wasn't very happy with Xavier. I was very upset with X because he said he was taking me to get checked out not to see if I was pregnant. That was something I had put away and never wanted to think about it or talk about it. The pain was great inside me and I was really pissed at Xavier. I felt him as he worried and searched for me and there was no way I was going to let him find me this time. I planned on making him as mad at me as I was with him. The anger drove me to walk every where to place my scent as many places that I could. I heard the Charger as he got close to the woods so I took off.

I know he searched for me for about a half an hour before he called in the reinforcements. All seven boys from the Great House and I knew this tactic, they were to split up and search more grounds. It wasn't going to be long before I was found so I kept moving around. LaStat found me first, "Piper where have you been, Xavier is worried sick?" he asked. "Stay away LaStat you haven't found me now go away." I said keeping my distance. "Aunt Piper please wait." he called to me. "Leave me alone LaStat." I thought as I looked at him with my eyes glowing green. I raced on leaving my scent many places before I finally stopped and put an end to Xavier's madness. I sat up on the hill side and watched them search for me with them all trying to connect with me. Poor LaStat couldn't stand it anymore he had to tell Xavier that he found me. "I'm sorry Xavier she got away from me before I could get hands on her. I think that maybe we should just let her come home when she is ready, you should have seen the look in her eyes." LaStat said. "Its alright LaStat I knew this would be hard." X said. Now I was even more upset and the storms moved in on us. "She's close now, I will be able to find her better her scent will intensify." he said knowing that he was really close. "Please Sweetness please let me find you." he thought to me. "I've stopped moving its up to you to find me." I thought back to him.

I sat there and watched them all look for me and soon Xavier found me, "Piper get down here right now we are going home!" he called up to me with demand. "I'm not ready to go home X!" I called back. "I wouldn't make me come up there and get you if I was you. Now stop this we are going home." he demanded. "Don't use that tone with me Xavier Matthews I'm really pissed right now." I said. By this time all the boys made their way to the hillside where I was sitting, "Piper I'm so tired of this nonsense I demand you to get down here now!" he said pointing his finger at me. That wasn't a wise choice because the winds picked up and moved everyone back. I stood up and walked off further up the hill. "That's it I've had it!!" Xavier yelled as he jumped the hillside and raced to my side with the others following him. He grabbed me and held tight, "Piper you are coming home with me right now!" he said. "Don't touch me Xavier you shouldn't have done this to me. I have put all this away and now it is fresh again." I said with tears forming in my eyes. He put his arms around me and face in my neck, "I am so very sorry Sweetness I had to find out if you might be. Cant you see that I can never lose you." he whispered up my neck. "Don't you see there are things I know and things that come to me when I least expect it I would have been able to give you the answers you seek in time, all you had to do was just ask me. But you decided to betray me and I hurt inside like the day when I told you that I couldn't give you any more babies." I said with the tears streaming down my face. The storm followed my hurtful emotions and when the hail started the boys moved in for shelter except for Bastian who watched his father work his magic on me. "I never meant to betray you or make you feel like this in any way, can you find it in your lasting heart to forgive me?" he asked still in a whisper up my neck. As he slid his hands up my shirt so our skin touched the weather started to come to an end, "Are you ready to come home with me now Sweetness?" he asked. "Yes take me home." I said now that I wasn't so mad.

Poor LaStat he kept his eyes down from me and I knew he was worried that I was upset with him, "I'm sorry LaStat I shouldn't have put you in the middle of this please forgive me?" I asked as I touched his face so our eyes would meet. "No harm done Aunt Piper just glad you are better now." he said with a smile. Bastian was wondering how Xavier could say the things he did with his tones and still bring me home. I turned to Bastian with a smile, "Your dad has his own brand of magic all he has to do is just touch me and I'm done for." I said. LaStat chuckled under his breath, "Like you said Bastian she's butter in his hands." he said. "Thanks LaStat." I said. "Sorry." he said lightly as we entered the house. I went to my room with X right on my heels, "Why did you make me look for you today, you had to know that I was going crazy?" he asked as I laid on the bed. "I guess I felt like you deserved it some for the way you made me feel. I sat up on the hill side and watched you search for me keeping you close to my heart." I told him. "You shouldn't lock me out when you hurt I want to feel you inside me always." he said as he touched me. "Would you like to feel what I'm feeling now?" I asked. "Yes and always I'm sure this is going to hurt I can read it on your beautiful face." he said.

I got up and changed my clothes without saying anything to him and when I passed him he pulled me to him, "Are you going to share with me?" he asked. "No I have put you though enough today and I want to forget it all." I said as I stepped away from him. He grabbed me once again, "Hey I love you." he said. "I love you always." I said with a smile. "Lets just hang out here for the day let me hold you." he said with his eyes glowing bright blue. "Anything you wish. So I take it your not mad at me anymore?" I asked. "The very minute I had you in my arms I forgot everything except you." he said as he pulled me on top on him. "X you getting me wet you should change your clothes." I said with a giggle. "Then I suggest that you get out of your wet clothes." he said with velvet words and very blue eyes. I ripped his shirt off his wet body and kissed him from his stomach to his neck stopping at his lips, "Your right I should change again." I said with our lips touching. "You shouldn't do that to me Sweetness now I will have you no matter what." he said as he grabbed me and flipped me to my back. He loved on me for hours without any words between us just the sounds of pleasure. The way he touched my body and our skin felt as we laid together I couldn't think of nothing but him. "Maybe we should check on the house." I said. "As you wish." he said trying not to let go.

We dressed and headed down the steps where Lucian saw me coming, "Pick me up Aunt Piper I want to hold you." Lucian said. I scooped him up and he put his hands on my face as he touched his nose next to mine, "You smell sweet you must be feeling better now." he said. I hugged him tight, "Yes Lucian I feel much better how is it that you know what I feel?" I asked. "Its when you are the most sweet smelling that's how I know you are feeling better. When you are sad your scent changes and than after a rain your sweet smell fills the room its very hard to ignore." he said. I kissed him softly and put him to his feet, "Go play and give your daddy a run for his money." I said with a smile. The house was back to normal with Bastian trying his luck getting near Kirsten and finding out that he was stronger than he thought. With the weekend coming to a close school and work was next and I planned on trying to stay busy. Xavier and I had many patients on Monday with Michelle working close to us and learning many things about me as I did the tastings. She would take notes so that our books for future covens would know our way and rules that Xavier set forth. Jade, Tiffany and Brie stopped by after school talking about dress shopping with their dad while I stayed back in the other room listening to them plead to take them shopping. The girls knew that Xavier was raised in the old world and the style was killing him slowly when he saw what they wore. "Awe come on girls please take your Momma or your aunts, I'm not good at that sort of thing." he pleaded. "But Daddy we need to know what a guy thinks." Jade said so sweetly. "Piper!" X called to me. "Yes Love?" I asked laughing. "This isn't funny I don't do dresses and stuff." he said not smiling at all. "Alright Ladies we will go tonight so get a move on I'll be there in a minute." I said still smiling.

The girls kissed Xavier and took off for home with him turning to me with arms crossed. "Did you put them up to this?" he asked. "No way they really wanted you to go and your advice." I said locking up. "I'm sure whatever they pick out will be just fine." he said as we walked home. "Ok well whatever they pick out you be happy with ya hear." I said with a smile. "You know what I will allow and what I will not stand for. They might be growing but they are my babies always and I wont stand for anything to revealing they will take it back." he said with warning. "Alright alright calm down." I said giggling at him. "I mean it Piper nothing that will make my head spin." he said now laughing at himself some. "I got it backless and strapless." I said picking on him something awful. "Hell no if they cant find something else they simply don't go." he said as I walked out of the room. "Piper!" he said walking towards me. "Love I got it I know the rules and trust me Brie will pick jeans." I said. "Then Brie can go the others better be covered up as well." he said following me down the steps. I kissed him when we hit the lower floor, "Make sure you guys eat and behave." I said. His eyes lit up, "Mmmmmm maybe I should just go along with you all." he said. "I love you Xavier." I said as I slid out of his hands.

We met Michelle at her house and headed for the mall for some girl time. Some of the things that they picked up I had to say no to because Xavier would have kittens if I allowed them to come home with that. This was taking a lot longer than I had thought with many dresses that passed me and poor Brie wasn't happy about anything, "Everything I like will make Dads blood boil so maybe I shouldn't go." Brie said as she took a seat on my lap. "Honey I'm sure you will find something that he will approve of. You cant tell Nikolas no after all the time it took you to say you would go with him." I told her. "Hey Brie how about a pair of coolots they have always looked nice on your Momma?" Michelle asked. "Whatever lets just get this over with." Brie said getting up. Michelle loved all my kids but Brie and Bastian had a special place with her and in her heart. Finally Brie found something that she could stomach to wear and tried it on, "K well I'm coming out." she said softly. "That looks beautiful on you Brielle it brightens your eyes." I said quickly. "Shoes next hurry Brie we ain't got all night." Jade said. "Awe I don't need shoes I have flops." Brie said dragging along. After many shoes and Brie rolling her eyes to every pair we was able to have dinner together and the trip home was make up talk. Brie didn't have a comment on the makeup thing she just sat and looked out the window the whole ride home. We dropped Michelle off and found Xavier waiting on the porch with a bright smile, "I have missed my Ladies did we have fun with Mom tonight?" he asked as he took our bags. "Yea and we cant wait to show you what we found." Tiffany said.

Chapter 42

Brie was the last one in the house, "Did something happen tonight?" Xavier asked watching her walk into the kitchen. "I'm not sure but I'm going to find out." I said following her. I watched her look out the window at the willow, "Hey Brie you feel like taking a walk with me tonight?" I asked. "Sure maybe some rain just like Bastian." she said as I took her hand. "You want the works tonight?" I asked. "For sure I do." she said lightly smiling at me. "As you wish Princess. When you are ready I'll be here waiting." I said as she laid her head in my lap. The thunder and lighting boomed all around us as she finally came around to talk to me. "Mom what I'm about to tell you I don't want you to get upset with me ok." she said. "I'm sure whatever it is I'll be understanding." I said. She took a deep breath, "What if I told you that I didn't want to be a princess of this house?" she asked. I thought it over thinking about shutting Xavier down until I could get the whole story but he was on me real quick, "Don't even think about it Piper I want to hear all of it." he thought to me. "Alright if you don't want to be a princess to the Great House then what do you want to be?" I asked. She looked up at me from my lap, "I want to be trained like the others like LaStat to be a protector to the Great House. I am very strong and quick I know I can serve you well if you allow me to try." she said. "Brie I just don't think...." I began as she sat up and stopped me. "Mom I know that I can be just as great as the others please let me try." she said. "Brie baby you were born to be a princess to the covens and nothing else. Bastian will need your help with the Great House as it grows." I said softly.

The lighting and thunder began to get close to us as I worried about her and looked into her future. "Mom why cant I try at the very least?" she asked noticing the weather. "If this is something that will make you happy than you shall be trained like the others. You will follow Bastian in the rule of the Great House and the covens at all costs." I told her. "Really I can fight like the others right beside them?" she asked with a large smile. "Your father and brother is going to flip over this but yes." I said as she wrapped her arms around me. I hugged her tightly, "Your father is coming and Bastian is following." I said. She quickly slid herself behind me as they approached, "Forget it Brie you wont be getting your hands dirty ever do you hear me!?" Bastian said with warning. "Brielle baby you don't have to take this path you will have many who will protect you." Xavier said. "Daddy this is what I want I have the right to chose my destiny. Mom is ok with this so why not you?" she asked softly. "Yea right Mom is ok with this, is that what you think? She will walk and make a hell of a storm you should have come to me first with this. We are one and have been since before we were born." Bastian said in royal tones. If I didn't know any better I would have mistaken him for Xavier. "Bastian that's enough it is was hard for her to come to me as is." I said. He stepped back with his arms crossed, "Brie I'm going to need you even if I have a queen." he said much softer this time.

Xavier searched my mind to see if I already knew her future, "Brie if this is what you want then it shall come to pass. Mik will return for training and he will treat you like any other so get ready for him." X warned her. "I know I can take what he hands me Mom did and she lived." Brie said happily. "More like Mik lived she could have killed him without any thought that day. Your mom is a different kind of Day Walker as you both well know, she can kill someone with just her thoughts." Xavier said. "Really!?" Brie and Bastian both said at the same time. "We are here for Brie." I said with warning. "I'm ready to go back if you are." she said looking at me. We walked back in the rain with the lighting flashing all around us as Brie and Bastian walked back arm and arm. I hit the kitchen and got Xavier and myself a cold cup and heated up. "Love have you found your fathers books that I wanted Bastian and LaStat to look through?" I asked. "Not yet Sweets but we can go look now if you wish." Xavier said. I took his hand as I was stopped by Bailey, "What kind of books of Kaleb's are you looking for?" B asked. "Just his old books that I think they should look over that's all." I said trying to move X faster. "No Piper you are lying, what books are they?" Bailey asked this time with more demand. Xavier stepped forward and I put my hand on X to stop him "Whoa B I'm not used to that tone from you." I said as I stepped in between them. "I meant no disrespect its just that Cyn said you know something that the rest don't. Then you ask for Kaleb's books for my son to look through and I have a right to know that's all." Bailey said much softer this time. "You are very right Bailey and if you wish to know than gather the guys and Xavier will explain everything to you." I said.

Bailey took off to get everyone together, "Why do I have to talk to them it is your vision Sweets?" X asked. "Because you are king that's why." I said with a smile. The guys waited on us to arrive with whatever I had seen, "Piper has seen things and as we know they have come to pass. As this house ages and Bastian takes over my rule, Piper and I will travel the world. There is no way we can stay as years pass and keep up the pretences of us being human. Bastian and LaStat will be confronted by night stalkers and there will be war of sides. Brie has asked to be trained to fight and this shall be done. My father had a friend that was a night stalker who helped him understand their ways. These books will teach them many things like their weakness other than sunlight. I have invited Mik back so the training will be intense this time." Xavier said. "How much time do we have?" Bailey asked with worry. "I'm not sure B we will know as the time gets closer." I said. "Are you sure that the New Breed will be able to handle this without you?" Mike asked. "Very much so and with your help I have no doubt. Bastian is his mothers son and he will grow into his powers, this blood line is very strong." X told them. All rose to take leave except for Bastian and LaStat, "Ummm Aunt Piper do you know my future after this is over?" LaStat asked. "What exactly do you mean?" I asked. "Will I return to finish my life as Bastian's loyal?" he asked as Bastian looked at me. "LaStat you will return and get everything your heart desires right at Bastian's side." I said. "Thank god I love you both." LaStat said as he hugged me tight. "Now off to bed I love you both." I said hugging him back.

I was never so glad for bedtime as the house winded down for the night. Everyone was in the rooms of choice and doing whatever. Bailey wasn't going to sleep tonight simply because he was trying to find a way to tell Cyndi about LaStat. Xavier grabbed a shower as I laid on the bed after picking out a movie to watch. Xavier came out of the bathroom wrapped in a towel and his body glistened with drops of water still on him. I watched him get dressed and he joined me on the bed, "I take it your not sleeping tonight?" he asked as he laid with me. I ran my fingers through his wet hair and down his back, "Sure well I'm going to try." I told him. "You put in one of your favorite movies and I know you wont even try until its over." he said as he pulled me closer and put his head on my chest. We watched the movie while I played with his soft hair and soon he was fast asleep. I really needed the time alone but with him having a death grip on me I knew that that was going to be near impossible. I had to try anyway and maybe just hang out near the window. I slowly slid his leg off me and then unwrapped his arms and moved his head from my chest. I laid there to make sure he was still asleep and them I slipped out the window. Brie had me worried and now the visions had me wondering if they would come to pass as I had seen them.

I saw Bailey walking around the yard struggling with himself and the future of his son that I had laid on him. "Hey B what's up?" I asked as I floated down to him. "Piper you should be in bed X will be worried." he said. "Lets not worry about me I'm more worried about you right now." I said. "Cyn isn't going to like this news very well, I hope she can accept LaStat's birth right. I'm very honored that he is Bastian's right hand but we thought the wars were over." he said. "I don't think the wars will ever be truly over, there is always someone who is going to want what we have and they are willing to die for it." I told him. "You have said that LaStat will be a great man and I know this to be true but this thing that they must do and without you and Xavier by their side, I just don't know . . . ." he said as he sat on the porch. "Bailey I have seen what will come to pass and as long no one changes it all shall be fine. As for LaStat he will return from this fight and have all that he desires I promise you that." I said as I patted his leg. "Truly my Queen you have seen LaStat return to finish his life to the fullest?" he asked. "Yes B I have he will return to be right here beside Bastian." I said with a smile. "Why cant you and Xavier stay?" he asked softly. "If we stay then it will change everything this is something they have to do on their own." I told him looking at the moon. "I'm trusting you with my son." Bailey said not looking at me. "I know." I simply said. Xavier stepped out on the porch and sat with us, "Bailey this is just as hard for us as it is for you, we think of LaStat as our very own son." Xavier said. "I know but if something were to happen to him Cyn would die and I would follow her." he said.

I stepped off the porch to have my own thoughts as they rose to join me, "Don't follow me this time I wont go far." I said not looking back. Both of them stayed on the porch with hands in their pockets waiting on me to think. Things were catching up with me now more than ever what if the visions were wrong what if I was wrong about their safety? I would never forgive myself and neither would Cyndi and Bailey. The rain started as I cried to release the worry and sadness, "Piper please I didn't mean to upset you." Bailey called as he started off the porch. Xavier put his hand on Baileys shoulder, "Not this time B you must understand its the rain of sorrow." X said softly. After I was finished Xavier walked out and held me tight, "You have never been wrong Sweets why all the rain?" he asked softly. "What if this one time I'm wrong what if something happens to any of them?" I asked. "Piper look at me you must learn to trust yourself as I do." he said. "I know X but what if . . . ." I started as he stopped me. "Sshhh Sweetness I know in my heart things will work out just fine." he said as he touched my skin. X led the way back to the house and when I stepped on the porch I hugged Bailey tightly, "I would never allow LaStat to be harmed I love him as if he were my very own." I said as tears fell on his shirt. "I know my Queen that you would give your life for his. I am very sorry that I have upset you please forgive me." he said as he hugged me back. Once back in bed it didn't take long for sleep to find me and the dreams wasn't as bad as I thought they would be. "Good morning Love are you ready for the day?" X asked. "Not really don't want to face Cyndi today, I'm sure Bailey had a talk with her." I said as I got up to shower. I tried to take my time so that all I had to do was hit the door but that didn't happen.

Breakfast was talk of upcoming dance and many other things as I ate quietly. I rose and took my plate to the dish washer and waited on Xavier by the door trying to avoid Cyndi. "We have to talk when you get home Sister." she said as she passed me in the hallway. "As you wish." I said softly as I went out the door. I hoped that the day would carry on so that she would forget to talk to me but some where deep down I knew that would be when hell froze over. Michelle was waiting on us when we got to work with her charts for the day, "Morning guys we have a busy day today." she said smiling. "Good I like busy." I said as I went in. Michelle was very right the day was busy with many patients and it was good to be back at work. I stopped seeing patients about an hour before time to go home to do paper work. I typed up everything that was done for the day and made a few follow up appointments for a couple of patients. "Hey girl I'm out for the day unless you need me." Michelle said. "Na you go on thanks for today. Tell Trev hi for me." I said. I slowly worked on everything that went on today and made a few changes that really needed to be done, "Hey Sweetness you about ready to go?" X asked as he came in. "I have a few more things to get done you can go on if you wish." I said still typing. "You know she will be waiting on you no matter the hour you return to the Great House." he said as he put his hands on my shoulders. "Fine lets go I can do this tomorrow." I said taking a deep breath.

As soon as we pulled up Cyndi waved to me from the willow tree, "I'll wait for you inside." X said. "Thanks chicken." I said as I walked slowly to her. All I could think about was that tree and the stories it held close to its own heart as I neared her, "I have been waiting on you." she said. "Yes sorry busy day today." I said as I took a seat with her. "That's alright I would have waited on you hope all is done." she said. "Oh sure all done for the day." I said. "Bailey had many things to tell me last night." she said. "I know and I swear that if anything changes I will have LaStat removed to protect him." I said quickly. "Piper you must trust what you see and no more sorrow rain. If you say he will return to me than it shall come to pass. Gina has helped me look into a few things and we see that same future you see so no worries." she said. "I love you Cyndi." I said as I hugged her. "I love you too my Queen now lets head back shall we." she said as we both got up. Bailey and Xavier was waiting on us to make way back to the house, "I see you did better than I no rain." Bailey said. "You have to know how to handle her that's all." Cyndi said as she was welcomed by Bailey. Bastian and LaStat was waiting on us all when we came into the house, "Things are just fine." I thought to them both, "Hey after dinner how about we hunt and I can show you guys something new." X said. "That would be great." Bastian said smiling.

During dinner I sat back and listened to everyone's day and the talk of the dance. "Mom what do you think Brie should do with her hair Friday?" Jade asked. I glanced over at Brie who looked like she was dying because of hair talk, "I think whatever makes her comfortable." I said. "I like it down around your shoulders like your Momma keeps hers." Xavier said with a smile. "Yea it looks pretty like that and you girls shouldn't try to change her or the way she looks." Mike said with a wink. We all knew what Brielle was feeling at this point, "We don't want to change her just fix her up that's all." Tiffany said. "Yes well let her go however she feel." Jon said. "Yea if you make her any prettier than she is now I'll be in fights all night. I already have a hard time with the way guys look at her in school." Bastian said. "Come on Bastian guys don't look at me they think I'm to smart." Brie said hoping to end this conversation. "Yes they do look at you like you are a movie star or something, but not when I'm with you they know better." Bastian said with LaStat shaking his head in agreement. "Whatever." she said. "You do look like your mom and she turns heads wherever she goes and I have to say I don't like it either." Xavier said with a smile. "Ok ok I don't want to talk about this any more I'm trying to eat and I think I'm going to throw up so . . ." she said turning back to her plate. I knew that Brie would hurry so that she could excuse herself from the table, "I'll clean up you guys go on and start the training." I said getting up. Brie watched the guys head out to the woods then she turned and went to her room.

Chapter 43

After I finished with the dishes I went to the woods to watch the guys teach the New Breed everything that could be. Xavier was very rough on Bastian and LaStat as he took them down making them get right back up, "Damn Dad not so hard." Bastian said as he got back up. "Do you think that you can tell your enemy to take it easy and they will, get up!" Xavier said pulling Bastian to his feet. "Fine get it again!" Bastian said. "Your mom learned this without any hands on, your not trying. Are you angry yet!?" X taunted. "I said hit it again!" Bastian said getting pissed. After about a solid hour of Xavier's total beat down Bastian and LaStat took him off his feet. "Bout time, what's going on with you boys are you afraid of me?" X asked. "Hell yes I'm afraid of you." LaStat said backing up. "There is no need, Xavier is teaching you he can place his anger away." Bailey said laughing. The guys gathered themselves up and started back to the house without ever noticing me. I slid down the tree and hung there so that I could grab either of them as they passed. Bastian and LaStat was talking back and forth as they passed me so I took the chance and took them both to the ground, "God Mom you scared the hell out of me." Bastian said as the elders came back to see what was goin on. "I thought I told you to teach them everything!" I said as I got up. "They are learning." X said quickly. "Yes learning to fall make them understand always be on guard even here in our own woods." I said walking away. "We are learning more than falling down." Bastian said quickly. I turned and flipped him over putting him on the ground, "On guard Bastian learn that then call me." I said backing away. "You upset Sweetness?" X asked as he gained on me. "Hell yes I'm upset, we don't know how long we have before we have to leave and you are playing around. By the way next trip bring Brielle with you she should be included." I said as he took my hand. "Playing around, those boys took an ass whippen from me today they are learning Piper. As for Brie I'll bring her from now on not that I like it one bit." he said. "Hey Mom wait up I want to ask a question." Bastian called. "What is it Son?" I asked. "Well I was wondering if you would share a power with me like you have with Dad?" he asked quickly and quietly. Both Xavier and I turned to look at him, "Is there anything that goes on in the Great House that you don't know about?" X asked. "Sure there is, so will ya?" he asked again. "No Bastian I wont." I said as I kept a steady pace. "Don't you think I'm strong enough?" he asked. "You are but the answer is no." I told him. "Why not Mom!?" he asked. "Your father is the only male I ever wish to bite and you still have human blood coursing through your veins." I said making way into the house. "Mom . . . ." he began to plead with me. "This conversation is over." I interrupted. I pushed my way through so I could get to my room and never hear of biting Bastian again, "You knew he was going to ask before to long." X said as I laid on the bed. "I fear him and there is no way that I would ever it would have to be a cold day in hell before I ever thought it. He has you in him and there is the human blood that calls to me no way." I said as he laid with me. "Oh trust me he has you in there as well, I can smell it in the mornings almost like when you were human." he said with a glisten in his eye. "Lets sleep Love I don't want to think about it any more." I said pulling him to me.

The next few days were the very same with work, school and training before the week came to dance night. "Mom I look like a freaking idiot" Brie said. "No you don't Baby you look great." I said as I thought to Mike for help. Mike walked in to save me just in time, "Hey Brie I thought this would look nice on you tonight." he said holding up a necklace. "Wow that is pretty where did you get it?" she asked. "It is from my past from my mother and I thought you would like to have it." he said as he put it on her neck. "Don't Tes want it?" she asked as she touched it softly. "There now you are complete, a princess warrior stylish yet loose enough to kick ass." he said. "Thanks Unk Mike." she said as she kissed him on the cheek and headed for her dad. "Your a life saver Mike thanks a lot." I said as we turned to leave. "Your welcome Piper, I don't know why she is so hard on herself." he said taking Tes by the hand. I set with

Xavier as the kids came in while Michelle took many pictures, "Lets see how many fight we are going to get into tonight LaStat." Bastian said as they came in. "None." I said quickly. "Yes my Queen." they both said. "Wow Ladies you are very beautiful, maybe I should come along and have the first dance with all of you." Xavier said smiling. "Daddy you cant come its for school kids only." Jade said sweetly. After the New Breed left for the dance the rest of us went to set up the bonfire. Soon I felt Bastian coming and fast so I waited on him at the bottom of the house stairs. He came through the door fast, slid on the floor and ran me over. "Sorry mom." he said as he jumped up, went up the stairs and slammed his door.

I went up and knocked on the door, "Go away I don't want to talk about it alright." he called through the door. I opened his door and went to set on the bed, "You know I might be able to help." I told him. "I don't know what happened we were dancing and having a great time and Kirsten smelled so good tonight." he said then stopped. "Bastian you didn't?" I asked surprised. "God no." he said quickly. "Then what?" I asked. He took a deep breathe and turned his back to me, "We were dancing laughing and joking then she asked me why I talk the way I do you know like we are from the old country. I told her that was the way I was brought up that you and Dad talk like that. You know what she said after that!?" he said almost yelling. "No what did she say?" I asked. He sat straight up, "She said something to the fact that we talk like those old vampires in the movies. I told her that was absurd and she got mad and wouldn't talk to me so I jetted up out of there. When she gets here tonight I'm staying in my room, I don't want to see her anymore!" he said yelling this time. "Ok then maybe you would like to tell her everything." I said softly. "Hell no I'm not telling her anything except I'm not seeing her any more!" he yelled. "Well something has to be said and I'm sure you don't want to break up with her so why don't you talk to your father." I said. "Just forget Mom I'll figure something out." he said as he flipped back over to his stomach. "Come on my prince lets have a drink and maybe talk to Dad." I said as I patted his leg. "You had me at drink." he said smiling this time.

The phone rang as soon as I hit the lower floor, "Hi Piper how are things?" my moms voice rang out. "Things are ok here how about you and Dad?" I asked knowing what this call was for. "Well we are ok here just wanted to call you and tell about his surgery date. Its Monday morning sorry to give you such short notice but they just called me." Mom said with worry. "Don't worry Mom I'll be there or shortly after he gets to the hospital." I said. "I know you will there is no need to worry or rush I know you have many to care for. I'm gonna go so I can pack your dads overnight bag. I love you Piper and tell all the others we love them." she said. "Love you both see you soon." I said as I hung up. I walked into the kitchen as Bastian and Xavier were talking. X was leaning up against the sink with arms crossed as Bastian was telling him everything, "Well Son this is going to happen to you and this is something I cant tell you what to do. She is curious that's human nature so with that said you have to make the right choice this time either tell her or avoid the questions." Xavier said with authority. "Dad!" Bastian said. "Either your girlfriend or the family you choose." X said. Bastian stood up, "Fine just forget it I'll come up with something thanks for nothing." he said as he stormed out. "Mom called Dads surgery is Monday." I said getting a drink. "Ok then I'll make a few calls and we leave early Monday morning." he said. "With Bastian and the worry I have for Dad I can feel a storm on the rise." I said looking out the window. "Yes I can smell it something about this one is going to be bad." he said as I turned for his touch. "Maybe you can wait just until the kids get home and have some fun then you can call the clouds all you want." he said softly. "They are coming home now so lets get this party started." I said trying to smile.

Mike and Jon was put back starting the bonfire as the kids came in, "Where's Bastian?" Brie asked. "In his room and leave him there until he is ready." X told her. When Bastian finally came out Kirsten was waiting on him, "Bastian can we please talk?" she asked. He walked over to her slowly, "Look I'm sorry about tonight but Mom and Dad are talking about moving to Ohio and well I don't want to go and maybe I took it out on you." she said. "Yea me to my grandfather is very ill, then there is what Dad makes me learn everyday then there is school so I have a lot on my plate that's all." he told her. "Soooo you guys are not in the mafia or the witness protection program right?" she said with a giggle. "Funny Kirsten but no just a lot that's all." he said with a smile. Xavier and I hung out with the kids for awhile before we went to bed. I laid there waiting on X to get into his shorts and pick put a movie thinking about many things. It didn't take long for sleep to take me with him wrapped all the way around me and his breathing. Dreams came to me in flashes as I slept some of the past and some of the future.

Moms phone call played over and over like a old movie, I worried about the twins and leaving them alone. The morning sun woke me from a restless sleep finding Xavier setting there watching me, "What did you see?" he asked. "Nothing that's the problem, come lets have breakfast." I said getting up.

Breakfast was hitting the table with kids running everywhere to get things together. "Brie after breakfast you will follow along." X told her. "Anything you wish of me." she said softly wondering what she might have done. Tiffany and Jade looked at her with wide eyes wondering why she was in trouble as well, while we all ate quickly so they could go. "Love you my Sweetness see you in about an hour. Come Brie now is the time.' Xavier said as he kissed me. Brie followed her father out the door looking back at me, "See you in a bit Baby." I said smiling. "Did she do something to get into trouble?" Emily asked. "Oh no just a talk that's all." I said as I cleaned up the table. "Why didn't she ask why she had to go I mean she looked like she was in serious trouble?" Emily asked. "In the Great House Xavier is never questioned that's all, you do as he asked." I told her. I set out back waiting in the New Breed to return so I could find out how Brie did today. Soon she came out the woods with LaStat and Bastian right behind her and them all laughing. "Well how did it go"? I asked. "Got em both on their backs first try." Brie said smiling. "Yea thanks for that I may never walk right again." Bastian said shoving her lightly. "Well done Princess I knew you had it in you now you go have some fun with your friends." I said as they hugged me and went on. Xavier made phone calls to Michelle and other patients so that Monday would be opened up for him to go with me.

The door bell rang out and Bastian and LaStat took off to see who it was, "Hi Bastian are the girls here?" a pretty voice sang out. I walked into the hallway and stepped in front of him, "Sure I think they are in their bedrooms would you like to go up?" I asked. "Sure if its not a problem Dr. Matthews. I'm Harley and this is my sister Sage sorry to just drop by like this." she said. "Oh its no problem come on I'll show you to the upper floor. Are you girls in the same classes as my girls?" I asked. "Oh yea that's why we stopped by we needed to get notes." Sage said. "Well then I shall leave you." I said as I opened the door to Jades room to let them in. "Thanks Dr. Matthews." they said. "You can call her Piper she would prefer it anyways." Tiff said. I came around the corner and ran right into Bastian and LaStat, "Are we lurking boys?" I asked.

"That was Harley and Sage." he said. "Yes I know but lets not forget about Kirsten shall we." I warned. "I remember but she has something about her that's screams my name." he said as I guided him back down the steps. He stood and waited on them to come down so he could open the door for her, "See you tomorrow Bastian." she said looking into his eyes. "Yea see ya." he said as he put on his bright smile. "We are going to lay we have a very early day tomorrow." X said as he took my hand. I showered with Xavier then laid on the bed while he dressed and picked out a movie looking at the ceiling, "Something you want to talk about?" he asked as he laid with me. "Not at this time but soon." I said playing with his hair. "Don't leave me if you feel the need to walk wake me." he insisted. "As you wish." I whispered to him. It didn't take long before the movie to start and me to fall asleep with dreams hitting me and I was trying to decipher them quickly.

Chapter 44

Morning came with me screaming myself and the rest of the house awake. Xavier jumped up and grabbed me, "Piper wake up!" he said as the others hit my room. "Get dressed we are leaving now!" I said as I jumped up. "Mom!?" Bastian asked. "Just go we will call you we have to leave." I said quickly as Mike moved them out. "What the hell is going on?" Xavier asked throwing on clothes. "We have to hurry before Mom and Dad leave they are going to have an accident they are going to die!" I said putting on my shoes. Everyone was in the hallway when we came down, "They are to go to school and we will call you just as soon as we know something." I said hurrying out the door. Xavier threw gravel and dirt as he tore out of the driveway knowing that we had a two hour trip to Virginia, "Sweets listen to me you have to find a way to calm yourself these feelings are killing me I'm not as you are." he said never taking his eyes off the road. "I'm trying just hurry please." I pleaded with him. He drove at top speed and soon we were over the state line. I shut my eyes so that I could find out if they had left yet when it hit me. I doubled over in great pain as did Xavier as my vision came true. I watched them hit the embankment as my father fell with a heart attack and them both passing over into the after life. When we reached the accident I jumped out and ran over to the car with a cop stopping me, "You cant go over there." he said. "Let me go that is my parents car." I demanded. "I'm sorry Miss there were no survivors." he said softly. I pushed him off and went over to Moms side of the car, "Oh my god!" I said. "Let me go to her." Xavier said as the cop moved out of his way.

X reached in and checked Mom and Dad for our own piece of mind, "You cant be here let the paramedics do what is needed." the cop said. "Come Sweets you have to go." he said pulling me to my feet. I sat in the car and watched them put my parents in body bags and loaded them into the back of the ambulance. "Call Aunt Barb." I said still watching. "Lets just ride over you shouldn't watch this." he said feeling my great pain and guilt. When he pulled up he came over to my side to help me out, "Are you coming Sweetness?" he asked lightly. "No you tell her then take me home." I said. "Deep in your lasting heart you know that you have to deal with this then I'll take you any where in the world you want to go. First lets get this part over with and I will make all the calls needed." he said guiding me out. I stepped up on the porch and he knocked, "Piper, Xavier what are you doing here I thought you were going to the hospital with your mom and dad?" Barb asked. "May we come in for a few minutes?" X asked. "Sure come in." she said moving aside so we could enter. I sat on the couch looking at the floor, "Barb we have some bad news. Patty and Ronnie were in a accident and they both didn't make it." X said. "This isn't true I just hung up with her." Barb said. "I checked them out myself I'm sorry but its very true." he told her softly. "What do we need to do?" she asked. "We need to make the funereal arrangements." I said dryly and walked out of the room.

Xavier followed me to the porch, "There is no need to rush Sweets." he said setting with me. "No we get this over with Mom and Dad wouldn't want a long drawn out process. We have to get this over before I kill someone, I'm so angry inside right now this is my fault." I told him. "This is not your fault this is their fate and you know this. Tell you what you stay here and get some fresh air and I'll make all the calls." he said as he kissed me and rose to leave. Aunt Barb came out on the porch, "Piper baby I'm so sorry I don't know what to say. What do you want me to do?" she asked. I laid my head on her shoulder as I cried, "I don't know what to do, I just want this to be over with. I need to call my kids and have them all down here." I said softly as she put her hand on my face. "Sweetness the gentleman at the funeral home would like to meet with us." X said as he came out to the porch. I shook my head and helped Aunt Barb up so that we could go. I let Xavier do all the talking and I sat there just listening to all the arrangements. As soon as the talking was over I rose to leave so that I could call my children. "Hey Mom how is everything?" Tiffany asked. "Hey baby things are not very good right now. Where is one of the elders may I talk to them please?" I asked trying to hold back any sadness. "Sure Momma as you wish." she said sweetly. "Piper what is going on I have tried to connect with you all day and you have me locked out?" Mike said as he answered the phone. "Mike I need you to pack up the family and make way here." I told him. "As you wish, may I ask why we are coming?" he asked with a touch of panic. "Mom and Dad were in a accident this morning neither of them survived." I said with tears slipping down my cheeks. "My god Piper is that what woke you this morning?" he asked. "Yes I tried to get here before they left but I couldn't stop it." I told him. "Don't worry about us we will be there in a timely manner my Queen. Would you like for me to inform them?" he asked. "Yes please tell them so that I don't have to talk about this. Thanks Mike this helps me out so much." I told him. "See you soon." he said and hung up. I sat back and looked into the Great House to see how Mike handled the responsibility of his new task. He called the family in the living room and sat them down as he told them everything he knew so far, "We are going to Virginia so pack quickly and bring dress attire. Piper needs us as a whole for the next few days Bastian so make sure you are on your best behavior. I'm sorry to inform you but our queen has asked that I do. Your grandparents were in a accident this morning, there were no survivors so please let us move quickly." Mike said to them all. "Well done Mike thank you again." I thought to him. "Piper please allow me to do this so that you don't have to worry about us." he thought back. "See you soon." I thought to him as Xavier came to the truck. "Piper your moms attorney said that he would like to meet with you as soon as possible, shall we go?" he asked. "Yes we shall before the children arrive so that all we have to do is feed them and I can go to bed until this is over." I said looking out the window.

Once at the attorneys office we were greeted by a nice gentleman "Mr. and Mrs. Matthews, I'm Byron Lakes please come in and have a seat. I'm real sorry to hear of your parents Mrs. Matthews they were good people." he said as he showed us in. "Thank you, this is my Aunt Barbara my mothers sister." I said as I pulled her close to me. "Please please have a seat." he said as he shook all of our hands. "How long is this gonna take if you don't mind me asking?" I asked quickly. "Just a few minutes, I have a few papers for you to sign and some things to go over if you will." Mr. Lakes said. "I'm sure whatever needs to be signed Xavier can do it." I said quietly. Mr. Lakes looked over at the both of us,

"It has been a very long day for her so far." Xavier said as he reached for the papers. "Sure I can understand ok then your parents have already set the funereal arrangements so there is nothing for you to do there. Here is a key that your mom asked me to give to you upon this event and a letter to you and her sister. Your parents said that everything were to go to you if you saw fit only that her sister should get the house since hers wasn't in great shape. Now do you guys have any questions for me?" he asked. "Sweetness is there anything?" X asked. "Not at this time." I said as I wiped the tears from my face. "Thank you guys and sorry to hear about your parents, please if there is anything I can do please let me know." Mr. Lakes said as we rose to leave. "Are you going to read your letter from your mom?" Barb asked. "No not right now maybe later." I said looking out the window.

We pulled up in front of the house and I got out looking the house over waiting for her to come out and greet us. "You know Sweets we don't have to stay here we can get a hotel room if you wish." X said as he put his arm around my waist. "Maybe we should stay here something is telling me its of great importance." I said moving closer to the house. "As you wish." he said following me. I went inside and up to Mom and Dads room so that I could start in there first. I called for Aunt Barb so that she could have whatever she desired as I went through Moms jewelry boxes. Soon the kids arrived and I called them to the bedroom so that I could give them something to remember them. I gave Brie a black onyx ring that she had admired many times Mom came to visit, "Are you sure you want me to have this?" she asked as she put it on her finger. "Yes and each of you are to pick something to take with you." I said as I handed Mike a piece of jewelry. "Piper I don't think I should take this they were Bastian, Brie and Jades grandparents." he said softly. "No please she would want you all to have something trust me. They both thought of you all as grandchildren and they loved you very much so please wear it and keep them in your hearts." I said trying not to cry. "As you wish as always." Mike said looking at what I handed him.

As I handed out something to each of them they began to ready themselves to leave, "Hey you know when I was little I would sleep in here when I was sick. Dad would try to tell me a story and he would start with the three little pigs and some how he would end up with the three bears. He would drift off to sleep and I would poke him in the side and he would ramble something about a wrong story, very funny stuff." I said smiling lightly. "Maybe we should let your mom rest for a bit before dinner." X said as he ran over my mind. The kids went down stairs and helped Aunt Barb with anything she needed while I laid with Xavier. Most of the time I laid there with Xavier holding tight letting things take over my mind. Soon Bastian knocked on the door, "Dad can I see you for a minute?" he said not looking at me. Xavier got up and went out to see him, "Its the hospital on your cell they have Grams and Pops personal effects they want someone to come and pick them up." Bastian said. "Alright then you go and take one of the elders with you, just come to me first when you get back." X told him. I feel asleep while he was gone and soon I woke up screaming as the nightmares of the day hit me. Xavier woke me up, "Shhhh Piper its over now." he said softly. "I have to get up and stay moving, just keep me busy." I said. I walked into the living room where the others were waiting on us, "Dinner should be here soon, Cyn and B went to get it." Jon said quickly. "Let me hold you Aunt Piper, pick me up." Lucian said. "Not now Lucian give her some time." Tesla said softly. "That's ok I need him to hold me for a few minutes." I said as I picked him up. He rubbed his nose next to mine, "You will heal very soon after your walk later this week. After it rains and you feel better inside I want you to hold me again ok, just so I can smell you." Lucian said. "I love you little man, I'll see you after the rain." I said hugging him. "I love you too very much." he said rubbing his nose to mine again.

As soon as he got to his feet he ran to his father, "You know you are the only one he does the nose thing with." Mike said. I shook my head yes and smiled at Lucian as Cyndi and Bailey came in with dinner. "Hey where is Bastian and Gina?" I asked as I set at the table. "They had an errand to run they should be back shortly." X said quickly. "Piper sweetie there are a few things I want out of my house and I was wondering if one or two of the guys would like to help me?" Barb asked. "I can stay behind if Piper and Xavier say that it is ok and help you." Jovi said. "Sure I can stay as well." Julien said. "Then it is settled you both stay and help her move things into the house when we leave." Xavier said as he rose and left the room. After a minute Bastian, Regina and Xavier came back into the room, "There you guys are come lets eat." I said as they came into the room. Bastian stepped up and hugged me, "Mom here are Grams and Pops wedding rings, I thought you should have them." he said holding his hand out flat. I looked at the rings and then at him, "Put those away and eat your dinner." I said and turned back to my plate. He put them in his pocket and took a seat without saying anything else. "You will stay the night?" I asked Barbara to break the silence. "Well if there is enough room I will, but I have to go to my house and get some clothes." she said softly. "I can take you and then we can watch a movie." Jon said.

Bastian rose and took my hand, "Come Mom lets me and you take a walk out back for a few minutes." he said. I went with him only because he had a death grip on me and wasn't giving up. "Bastian where are you taking me?" I asked. "Mom why didn't you take the rings when I brought them to you? I only ask because I know that I will never have the same feelings as humans do and you still have so many left." he said. "I don't know I just don't think I'm ready to have them that's all. You keep a hold of them for awhile and when I'm ready you can give them to me." I said lowly. "No I think it is best if you take them and start dealing with this. There is a storm on the rise I can smell it and its going to be very bad." he said in his royal tones. He took my heart locket off and slid their rings on it and put it back on my neck, "There next to your heart forever they will be my Queen." he said as he kissed me on the cheek. "You know son I don't think you are going to have to worry about being great because you already are." I said as we made way back to the house. "Well done my boy." Xavier said as Bastian handed me off to him. I walked back into the kitchen and took a drink out of the fridge, "Ya know every room has a story of some kind. Like we used to have two kittens and Dad taught them to run up his pants legs and hang there like guns. He would feed them something special when they did that. Well one night he was in his shorts and when he got in the fridge the kittens thought it was snack time. They ran right up his bare legs and hung there with him screaming "Get em off Patty!". But Mom was laughing so hard she couldn't do anything about it. Maybe I shouldn't be remembering things like this I only hurt more when I do." I told them all.

Everyone left Xavier and myself so that I could finish all that needed to heal, "You should always remember the great stuff those are what make you the way you are now. The way they loved you and the life lessons your parents gave you made you great. I thank god for them everyday because they made you for me." he said. I cried more at the way he said that, the sad tone he used made my heart break for some reason. "I'm sorry Sweets I didn't mean to make it worse on you." he said feeling my sadness. "No I'm fine the more I get this out the better." I said wiping tears from my face. When Jon returned with Barb the movie started and soon all went ways to rest with Xavier and I falling asleep on the couch. I could hear someone calling my name and when I woke up I saw Mom standing in front of me and motioning for me to follow her. I stood up to follow her, "Sweetness where are you going?" Xavier asked as he caught my hand. "Its Mom she needs me, I'll be right back." I whispered. "Piper wait I'm coming are you sure its her?" he said getting up. "Can you see her X, isn't she beautiful in the glowing light?" I said still whispering. "Yes I can see her." he said catching up with me. She floated in front of me smiling softly just like I remembered when she would care for me. "Piper baby things are the way they are supposed to be, this is life we are born to die. You must not let yourself slip into a depression we are fine and we will watch over you always. Your children need you in the worst way and you must stay strong for them. I will love you forever and my beautiful grandbabies. Take good care of my baby girl Xavier and love her with all your heart and soul. I have to go now and I will never visit again for this is the very best thing for you." she said with her voice sounding like a song. "Mom wait please I'm not ready to let you go, please stay." I pleaded with her. She floated close to me, "Piper I have to go you know I cant stay now your father is waiting for me. Take her now Xavier and let her do what is needed to heal inside." Mom said softly as her light slowly went dim and then out.

I sat in the floor and cried hard as I heard the thunder coming over the hillside. "Outside Sweets now you have to release this and I want you to give me all you have inside you!" X said as he pulled me to my feet. I went outside and let it storm like no other before and cried as it rained on me and X. The others came out to be with me as I stood there with the mixed weather beat down on all of us. Bastian started towards me and X held him back, "No Bastian she needs this and if you go near her she could hurt you. She hurts deep inside right now and this is for the best." X told him. "I wish I could feel her, she has shut me off from her feelings." Bastian said. "No you don't I'm having a hard time standing here as is." X said. I turned and walked over to Bastian as he took steps back to get out of my way. I put my hand over his heart, "Hold her tight Bastian this is going to hurt." X said. I let the feelings run from me into Bastian as he held tight to my wrist.

I pulled him to the ground and we sat there while I let him feel my human feelings. "Mom that's enough I cant take anymore." Bastian said with great pain. I didn't stop I let the feelings run hard from me until I was finished. "Piper let him go." Xavier demanded. I let him up and we both laid on the ground in the rain, "See this is the very reason I have shut you down from me. This is the very last time you will ever feel this kind of pain." I said as I caressed his perfect face. Morning came over the hillside with me laying on the ground and Xavier setting beside me, "Sweetness shall we go inside or would you like more time?" X asked. "I'm finished until I get home and walk, and when we get home nothing changes I want the same as always." I said getting up. "As you wish." he said walking with me.

We went to shower so that this day could get started and I could be closer to getting back to the Great House. "Mr. Brooks from the funereal home has called and asked that we come along." Cyndi asked. I gave her a heads up when I came in the living room, "Did you forget Aunt Piper?" Lucian asked. "No Love I haven't forgotten come and I'll hold you." I said. I scooped him up and he put his arms around my neck hugging me tightly then rubbing his nose next to mine. "Almost but not just yet you have to walk and then it will be over. You will smell the way you are to smell to me." he said with a smile. "You are something else Lucian and your right it will be over very soon." I said as he played with my hair. Once at the funereal home everyone got out except me, "You coming Piper we can go in together?" Aunt Barb asked. I shook my head no at her with Julien coming up to us, "She will be there in a few minutes maybe I could escort you inside." Julien said softly. She slid her arm into his and they walked away with Xavier opening my door, "Now Sweets you have to go, this day and the next then we go home." he said holding his hand out. I took his hand and got out to walk into a empty room all except for the family, "Mr. and Mrs. Matthews please allow me to express how sorry I am, your Dad and I were pretty good friends they were great folks. If you would like to view before everyone arrives I can show you the way." he offered as he put his hand on my back and slightly moved me forward. "If you wouldn't mind Id like to go last, make sure the others go then I shall." I said as I dug my heels in floor. Mr. Brooks looked at me then Xavier, "I'll make sure she gets there before it gets to busy." Xavier said. As soon as Mr. Brooks was out of sight I turned to leave, "Oh no you don't Sweets, we have to do this. I never got to say goodbye to my parents and I regret it everyday just like I know you will." he said softly as he touched me. "What if I freak out?" I asked still trying to leave. "Just don't leave my touch and I'm sure you will be just fine." he said taking my hand.

Chapter 45

So many people showed up to pay their respects to Mom and Dad. Before to long the long night came to an end and many left, "Are you ready to go and maybe get something to eat?" Bastian asked. "Yes please take me out of here I don't want to be the last ones here." I said getting his arm. We sat in the car and waited on Xavier to finish, "Hey Mom do you feel those kind of feelings that you shared with me all the time?" Bastian asked softly. "Yes everyday all day that's the reason I shut you down from me. Lets not forget when you feel LaStat also feels and he is different than we are. Why do you ask Love?" I asked looking in his blue eyes. "Do all humans feel like this over things big or small?" he asked not looking at me. "No they don't feel as deep as I do but they hurt and heal, where is this leading?" I asked tracing his face. "Maybe this isn't the right time, maybe we can talk after you had your walk." he said quickly. "Maybe you should just tell me and we can work this out now." I said. "Alright I ask because I never want to make anyone feel like that." he said and stopped. "Who could you possibly make feel that way?" I asked looking him over. "Kirsten I mean I like the girl but not to marry to make mine forever. I knew when Harley stopped by that she was the one, but I hate to think that I might make Kirsten feel like that." he said with a touch of sadness. "Awe Baby if Kirsten isn't the one then you need to end this now before it goes to far." I told him as Xavier opened the car door, "Shall we go and have dinner?" he asked.

I looked at Bastian who had this look on his face of don't tell dad, "Yes please." I simply said. "Is there anything I can help with?" Xavier asked looking at both of us. "No Bastian just thought maybe we could go hunt that it may do us some good." I said with a smile. X narrowed his blue eyes at me, "Your lying Sweetness." he thought to me. "Yes well we can speak of it later." I thought back to him. Dinner came and went much to fast for my liking only because I had to return to my parents home. The house was dark when we pulled up and everyone got out but I held back, "Would you like for me to go in first and turn on some lights?" Jon asked. "Thanks Jon she never liked the house dark." I told him. I watched all my children enter the house as I sat in the car, "Is there anything I should know about our son, he shouldn't bother you right now?" X asked. "He didn't bother me Love you know that I would rather deal with his problems instead of mine. He was asking about the feelings that I shared he wondered if humans feel as deep as I do. Its Kirsten she isn't the one Harley is." I told him. "Somehow I knew this would come up, is he alright?" X asked. "Oh sure he is your son and he will make the right choice like you have." I said walking into the house. "Momma do you have another story about Grams?" Jade asked carefully. "Allow me to change clothes and I will tell you all something else about her alright Baby." I told her as I touched her face.

I changed clothes and went back down stairs to find all in the living room waiting on me. "Ok well one night Mom and Dad were in bed when she was woken up by a strange sound. When she woke she found out that there was a bat in the house. She jumped out of bed and flipped on the light shutting the door behind her. Dad was locked in the bedroom blinded by the light she told him to get the bat out of the house and then she would let him out. He was on the other side of the door screaming "Let me out Patty!" as she was held the door tight. Well he shut the light off which in turn let the bat see very well. Dad finally caught the bat and put him out then she opened the door for him. He was upset with her but only for a few minutes. Another thing she would do she would send him on to bed while she made rounds in the house to make sure that the house was locked up and I had all I needed then she would get into bed. He was nice and warm and she would put her ice cold feet on the back of his legs sending him right out the other side of the bed. You had to keep a very close eye on her at all times." I told them laughing some. "Now I know where you get it and it is very nice to see you smile." X said. "It feels good to smile some I guess. I'm really tired so I'm going to lay here for a few minutes." I told them. "I'm going to go to bed if you all need anything come and get me." Aunt Barb said. As soon as she was fast asleep we went to hunt as a family. I waited and watched while the others hunted. It was amazing how Xavier and Bastian looked the very same when they pounced after their prey.

I sat under a tree and slowly fed on mine when Jovi came and sat with me. "How are you holding up my Queen?" Jovi asked softly. "I'm ok just another day then I can put this behind me." I said as I laid my prey down softly. "May I ask a favor from you?" he asked. "Sure what is it?" I said looking at him. "Please don't go to bed and stay for many days. I sat outside your door many hours just in case you needed me for anything. You are so very important to us all." he said not looking at me. "I knew you were out there and I'm very sorry that I stayed in bed. I'm going to try to keep my feet flat on the ground this time." I said putting my arm around him. "Allow me to escort you to Xavier." he said with a smile. Bed time came as soon as all was in the house with Xavier and I on the couch. "This reminds me when we came to tell your parents about us having the twins." X said as he pulled me close. "Yes I remember Dad was mad as hell." I said relaxing some. "I love you like no other can." he said falling into a sleep. "I love you Xavier." I whispered to him. When the sun rose over the horizon I slipped out of his arms and got ready for the day. Mike was next to hit the lower floor, "Good morning Piper did you sleep?" he asked. "No not at all, how about you?" I asked as he lead the way to the kitchen. "Not very well mostly I thought about the pain you were in. You have showed Bastian and Xavier can feel you most of the time I was wondering if you would do the same for me?" he asked softly. "Mike why would you want to feel such horror you are made different then Bastian and myself it could kill you?" I asked. "I don't know why I want something like this, please I have never asked you and I really want to know." he said setting with me.

I set myself inside his mind and heart as I put my hand over his heart, "As you wish hold tight to me." I said softly. I let some things go into him with his grip getting tighter on me and soon he began to stop breathing. "Please, please." he begged. "No you have to feel it all to understand I'm so sorry." I said crying that I placed him in great pain. We both went to the floor as I finished letting him into my bleeding heart and then I stopped. I sat with him until he began to move once again, "Are you alright?" I asked. "How do you get out of bed, is it like that for you everyday?" he asked as he set up. "Yes most days but you need to know that you only got the baby thing and my parents." I told him. Xavier came into the kitchen with a unhappy look on his face, "What the hell did you do to him Piper?" he asked helping Mike out of the floor. "Nothing I didn't ask for Xavier I begged her to allow me in." Mike said as he got to his feet. Everyone started to come in and ready for the day, "Should we leave now?" Brielle asked. "Yes then when this is over we should be heading back to the Great House." Xavier said. "Why do you have to leave so soon?" Barb asked. "I have patients that I'm sure needs my attention and Piper needs to get the proper rest. Julien and Jovi will stay behind so that you get the things moved around to fit your needs then they can return home." Xavier told her. We loaded the cars up and headed to the funereal home and I was last in my seat up front. We listened to the sermon and soon it was time for my seven boys to help as pall bearers to carry Mom and Dad to be buried. I had nothing to say on the drive up to the burial site just looked out the window. That day was the day we put my parents to rest beside my Grandmother and Grandfather. I handed flowers to all of my kids as they made way back to the car and I stayed behind to talk to them once more. "I will love you both for the rest of my days keeping you in the hearts of all my children. If I had been here in time I would have been able to stop this from coming and I would have you here with me. Please take care of one another and I will visit from time to time but there will be a time that I cant but you will be in my memories." I said standing there alone. "Come on Sweetness you have to leave them here. Their souls will be taken very good care of it is just their temples that lay here." Xavier said as he led the way to the car. I didn't stay long at the house before I wanted to get back home. I kissed Aunt Barb and took the things my parents set forth for me to have and waited on Xavier in the car. "Michelle is waiting on us she is worried that we haven't called." X said as he got in. "Yes I have known for a day or so that she is looking for clues to where we are. I should have called her ya know?" I said. "She will understand as always. Why don't you try and rest while we make way home." he said. "No Id rather not ever sleep." I told him.

Michelle was waiting on us when we arrived, "Hey I used the key to let myself in hope that's ok? Where have you been I called both phones I was worried sick?" she asked crossing her arms. "We had a few things to take care of sorry we didn't call." he said as I went to my room. I laid on the bed with the flowers I took and cried what I had left in me when Michelle knocked on the door, "Piper honey I'm so sorry, Xavier told me what happened. Is there anything I can do for you?" she asked. "Will you hang these upside down so they will dry?" I asked as I handed her my flowers. "Sure thing, would you like something to eat or maybe one of your cups?" she asked. "I'm sure X will be coming up soon. Forgive me for not calling I was so well you know." I said softly. "That's ok but I'm gonna put a GPS on you so I know where you are from now on." she said with a laugh. "Hey Michelle how was the office while I was gone?" X asked as he came in with a warm cup. "Fine most I took care of the other I rescheduled." she said as I drank. "Will you be staying for dinner?" I asked. "Thanks girl but I know you have to walk so lets get together tomorrow." she said with a smile. "Sounds great girl steaks on the grill." I said perking up some. She hugged me and left. "Would you like to read your letter before your walk?" X asked. "You read it and sum it up for me." I said as he took off my shoes. "That is a personal letter from your mother and there is no way I'm reading it alone. We can lay here and read it together but I'm not reading it for you." he said. I took the letter and very carefully opened it as we laid there together. He put his arm around me as I pulled it from the envelope.

Dear Piper,

I hope this doesn't cause you pain but I was compelled to write you something. You have been the light of my life and I could have never imagine what it would have been without you. Your dad and I love you so very much and we knew that you would turn out great. We are very proud to be your parents and the grandparents of all those children you and Xavier care for. Bastian, Brielle and Jade have been a blessing to us and we thank you both for them. Now don't hover over them let them spread their beautiful wings and grow into what I know will be great adults. They say that there is someone out there for everyone and I think you have found your eternal soul mate. Love Xavier with all of your heart, respect him and in return he will do the very same. Take care and love each other like there is no tomorrow. Give the kids a life lesson that they will carry with them and love them unconditionally and they will be as great as you both are. I love you my baby girl.

Love,
Mom and Dad.

Xavier took my hand and led me to the window knowing now was a good time to walk. Walking in our own woods felt good to my soul even though I felt like this was my fault. If I had taken the time and went the night before I could have prevented this from coming. Leaving Mom and Dad in Virginia was the best thing knowing I wouldn't be here always. I finally slowed enough for Xavier to walk with me, "Take me home." I said softly. "You need to put this away so that it doesn't take you away from me. If you allow this to bring you down I may never get you back." he said as he took my hand. "I have put this away it will burn in my lasting heart for many days but keeping busy will help." I told him. "And sleeping do you think you might?" he asked. "I hope so I have shared many things the past few days and when I do I usually sleep." I told him. "Yes poor Mike and Bastian the pain you gave them was horrible." he said with a smile. "Mike will never ask again for he will remember always. Bastian on the other hand he needed this so that he can understand himself and humans as they come to pass in his life. Please don't say anything about Kirsten let him come to you." I told him. "As you wish always my Queen." he said with a smile. I kissed him on the cheek and took off laughing as he began his chase, "You are supposed to say go or something!" he called after me. I ran as fast as I could knowing he was a few clicks behind me making into the back yard first hoping to make the house. I ran LaStat over as I came around the turn, "Trying to win the race again Aunt Piper?" LaStat asked as we laid in the yard together. "Yea but not going to happen today huh?" I asked with a smile. "You should keep your eyes open Love you could get hurt." X said as he walked over to us. "Don't you mean hurt someone?" LaStat asked as he helped me up. Dinner was on its way to being done and I wasn't very hungry but I ate so that I could hear of the upcoming events from the children. Bastian had many things running through his mind about Kirsten and Harley. He worried that he would hurt Kirsten and make her feel like I showed him while in Virginia.

Chapter 46

I helped with the clean up as Bastian came back in the kitchen and taking a seat, "Hey Bastian would you like to go to the store with me?" I asked. "Isn't Dad going like always?" he asked putting his head on the table. "Nope he has things to do so you can go with me this time. Come on we can take the Charger wanna drive?" I asked as I pulled on his hand. He jumped to his feet and pulled me along, "Bastian!" X called as we hit the front door. "I know I know be careful." he said as we went out. He drove along with a huge smile on his face, "I thought Dad would never let me drive this car he always says take the truck." he said happily. "That car is his baby I have only driven it a few times myself." I told him on the way inside. We walked through the store and filled it with junk food and a few household items we needed, "Hey Mom I need a new pair of kicks would it be alright if LaStat and I head to the mall one day this week?" he asked. "Sure that will be fine just you two?" I asked. "Yep no sisters." he said with a smile. "Hey Bastian where have you been, I've missed seeing you at school?" a small voice rang out. "Hey Harley had some family business to tend to. What are you doing here?" he asked holding his breath. "Hi Mrs. Matthews, just grabbing some junk." she said with a smile. "Harley so nice to see you again." I said hoping she would call me Piper. "Family business everyone alright?" she asked kindly. "Na my grandparents passed away and we were in Virginia the past few days." Bastian said looking at me. "My heart goes out to all of you. If there is anything I can do let me know." she said as she touched my arm. "That's is very kind of you." I said softly.

"Hey Mom this is Bastian and his mom Dr. Matthews." Harley said as her mom approached us. "Nice to meet you, I'm Becky." she said as we shook hands. "Your girls are invited to a sleepover this weekend if you wish." I told her. "Well maybe I usually like to meet the family first." she said quickly. "Then feel free to stop by anytime you are most welcome." I told her. "Mom they have like fifteen kids they have adopted so many that have no where to go, it has to be great fun." Harley said just as quick. "Where are the boys when the girls are sleeping over?" Becky asked. "They hang out for bonfires and movies but when bedtime comes they are to stay in their rooms. I have strict rules about that and Xavier and I are always there during movies." I told her. "Alright then maybe we can stop by Friday if that is alright." she said looking at the girls. "Yesssss!" both Harley and Sage said together. Bastian laughed under his breath, "See you Friday then." I said as we shook hands again. "Mom you should see her husband he is as gorgeous as Bastian." Harley said as they walked off. "Harley you should keep your comments to yourself, she may not like that." Becky said. Home again and Bastian couldn't wait to tell LaStat his news on the girls coming over, "Help me then you can inform LaStat, I know you are about to jump out of your skin to tell him." I said with a smile. "Ok hurry I'll carry all the bags if need be." he said getting most. "Just go and send someone out to help me." I said as he kissed me on the cheek and headed for the door.

Bailey came out looking back at Bastian, "Would you like my help?" He asked. "Yes please I was ditched for LaStat again." I said handing him bags. "What's the rush?" he asked. "Girls." I said. "Have mercy those boys are something else." he said as we landed on the front porch. "Wow cleaned out the junk food isle did we?" X asked as he took my bags. "I have learned to never take Bastian junk food shopping that boy can shop. Oh by the way Bastian and LaStat wants to go to the mall this weekend for shoes." I said. "He can take the truck not my Charger." X said quickly. "He knows that you love that car more than anything else in this world." I said knowing I would get a reaction from him. "Sweets!" he said and quickly turned around. I met him with a smile "Just giving you a hard time that's all." I said. "It will be his soon enough, I'm gonna miss that car." he said leaning up against the sink. "Who says we have to give him the Charger he can have the Camaro." I told him. "And what of the girls what shall they drive?" he asked. "Maybe it is time we find them something of choice." I suggested. "As you wish we can do it this weekend." he said with a smile knowing he was keeping his Charger. As the week closed Xavier worked everyday with me hanging around the house watching Ely and Lucian grow at top speed and soon they would be as big as the others. We never put the children in school until their growing slowed at a normal speed but they were as sharp as the others.

Lucian came into the living room, "Aunt Piper the time has come for me to hold you now." he said. "Alright little man lets have it." I said holding out my arms. He ran up to me as I picked him up, "This is the scent I love from you. You feel much better now don't you?" he asked as he rubbed his nose next to mine. "Yes all has been put away hope they stay like that." I said. "Locked tight in your heart and they will stay. You have to push yourself hard to live everyday and do the things you love the most. You are most needed here and soon you will have to leave but not before you have taught us everything you and Unk Xavier knows. Please don't worry you will come back in our hour of need as always." he told me as he played with my hair. "How is it that you know these things Lucian?" I asked. "I don't know when I sleep I can see things as if they are happening at that moment in time. You and Xavier will have many great adventures together." he told me still loving on me. "You are very strong minded and very smart use them well." I said. "You know what, I will be very important to Bastian during his rule and I am proud to be by his side." he said. "You are your fathers son never allow anyone to cloud that." I said as he smiled and slipped out of my arms. I finished cleaning up the house and putting laundry in before X got home when I heard a knock at the door. I opened the door to find Becky, Harley and Sage coming to visit. "Good afternoon Ladies please come in." I said showing them in. "I hope this is ok?" Becky asked. "Oh yes always glad to have you." I said.

The human scent always brought everyone near so that I was watched over. I introduced each as they came into the living room starting with Mike. "Wow you have a lot of names to remember." Becky said with a laugh. "Yea its easy I guess." I said with a smile. My girls took Harley and Sage with them so that the night could get started when Xavier came in wearing his blue scrubs, "Hey Sweetness missed you today." he said as he kissed me. "Missed you too. This is Becky she is Harley and Sages mom." I said. "Nice to meet you." he said with his velvet words. Bastian was next into the room, "Wow you look just like your dad." Becky said with wide eyes. "Yes Ma'am I have been mistaken for my father a few times." he said a bit shy. "This is LaStat." I said as he came in late. They both kissed me and took off to Bastian's room, "They seen to love you." she said. "Yes and I love them each." I said. After some small talk I walked Becky out coming back in meeting X, "You should have read her mind wow." I said smiling at him. "All I could think about was you and the way you smell. Been drinking Cherry Dr. Pepper today Sweetness?" he asked. "What makes you think I have been drinking that today?" I asked slyly. He took me in his arms and smelled all the way up my neck, "Id say about two cans today yummy." he whispered.

I smiled and headed up the steps knowing he wanted to change into street clothes almost running over Harley. "I'm sorry Honey are you alright?" I asked with Xavier right behind me. "Sure where's the fire Piper?" she asked. "Just trying to win that's all." I said with a smile. "Tiff said I can grab a drink?" she asked. "Help yourself to anything you like we order pizza in a bit." X said giving me a slight shove forward. "How was your day?" I asked as I laid on the bed. "Things are well I miss you cant wait until you get back. How was your day?" he asked sliding into his jeans. "Things were well here just a bit down nothing to worry about." I said as I ran my hands up his naked back. He shut his eyes and tightened his hold on me, "Sweetness maybe we should wait until you feel better, I don't want to rush you." he said whispering. I knew what I was doing to him, "No I don't want to wait I want you to love me." I demanded in a whisper up his neck before I kissed him. "As you wish my Queen." he said with his face in my neck. He lifted me into his arms and made his way to the bed. He was so soft with the way he made love to me. His touch made me forget everything I had been through the past week. We tasted each other and our bodies trembled as we touched one another. His hands felt so good to my body and I loved the way his body felt under mine. "I love you Piper." he said as we came to a finish. "I love you Xavier you don't know how much I needed you to touch me today." I told him. "Yes I knew but I didn't want to rush you and I have a way of getting what I want so badly without any thought." he explained. "I know all to well that you get what you want but you must remember that I always want you no matter what the day holds. The way that you love me makes me forget everything bad and your touch is complete heaven to me." I told him. "Heaven huh? You are my heaven everything about you." he said as he ran his fingers up my arm.

We both got up to get dressed "How about a cup before we order dinner?" he asked. "Race ya." I said and hit the door. I met all the kids in the kitchen, "Hey Bastian how about you and LaStat go ahead and get your shoes you can grab dinner there." I said. "Yea that would be great my shoes are about to fall apart, I hope I can find another pair like these." he said as X came in. "Where you guys going?" he asked. "Mall Mom said to go on and get shoes." Bastian said quickly. "You can give me a few minutes before you leave." X said as he handed me a cup. "As you wish." Bastian said looking at LaStat. "Your mom and I have decided to get you all cars of your choice. You can have the Camaro I'm keeping the Charger sorry Bastian." Xavier said with a grin. "You should let me have the Charger Dad you and Mom can take the truck it has more room." Bastian said with a very evil grin. Brie's mouth fell open, "I wanted the Camaro that's not fair." she said. "Fine then you can have to Camaro and Bastian can have something else." Xavier said. "I want a Hummer H2 lime green." Tiffany said. "I want everyone to look on the net and when we all find what you want we will go and get it." X said.

I looked over at Jade who kept quiet this whole time, "Jade you haven't said what you wanted." I said. "Yes well that's because the car my heart desires Dad will say no to." she said getting up. "What kind of car is it and let me look it over then we shall see." X said. "I want the Bugatti Veyron." she said backing up just in case. I felt Xavier tighten up and Bastian choked on his drink, "Hell no Jade why cant you ask for the Cuda or the Roadrunner?" Bastian said quickly. "I don't want those cars I want the Bugatti Veyron." she said with narrowed eyes. "No Dad don't give into her she's gonna kill herself and I forbid it." Bastian said with arms crossed. "Bastian this is up to your mother and myself. We can talk about this later." Xavier said. "No I want to talk about this now because she isn't getting that car." Bastian said standing his ground. "You know what Bastian I think she is responsible enough for this car and if she wants it then she can have it!" Xavier said getting upset with Bastian's tone. "Whatever you say Dad!" Bastian said throwing his hands up. "Maybe I can think about it some more if that would please you." Jade said softly. "Come on Jade let me show you something you might like." Bastian said getting her hand. "I'm not getting the Volkswagen Beetle so forget it." she said on her way out with him. "LaStat would you like to run and get the pizzas this time for me while Bastian is busy?" I asked. "Anything for you Aunt Piper." he said with a smile. "Sage would you like to go with or do you think your mom might get upset with me?" I asked her. "I'm sure she wont mind its just pizza." she said with a smile. LaStat held out his hand and she put hers in his with a an excited smile. I gave LaStat a warning look, "Don't worry she will be safe with me." he thought to me.

When LaStat and Sage came back he was more than ready to get going, "Come on Bastian lets get going!" he called out. Bastian came in and grabbed LaStat by the arm, "You coming slow poke?" He asked laughing. "Hey Mom what kind of movie tonight?" Tiffany asked. "I'm sure whatever you girls pick out will be fine. The moon will be half tonight so not very bright." I said not thinking. "Is there something pressing you?" Xavier asked. "No why should something be pressing?" I asked. "No bright moon." he simply said. "Everything is just fine half moon that's all." I said forgetting about Harley and Sage. "Why ask if she is upset not like she can make the moon full or anything?" Harley said. Xavier took his cup down from his lips slowly as I looked into both girls future. "Well Piper is very special so to speak, a woman of many wonders." X said softly. "Sooo she can control the moon then right?" they both asked at the same time. "Yes she can and many other things but you must never tell." X said. "We would never tell ever!" Sage said quickly. "Please show us Piper." Harley said. "If I show you and you tell anyone I will come for you while you sleep understand. We are vampires in this house and I can come like a thief in the night." I warned. "Never not one word." she said with Sage looking like she was going to pass out. I walked out in the back yard looking up at the moon making it brighter. "That is the coolest thing I have ever seen, what else can you do?" Sage asked. I shook my head at her and let the thunder roll over the hillside, "That's all your getting." I said and returned to the Great House. Xavier led the girls in with them smiling, "Bastian is returning you must not tell him that you know he likes to keep this to himself. When he is ready he will tell you if he so desires." I warned. "How do you know he is coming?" Harley asked. "I can feel him getting close to me." I said as I went to meet the boys at the door.

Bastian and LaStat came in showing me their new shoes, "Check these kicks Mom cant wait to break them in." Bastian said. Brie came in with many loose thoughts running through her mind and Bastian swallowing very hard. "Is it true Harley and Sage knows about us?" Bastian thought to me. "That's right Bastian, Mom and Dad let the cat out of the bag." Brie thought quickly. "Sorry Son it was a true accident." I told him. "Harley maybe we should take a walk if you like." Bastian offered. She held out her hand, "Only if LaStat takes Sage." she said with a smile. LaStat took Sage by the hand and the four of them took a walk, "Only answer what they ask offer nothing more." I thought to both of them. I kept up with them as they walked and talked about a few things, "How do you guys eat or whatever?" Harley asked him. "What you mean we eat like everyone else." Bastian said. "I mean do you bite people?" she asked lightly. "Hell no we don't go around and bite people!" he answered quickly. "I'm sorry Bastian I didn't mean anything by it." she said softly. "No I'm sorry this is kinda hard for me, if you know what I am then you might be afraid of me that's all. Look we have to have a blood source and we get it from a special blood bank and we hunt wild life but never humans ever, my father would flip his lid." Bastian said smiling.

Soon they came back to the house and the girls met up with my girls, "Lets watch this movie Ladies." X said with velvet words. Most of the blankets were brought out by the girls while Bastian and Harley were talking. Everyone was in the movie so when Kirsten walked into the house no one noticed until it was to late, "Bastian what the hell!?" Kirsten said loudly when she saw Bastian laying with his arm around Harley. "Kirsten what are you doing here I thought you were out of town this weekend?" he asked as he jumped up. "Well I can see why you would think that!" she yelled as she turned to leave. "Wait let me talk to you!" he called to her. "No stay away from me Bastian Matthews I wouldn't care if I never saw you again!" she said walking as fast as she could. "No you will wait we have to talk about this!" he said with authority. They walked the yard and talked with everyone watching them. "I'm sorry Kirsten I never meant to hurt you like this." he said softly. "Maybe I should have called or something I just kinda showed up. Look I have no right to ask you for anything we were mostly friends in the long run." she said as she took a seat in the yard. "That's not true Kirsten I do love you and . . . ." he started. "We are moving Bastian to Ohio." she said quickly. "What?" he asked a bit taken. "Yea my Dad took a job and we are leaving in a week." she said as her tears showed up. "Ohio isn't that far away and its not like we can text or call some." he said. "Yea I know but I love you and your family I'm gonna miss you all so much." she said. He put his hand on her face to wipe the tears away, "I love you too and I will miss you deeply. So now what happens?" he asked. "I guess we end this like it started as friends how's that?" she asked with a weak smile. "Friends yea that sounds great." he said as they came back to the group of kids. Xavier and I walked back into the house while they finished up talking. Bastian was shortly behind us, "Man that sucked she was hurt I could feel her." he said as he dropped his head on the table. "I know Son but you must start dealing with these feelings, you are going to feel them with everyone." I said as I put my hands on him to calm him some. "Piper you are putting him to sleep." Xavier said softly. "He hasn't slept in a day or two so let him rest." I said with a smile. Shortly after the girls came in laughing and made Bastian jump out of his skin, "Come on Ladies have some respect, I was sleeping here." he said getting up out of the floor. "Why are you sleeping in the kitchen any ways?" Brie asked. "This is the room with the food so I can eat when I want." he said with a smile as he opened the fridge door. "So where is Emily is she coming over as well?" LaStat asked. "Yea she should be over soon she had to finish her room before she could come over." she said softly. Movie time was back on and I laid with Xavier falling asleep for the first time in a few nights.

Chapter 47

The very next thing I knew I was waking up in my bed with the sun light coming in, "How did I end up in here?" I asked as I stretched. "When I carried you to bed Sweets. Ummm is there anything you would like to talk about?" he asked with a smile. "Nope should there be something to talk about?" I asked. "You talked all night last night very entertaining stuff." he said with a chuckle. "Is that funny to you or something?" I asked not joining in the humor. "You have never did anything like that before, I very much enjoyed it." he said as I flipped him on his back and held him down. "Well it will never happen again if I can help it." I said. "So are we talking about it or what?" he asked as he put me on my back. "There is nothing to talk about." I said quickly. "You are lying to me again Sweets." he said in a whisper up my neck. "Xavier please I don't remember dreaming last night." I pleaded with him. "We can get up on one condition." he said still close to my neck. "What did you have in mind?" I asked. "You have to hunt with me this morning." he said as I ran my fingers up his naked back. "As you wish." I said softly as he closed his glowing eyes. "Sweetness what do you think you are doing, you know what your touch does to me." he whispered. "Would you like for me to stop?" I whispered. When he kissed me I bit his skin softly, "You have the most exciting way of asking for something." he said in between biting the buttons off my shirt. He made love to me for hours with our hands never leaving each others bodies. "Maybe we should hunt before the girls get up." I suggested as I got up to dress. "I'm sure Bastian would like to hunt this morning." X said. "Speaking of Bastian you need to get back in training with the boys. It is almost June and we have to leave the day after Halloween." I said as I sat on the bed. "We could leave before our anniversary and let that be that." he suggested. "I wanted to be here for one more birthday for all the children and I wont get to see them finish growing." I said sadly. "I knew this would come up we talked about this last night while you were sleeping." he said as he took a seat with me. "I'm sorry Love they all mean the world to me but . . . ." I said as he stopped me. "Look Sweetness you saw this for yourself and you know we will be back. I'm very sure that you will keep your thoughts on them all while we are gone. Come on a walk and a fair hunt will do us both some good." he said pulling me into his arms. "Alright I'm coming lets get going." I said taking his hand. We walked to the kitchen finding Bastian waiting, "What are you doing in here alone?" X asked. "Waiting for you all to get up. Hey Dad you want to go hunting this morning?" Bastian asked. "Well yea your mom and I were going if you want to join us." Xavier said. I walked behind them as they chased each other laughing making the birds take flight. If it had been dark and I didn't know any better I would have been scared. I watched them hunt them found something for myself.

The smell of bacon led us back to the house finding it awake with laughter, "Hey were have you guys been we waited on you?" Sage asked. "Hunting and training mostly hunting." Bastian said as he walked past. "You should have came and got me I would have went with." LaStat said. "Yea I would have loved to watch you Bastian." Harley said with a smile. "Well that wont be happening any time soon so just forget it." Bastian called from the hallway. "Why not I would find it fascinating." she said. He came back in the kitchen with his eyes glowing mad, "That is something that you wouldn't understand so just leave this alone!" he yelled and stormed out. "What did I say?" she asked with a hurt look on her face. "Its ok Harley just give him some time to calm down, its hard for him to have humans to know his secret. Besides the hunting trips are very difficult to watch and I'm sure he is worried about you seeing that. Bastian has a strong soul and he likes to be in charge of many things you will learn that about him." Xavier said softly. "Well he needs to know that I'm just as different as he is I'm not like other girls and I don't scare easily. I know there are things he has to do to stay alive and I'm not afraid of any of you." she said a bit upset with him. Bastian stormed back into the kitchen, "You wanna see, fine lets go!" he said as he grabbed her by the arm a bit rough. "Bastian!!" I called as he began to pick up speed. "You stay I'll make sure she is safe." X said as he took off.

I watched from the house as he tracked into the woods and Xavier right behind them. Harley was holding tight as he carried her and put her in a tree, "Sit and don't move you will fall out!" he said hatefully. "Just go Bastian do your thing!" she told him just as hatefully. Xavier kept close just in case she might have fallen off the branch that Bastian put her on. It didn't take long for Bastian to find his prey and chased it down at top speed. He took it down in front of the tree that she sat in so that she could see for herself. She made her way down the large tree and sat with him while he finished his prey. He took a deep breath and wiped his mouth, "See it is very brutal this is why I didn't want you to watch. I can only imagine what you think of me right now." he said softly. She put her arm around him and kissed his cheek, "I think that was amazing." she told him. "So your not freaked out or think bad of me?" he asked. "Hell no I know that you have to do this to live and I'm cool with it." she said with a smile. "I'm sorry that I was a jerk its just we hunt as vampires never humans who wouldn't understand." he told her. "Well its neat like the way we made it here without you getting out of breath, will you be taking me back the same way?" she asked. "As you wish hold on tight." he said as he picked her up. Xavier was first into the back yard of the Great House as I waited with my arms crossed, "Be easy Sweets he's young." he said as he kissed me on his way in. "As you wish." I thought to him. Bastian came through the trees holding to Harley, "Oh damn I'm in trouble Mom is pissed." he said as he slowed and put her to her feet.

I gave him a look, "Hey Toots wait for me inside." he said. She smiled as she passed me and I tried to give her a warm smile back, "How dare you take her like that, you know better!" I said loudly. "I don't know what happened she said she wasn't afraid and I wanted to show her what I really am. Please Mom don't yell at me it hurts when you do." he said softly. "Don't ever forget who you are and never allow yourself to do that again. The damage she could cause for this family is unspeakable do I make myself clear!" I said still yelling at him. He put his hands in his pockets and looked at the ground, "Yes my Queen please forgive me it will never happen again I swear it." he said softly. "Eyes on me Prince Bastian." I demanded. He looked up with crystal blue eyes, "Forgive me my Queen I shall never forget my place." he said. I put my arms around him and loved on his face, "Now what do you think of her?" I asked softly. "I love her and she can love me unconditionally, she is the one for me. Just like you and Dad love me even when I'm a pain in the neck." he said as he loved me back. "That's good Bastian make sure you tell her that and love her just the very same. She has a lot to learn and might have a hard time understanding, just be patient with her. You will have to learn to put that temper away with her as well." I told him. "Dad don't with you all the time." he said quickly. "Yes well your dad and I understand one another, our love is not like any other and I hope that you can have that one day." I said as we made way back into the house. "Me to Mom me to." he said.

Harley jumped up when we came into the kitchen, "Piper please don't be upset with Bastian this was more my fault." she said. "Harley the things you and Sage learn here in the Great House must be kept close to your hearts I have warned you that I will come for you both while you sleep and I meant every word of that. I will not stand for insubordination when it comes to my family and I will find out for I know everything." I warned her again. "Yes Ma'am I would never tell I swear." she said as she moved closer to Bastian. "Harley she would never hurt you but be warned even the smallest mistake will make her come for you." Bastian said smiling. "Did you see her eyes change colors when she was talking to me?" she asked. "Yes well she means every word of it." he told her. The day carried on with the kids doing whatever and Lucian and Ely looking like the others. X and Jon looked over the mail and I paid a few bills on line, "Hey Jovi and Julien should be back today and Aunt Barb is sending something back to you." Regina said as she hung up the phone. She spun out of the room and I knew that she was looking up Xavier to warn him about the something that the guys were bringing back to me. The girls came in and asked if they could go for a walk in the woods close to home. I let them go reminding them that Harley and Sage couldn't move as fast as we could.

Michelle and Trevor came by for a visit, "Hey girl how have you been?" she asked. "Alright here how about you guys?" I asked as Trevor went to find Xavier. "We are good just saving so we can tie the knot." she said with a smile. "Michelle I have something to tell you, my very best friend." I said softly. "Oh no what's up?" she asked. "The end of October will be the last of Xavier and Piper. We are leaving and never to return and if we do it would be for such a short time and no one would ever know." I told her. She sat there looking me over for a short time without speaking, "Hell no your not leaving you have to stay till I die." she said with tears forming in her eyes. "Hey now don't get upset, its not like we want to we have no choice this time. It will be Bastian's time to rule the Great House and we must leave." I told her trying to hold back my tears. "It cant be his time I need you here." she said with tears falling on her cheeks. "I'm sorry Michelle it has to be this way I have seen it." I told her as the clouds made it over the house. Bastian came sliding into the room, "Mom everything ok in here?" he asked with the same pain I had. "Yes but would you and LaStat go find the girls bring them home now please." I said quickly. "Where the hell is Xavier I'm talking with him." she asked as she got up. "Michelle honey this isn't going to change anything." I said following her into the kitchen.

The rain came with thunder and lighting as my heart broke right along with hers, "Tell her Xavier she isn't going anywhere she has to stay here." she yelled at him. "I'm sorry Michelle we have to leave as she has foreseen." he said softly. "No this cant be, you both have been through so much and now that it has calmed down you have to leave, this isn't fair!" she yelled and cried. Now with the storm coming in with a force and still no kids, "Jon you and Mike go find my children bring them home." I said softly. "Its ok Michelle I'm sure she will keep in touch with you." Trevor said as he tried to calm her. "I know this is a shock but if we stay the house will fall it is time for the children and for some reason we are not included." I said as I hugged her. "Please don't go far stay close so we can see each other." she pleaded as the kids came in soaking wet. "Michelle . . . ." I began. "Sweetness before you speak you should calm the weather." Xavier suggested as he slid his hands up the back of my shirt. I brought the thunder and lighting to a stop with his touch while Bastian, LaStat, Harley, and Sage watched. "Alright I'll tell you what, we can try and stay close but Piper wants to see Egypt and that's where we are going first. You know she will be in complete contact with you and all you have to do is think of her and she will call you." X told her. "You swear you will call every time I need you?" she asked. "Every time Girl I swear." I said. "You know something Aunt Michelle we will be here for you anytime you need us." Bastian said with his hand out. I walked out to clear my head being followed by Harley, "Piper are you ok?" she asked softly. "Yes I'm fine but you should go back inside for a few minutes." I said not looking at her.

Bastian came back out, "Hey Toots you should leave Mom when the weather is like this she can be very dangerous." he said. "She shouldn't be left alone Bastian she is very upset." she said as he pulled her inside. "Baby are you coming in she is better now?" Xavier asked. "Yes I'm coming. Hey what did Jovi and Julien bring back from Virginia?" I asked. "Lets deal with one storm at a time shall we." he said. "You mean you didn't intercept it and look it over?" I asked looking in his blue eyes. "Yes I did and its the lock box that the lawyer told us about. I thought we can see the contents at a later time tonight." he suggested. "As you wish." I said as he took my hand and led me inside. "Here Piper, Bastian fixed this for you everything ok now?" she asked. "Much better now no more worrying about me go and have fun with the girls." I said with a hug. I walked in as Bastian rose from Michelle, "So you mad at me?" I asked. "Yes and no but I will deal with it. That nephew of mine is very convincing when he needs to be." she said as I took a seat with her. "He is very much like Xavier in that department." I said smiling at her. "Egypt I mean I knew you liked places like that but that's far away." she said. "Yes for sure I would love to go to Egypt, I have been obsessed with mummies and things like that forever. You know what I never told him about me liking Egypt I wonder how he knew?" I said thinking out loud. "Come on lets go ask him now you have me curious." she said pulling me to my feet. "Hey X how did you know that I wanted to visit Egypt?" I asked. He smiled and looked at me, "I just know everything about you Sweetness." he said with a wink. "That's not going to work this time my handsome man I wanna know." I said walking over to him. He pulled me into his arms and I ran my fingers through his wet hair, "Sometimes and only sometimes I can get your memories and your thoughts from your past when I bite you. You have been so open a lot this past week so I have got many new things about you." he said holding tight to me. "Why haven't you said anything to me you know I wouldn't have minded?' I asked as I kissed up his neck. "Awe Sweets don't do that to me right now please." he pleaded. "I'm sorry Love but you are still wet from the rain and I cant help myself." I whispered with a smile. "I love you but you are going to have to wait this time." he said putting his hands on my face.

Dinner saved Xavier from complete agony this time as he made sure all washed up. Jon held back some so I walked to him, "Hey you and I don't talk much any more is there a reason for that?" I asked. "No I don't think so just been laying low that's all. I learn from everyone else no need to bother you and Xavier with the little stuff." he said. "As you well know we wont be here much longer so if there is ever anything please feel free to come to us. You and the others are Xavier's brothers and soon to be my sons loyals and I want to make sure you have everything to help him be great." I said. Jon pulled to the side, "Piper he is already great he just has to see it for himself. He is young and he thinks he cant live up to his fathers legacy but soon find out other wise. When you leave us please don't go with a heavy heart things will be great here and we will call if you are needed. I swear to you my Queen he will have the very best protection a king can have." he told me. "Please Jon I'm just Piper here in the Great House." I told him. "No you will forever be my Queen no matter who takes your seat in your absence." he said. "Thank you Jon you have made me feel so much better now lets eat before its all gone." I told him as we walked together.

Chapter 48

Soon it was time for the bonfire and movie like so many nights at the Great House and these were some of the moments I was going to miss deeply. "Bastian lets get the fire wood." LaStat said in Latin. "Wow when did you learn a different language?" Sage asked. "I know many different languages I was born this way." LaStat said shyly. "Is that all you can do?" she asked. "Na I can read minds like the rest of us. I can feel what Bastian feels most of the time so if he is mad or upset I feel like that as well, and I'm very fast and very strong." he said with a smile. "That's too cool." she said smiling back at him. Now with the sun all the way to rest I was getting very impatient for what the lock box held for me. Mom never kept many secrets from Dad so I could only guess that whatever was in the box had to be bad. What if she wasn't my real mother or something how would I deal with that news? "Sweets you know that your mom was in fact your real mother. Now after the kids go to bed we can do it together or I can leave it to just you." he said holding tight to me. "No I don't want to do this alone please don't leave me." I said quickly. "Come we do this now before your head spins off your shoulders." he said with a chuckle. He led the way to the bedroom and sat me on the couch, "You wont leave me no matter what the box holds right?" I asked. "Not even if you were raised by wolves your first year." he said with a laugh. "Not funny Xavier what if there is bad stuff in there?' I asked. "Your getting yourself worked up over nothing lets take a look and go from there." he said as he put the box in my lap and handed me the key. I took a deep breath and slowly put the key in secretly hoping that I was taking to long and he would just do it. I opened the box to find a single letter with my name on it wrapped in a red ribbon.

Dear Piper,

    I'm writing this letter to you so we didn't have to do this face to face. I wanted to tell you that I know your and Xavier's little secret and have for some time now. I have asked questions in hopes that you would tell me but you never did. I know that you and the rest of your beautiful family are in fact vampires. The reason I know this is because you come from a long line of powerful witches. You have had powers in your blood line since you were born. Have you ever wondered why people tell you things that they would never tell? I bet you are very powerful at this time and you can do many things with your mind at the same time. Your dad never knew this secret about me because he would have never understood and I should have told you years ago, in fact I had to work very hard to avoid your power. Now that you are vampire I hope that you use your magic for good just as I have. You are a very special breed now that you are vampire, witch, and human all in the same body. Bastian, Brie, and Jade will share this with you having all three running through their veins. Be careful if you bite Xavier he will begin to dream just as humans do and it will be hard for him to understand why. I hope you share this with him it will serve you well and he will understand and I hope you can forgive me for not telling you. Your dad will never know the truth about me or you so no worries. Your father and I are very proud of you in whatever you choose to do with your life. Be understanding with your babies they might have a hard time dealing with this information and coming into their powers. I knew that one day you would be found by Xavier, I saw your future. Piper he had to have you and he would have done anything to have you. I'm glad you gave into him because he would have had no choice but to bite you anyway. You hold his heart so tight that if he couldn't have you he would have died. I can feel the love you both share with each other every time I'm around and it is electric. He has to have you in his life and he has to feel you near him always or he would fade away and now so would you without him. No one knows what the future holds for any of us but I know in my heart that whatever happens you and Xavier will go together. I should close this letter now so I love you both and all of the children you have brought in our lives. Love each other with everything you have inside yourselves. I love you Piper and Xavier so very much and I will keep you forever in my heart.

Love Always,

Mom.

I sat there with the letter in my hand not knowing what to say to her words and to tell the truth neither did Xavier. "How, when, I . . . . ?" I said looking at the letter. "Sweetness I don't know what to say other than it makes sense now. The way you and the kids have three scents about you and the powers. She is very right I would fade away without you and I do love you with all that I am. I cant believe this I married a witch . . . ." he said drifting off and walking the floor. "Is it true that if I had said no that you would have bitten me anyway?" I asked. "To tell you the truth I don't know you gave in to me so easily." he said as he stopped. "And me being a witch is that something you would be ashamed of if any one knew?" I asked not looking at him. "Hell no I would never be ashamed of you or what you are. The powers you have gained and shared with me are amazing and the dreaming is wonderful nothing have I ever had before. All that matters is you are forever mine and I will keep you." he said as he touched the tears on my face. "Should we tell the kids?" I asked. "I think that this is your news and what ever you say I will stand with you always." he said getting up. I took his hand and we went down to find all the family waiting on us to see how I was smelling the rain coming. Bastian was always searching the truth about me with the look the worry on his face. "We need to talk tonight just the family." I told him. "Cant we do it now everyone knows about us anyways?' he asked trying to get into my thoughts. "Maybe we should follow your Moms wishes and let her put this in the right folders." X told him. "No humans not even my dearest friend Michelle." I said in a fashion that he wouldn't say anything more. "As you wish my Queen." he said not very happy with me.

Everyone went back to their friends with X and I hanging back in the house, "Would you like to walk even if it means that I let you go alone this time?" he asked as he rubbed my arm. "No and even if I did I don't want to go alone this isn't about just me any more. They are all so proud to be vampires and now they are witches as well." I told him. "They will understand they are very much like you. Besides you are their queen and they would never go against what you put forth." he said with pride. "I'm am their mother not their queen and you know that. I just don't want them to be upset with me." I said. "If there is any problem it will be Bastian he is the most head strong." he said. As to my wishes everyone went home this night so we could have a family meeting. Bastian was about to go nuts trying my thoughts many times over to get a heads up on what was going on. "Alright lets have it I cant stand it any longer." Bastian said as he came into the living room. "As you well know I have a great deal of powers and no one knows why. I have just found out through a letter that I am a witch." I told them and stopped. You could have heard a pin drop with the complete silence, "Well isn't someone going to say something?" Xavier asked. "Are you sure I mean there could be a mistake in this?" Bastian asked. "There is no mistake it came to me in a letter that was in a lock box from your Grams." I told him.

Mike stood up, "I can do all the research for you if you wish." Mike offered. I looked at Xavier not knowing what to say, "Yes dig deep into her family tree and miss nothing." X said. Mike kissed Tes and hugged Lucian, "Come Bailey I'm going to need help on this one." he said. Bailey rose and left with him after kissing Cyndi. "We will return in a few days." Mike said as he and Bailey took their leave. Jon took the others out only leaving the three children and X and me, "Bastian I never told any of you but you three have three scents about you human, vampire and the other I could never pick up on, now we know what the other is." I told him. "What does this mean for us?" Brie asked. "I guess as you grow so will the powers in the bloodline and all of you are human, vampire and witch just like I am." I said. Bastian rose and walked out without saying anything, "Bastian!!" Jade called to him. "Just leave him Baby Girl he will work this out on his own." Xavier said. "I think it is cool that we are more than vampires I'm proud to be a witch and your daughter." Brie said softly. "Me too." Jade agreed with her. "Thanks girls that means a lot to me." I said as they kissed me and left. "Well that was brutal." I said as I took a seat. "Come lets at least lay so that maybe rest will come to you." X said taking my hand. "If you had known about me would you have asked me to marry you so quickly?" I asked. He laid with me touching me making me feel better with every touch, it was like heaven to my body. "Yes I would have and I could ask you every day just so you would say yes to me. You know we could do it over again if you wish I could have someone here in minutes." he said with a sly smile. "I think the next time we should do it on a beach somewhere although I would love to have the kids with us." I said. "So you would marry me again?" he asked. "Yes I would have married you the very first day we met and I would do it over and over again." I said breathing him in. "Alright then one last party before we leave." he said. "As you wish." I said watching him fall asleep.

I waited patiently on Bastian's to make his way to my room and soon his long awaited knock came to the door. "Mom can we talk for a few minutes?" he asked as he stuck his head in. "Sure." I said as I patted the bed beside me. "I'm sorry for the way I left tonight, I just didn't know what to say or think that's all." he said as I played with his satin hair. "Its alright I don't know what to say or think." I told him as Xavier started to come awake. "Does this mean I will have all those powers?" he asked. "I'm not sure what you will have but I have seen that you will become very powerful in your days to come. It may be broken up between your sisters and you so make sure you listen to them and your queen." I told him. "Right my queen?" he said. "What's that supposed to mean?" I asked. "If it is Harley that is to take my side, what happens to her when I bite her?" he asked. "When that day comes she will be vampire like the rest." I said. "What if you would bite her would she become all three like me?" he asked. "No you are this way because you come from mine and Xavier's blood not venom. That's not to say that you might be able to share with her in time." I said. "Thanks Mom see you in the morning." he said as he got up to leave. "Love you my prince." I said with a smile.

Many days went by with school and work and no word from Mike or Bailey. "Maybe I should try to get a hold of Mike." I suggested on our way to work. "Let him do his job he will not make haste, trust him Piper." X said. "I do trust him completely its just I hate to wait that's all." I told him. "Not nice to hate." he said laughing. I tried to work and leave Mike to his objective but I knew after work I would at least try to call on him. "Hey I think I wanna walk home today." I told X as we closed up on that Wednesday evening. "As you wish would you like company or just you today?" he asked. "You can come I just want the fresh air that's all."

I said putting my arm through his. I really didn't have anything to put away this time. I have grown in the things that I have learned in my days and I was comfortable in my skin for the first time in my thirty years of life. "Hey Mike and B are back come on lets hurry." I said pulling him along. We came into the living room finding Mike by the window with arms crossed and a look on his face. Bailey handed X a scroll and took his leave, "Mike what did you find?" I asked walking to him. "Piper take a seat please." he said not looking at me. "Mike!?" X said quickly. "Do you know how old your mother was?" he asked. "She was 55 at the time of her death, why?" I asked. "Try 105 at her death. We found out that you shouldn't even be." he said softly.

"What are you saying?" X asked standing up. "I'm sorry X she should have died when you bit her, and the children shouldn't be either. There has never been a witch from her bloodline that has survived a vampire bite and I have searched everything. The last two witches I looked up one went insane and she was put to death and the other female died shortly after the bite. The powers that Piper has never been spoken of in any thing I have read." Mike said with some sadness. "That enough I don't want to hear any more and this conversation is over never to be spoken of again in the Great House!!" X yelled and walked out. "How long Mike?" I asked. "Not sure there were a few things missing I'm guessing two or three years, sorry Piper." he said as I turned to find Xavier. I looked every where for Xavier and finally found him in a tree near our window, "X we need to talk so are you coming down?" I asked. "I'm not talking about this Piper leave me alone!" he said hatefully. "You are impossible we really need to talk about this." I called from the ground. "No leave me." he said still hateful. "Damn—it!" I said and walked off. "Hey Aunt Piper wait up what's going on?" LaStat asked as he and Bastian ran up to me. "Nothing and leave your father alone." I said still walking. "Mom what did Unk Mike say?" Bastian asked. I spun around with my eyes glowing, "I can see you are not going to let this go so here is the hard truth. I should have died when your father bit me and you three should never even be. One witch was put to death when she went crazy and the other died about two or three years after being bit. Now here we are and I'm on the verge of the third year mark so we shall see." I said and quickly walked off leaving them standing there with wide eyes.

I walked until I found the flat where the moon touches the grass and I laid there looking up in the sky. I hoped that I didn't die within the next year and I had almost went crazy with the powers I gained not to mention never having more children. "Sweetness." I heard Xavier whisper. I never answered him I just laid there, "I'm sorry I was hateful to you but you can never leave me and I didn't want to hear of it." he said softly as he laid down with me. "I'm almost at my third year mark." I simply said. "I don't understand." he said rolling over to look at me. "Mike said two or three years after being bitten is when the other witch died." I said and got up to leave. I walked back into the house with Xavier close on me and many thoughts running through his mind, "Piper can I have another minute please?" Mike asked. "Can we do this later?" I asked and walked off. Xavier shut the bedroom door behind us, "Piper let me bite you and see your future." he demanded. "No not this time." I said backing up from him. "Either you allow me to do this or I will hold you down and do it." he said with royal tones. "I don't want to know and I don't want you to know so don't touch me." I said trying to back up more. Mike knocked on the door and let himself in with out waiting, "Piper you left before I could finish there is more. There has never been a witch that has been bitten by vampire that is still human in her. You are unique and very powerful, but no where in the history of your family that has the human part left." Mike told us. "Thanks Mike." I said as he left. "Sweetness are you going to allow me to find the answers we both seek?" X asked more calmly this time. "I have said no if it is death you find what will you do about it?" I said still keeping my distance. "Damn—it Piper!" he yelled just before he grabbed me and bit me deep and drank hard. "That's enough!!" I screamed and pushed him off. I went out the window and the clouds came in with force black and heavy. I sat out in a flat area of the yard letting the rain pound on me. I felt betrayed by Xavier once again but this time was deeper than before. Everyone came out to be with me, "Sweetness would you like to come in so I can talk to you?" X asked. "Stay away from me all of you." I ordered. Xavier reached out to get a hold of me and I struck lighting in front of him as he backed up quickly. "I'm warning you Xavier!" I said looking at him through thin slits.

X backed everyone up, "The storm is very bad this time everyone back inside, I'll stay with her." X said as Lucian got closer to me. "Aunt Piper look at me." Lucian said. I looked up and narrowed my eyes,

"What do you want?" I asked more hatefully than I should have. "Don't you believe in what I told you. I said you and Unk Xavier will have many great adventures there has been no change in that." he said. "Back inside Lucian before you get hurt." I said and looked down. "Look at Xavier he is hurting because you are he needs to touch you to heal both of you. Can you feel him? Please back inside with me I'll help you." Lucian said. "Thanks Lucian but I think I need this go on now." I said with a smile. He rose and walked back to the house as I looked deep into Xavier's feeling and I could feel that he was very sorry for what he had done and his pain was great. "Piper please look at me." X said as he took a seat on the wet ground. I glared at him, "What could you possible want that you haven't taken already? As a matter of fact I don't care what you want or need just like you didn't when you went against me. Do you hurt, feel it deep in your gut?" I asked. "Yes Sweetness I do." he said as he reached out to touch me. "Don't you dare touch me either! I'm glad you are hurting you deserve it for the betrayal you laid at my feet!" I screamed at him. He never said anything he just took my anger as I dished it out to him. I knew what he was feeling at the time and if he could have cried himself he would have. I stood up and walked away from him so that I could rip something up.

He ran up behind me and grabbed me hard, "I am still king of this house and you will give me what I want! I will touch you any time I damn well please you understand me!" he yelled at me in royal tones. "Say your piece and leave me be King Xavier." I said in a smart ass tone. "Don't speak to me like that I am your husband for most not your king!" he said loudly. "You were the one who brought up the king thing I was just giving you what you wanted." I said still with sass. "I have seen your future and there is nothing that suggested death so we can calm down." he said a bit softer still touching me. "Glad your happy now may I go?" I asked not looking at him. "Hell no you cant go unless it is inside with me! I'm not giving you what you want this time you will have to be pissed at me in the safety of the Great House!" he said with warning. "Fine take me home and put me in my room alone!" I said pushing his hands off of me. "If that is what you want then so be it!!" he said loudly. This time the thunder came on his demand, it was so loud that it shook the ground. He grabbed me by the arm hard and pulled me to the house, "Things better now?" Jovi asked. "She isn't allowed any visitors until I say this mean you Bastian understand!" he warned the family on our way though. "Also if she calls for any one through her thoughts no one answer her fear the day you disobey me this time!" he said up the steps. The lighting flashed so bright that the others turned away from the light. He put me in my room and slammed the door and there he left me. I knew he was outside the door I could feel him and I sat on the floor in front of the door. I needed to feel him just as bad as he needed but I wasn't about to tell him that right now.

Chapter 49

Most of the evening was spent with the both of us setting in the floor till I feel asleep. I could smell his sweet scent when he came through the bedroom window, "Come on Sweets lets lay down." he whispered as he picked me up. "You know that I would have given you the answers you seek in time all you had to do was wait." I told him softly. "I know I should have trusted you and waited but cant you see that I needed to know if these are our last days." he said as he pulled me close. "Even in death we shall never part." I said as I touched his soft skin. "When I let my emotions go and the thunder came it made me feel free." he told me. "I know it feels great to let all your anger go in something so powerful." I said before I fell asleep. Morning came through our window waking me refreshed and I couldn't wait until I had a cup. "Come on X I'm hungry get up." I said as I rolled over and nudged him almost out of bed. "Alright, alright I'm coming just one more sec." he said with a smile. "Either get a move on or I'm leaving you in bed buddy." I said getting in my jeans. I watched him roll out of bed and hit the floor as I reached for the door knob, "Wait I'm coming." he said with a chuckle. I walked as slow as I could so he could catch up with me, "I want you and the kids to go and get the cars this weekend." I said as I went into the kitchen. "What are you planning to do while we are gone?" X asked. "I'm not for sure maybe just lay in bed." I told him. "I forbid you to lay in bed Piper I mean it find something else to do while we are gone." he said with a little bit of warning. "Ok maybe Michelle and I can get Becky and go to the Bash or something how's that sound?" I asked. "Well I'm not in love with it but I'm sure you will be safe." he said getting a cup.

As the kids came in we fixed breakfast and ate together, "Kids Mom wants us to go get your cars today so lets not make haste get ready so we can get back." he said not really wanting me to be alone. "I'll call Michelle and Becky." I said putting my plate in the sink. "Yes I have to make a few calls before I leave." he said not making eye contact with me. I made the calls I needed then headed for the shower soon being joined by Xavier. "Who was on your calling list?" I asked. "No one special just calls." he said hurrying up so he could get out and avoid me. Michelle and Becky rang the door bell as the kids got ready to go with Xavier. "I'll be ready in just a minute let me tell the brood goodbye first." I told them. I kissed everyone on their way out, "Please promise you will be safe and keep your senses sharp." Xavier said before he left. "Go on and have fun with the kids no need to worry about little ol me, I will be just fine." I said as I shoved him softly out the door. "I cant believe that Xavier is letting you go alone without ya know." Michelle said as we got in the car. "I'm sure I wont be alone." I said with a wink. It was a full house when we got to the Bash, "Brad what are you doing here?" I asked. "My Queen pleasure seeing you here this evening. Where is Xavier will he be joining you?" Brad asked. "No it is just us ladies tonight." I said as we took a seat next to him and his three sons.

Most of the night I sat there with Michelle and Becky talking back and forth all the while watching a gentleman as he watched me. "Maybe we should leave, he looks like he means business Piper." Michelle suggested. "He is vamp and he hasn't taking his eyes off of me I'm sure we are in trouble, come on lets get out of here." I said as I looked over at Brad. "Shaun, Timmy and Bryce will follow you home." Brad thought to me. We got in the car and the man came out keeping his face in the shadows so I couldn't see him, "I will follow you to the driveway of the Great House so that Xavier can get you in." Brad said as he got in his car. "No Xavier isn't home please take me the whole way." I thought to him quickly. My phone rang with Xavier's voice full of worry, "What is going on? I'm coming stay moving don't get out of the car." he said before I said hello. "Stay with the kids I have Brad and his boys, I mean it X this is important to them." I said. "Becky you will let Bryce take you home and there you will stay understand." I said softly to her. "Yes Bryce can take me." she said under my spell.

I pulled up in the driveway and the three of us got out before Brad could stop his car, "Bryce take Becky then come back." Brad said. "Yes Father as you wish." he said quickly getting Becky in the car. "Maybe we should go to my house My Queen the Great House is so large." Brad suggested. "No this has to take place here and you will stand back this has to be done by me." I told him. "It is my place to die for you no matter the fight please allow me to fill my destiny for you." he pleaded knowing Xavier would be pissed at him. "Not today Brad you will stand back this time. You have other things to fulfill before you leave understand." I said as I took a seat with Michelle. "What's going to happen if he shows up?" Michelle asked with everyone looking at me. "When he shows I will simply ask him to leave. If he refuses I will kill him myself. You are to stay out of the way don't watch." I said not looking at her. I knew that she might fear me after she sees me fight like I knew I was going to have to. Soon the front door swung open and walked in a large man, "Piper Matthews I have come for your only son!" he man said loudly. "You cant have him you should leave." I said calmly. "Give him to me before I kill you and take him anyway!" he said as he came in the room. I gasped when I saw his face, "Dakota is that really you?" I asked taken back at the sight of him. "Yes Piper its me, where is that boy of yours?" he said. "Why have you come for Bastian?" I asked. "You and Xavier own me Prince Bastian for the death of my brother. I have many plans for that boy he is important to me and my future." he said with a hiss. "Awe yes Brandon how is he oh yea he's dead for real this time isn't he?" I said with a smart ass tone. He took a deep breath and stepped forward, "Where is that boy?" he asked as Timmy and Shaun stepped forward. "Guys this is between Dakota and myself please step back." I said as I rose to my feet.

Both boys looked at Brad and moved back, "Look here Dakota this has nothing to do with you or Bastian so please leave my Great House and never return. Brandon got what was coming to him because he came in the night and stole my girls and it felt good to watch him pay for what he did." I said moving closer to him. "Stay away from me Piper I know what you can do with just a touch. I will kill you if you get close enough." he hissed at me. "I don't want to touch you Dakota I want you just as your brother." I said never stopping. "Piper I'm warning you." he said taking a step back. "Come on Dakota what will it take besides my only son for you to leave?" I asked. "Just Bastian that's it where is he?" he asked falling under my spell. "Not here sorry you wasted your precious time." I said. He shook his head and closed his eyes then grabbed me by the throat, "You got close to me didn't you?' he said with a evil smile. "I have had enough of this!" I said and pushed him off of me with winds. He fell to the ground getting to his feet quickly and ripping my stomach opened with his fingernails. I jumped on him pushing him to the floor then I reached down and ripped his throat opened with my teeth tasting his blood and spilling the rest on the floor. I sat over him making sure there was no coming back for him like his brother as Xavier walked in with the kids. "What the hell is going on here? Tell me why it is your Queen covered in their blood?" X asked with anger in his eyes. "I apologize my King it will never happen again." Brad said quickly.

I took this time and walked out so I could get a cup and start my healing. "Piper you need something more than just a cup." Bailey said. "I'm fine I think." I said almost not making it to the table. "May I take you to hunt something richer my Queen?" Bailey asked. "No I will take her this time, leave us." Xavier said as he came in. Bailey quickly took his leave as Xavier picked me up and headed for the woods. I was at the point of no return leaving Xavier to bring me something to feed on, "What the living hell was that about Piper you should have known better!!" he said not happy with me. "He was waiting on Bastian he was going to take him." I said after I drank the prey he brought me. "Tell me who he was for you to allow that close to you?" he asked trying not to get upset. "Brandon's brother Dakota he came for Bastian because we killed Brandon." I told him trying to get up. "Sit down and finish the story. Tell me about Bradly and why they all stood there and watched you defend yourself?" he said with authority. "On my way home from the Bash I saw this fight between Brads coven and there would have been no survivors. There is something of great value about those boys of his and I needed them to survive. Please Xavier don't be upset with me this was the only way." I told him. "As you wish on the condition that this will never happen again understand." he said helping me to my feet. "As you wish my King." I said walking with him.

The house was still talking until we came in, everyone fell quiet, "Much better now Piper?" Michelle asked as she walked closer to me. "Yes all better." I said as she raised my shirt and took a look for herself. "Mom what happened here?" Bastian asked. "He came for you and I had to stop him nothing for you to worry about." I told him. "King Xavier please allow me to express . . . ." Brad began. "Piper told me why this took place." X said as he put his hand on Brads shoulder. "You and your boys are very important to me, all is well Bradly." I said with a smile. "We shall take our leave if there is nothing else?" he asked. "Thank you for getting them home tonight." X said as he walked them to the door. Jon asked to take Michelle home as I went to rest upon Xavier's request. "I want to see your stomach." he said as he came in the room. "I'm fine all healed up." I said looking him over. He never stopped as he came to the bed and pulled my shirt up, "Piper do you have any idea what could have happened?" he asked as he ran his hand over my belly. "Nothing would have happened I had Brad, Shaun, Timmy and Bryce here and they would have never allowed it to get out of hand." I said knowing what he was thinking. "Yes but he could have gotten the best of you before they could have made a move." he said. "Xavier you know as well I do that there is no chance in another child together. Please you allow this to linger in your ever lasting heart and it breaks mine when you feel like that." I told him. He got up off the bed and walked away, "Sometimes I hope that our future will change so that we may someday have another powerful child together but I know that we shall never." he said sadly. I walked over to him resting my head on his back and my hands up his chest, "Never shall it I have seen it more than once both ways." I whispered. "Come lets talk with the house." he said taking my hand.

When we walked in the living room the kids gathered and took a seat. "Now that August is upon us we have many things to get done. Mik is going to return and train each of you also training Harley and Sage. He will be rather rough with your sisters and with the human girls the both of you will control your temper. LaStat you will take Sage hunting with you she must see the true you. Once we leave Bastian will have to take your fathers seat and rule over many. The elders will be here for any assistance you may need and your sisters will have some say so if it calls for it. There will no turning of the human girls until after graduation this is your fathers rule and you will abide by it." I said looking at them all. "When would you like me to take Sage?" LaStat asked with a worry look on his slender face. "It shall be done today so you better prepare yourself." I told him. When Sage and Harley showed up LaStat rose to greet her so that he could inform her of what was about to happen. "Piper said I'm to take you hunting with me today." he told her. "I really don't need to see any of that I mean I already know about you." she said with wide eyes. "I'm sorry but if Piper says for me to then I have no choice." he said taking her hand.

Bastian came in the hallway, "Mom if LaStat isn't ready don't make him show her." he said looking very worried. "I'm sorry Bastian he has to she will be fine trust me." I said softly. "Maybe he can do it later or something." he tried again. "Nothing more on this Bastian it shall be done get them ready we are going now." I told him putting a comfort hand on him. He walked off unhappy with me like most times that I don't give in to him. Xavier and I waited on the large family to gather at the back yard to hunt together. "X and I shall make way first so that I can be at hand if needed." I said starting my run. Xavier found his first and I soon followed suit by quickly draining my prey, "We must hurry so that I can be there for Sage. She isn't as strong as her sister and she will make LaStat feel bad not meaning to." I said pulling at Xavier. "Ok ok I'm gonna have some fun with Bastian while you are laying charms on the humans." he said with a sweet smile. I followed him back to where Sage was waiting with LaStat, "Go on now she is with me." I said to him in the dead language. He took off with great speed and found something to chase down, I stood there with my arm around Sage.

When he made the kill he was as gentle as his hunger would allow him to be. Sage tightened up on me and held her breathe, "Its alright Sage this has to be and one day you shall be the very same, his life would be slowly taken if he did without." I told her. "Please don't say anything to him please Piper." she pleaded with me. I smiled and walked away when he came close to her, "See I wish you didn't have to endure that." he said softly. "I think it was neat and you move faster than any other time." she said as she kissed him on the cheek. Xavier blew past us with Bastian and LaStat joining in the cat and mouse games that they so loved. I walked back with the girls picking up the scent of our dearest friend Mik. "Mik my old friend how are you?" Xavier asked as he came to a sliding stop. "I'm well and you?" Mik asked. "As you can see." X said with a smile as we all entered the yard together. "Humans on a hunting trip?" Mik asked surprised. "Yes things are a little different these days. Is it alright that we ask you to train them with the others?" X asked. "Sure just I'm not going to take it easy with them just cause they are human so we can keep Piper at bay?" he asked with a smile looking at me. "You can try." Xavier said as the family laughed. "Lets begin." he said taking Jade in his arms with a knife to her neck. Bastian took a step forward, "Lets have it Boy." Mik said with a evil looking smile. Jade knew that Bastian could have hurt Mik with that look on his face so she flipped him and sat over him taking his knife, "How was that?" she asked sweetly. "Very good Jadey very good." Mik said carefully. He knew that even with us friends we could lose sight of our temper and hurt him.

Chapter 50

Many days and weeks went by just the same with training, work and school. The kids went to school with little sleep and sore bodies. Mik taught many things to the human girls and they were learning quickly. "Today Sweetness I'm taking Bastian to the store while you get a few things finished up here at the house, is that alright?" he asked with a smile. "You know if you take Bastian he will clean out the junk food isles." I told him. "Yes well I'm going for steaks and I have a special run to make." he said turning to walk out of the room. "What's the special run what are you going for exactly?" I asked walking to catch up with him. "Never you mind, I'll be back soon. I love you." he said kissing me quickly and leaving. I took the time and wrote many letters to the children and put them in a place where I knew they would be found when the time was right. I placed things that I wanted to take with me in the lock box making sure that I had my drawing book from Xavier. I changes the bed and packed a few clothes so that much was done when time came. "Come to me Sweetness." Xavier whispered inside my mind. I came down the steps and found him waiting on me with a smile. "Are you ready to start dinner we are having guests soon?" I asked. "Yes so ready." he said taking my hand. He started the grill and I wanted to talk to the children to make sure they were well. I saw Brie's face light up when Bradly and his strong boys showed up, "Good evening Queen Piper how are you?" Brad asked. "Very well and you?" I asked. "Shall I take you to a seat Queen Piper?" Shaun asked. "Please just Piper in the Great House and any where else we shall meet." I said with a smile as I slid my arm into his.

Brad took a seat with me while Shaun and Bryce went to hang out with Bastian and LaStat. "Bradly you will help watch over my young ones wont you while we are on leave?" I asked. "Yes everyday I shall keep watch." he said with a smile. "Timmy if you would like to join in the fun help yourself." I said when I noticed him standing tight to his father. "Thank you Queen Piper but of it would be alright I can just stand here." he said not looking at me. "Eyes on me Timmy please and just Piper no need to be so formal." I said. He brought his blue eyes to mine and I gave him a smile. Brie started her walk over to us, "Brad so nice to see you again." she said looking at Timmy. "Princess Brie you have grown into a very beautiful lady." Brad said with a smile. "Hi Timmy." she said with magic. "Princess Brie." he said softly and with glowing eyes when he seen her. "Would it be to much trouble for you to take me to my brother? Oh and please just Brie if that's ok." she asked knowing his answer already. He smiled at her as she slipped her arm into his. "Timmy will be of great use to Bastian when he is needed." Brad said. "Yes he shall and to Brie as well." I said watching him with her. I gave Xavier a heads up when he walked over to me and Bradly, "Awe I see Brie has found someone who she can be herself with." he said as he handed me a plate. "Yes and I shall ask him to take his rightful place in the Great House today." I thought to X. He smiled at me as he called the kids for dinner and them fighting for first place in line.

Once around the tables Mik was killing the kids with more work outs after this night was over, "Come on Mik we are sore enough as is." LaStat said with a smile. "Not sore enough your still walking ain't ya?" Mik said with a evil smile. Brie was glowing having Timmy with her and they seemed to make great friends from the start, "Timmy I have seen many things and now is the time for you to take you rightful place within the walls of the Great House." I said giving Brie a wink. "Truly he is to stay here?" Brad asked looking shocked. "Yes that is if he wants to and you allowing him." I said softly. "Who am I to say if this is what you wish then he shall." Brad said quickly. "Bradly you are his father and have final say so over him it is an invite the both of you have free will." I told him. "Father I want to I know that I can serve Bastian well." Timmy said looking at both of us. "Very well then it shall be done." Brad said. Shaun and Bryce had a look of great shock on their faces as they looked at their brother. I smiled at Shaun who I knew wanted to be in the Great House with all his heart. It is a great honor to be invited into the strongest coven to live most everyone knew that.

After eating and kids hanging out I was tired and took my leave to rest, "I'm going to say good night see you all in the morning." I said as I passed the kids. "I'm coming let me finish here wait for me." X thought to me. I laid on the bed getting visions of the future and some were very sad to me knowing that I would miss many great things my growing children would do. I took the drawing book out so that I could sweet talk X into drawing something new for me. "What are you doing up here alone Piper?" X asked as he came in with a warm cup. "Just wondering if you would draw something for me?" I said as I looked at the pictures. He had put in the day that I put my parents to rest. It was black and white except the purple rose that I held tight as I stood there alone. "What shall I put in there for you?" he asked with a smile. "I want you walking over to me. You take my breath away when you come to me the way you do." I told him. "Ummm not sure if I can do that I've never seen myself walking to you." he said as he laid on the bed with me. "I'm sure I can help you with that if you wish." I said running my fingers up his back. "I will give you anything you wish if you keep touching me like that." he said with glowing eyes. I got close enough for him to taste me as I let the memories of him walking into any room where I was and I allowed him the feeling that he gives me. With him getting that close to me never took long for us to become one with his soft hands touching my body all over. "Would you like to watch me while the memory is still fresh?" he asked. I handed him my book and a pencil with a smile. He drew it with ease and quickness, "There how's that?" he asked. "That is amazing you didn't miss anything." I said as he closed the book. Sleep came to me with ease and I carried out most of the night without to many dreams.

I was the first to wake up and tried to get out of bed, "You are luscious this morning, where do you think you are sneaking off to?" X asked as he tightened up on me. "We must get moving around we have many things to get done." I said looking him over. "Fine if we must, but may I ask if you dreamt last night?" he asked. "As with many nights why do you ask?" I asked. "Mine was different again I have never had this before. It was like I was inside your dreams, did you see Brie with a sword?" he asked carefully. "Yes I did and she is very talented just like you." I said as I hit the floor. "Then today we shall see if the dreams are correct." he said as he got dressed himself. Breakfast came and went with Timmy learning many things about the family quickly, "Ok guys hit the training so we can rest some before Mik brings it to ya again." I said as I cleaned up after everyone. "Brie I have something new for you today are you ready?" X asked. "Ready as ever I guess anything has to be better than having Mik kick our ass." she said giving Mik a playful shove. I watched them move the back yard with speed with Timmy hanging back some, "Are you not going to take part today?" I asked. "Just making sure that you are not left alone that's all." he said softly. "I'm just fine you are needed out there today have fun." I said. He smiled at me and as soon as his feet hit the grass he bent trees down with his great speed catching up to them quickly. I watched them as I slowly walked to where they were training finding a tree to hang out in. Brie watched as Bastian and LaStat took some punishment with a smile on her face even through she could feel Bastian's pain. "Your turn Baby Girl." X said as he tossed her a sword. "You want me to use this I don't know how to use it!?" she asked with surprise. "Oh well you better figure it out cause I'm coming for you." Xavier said swinging his sword hard at her. She put hers in the air to block his from hitting her and she pushed him away from her. "You ready?" he asked as he come to her fast and hard. It was like she was born with that sword in her hand everything just came to her. She went a few rounds with X as he got harder and harder on her taking her to her knees a few times. "Get up defend yourself before I cut you through." he said knocking her over to the ground. "Damn it!!!!" she yelled as she got up. "Dad chill out don't hurt her." Bastian said. She went after Xavier with anger in her eyes but he was more skilled than she was. "Breath Brie come on this is gonna hurt unless you defend yourself." X said taking a step towards her. I watched them dance around clashing swords together for some time until he took her to her knees once again. He walked over and got himself another sword leaving her to just one, "Don't make me Brie I will, this is what you wanted." he said coming hard to her. She got up taking herself another sword as well and dancing around with him soon making her point as she took him off his feet. "Very nice My Lady are you sure you never used one before?" Timmy asked as he walked her back to the house. "Dad has never hurt me like that I was afraid of him." she said. "He has to make sure that you feel some pain so that you are ready when time comes I'm sure." Timmy said.

I was pleased that he didn't take it easy on her knowing what they were going to face in the future. I was last back to the house letting things run off of me as I walked slowly, "Did you see what I did to Dad?" Brie asked. "Yes Baby Girl very nice job." I said as I hugged her. "Mom how much longer are you allowed to stay?" Bastian asked with everyone gathering around. "We must start making plans to leave soon I'm sorry but our time has came to an end here." I told them as Xavier put his arms around me knowing I was hurting. "Shall we have a farewell party?" Cyndi asked. "Yes so that we can see our friends on last time." X said. Nothing pleased Cyndi more than a great party that she could be head of. I hoped that she would invite our dearest friends including Becky and Chris. I had already made sure that Bradly would come back for Timmy's sake even though we were vampires didn't mean we didn't love our families. I would pack clothes that I needed for our trip and some of the things dear to my heart that I couldn't live without. "When are you coming down we have our friends arriving?" Cyndi asked. "I'll be there in a few minutes." I told her as I took a long last look around.

I took a deep breath while closing my eyes making sure I could remember the smells of this Great House and where I loved all my children so deeply. I quickly flipped through the pages in my mind to make sure I had every memory possible taking each with me. I slowly walked out of the room that Xavier and I had shared so many things together in and I closed the door to that chapter in my life for the last time. I held back the storms and tears as I walked the great halls and looked into every room that held different memories for me and went down the stairs to greet the family. "Shall we be having rain this evening Miss Piper?" Shaun asked as I came into the hallway. "Lets hope not. Would you be so kind as to take me to Xavier please?" I asked as I slid my arm into his. "My pleasure, is there anything that I can help with before you make way?" he asked. "No but I'm very sure that you will be of great help soon enough." I said before he handed me off to X. "Please Love I don't want to talk about it right now." I said when he looked at me with hurt in his heart. "As you wish." he said. There was dancing and laughing among our friends while I watched all closely. "Michelle please stop by often and check on my babies make sure they are behaving and maybe crack em one if they are not being good." I said with a light smile. "You know I will, man I wish you could be here when I get married to Trev." she said with tears in her eyes. "Yes me to maybe I can sneak back and watch from a tree top I cant be seen here once I leave you must understand." I told her. "I do I guess just text me later if you do let me know." she said. I hugged her tight letting her know I would try to be here. "I believe the time has come and the hour is short, shall we Sweets?" X asked.

I hugged everyone that I could telling each something that they would keep with them, "I just got parents and now you are leaving." Tiffany said. "We will be close to you Cutie please we shall be together once again." I told her as I loved on her face one last time. Brad and his boys came to say goodbye and I hugged them as if they were my blood as well, "Take care and no worries here." Brad said. Bastian held back for as long as he could before he had to make way and take leave staying on the porch watching. Mike was last as always with him coming to me this time, "I'm leaving them in your hands love them as if they are your very own. They will listen to you when the time comes, use careful hands with Bastian he has a lot to learn and he is quick tempered. Make sure dinners are at the table with everyone sharing their day or I'm coming back to get you. I will be watching and only come back in extreme emergencies allow them to try and fix anything they mess up. I love all of you take care." I said as I hugged him tightly. "I swear it shall be done just as you wish as always my Queen. Like Jon has said don't leave with a heavy heart they are good protective hands." he said with a smile. Xavier helped me in the truck with me loving on Bastian, Brie, Jade and Tiffany one last time as he started the engine. He slowly pulled off with me turning around in the seat so I could watch my family fade into the night. "Sweetness?" X said as he took my hand. "I know so lets go and have a great time doing what we love best. Take me away, show me new memories of forever together." I said pulling myself closer to him and us driving away into the darkness.